GATHERING SHADOWS
THE WEBS OF FATE
BOOK ONE

C J WALLINGSFORD

TRIGGER WARNING

This book is intended for mature audiences. This series will contain explicit content and dark elements that may be triggering to some. It will include a magical race of beings known as the Seraphinus that has two factions with extreme prejudice against each other.

Additional warnings:
Violence / Mature Language
Contracted Servitude
Emotional / physical abuse
Substance abuse
Sexually explicit scenes* / Dub Con

*While not included in this book, this series will feature a MMF relationship

For anyone who needs an escape.

*

Whether it's simply to escape from the reality of life,
Or looking for a hot alpha shadow daddy,
I hope you find your escape.

THE CONTINENTS

AVGORA MOUNTAINS

ISLANDAL

SERPENT MOUNTAINS

ILBUIO

VALLEMON

NARWAL

MOLANCH

SERPENT RIVER

THE ISLES

THE COUNCIL

ARID PLAINS

INVECTUM

KIPNOP

HAPSFORD

MIKKANOS RAINFOREST

SALT BATHS

JULIQUIAN

BRISHMAM RAINFOREST

DI AURATUS

SALTINA

IZUL

GLINTING MIRAGE

RUNE DIAL

The Continents Calendar

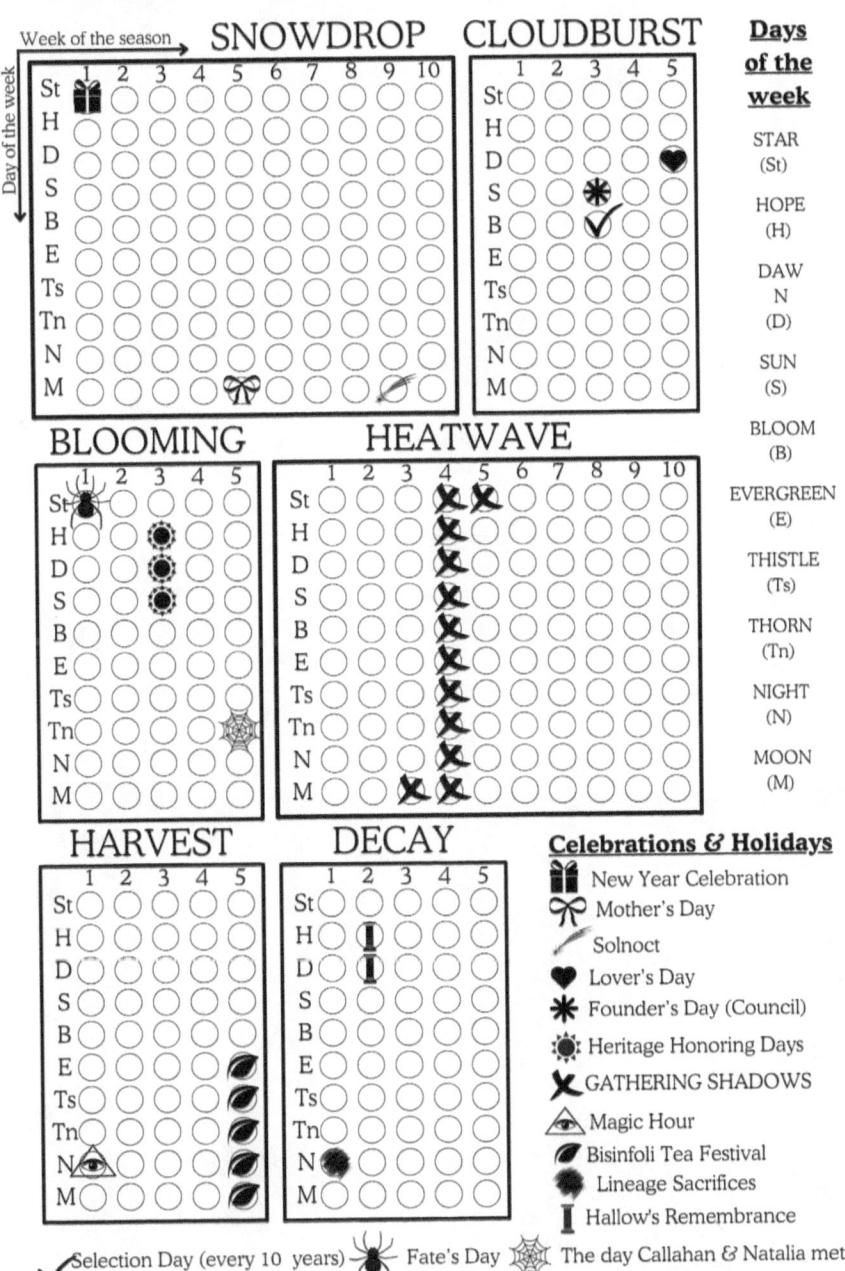

Week of the season →

Day of the week ↓

SNOWDROP

	1	2	3	4	5	6	7	8	9	10
St										
H										
D										
S										
B										
E										
Ts										
Tn										
N										
M										

CLOUDBURST

	1	2	3	4	5
St					
H					
D					
S					
B					
E					
Ts					
Tn					
N					
M					

BLOOMING

	1	2	3	4	5
St					
H					
D					
S					
B					
E					
Ts					
Tn					
N					
M					

HEATWAVE

	1	2	3	4	5	6	7	8	9	10
St										
H										
D										
S										
B										
E										
Ts										
Tn										
N										
M										

HARVEST

	1	2	3	4	5
St					
H					
D					
S					
B					
E					
Ts					
Tn					
N					
M					

DECAY

	1	2	3	4	5
St					
H					
D					
S					
B					
E					
Ts					
Tn					
N					
M					

Days of the week

STAR (St)

HOPE (H)

DAWN (D)

SUN (S)

BLOOM (B)

EVERGREEN (E)

THISTLE (Ts)

THORN (Tn)

NIGHT (N)

MOON (M)

Celebrations & Holidays

New Year Celebration

Mother's Day

Solnoct

Lover's Day

Founder's Day (Council)

Heritage Honoring Days

GATHERING SHADOWS

Magic Hour

Bisinfoli Tea Festival

Lineage Sacrifices

Hallow's Remembrance

Selection Day (every 10 years)   Fate's Day   The day Callahan & Natalia met

Welcome to Jibuto all the fresh blood
and those who have lived long enough to return.

In accordance with our laws, the Gathering of Shadows Ceremonies
are to determine who should be your next Dark King.
Every contractor who has proven enough strength
to garner contracted is entered into the games.
You are warranted one who contracts their life to yours for assistance,
proving not only your strength but that of those you control.

CHAPTER I

NATALIA

FIFTH THORN'S DAY, BLOOMING 4049 6TH MILLENNIUM

I AM GOING TO THROW UP OR PASS OUT. I'M NOT SURE WHICH.

Bright morning light shines through floor-to-ceiling windows at my back. It's mellowed to yellow lighting, which means that both suns have risen. Several machines whir as a dull background to dozens of voices. Some overly chipper woman is taking a drink order from a large man who is one notch down from bellowing.

The world is bright and loud, grating my brain like cheese against a grinder. My stomach churns. I exhale, my breath tangy like I swallowed mouth wash and I keep burping it up. I grimace, waiting for the scent of roasted beans to overcome the wretched smell burning in my nasal cavities.

I close my eyes and try to find enough fortitude to keep the acid in my gut from coming out of me. Steam hisses. Warm, delicious air wraps around me.

"Tallie?"

The sound of my name fills me with relief. My order is ready. Blessed caffeine will soon be ingested from the largest disposable cup the café offers on their menu.

I reach for the beverage, trying my best to smile at the woman, mostly leering in the groggy throes of a massive hangover.

It's not my fault. Thistle's night drink specials are too enticing to pass up. There's no other night I can get drunk in exchange for a reasonably priced tab.

Heat radiates into my palm from the coffee through the stiff paper as I close my fingers around my prize. I draw it in close, inhaling the delectable aroma of freshly brewed coffee with milk and drizzled with caramel. The space under my tongue salivates with tiny pin pricks of anticipation.

"Thank the fucking Mother," I whisper at my salvation, turning toward the front of the café, navigating my way out of the milling people.

I need to get to my job, although my boss is used to me being late and possibly even still drunk on Thorn's days. He's Magia too, about twenty years my senior, but he knows my life story. He understands why I need alcohol, and that he doesn't pay me enough to support my drinking habits.

Tony pops into my head unbidden. It gives me an urge to smack my forehead against something solid in an attempt to remove the thought. Ignoring that impulse, I shoulder the door open, a warm breeze of the Blooming season streaks past me into the shop, fluttering the loose waves of my dyed hair. The bottle said lilac, but it's more a silvery color reminiscent of irises.

A blinding flash of light erupts, followed by a deafening boom. My eyes narrow against the jarring attack on my senses, as my head shies away at the shock wave ripping through the air. A single heartbeat squelches in my ears as I pretend like that was lightning.

It wasn't. It was a smite, a powerful attack conjured by a Light Seraphinus.

I ignore that annoying inner voice in my head telling me to do something. I'm Magia. Magia protect humans from the Seraphinus, who treat humans like an uninvited spider in the shower, squashing them as pests.

Bright spots dance in my vision as I squint around. Others are recuperating, getting to their feet. A few of them stand there glancing around, while the most intelligent individual of the group is running as fast as she can in the direction away from here.

A tall, slender man stalks forward. I assess him with pursed lips, taking a drink of my roasted, liquid caffeine.

Pale skin. Blonde hair. He's dressed in white and beige. Those details aren't as important as his eyes. Lighters have a full white eye. It's too hard to tell at a distance; however, I don't need to see his eyes. The golden Light wrapping around him is a dead give-away that he is a Lighter–a Light Seraphinus.

Little zaps of electricity *zzt* in the air around me as I follow the Lighter's line of sight to a man sprawling on the ground nearby in the array of knocked over tables and chairs. His eyes are closed, and there's blood leaking from beneath his eyelids and out of his nose. The ichor stains the corners of his full, pouty lips while his gray button-up shirt has a growing dark splotch across his abdomen.

I had noticed him walking in, my eyes lingering on his handsome face, trying to check out his lean build. He'd been sitting alone at ease, staring at nothing. The black sunglasses he'd been wearing are on the cobble stone next to him, one lens cracked.

The pulses of electrical energy speed up, warning of a building smite. Another strike is impending.

On the ground, the handsome stranger lies still, his chest rising and falling steadily. I'm not sure how he's alive, but at least he's unaware that his life is about to end.

I question what he did to annoy the Lighter enough to warrant being smited, especially a second time. The act seems like overkill times a thousand. The poor bastard could have just been sitting where the Lighter wanted to enjoy his morning drink of choice.

I could be late for this. My boss would commend me for defending a human. For half of my life, I've trained to harness my

3

Ki and protect those who can't defend themselves from the Seraphinus. I have an obligation to react.

Humans are the weakest race, and the Seraphinus abuse their strength, considering themselves gods who get to do whatever they want. For me to ignore this would be a breach of everything the Magia are supposed to be.

On the other hand, my head is pounding, and I haven't drunk my coffee.

Sighing, I force my fingers to release their grip and drop the cup of precious liquid. If he was cute enough for me to check out, I should save him from the wrath of the Lighter.

Breathing in deep, I straighten my spine, stepping over my discarded drink while the sacred geometry along my spine sears with heat as I call on every bit of my Ki.

The world goes white, and I take the hit, absorbing the magic of the smite. It rushes from my scalp, through my veins into the soles of my feet, like the rush of a million cups of coffee. My pounding headache is gone. The grit in my mouth disappears. Silvery Light rushes over my skin, drawing prickles of chilled bumps in its wake.

I grin, meeting the colorless eyes of the Lighter.

His gaze widens, his jaw going slack in shock.

Someone rushes forward, black tendrils like shadowy, writhing snakes reaching toward the Lighter.

I jut an open palm at him, sending his magic out of me and back to him. A shield of Light forms, an arc meant to deflect the attack I redirected, but it's useless. Seraphinus can't protect themselves from their own magic.

My retaliation ripples through the block and into the Lighter. His eyes roll into his head, his knees giving way as he crumples.

Two figures move into my view, their skin deep, cool brown and black wisps coil around them. One checks the human man I protected. The other kneels over the Lighter then glances up at me. His inky black eyes peg on me, accusatory confusion contorting his features.

These are Darklings, the other kind of Seraphinus. They aren't friends of the Lighter. Dark and Light hate each other, but they aren't friends of Magia either.

I brace, preparing to fight, but wait. My hangover might be gone, but I'm not risking my life trying to take on two Seraphinus at the same time without due cause.

The man inspecting the human says, "He's alive."

The man staring me down sneers. "Grab him. We need to get him back." He shifts upright then kicks at the Lighter. "This is dead."

My lips twitch. I didn't intend to murder the Lighter. I'm not sorry, but I'm never thrilled with killing anything.

The Darkling focuses his attention on me as the other grabs the unconscious man, throwing him over his shoulder and standing.

I hold my hands up, taking a step back. If it attacks with magic, I have the upper hand and can win. If it doesn't, I'm at a disadvantage.

While Magia carry bloodlines of both Light and Dark mixed together, we inhabit human bodies. We are fortified by our magic, but still more fragile and weaker.

The Darkling sans human sneers. "You're coming with us."

Trying to keep a cavalier tone, I force a smile. "Woah. I'm not involved with this. Wrong place, wrong time."

The Darkling steps over the Lighter. "He'll want a word," he says, grabbing my wrist.

It's like hardened metal binding around me. I grit my teeth at cartilage rubbing together in a painful grind.

I try to yank free. "Who will?"

Twisting my limb in his grip, he pivots, dragging me forward. "Him," the Darkling says, jerking his head at the unconscious man.

Digging my heels in, I lift my voice. "Wait, what the burning afters is going on? Why is that human so important?"

The Darkling glances over his shoulder with eyebrows pulled together in irritated daftness. "What human?"

Horror fills me. I stare, frozen in shock, unblinking even as the Darkling yanks me toward a waxed and polished, shiny black vehicle. Seraphinus appear human at first glance. The eyes are the most telling and obvious sign of what they are.

He'd been wearing sunglasses which obscured his eyes, and then they were closed.

I didn't rescue a human. I saved the life of a Darkling.

Oops.

CHAPTER 2
NATALIA

I SIT OPPOSITE THE MAN I MISTOOK FOR HUMAN. A BROAD CHERRY-red tinged wood desk spans the space between us. The surface is neat, a few envelopes unopened and several thin stacks of pages litter the polished surface. There's not a single speck of dust or dirt evident.

Swallowing my nerves, I worm my fingers together, shifting in the leather chair. The upholstery makes a squeak as I drag my butt against it in search of comfort. It's the only disruption of silence, adding to the mounting discomfort.

He's tall. Even with both of us sitting I must lift my chin to meet his gaze. His complexion is his tan, warm with muted tawny tones. He blinks his eerie eyes, full glittering black with their hazy, gray irises barely discernible. It's the only warning he's a Darkling.

He passed for human sitting in front of the café, sipping from a mug in sunglasses. Had I seen his eyes, I would have known better than to get involved.

I wouldn't have been dragged from the café, shoved into a car, brought to this mansion, then woven through the halls and up several floors to this frigid, yet immaculate, office. Everything in my possession was stripped from me, including my phone, wallet, and car key before I was instructed to wait. It felt like three runes passed before the man I misidentified entered the room.

I sit, waiting like a well-behaved captive. I could win a fight against one Darkling, but there are more than enough waiting on the other side of the door that would take me down. One-on-one I'm confident in my abilities. I'm not sure I can survive fighting my way out of this estate.

Lifting a hand, he rubs it over his mouth and settles into a confident ease. Four lines of scrawling script spans the back of his hand, dropping out of sight before I can read the words.

He smiles with pressed lips, the motion forced. "You saved my life."

I've been sitting here alternating between staring at him and the four bare walls painted charcoal, listening to my life waste away one heartbeat at a time for what feels like half the day, just for him to state that fact. I'm torn between laughter and tears.

It was stupid, incredibly stupid. So, so foolish of me. I broke Magia Law. If any other Magia finds out and reports me to the Assembly, I'll be branded a traitor, facing punishment that can include death.

Taking a deep breath, I say, "I see you're going to make me regret it."

"You're funny. I like that."

"Not particularly, no." I clear my throat and cross my legs, pressing my hands together while forcing my half numb fingers between my thighs for warmth. "What can I do for you?"

His eyes narrow, the inquisitive stare melting as he glances up at someone entering behind me. The presence makes the hairs on the back of my neck stand up.

The voice behind me is more musical, but deep. "The new machine is here."

"Thank you, Ramon."

That was it. The presence leaves, the tickle of skin dissipating with their departure. I pull my hands free, my palms clammy and my fingers trembling as I grip the armrests of my chair.

I begin to push myself to my feet. "You seem to be busy, so I'm just going to–"

"Sit."

I drop into the chair again, crossing my arms and legs to preserve warmth. "Guess I can spare a few more fractions of a rune."

He steeples his fingers, elbows bent on his armrests, as he bows his head. His fingertips press into his lips as he studies me, eyes steady with an unrivaled intensity.

Between the strong jawline and high cheek bones, he's a classic pretty boy. His thick black hair is a bit longer, loose waves that cascade from his head. I should have realized he was a bit too alluring to be human even with his eyes covered.

I lift an eyebrow. "Is there a point to this?"

He makes no response, just sits there in his tailored black button up shirt, the sleeves rolled back to expose more of his reddish-brown skin. A watch graces his right wrist, black and sleek. I'm tempted to ask what rune it is.

He is intense. Everything about him. His jet hair, his clothes, even that wicked stare.

I can't help but to think he should have been wearing black earlier to avoid the bloodstain that ruined his gray shirt. I'm not sure how he's upright after the impact he took before I interfered. Not that I expect him to be dead, but he doesn't seem fazed in the least.

My stomach knots as the predator's mouth presses, the corners twitching down, eyes narrowing in pinched deliberation.

Footsteps fall to a stop behind me, another male voice speaking, "You wanted to see me?"

"Massimo," the man staring at me says. "Yes, meet Natalia." He gestures an open hand to indicate me.

"Tallie," I correct him in a hurry, a bit of discord sliding through me that he knows my name. They have my wallet, therefore my official issue registration. It's not a surprise, per say. It's just unnerving that a Seraphinus would care to know my name.

I crane my head to meet the eyes of a second Darkling as Massimo steps next to me. Hitching a smile, I do my best to quash the growing unease. This one is twice as muscular, not lean like the man sitting behind the desk.

Massimo looks down at me, inclining his square shaped head. A thin, white scar runs from temple to cheekbone, glistening in his rich skin of cool brown. He looks like he might be able to survive by eating gravel, which does nothing to calm my ever-growing anxiety.

I lift my eyebrows. "Hi?"

Turning back to the man in charge, Massimo asks, "This is it?"

"Yes."

Sliding his hands into the front pockets of his black jeans, he asks, "What would you like me to do with it?"

I bristle with indignation at being referred to as 'it', screwing one side of my face up to show my displeasure. "It?"

Silence fills the room.

I get to my feet, wanting to exit this situation. I'm late for work. As soon as I leave, I can put this all behind me, forgetting about this disaster. "This has been some kind of morning, but I'm going to leave now. Thanks for," I glance around, not sure what I'm expressing gratitude for. They shoved me in a car, stole my things, and brought me here without consent.

He should be thanking me. Maybe. I got involved unnecessarily, sticking my foot somewhere it never should have been.

"Yeah," I say with a shrug, starting to turn away.

Massimo reaches out, grabbing me by the upper arm without bothering to look my way. His hand encapsulating my bicep is like steel, and I wince. I know Seraphinus of both kinds have superior strength, but I'm less than fond of garnering firsthand experience with their bruising grips.

"Um, dude," I say, using my available hand to push the lilac strands of hair away from my face. "First and final warning, let go."

The man in the chair almost smiles. The corners of his lips twitch as if he considered it then decided better.

Massimo's hand tightens, threatening to snap my humerus. "Try it little Seraphim."

"Woah, hold up, no need to get nasty." I wrinkle my nose. "I'm just trying to get by in life while staying out of the way of your kind."

"Our."

"Your," I repeat, adding force. "As in you and you." I wag a finger between the Darklings, then point at myself. "Not me and mine. The other kind, not the same as me. As in, no wings." I point over my shoulder at my back.

Massimo chuckles. "You killed a Light. That takes serious punch. Humans aren't capable of that kind of power."

I'm not human or my bones would have shattered in his grasp when he clamped down. I lift my eyebrows, cocking a grin. "It was an accident?"

Massimo chuckles, even desk-chair boy smiles behind his fingers.

"Seriously," I say, nodding. "It was pure dumb luck. I thought I'd save a cute guy from your kind's bloody war. No idea who you people are, or anything at all," I tug on my arm in the iron grip to no avail. "How about I just walk out of here, and you never have to see me again?"

The man in charge points at the chair.

Massimo shoves me into.

I grit my teeth, glaring at him. "That's nice, men tossing women around."

"If you hadn't saved his life, you'd be dead. Consider yourself lucky."

"Why?" I yelp, trying again to get to my feet, desperate to run as far from this place and these Darklings as soon as possible.

"We are the Dark. Light fucks don't usually get polite conversation, Seraphim or not." Massimo shoves me down with a hand on my shoulder, bearing down with his weight to keep me in place. "Stay."

I gawk at the man in charge. "I'm going to say this nice and slow, so you follow along. I...am not...nor ever have I been...a Seraphinus...or Seraphim...if there's a difference between the two."

The man's lips hitch back on one side as he drops his hands away from his face. His broad shoulders roll back into the chair, the top few buttons of his shirt undone, leaving a patch of smooth, tawny skin to peak through.

"There is."

The world is run by the Seraphinus, which are split into two factions of Light and Dark, a difference that doesn't even extinguish if they were evil or good. Like humans, the good and the bad come in all shapes and forms, each looking just like the rest.

I blink, tilt my head. "I didn't even know that." I try to stand.

Massimo shoves me down again.

Expelling air in a harsh sigh, I hold my hands up. "All right. Tell me what you want from me. I'll do it to keep my head attached, then we can all just walk away. Yes? Good." I give a curt nod to the man in charge.

"Take your shirt off," he says.

My heart skips a beat, eyes widening. "I beg your pardon?"

"Take your shirt off and turn around."

My eyes drop to my breasts. The request isn't untoward or sexual. He's interested in my back. I cock my jaw, considering if the fight is worth avoiding giving him what he wants.

If I show them my back, they'll see the Magia sacred geometry inked into my skin from my neck to the top of my butt. They might kill me for being what I am.

I shrug off Massimo's hand before turning to sit backward in the chair. Crossing my arms while gripping the edge of my tee-shirt, I pull it up, ducking my head to show off the expanse of my back. "Happy, dick for brains? May I put my shirt back on now?"

One warm finger settles on the top of my spine, the bony knob that sticks out at the base of my neck. That had been the absolute worst part of what he is no doubt inspecting, the dead center of the eye that was nailed into my skin with jade ink. It taps twice, then disappears.

"Satisfied I'm not Seraphinus or Seraphim?" I ask, knowing I don't have whatever he's searching for.

Someone else enters, a brunette man with tan skin. He has human eyes. That's a relief. He shifts his brown gaze beyond my shoulder. "Marius is here to see you." He inclines his head, turns on his heel, and leaves.

Desk-boy calls after him, "Thank you, Thomas."

I've heard one too many names. I release my grip, the loose fabric of my shirt slipping down into place. I spin on my butt to face the man in charge. "May I go now?"

"No. Massimo, take her to a room. Keep her secure until I decide what to do with her."

My jaw drops as Massimo grabs me by the arm again. "What? Hey, dude, no, what is this? You can't just–"

"I can," he shrugs, the ghost of humor taking hold of his chiseled features.

Massimo chuckles, pulling me toward the door. "Come along, Little Light Bug."

"Bug," I repeat, aghast. "Do I look like a bug to you? Do I have big eyes and six legs? No. Let go. I'm not going anywhere with you. I've been patient, but I'm leaving now."

The man behind the desk ignores me, leaning over, staring down at a folder that he flips open.

"Damnit," I grind out, trying to dig my heels in while trying to peel Massimo's fingers from around my arm. "You can't do this."

I center, straightening my spine and tightening my abdomen as I inhale deep to expand my ribs to draw on my Ki. Light flashes, brilliant, pure, and blindingly bright.

Massimo snarls, face scrunching and eyes narrowing as shadows curl off his body. His hand clamps tighter. I shove my hand to the middle of his chest.

He might be Seraphinus, but I'm Magia with the marks down my spine to prove my bloodline and training. He had fair warning. He saw my back.

The crack of my hand into his chest sends him flying. His grip on my arm rips free. I stumble, blinking away the bright dancing stars in my vision.

Massimo picks himself off the floor, swiping at leaking, glistening dark blood from his nostrils. His eyes glitter with the promise of pain and the man behind the desk is on his feet. Both sneer at me.

Standing in a room with two Darklings then attacking one is probably stupider than saving the life of one. I can't undo the action, so I head for the door, hoping to run for freedom.

Massimo heads me off. Shadows wrap around him that streak toward me. I shield. The translucent Dark tendrils drive into glistening arcs of my block, twisting and unfurling like ink in water against the barrier.

The Dark coils wrap around his fist and wrist as he swings. I try to stop my forward movement, praying to the Mother I can avoid the hit, but fail. Massimo's fist slams into my face. The world tilts, then everything goes black.

CHAPTER 3
CALLAHAN

THE ROOM GOES BRIGHT. I LIFT A HAND TO SHIELD MY EYES. MY magic hisses, despising the Light. It leaks out of me as soft tendrils that curl around me in protection. Their inky darkness is stark against the illumination emitting from Natalia.

My eyes adjust, narrowing against the brilliant glow from her as she stares down Massimo. I'm half blinded by the sheer, overwhelming power slipping free of her control.

I squint burning eyes as she reaches out, putting her hand to Massimo's chest. He flies away from her, then the Light goes out, plunging us back into the softer glow of electric bulbs.

Frowning, I drop my hand as Massimo gets up.

Natalia takes two steps toward the door. She's running. It seems odd. It's a smart choice, but not the one I expect from a Light.

Massimo strikes with a single swing of his fist and a grunt. She crumples like a fragile child's doll. I flip the folder shut with a slap of my fingers against the desk, shadows seething from the tips.

Pulling my ears back in displeasure, I drop my gaze to the woman on the floor. I stalk around my desk to Massimo, grabbing him by his shirt, dragging him away from her, and slamming him

15

against the wall. Pinning him with a forearm, I curl my lip. My Dark seeps from my skin, spreading out across Massimo's chest. "She's a woman who saved my life."

"She attacked me first," he snarls, not fighting back. Massimo knows not to piss me off.

"Deal with it nicely. You can handle her without resorting to either killing her or causing significant injury." I shove away from my man. "Pick her up, put her in a room, and keep her there. I have to go deal with Marius. I'll decide what to do with her after."

I straighten my shirt as I check what rune it is on my watch, then head from my study to the front room of my home. This is not what I intended to do with my day.

Marius stands when I enter, running a hand down the buttons of his shirt then crossing his arms. Jacques, Marius's contracted, remains slouched in one of the black leather armchairs.

I stop short, meeting Marius's eyes. They are full black with a foggy gray iris like all my kind, although a fleck of red resides in his right eye, a sign of his race. His eyes are stark against his pale skin, his features pinched in the middle of his face.

I lift my chin. "To what do I owe this displeasure?"

He rolls to the balls of his feet, grinning wide. "Word is out that you're a contender for the Dark Throne."

I check my watch again chalking this up to a waste of his time. "I realized that. How's your father's health? Still declining rapidly?"

"Our King is still ill." Marius's grin widens. "As a matter of fact, the old bastard isn't dying fast enough if you ask me. Would be nice if he went to the afters in the next few weeks. We wouldn't have to go through another Gathering Shadows."

I wouldn't mind forgoing another Gathering Shadows. It's an annual event in the Dark Capital that I've had to endure for nearly three centuries. For twelve days, the strongest of the Dark compete to prove who are the strongest, the top five being assigned as contenders for the Dark Throne.

Rubbing my jaw, I shrug. "We'd have to go through the contest."

Marius smooths his combed over black hair to one side then drops his hands to his hips. "That's inevitable. There is an interesting rumor from this morning. A Light came to your aid."

"What a ridiculous notion that is," I reply, forcing a tight smile.

"Something killed the Light."

Rolling my shoulders back, I cross my arms. "That is what I am told."

"Bastard caught you off guard," Marius says, chuckling.

"That tends to happen when enemies know a secret they shouldn't. I question how they knew."

"Someone must have talked."

"Someone always talks. I'll be cleaning house, though I doubt this came from within."

Marius's voice is paper thin but smooth as silk. "Yes, everyone is loyal to the Great Cal. Or is it Callahan the Calm? You'll need to pick one."

I'd take his quip as a compliment if we weren't both on the contenders list. We are two of those five once his father, the current Dark King, dies. One of us is going to die before either of us wins the throne. The precocious titles are mockery, not genuine assistance.

I lick along my front teeth. "At the moment, cranky is more fitting. I had a smite dropped on me during my morning cappuccino. Didn't even get to finish the fucking thing."

"How very unfortunate."

"Was there anything else?"

Holding my gaze, Marius shakes his head. "I heard she was a pretty little thing. Killed that Light fuck a little too easy."

An image of Natalia flickers through my mind. The woman is lithe with purple hair and silver eyes that flash with vigor. Pretty little thing is an accurate description. "The universal truth is 'Light burns out the Dark, and Dark snuffs out Light.'"

Marius shakes his head. "I see I'll be getting nothing from you. Somewhere out there someone knows something though. It's only a matter of time until she's found."

I fight responding to the bait, even giving him my most charming smile. "Do you know how most rumors start? An over-active imagination."

His eyes twitch as he glances down and back up my body. "Fair enough. If it hurt you too badly, you wouldn't be upright. Smites sting. Un-countered smites are deadly, even to Callahan the Great. That one has a nice ring to it."

"If that is all?" I turn away. "I have business to attend to."

A throat clears as Jacques interjects, "One more thing, Callahan."

I stop, turning my face to glance over my shoulder. Jacques is on his feet, shoulder to shoulder with Marius, a letter is extended in his grip.

I curl my lip at it, then meet his narrow black eyes. His cheek bones protrude, his features sharp. Next to Marius, he appears frail, built thin with wiry limbs.

He tries to smile, his thin lips closed and curving upward at the corners. "The escapade you enjoyed this morning didn't go unnoticed. The Council sends their regards."

I snatch the envelope, baring my teeth at the red wax seal stamped with crossed swords, a crown above and below them. "Why am I being summoned? I was attacked."

Marius withdraws, chuckling. "It's the Council. Everyone knows it's nothing but a waste of time."

Jacques shrugs. "As a member of the Council, I must remind you that any infractions to our laws are investigated, then appropriately addressed." He rubs the back of his neck, staring at my shoes as his shaggy blond hair falls forward into his face. "It should be routine, simple questions."

Marius whistles in a sharp signal to follow. Jacques lifts his pointed chin at me, then spins around, quick to obey his contractor. I eye them leaving as I tear the parchment open to pull the card out.

Flourished script in deep red is stark against the waxy white surface, the scent of decay wafting from the page. I curl a lip at the Council's fondness for writing in blood, skimming the words. It's a summons to the Common Ground Citadel for allegations of peace disruption.

I crinkle the letter in my hand, glaring at Thomas, a young Seraphim approaching.

He stops short, frowning. "What can I do for you?"

"Get away from me," I grunt, the summons shaking in my fist. "Then tell everyone else who shows up to fuck off."

I return to my study, tossing the crumpled letter onto my desk. Millennium ago, the Light and Dark met to agree on common ground, establishing a council to bridge between us. It was designed to end the continuous wars between Light and Dark, evolving to use laws to determine who lives and dies, resolving disputes with politics and negotiations rather than with blood and death.

The summons I have is nothing more than political nonsense. It was issued to cover the Council from any recoil or backlash. There is no legal case against me. I was attacked, not responsible for the clash between Light and Dark, nor responsible for killing my attacker. Other than the annoyance of being forced to appear and answer, which is nothing but a time-consuming endeavor to report those facts, I have little care for this interruption of my life. I'll share the story before being excused.

My concern is that someone opened their mouth, releasing my name as a contender for the Dark Throne. Two-hundred and eighty-eight years ago an entire contender's list was wiped out by the Light.

My Dark twists around me in fury and hatred alike.

The Dark King is dying, his health deteriorating rapidly, and the Light will be eager to cause disruption for the weakening

Dark. The Gathering Shadows ceremonial games are approaching, which is hassle enough, but I have a more pressing problem locked up in a room somewhere in my home.

I grab the back of the chair Natalia sat in, leaning into it as a support while hanging my head to stare at the floor. There are already rumors about her, and she has no idea what she is. Her power is undeniable, yet she has no wings, or, at least, no scars on her back.

All Seraphinus have wings, regardless of Light or Dark, lineage or heritage. It's a manifestation of our magic. When it rips through our skin and retracts it burns, leaving behind scars. Granted, Natalia is young, so her magic may not have developed enough to be capable of exhibiting in that way yet.

My confusion ticks higher. Her magic has developed far enough to be capable of taking down a fully matured Light Seraphinus, so wings should be an easy feat.

Standing up, I shove the chair toward the desk. Natalia could be a Seraphim, in which case, she would have no wings. If so, she shouldn't possess the strength to bring down a Seraphinus.

I'm not going to unravel that riddle yet. First, I need to deal with the release of my name on the contender's list, to determine if I have a vassal in contempt of their contract.

I press a hand against my abdomen, breathing out sharp at the tenderness of the wound. Marius was right about one thing. Smites sting. I'm no fool though. A man in my position can't afford to walk around without protection. As blindsided as I was by the attack, the protection spell I wear had done its job. I'm alive, and Natalia had neutralized the threat against my life.

Natalia can stay locked up. She'll be safe enough that way for now. The gods help either Light or Dark that decided to piss her off, though. The woman killed a Light and took down Massimo. Whatever she is, to be toyed with isn't it.

CHAPTER 4
CALLAHAN

I SPENT THE DAY INVESTIGATING MY CLOSEST CONTRACTED, ensuring their compliance to keep my secrets. I found no reason to suspect any of them are in contempt. Running a hand down my face, I collapse on the couch, staring at nothing in the air.

Checking the time on my watch, I realize it's almost Night's rune. My entire day was wasted by this mess.

My abdomen pulses, and I go back through this morning in my mind, reviewing what I missed, how a Light managed to get the drop on me. The room darkens, shadows swirling, and the blessing of night descends upon the world.

Massimo steps into the open archway of the room, crossing his arms. He scowls at me, and then drops his arms, turns, and grabs a decanter. Settling on the other end of the sofa, he pours two tumblers, sliding one across the smooth surface of the low, wood table. "The lightning bug is annoying."

I glare at the drink out of reach, clenching my jaw. The Light is locked up in a room of my house. It's in my home. It's agony. I want it gone, or better yet, dead. I can't reasonably kill it, no matter how tempting. It wouldn't be fair considering it interfered to prevent my death.

"Leave it. I have to figure out what to do with it."

A throat clears, so I lift my eyes under drawn brow to Thomas in the doorway. "Would you like the messages left for you?"

Cocking my jaw, I consider him. He's thin and lanky, with skin that carries a faint tinge of color and brown hair. He is the sole Seraphim I have contracted to serve me. Thomas's father was a vassal of mine who raped human women. Apparently, he did so frequently until I caught onto his actions. I sent him into the burning afters with joy, however, one of the humans gave birth to Thomas.

I accepted responsibility of him. His father was my contracted, therefore the results of his actions were my problem. I raised him into adulthood, sheltering him under my wing, and then when he was old enough to comprehend the world, I signed him to a life-long contract.

Seraphim aren't strong, although they will manifest with the Light or Dark according to their ancestry. He's never going to be able to fight for me, but he's as much of a son as I have.

I ask, "How old are you, Thomas?"

His gaze falls to the floor, his lips pinching. "One-hundred-and-twenty."

"When did you develop the Dark?"

He cocks his head, eyes rolling to the ceiling. "Ah...ha, it was later than Seraphinus. I think about..." He lifts a level hand and wiggles it side to side. "About twenty?"

"You aren't hiding any great abilities from me, are you?" I drop my chin to my chest, staring from the tops of my eyes.

He laughs. "Not in the least. Is this about that lightning bug? Is she a Seraphim too?"

Putting a hand to my stomach, I rock forward far enough to snag the glass, then settle back. "Who stopped by?"

Thomas checks the small pages in his hand. "Jezabelle, Sterling, Chlem, ah," he stifles a smile, "Telra, and Lazarus."

My face screws up. The first four names make sense. Jezabelle,

22

Sterling, and Telra are three other contenders for the Dark Throne, with Chelm trying to reclaim his place on the list since he got knocked off it. I'm bored by their presence, no doubt looking for answers about this morning as Marius had been. The last name is unfamiliar, though.

"Lazarus," I repeat.

Checking the page, Thomas nods, "Yes. Lazarus Baron. He requested to speak with you. I gave him the requested response the same as the others."

I take a drink, grinning behind the rim. "I'm sorry I didn't get to see their expressions."

A wistful haze takes over Thomas's face, halfway to a smile frozen by death. "Ah, I was pleased to deliver that response to Telra most of all."

Massimo laughs. "Wish I would have gotten myself in trouble and been answering the door today."

Ignoring their disdain for Telra, I ask, "Did Lazarus say what he wanted to speak with me about?"

Thomas shakes his head. "He declined to give me details."

I cut my eyes to Massimo. "Any ideas?"

"No." He settles back, resting his glass on his thigh. "Don't know the name."

"I don't care then." I meet Thomas's eyes. "Any other surprises for me?"

"No, sir."

I jerk my chin. "You can have the rest of the night."

"Thanks, dad." Thomas grins as he spins on his heel, leaving me to Massimo and the booze.

Sipping on the liquor, I savor the burn over my lips and down my throat. I down the rest in a single mouthful then fiddle with the glass.

Massimo asks, "What am I doing with the lightning bug?"

I breathe out slow, getting comfortable by tipping my head back and closing my eyes. "I haven't got a fucking clue."

"Do we believe her?"

"It's the Light. I don't trust it."

"It says it's not Seraphim, and it has no wing scars."

"If you're only going to tell me what I know, why are you here?"

Chuckling, he says, "For the good stuff."

I pick my head up, glancing to see him lifting his half-full tumbler. Extending mine without a word, I expect a refill. "I hate the Light."

"We all do." He takes my glass, pouring three fingers, and passing it back like a well-behaved vassal.

Sighing, I take a drink, licking my lips. The Dark and the Light are instinctual enemies, but I have reason to hate the Light more than most. It cost me my father in every possible way. I throw back the liquor to chase those damned thoughts and memories from my mind.

I tap the empty glass against my leg. "I can't kill it."

"Well…" Massimo laughs, "You could, but it wouldn't sit right with our honor code." He turns to me and winks. "I wouldn't tell on you though."

I pull back one side of my mouth in lazy humor. "I'd know, and as much as I loath to admit it, the lightning bug earned respect."

"Guess we know the spell worked at least."

I reach behind me, reaching beneath the collar of my shirt to rub the space between my shoulders. "It's there. We already knew it worked."

"No, we knew you put stupid marks on your back."

"Shut up, it worked. I'm a genius for it." I flash my teeth at him in a faux grin. "Speaking of marks…"

"Don't ask me." Massimo grunts as he drains his glass. He reaches for mine, filling both tumblers before returning it.

"Are you trying to get me drunk?"

"Your ass got smited. Yes."

24

I laugh. "What the fuck is down her back? Is that just stupid human shit?"

"I said don't ask me. No fucking clue what it was, but I get the feeling she didn't want to show her back because she was hiding them."

Rubbing my jaw, I stare at the wall before us. The liquor is kicking in, the edges of my vision fuzzy. In all the madness of the day, I'd never consumed anything. I hum, picking at that thought.

What I thought was an inconvenient detour in this day of my life may be a potential benefit. "I could feed from it."

"I believe we established that we weren't killing it."

I throw back the bourbon, not believing I'm about to speak these words. The idea is taboo, yet my father did it. I can't believe I'm even considering this idea, so I'm blaming it on the alcohol. "I don't kill it. In fact, I keep it. I'll contract it."

Massimo spits his mouthful out, the air before us filling with a fine mist of expensive liquor. He chokes then smacks himself in the chest with a closed fist. "Excuse the ever-loving fucking Dark out of me, but what did you say?" He lifts his glass, eyeing the contents.

I smirk. "You heard me right. I keep it with a contract."

He's sitting upright, twisted to me with fury, yelling, "It's the fucking Light."

Shrugging, I wince at the stinging in my abs from using torn muscles. "Yes, we established that we believe it to be Light. Are you going to continue to tell me things I already know?"

"You're out of your fucking skull," he says, his voice hoarse. "That smite shorted something in you."

Grinning, I offer my glass. "Maybe, or it's the liquor."

Massimo rips the tumbler from my grip, hurling it across the room. It shatters, busting the plaster of my wall.

I narrow my gaze to scream at him with my eyes. "You're going to clean that up and fix the damage personally."

"Worth it."

I extend my hand for his glass. "I hope so."

Pouring the contents down his throat, he places the empty tumbler in my open palm. "I think you've had enough."

I'm not going to laugh at that, although he's probably right. "Don't make me be an ass and use your contract." I lift my right hand, showing the back of it with his worn agreement in my skin.

He plucks the tumbler up, filling it to the brim, and dangling it in front of me by his fingertips. "Yes, *sir*."

"Don't." I grip the base as he withdraws his hand.

"You have lost your wits. You can't contract the Light."

"There are no laws against Dark contracting Light in service."

He shakes his head, getting up for another glass from the liquor cabinet. "There are."

I lift the drink to my lips, taking care to avoid spilling the contents. I've been studying the laws, committing them to memory for decades in preparation of being the next Dark King. "There are laws against me coercing the Light into servitude, but if it agrees willingly, then it's legal. At least, there's nothing illegal about it."

"There are no laws about it because it's impossible. The Light is never going to willingly and knowingly agree to serve the Dark."

"Light doesn't save the Dark. It burns it out until it no longer exists," I say, breathing out through my nose, relaxing into the fuzz filling my skull. "It saved me. It isn't acting like the Light."

"I don't give a fuck what it's acting like." He leans forward, face in his hands, groaning. He rubs his face, then reaches for the decanter. His Dark stretches in tendrils through the air to pick up and deliver a new glass into his hand. He fills the tumbler partway, then throws it all down in a single gulp. "You're going to fucking do it, aren't you?"

"It solves a problem in my life. I don't have to figure out how to get away with murdering a Light fuck every time I need to feed on the Light."

He pours another shot, forcing it down before shaking his head. "It'll kill you. Even if the host agrees, the Light hates us. One of you will kill the other."

I hum in response. I have firsthand experience that he's incorrect in the assumption. At least partially wrong. My father had a Light Seraphinus to feed from. It caused his demise, but the Light he fed on isn't what killed him.

Massimo might be right about the smite damaging something in my brain. What my father did revolted me, and here I am, heading down the same path. Albeit, I have no partner to betray, and I don't foresee falling in love with it. Fucking it, though. That's an option.

My eyes widen as I stare at my cock. That was entirely it's decision, so I'm putting it in time out now. It makes stupid choices.

Turning to Massimo, I say, "Go get another bottle. I'm going to need more bourbon."

CHAPTER 5
NATALIA
5TH NIGHT'S DAY, BLOOMING 4049 6TH MILLENNIUM

TRUTH BE TOLD, THE ROOM I'M LOCKED INSIDE IS GORGEOUS. Waking up in the middle of the enormous bed wasn't a terrible experience. Everything is dark wood, gray, middle of the night blues, and blacks. There is a waterfall shower in the attached bathroom, the walls glittering dark, and this suite is larger than my entire rented house. I might be a prisoner, but it's not a four-by-four foot, dank, dark, and moldy cell.

Gilded cage or disgusting hovel, a prisoner is a prisoner, even if this single room is more like my own personal palace. After a few deep breaths while taking a look around yesterday, I decided to enjoy myself. Eventually running out of patience, I banged on the door, screaming to be released. It left the side of my hand and forearm-tinged blue with a deep bruise this morning. Both things were easy enough to heal with Ki, but my efforts got me nowhere.

The most I got for my troubles was informed to cease and desist and a door slammed in my face. The only other time the door was opened was to deliver an evening meal. It was so damn good I had licked the crumbs from the plate.

Today, I get a delicious breakfast, a scowl when I put in a request for vodka, and the door slammed in my face again. I relax then stretch, moving through poses until my muscles are quivering mush, before slipping into the bathroom to enjoy the grand shower. Soaking in hot water and steam, I meditate under the luxurious spray until my fingers prune.

I lay in the middle of the glorious bed, like a massive cloud that I sink into, eyes rolling in pleasure. As much as I'm getting restless, I'm trying to deny the fact that I'm content to remain his prisoner. Working fingers through my hair, I detangle the knots, then masturbate to kill time.

At first, I try to avoid thinking about that man on the other side of the desk, but my restraint fails. Darkling or not, the man is more than attractive. Casting aside the moral qualm, I daydream about the things he could do.

Drifting in a half-conscious state, I ride out the bliss of my orgasm in this incredible bed considering how I got into this mess. All I wanted was a little caffeine to help start the day. If only I had walked away to let the Seraphinus tear each other apart. I wouldn't have wasted six coin on coffee by dropping the cup to defend him.

I roll over, curling in a ball and tucking my hands beneath my head, then sigh. It's only the second day, but the suns are setting. The sky is teal, the orange sun gone from sight, the smaller red nearly dipping below the horizon.

This could be worse. Aside from being cooped up, it's a haven from my life.

The door opens, and the man in charge steps into the room in dark, tailored clothes that do nothing to conceal the strength radiating off his body. His black gaze settles on me as he closes the door behind him.

I should have put my clothes back on.

Clearing my throat, I sit up, gripping the sheet to my chest. "Do you know this is illegal?"

He takes a few steps closer to the bed, features bored. I already know Seraphinus don't answer to human law, but I'm going to make a point.

"Dude, I'm serious, I need to know if you're an asshole or a dumbass. I need to know what I'm working with here."

His eyes drop from my face, lowering to my body, then lift back to meet my gaze. "An asshole."

"Oh, good," I say, adjusting to ensure I'm covered. "Can I go home now?"

"No." He didn't even take a breath before he spoke. It was absolute and without mercy.

I turn my face away, cocking my jaw as I consider what to do with that. "Then tell me what you want from me."

He stares, then slides his hands in the front pockets of his dark washed jeans. "Light does not save Dark. It burns it out until it no longer exists."

I hang my head, snorting through my nose. "I'm not a Seraphinus, so I'm not Light or Dark."

"If not Seraphinus, then Seraphim."

I fight a smile, managing to keep my lips pressed. "What the burning afters is a Seraphim?"

"You don't know?" He lifts a single eyebrow, watching me like he doesn't believe me.

"No."

"Half Seraphinus, half human. What do you think you are?"

I perk up, straightening my spine and rolling my shoulders back. I assumed they knew. They'd seen my marks. "Magia."

He stares at me like he doesn't understand, head leaning to the side.

"Magia," I repeat, eyebrows drawing together. "Hereditary bloodlines of magic, stuck between the Light and Dark. The mixed blood of Light and Dark Seraphinus imbued into humans." I mesh the fingers from both hands together. "It was a task carried out as a way of unionizing the Light and Dark. It was an accord of peace that was later shattered, although the Magia remained. Any of this ringing any bells?"

The man takes a deep breath, torso swelling, the blood red button up shirt stretching tight across his chest. "The old stories of Magia tell of great power, but the bloodlines were diluted. There hasn't been a Magia as far as the Seraphinus are concerned in a very long time. They were destroyed."

I run fingers through my hair, tossing the locks out of my face. "Sure, whatever you say. We avoid your kind unless we are trying to stop you from killing humans, hence me trying to save you," I wave a hand at him. "So, are we good now? I can go?"

He presses his lips together and shakes his head, face dropping to the floor. "Natalia..."

"Tallie," I correct him.

"...I don't think you are comprehending the magnitude of what you did."

"I've been locked in this room for two days. I'm getting the message loud and clear. Trust me, I know better than to get involved with your kind. It won't happen again."

The man lifts his gaze to me. "You're involved now, like it or not. By now everyone has likely heard the rumors. Light will be angry. Dark will be curious. Both will be looking for you."

"Me?" The word is a sharp shrill squeak from the back of my throat as my eyes get wide. "Why?"

He shrugs, "To kill you, enslave you," his voice drops as do his eyes. "Use you."

The fact that I'm naked registers, sparking fantasies about him using me. I wrap the sheet tighter, adding a couple more layers for extra protection against his wandering eyes. "I'll figure it out. It'll be okay. I don't even know your name. You can just let me walk right out of here knowing nothing about you or yours or whatever goes on here and whatever happens is my problem."

"Callahan."

I throw my hands in the air, then rush to grab the sheet before it drops any lower. "Why'd you go and do that?"

31

He smiles, a dimple in his left cheek. "You kept me alive. You should know who you saved."

"I don't want to know! I don't want to know a damn thing. I just want to go home and forget the fact that I saved a Dark Seraphinus because my nana will kill me if she ever finds out. A fucking Magia heiress saving the life of a Darkling? Mother have mercy, it'll give her a heart attack and she's a hundred and thirty-seven these days." I dot the triangle of the Mother from chin, to right shoulder over to the left and then up to the top of my nose as I roll my eyes.

Callahan takes the last couple of steps and then sits on the edge of the bed. "Mind if I lay down?" He leans back to lower himself to lay flat before I can answer, head near my bent legs so he looks straight up at me. "I'm not fully healed yet, this is easier."

I frown. "I'm fine. Enjoy the view up my nostrils."

His eyes close as he rests in ease. My heart skips a beat staring down at him. He has chiseled features, and from what I can discern, lean cut muscle in skin that draws the scent of cinnamon to mind.

I grip the sheet harder in both hands, rolling my right shoulder in a nervous tick. I shouldn't be drooling over a Darkling. "I didn't think Seraphinus were so easy to hurt."

"I'm not." He's unamused, voice terse. "And I'd take you down even injured, so don't try it."

"I'm not exactly dressed for a fight."

"I noticed."

Shifting to make sure I'm covered again, I bob my head. "I can, uh, help you," I offer. I'd already broke the rules by saving his life. Healing him would be more like bending the rules.

One of his eyebrows ticks up while his eyes remain closed. "I was about to say the same."

"What's going on here?"

"I have a use for you, and you have a use of me."

Blinking rapidly, I lift my eyebrows. "Excuse me?"

"You embroiled yourself in things you do not understand without the ability to even recognize the danger you are in because of what you did. I am in a position where I can use you for my benefit and can manage threats for you in return for your compliance."

It was rather straightforward of him, albeit abrupt to outright acknowledge he wanted to use me. I frown, picking at a frayed string on the edge of the sheet. It's the first imperfection I've seen since I arrived. "What are you saying?"

"You need me, and I can use you."

"Need is a strong word."

One side of his mouth curls back, eyes opening. "You need me. Wolves are coming for you, Lightning Bug, and make no mistake they are hungry."

"I'll manage," I say, my voice lacking confidence. I'm not sure how long I'd last if Seraphinus came for me. A one-on-one fight I can manage, survive, maybe escape, but his words imply more than that.

"You'll end up dead or on your knees in chains serving."

"And you'll use me," I snap back, huffing. "I'll take my chances on my own."

Callahan grins. "Yes, I'll use you, but you may find my treatment of you is less ugly."

I glare down at him. "Your man knocked me out."

"I dealt with Massimo."

"Oh." I'm not sure what 'dealt with' means, but it leaves me inferring he noticed and was displeased. That's sweet.

"You have my word it will not happen again as long as you follow orders."

Any tenderness his previous words invoked disappears. "If I don't follow orders?"

Tipping his head back, he smirks, but his tone remains aloof. "Then you'll have to deal with me, and you'll be glad it was Massimo the first time."

I sigh, pulling fingers through the underside of my hair while turning my face away. Although staring at him is enticing, he was accurate in his admittance of being an asshole. At least he is honest.

Tony pretends to be otherwise. He holds tight to his belief that he is righteous, a good man of strong faith in the Magia, a paragon of what they stand for.

Frowning at the wall, I ask, "I'm not being given a choice, am I?"

"You are. I'm assuming you'll make the smart decision."

"Which is letting you use me?"

"There will be a contract," he says, shrugging his shoulders, "You will be a vassal of mine, and in return I will protect you."

"Isn't vassal just a really fancy word for servant?"

"Yes," he laughs, "but it isn't slave."

"Pretty sure it's slave with payment."

He's smiling. "Isn't that the same as what humans refer to as employment?"

I laugh this time. "Pretty much." That sobers me. I'm probably fired for not presenting to work. There is no way I can explain my whereabouts. If I confess to saving the life of a Darkling, my life gets worse than losing my job.

"I can throw you out, leave you to your demise or," he hesitates, "you agree to pay me ten years."

Ten years puts me closer to forty, almost at the end of my possible childbearing days. "Can't do ten. How about two?"

"Ten."

"Five?"

"Ten, my standard contract is twice as much, with those who take it usually asking to increase it."

I shake my head. "Your standard contract is probably for Seraphinus, who live for centuries."

"Your nana is over a century."

I smile. "Nana is a hundred and thirty-seven, and still going strong."

He gives me a humored expression. I tip my head back, staring at the ceiling to concentrate. Magia live longer than humans, as we age slower due to the Seraphinus blood, however, we still couldn't have children forever. I have obligations, a duty to produce an heir.

"But," I drawl, "I'm almost thirty, and I can only have children until forty-five on average."

"That's plenty of time when I'm done with you."

"Golly gee, that's fucked of you, but that's only if I survive the ten years, with a maybe I have time if I'm average, plus Tony will flip his shit if–"

"Who is Tony?"

I sink my teeth into my lower lip, wincing, knowing I shouldn't be discussing these things with a Darkling. This is Magia life. My life. I glance at the ring on my left hand, the obvious symbol I can't hide. "My fiancé."

Callahan twists up, leaning on one arm to glare at me. "A union? That ends when you enter my services."

I frown, twisting the ring. The gem was large enough, but Tony didn't go for anything extravagant, just the round stone on a silver band. It was nice that he bought me a diamond when he didn't have to buy anything at all. Sometimes I might be too hard on him about our relationship. "My personal life is none of your business. You don't get to control it."

He stares with putrid rage. Black tendrils curl from under his shirt, wrapping around his neck like black fog. "When you serve me, you don't get a life beyond my needs."

I blink at the shadows twisting around him like smoke. "I'll take my chances."

"What would Tony do if he knew you were in bed naked with me? What would he do if he were to find out? If I were to tell him?"

His threat is evident, but it rings hollow. I shrug with a wide, faux smile. "Not much, you could tell him if you really wanted."

The fog darkens, almost solid, creeping over his collar, wrapping up his forearms. "If I heard my intended mate was in bed with another man naked, regardless of circumstances, I'd kill the other man then chain my woman up where no one but me would ever see her again."

There's a rush of heat through my core at the idea of being chained up at the mercy of the man before me. I shake the daydream away. It's far too arousing, and I already got off on the fantasy of a Darkling. I need to step away from the ledge, not off it.

"That would be if Tony cared enough, which he doesn't. It's not like that, but I can't break the engagement. This is Magia stuff–bloodlines–I'm an heiress–an original family ancestry. This is shit that I don't have a say in. So, five years and the engagement will stand, or I take my chances out there," I jerk my head toward the windows.

He considers, then shrugs, lying flat again. "Seven for the inconvenience of your split attentions."

I almost laugh, choking on a scoff of humor instead. Callahan lifts his eyebrow as I recompose myself. "I'll think about it."

He closes his eyes, lacing his fingers over his stomach. "Think fast, Little Lightning Bug. You do not have time."

I pull my knees to my chest and stare out the windows. The view overlooks neat shrubbery, a miniature hedge maze with a pergola in the middle, cherry trees in blossom line the massive square garden on the other side of the windowpane. The white flowers seem to almost glow in the soft light of dusk. Between the gorgeous room and the promise of spending time in that garden, I'm almost willing to sell my soul to live like this.

Almost, just not for the price of my freedom. Not even what little I pretend and claw to have. "No," I say, the word a breath of air released from my chest without conscious thought.

"You're going to walk out my door to the imminent threat of death or enslavement of all manner?"

"I think you're just trying to scare me because you want something from me." I do my best to keep my voice from trembling.

He sits up, hunched over so his elbows rest on his legs, his head bent forward. "Then the very least I can do is give you a ride home in exchange for standing against the Light on my behalf." Callahan stands up, heading for the door. He grabs then twists the knob, opening the door. He pauses, glancing back at me. "You have a tenth of a rune while I collect your things. I suggest you get dressed."

CHAPTER 6
CALLAHAN

I DRIVE NATALIA HOME RATHER THAN SENDING SOMEONE TO DO THE job. While I have plenty of vassals at my disposal, I want more time with her. My potential use of her is enticing, which means I need a way to convince her to accept a contract. Information is key, so I sit in the driver's seat with Massimo in the backseat as an extra precaution. In another day I'll be healed. I could survive on my own, but I have no reason to strain myself.

Natalia sits in the front seat next to me. She is dressed again, staring out the window. It helps to subdue the distraction of her. Her pleasant features and build make it difficult to concentrate with the memory of there being only a thin sheet between us earlier.

I hate that she's appealing. She's the Light.

My eyes keep flicking to her unbidden by my logic. I struggle to keep my gaze on the road, even as I have to swerve to stay on it.

She's chosen death instead of servitude. It tells me something about her. She is stupid. That fact isn't going to deter me. Knowledge can be taught.

Her phone rings. As she lifts the phone, I check the display.

Tony is calling. She rejects the call, then goes back to staring out the window. He calls again.

She sighs, accepting the call. "Hello."

I reach out, grab the phone, put it on speaker, and hand it back to her. If she is going to be in my car, I have the right to know what she is discussing. Natalia takes the phone back, giving me a snide glance of irritation.

"Hi?"

"Bad day or just because it's me?" A terse male voice comes through the speaker.

"Long day."

"Oh," he laughs, sounding surprised. "Cool, dinner? Next Thorn's day?"

My gaze shifts from the road to Natalia. She seems confused as well. "A week from now?"

"Today's Night's day. How much have you drank?"

"Whatever, basically."

"You in?"

"Yeah, that sounds–"

"Great, my mom wants to see you."

The confusion on Natalia's face becomes disgust. "Sure."

"The Gardens, next Thorn's day at Thistle rune, oh, I saw the purple, not your color, change it before dinner. It'll give my mom a stroke to see you like that."

I steal another glance at her. She shifts, crossing her arms over her stomach like she wants to hide herself. "I kinda like it." Her voice carries defeat.

"Nat," Tony says. "Come on, do you own a mirror? You look like shit. Not like–I just mean sick, like you're not feeling well," he trails off. "Just stay blonde."

Natalia points left as I approach a traffic direction light, so I shift to the turn lane. "Sure. Anything else?"

"Wear something nice, okay? With heels. Maybe put a little

effort in? Not like you just rolled in from the shop again please. It was embarrassing."

I brake, stopping the car, waiting for traffic to slow for a chance to turn. I listen, frowning. The tone of the call seems tense and terse. It strikes as odd given their relationship.

Natalia shakes her head, turning to stare out the window again. "I'm sorry my job is so embarrassing to you."

"It's okay, you'll quit soon enough. Seriously, put your notice in, pick a date, my mom's been practically begging—heads up, she wants grandchildren like yesterday. We need to just do this. Stop dragging your feet."

Natalia flips the display off, middle finger up, thumb out. "I'm not ready to pop a couple kids out yet, okay?"

Her words are clipped, her tone full of vinegar. In the bedroom she'd been adamant about her ability to have children. My eyebrows come together as I turn to her. She meets my gaze then flips me off too.

Tony lets out a bark of laughter. "What, like going out with Ness and getting shit faced is really what you should be doing? Fuck, you're wasting your life. You were all business until you earned your marks, then dropped everything afterward."

Natalia sucks in a breath like a reverse hiss. "I'm just supposed to be okay with everything? Nicky and Nat and this?"

There's silence, a lot of it from both participants. I check to see if the call is still connected. The fractions of a rune tick by on the display.

"You know what," Tony sighs through the speakers, "I know this ain't what we wanted. You aren't what I wanted, but I'm trying. I'm actually fucking here, trying but you aren't even working with me on this. You're fighting this, me, our union the whole way because why?"

"You know what's wrong here, so fuck you."

There is a long silence. "Sure? Eventually we have to," his voice drops away, muffled but still audible as he says, "fuck that's going to be awkward." He clears his throat, "I'm serious. You have impressive skills that you aren't doing anything with. You just gave up on everything. When's the last time you gave a shit? Even saved anyone from the winged fucks ruining this world?"

My grip tightens on the wheel. A glance in the mirror as I make the turn tells me Massimo is as annoyed as I am by that statement.

Natalia shakes her head. "Funny story, I did save someone recently."

"Fucking finally, good for you, hope you killed the fuck. Darkling or Lighter?"

Natalia smirks. "Actually, I killed–"

"Yeah, awesome, look I have to go," he laughs. "Holy fuck dude! No way! Sorry Nat, I gotta go. Thorn's day, Thistle, Gardens, wear a dress for fuck's sake–" he laughs "–fuck yeah, oh, and fix your hair."

He disconnects the call. The car fills with silence. Natalia scowls at the phone in her hand, then chucks it to the floorboard.

Tony. Union. Something is very wrong there. It could work in my benefit. Maybe she isn't stupid, maybe I need to find the right leverage to get what I want.

Natalia doesn't say anything other than to give directions until I pull in front of a rundown house with a front light illuminating the brick façade in the dark of night. It's minuscule, maybe a couple hundred years old with ivy growing over one side.

She glares at it, grabs her phone off the floor, then tugs on the door handle. Shouldering the door open, she gets out of my car.

The front door flies open with a bang. A dark-haired woman sticks her head out, mouth open, jaw hanging low in the dim glow of the electric light. "Holy shit, where the Mother have you been? I thought you died!"

Natalia slams my car door as the woman comes running out of the house into the night as Natalia heads toward it. The woman throws herself at Natalia, wrapping her arms around her.

41

"Two fractions of a rune," I say, not taking my eyes off the women. "If I swing, come help me." I get out of the car and walk to them.

The dark-haired woman is taller, long legged with black hair and brown skin. "Seriously, where've you been?" She holds Natalia at arm's length, then glances at me, her eyes growing wide. "Hellllllooo gorgeous!" She whistles.

I stop short, contemplating her with eyebrows pushed together. "Natalia," I say. She turns, I extend my hand, redirecting my eyes from her to the other woman. "Phone, and who are you?"

"Ness," the dark-haired woman says, "and holy shit, you went big for the first time." She nudges Natalia.

"Whatever you're thinking, no." Natalia turns to me. "Why?"

"In case you change your mind."

"I won't," she says, disappearing into the house.

Ness smiles with confusion, only half her face working. "What happened? Why is she in a shit mood?"

"She had a phone call with Tony."

Wincing, Ness wraps her arms around herself. "That'll do it, probably should go stop her from chugging vodka now." She lifts her eyes to meet my gaze, then stumbles back a few paces. "Oh, fuck."

I blink at her, saying, "She should change her mind. Take my number, change her mind, then call me."

Ness scowls, fists clenched at her side. "Buddy, I'm supposed to kill you. I don't know what happened that she just got out of your car and walked away, but you get one free pass, which expires as soon as you get in your car."

Narrowing my eyes, I ask, "You're another Magia?"

Her frown deepens. "Yes."

"Are you as strong as she is?" There is a chance I have other options, maybe less difficult choices.

Ness blinks, face going slack. "No, absolutely not. She's a Swan, the last Swan too. No one's as strong as she is. Now fuck off and get out of here before someone sees you." She glances side-to-side, eyes shifting around. "If they hear you were here and that we let you walk away, they'll label us as traitors."

"Interesting." I glance in the direction Natalia disappeared to. The screen door is hanging off one hinge, the blue paint peeling off the front door. "If it comes to that, maybe you could use someone to call."

Ness stares down her nose, head leaned back, eyebrow lifted. "If it gets you off my front stoop," she pulls her phone out, "digits?"

"353 15108 63368."

She taps on the phone, then slips it into the waistband of her shorts. She crosses her arms, jutting a hip out with attitude to stare me down.

"You wouldn't win," I assure her, turning my back.

Massimo gets out of the back, stepping to the front passenger door. I lift my chin as we both slide into the front seats.

I stare at what I will refer to as a house. The dilapidated construct is so worn if wind blew hard enough, I'd expect bricks to fly free. This place is a shithole that makes my skin crawl.

The land it sits on belongs to me. The whole city and outer lying grounds are titled to my family's lineage, although humans are allowed to use it for a price. They pay living tithes and property taxes to me to compensate for their presence. They still irritate me.

The friend stays where she is, frowning, as I back out of the drive.

Massimo asks, "Are you sure letting her go was the right choice?"

"I need her to submit willingly. It will make her more useful. If she won't sign a contract of her volition, then she becomes more of a problem than I want."

"I get that, but you gave up, which doesn't happen, and easier than I'd even expect if you did."

I smile. "I'm not giving up. She'll change her mind, and when she does, I have leverage. She'll get a contract that more suits my desires."

Massimo turns to me with curiosity but doesn't ask. That's fine. I don't want to answer those questions.

My standard contracts are for vassals that I rarely deal with. That's ideal. There are a few I see regularly, with a bit more of a personal relationship that have a bit more detail to them like Thomas. Then there are my worn contracts, like Massimo. His contract is four lines, and yet by far the most indenturing and complex contract I carry.

When Natalia signs a contract, she would get a few extra rules for my personal benefit, starting with a termination of her intended union to Tony. I don't like sharing my toys.

I glance over my shoulder to change lanes and speed up, heading for the outskirts of the city where my estate lies. "Magia, how much do you remember our lessons from childhood?"

Massimo chuckles. "That was a while ago." He rubs a hand down his face replying, "Ah, not much, they aren't relevant. Basically? Humans that were imbued with the Light and the Dark to run the Council between us. We got rid of them."

"Natalia and the other claim to be Magia." I strum my fingers on the steering wheel, waiting in a line of traffic. I have nowhere to be, and I need to think. I can do that sitting right where I'm at. "Find out what you can, we may need to know more once she changes her mind."

"You're sure she will? I'll say it again, I'm strongly advising against this."

"I know, I just don't give a fuck. I hold the contracts, I decide, and I've decided she's going to change her mind. I'll make sure of it."

He winces then faces away. That's fine. Sometimes he needs a reminder of who is in charge.

44

CHAPTER 7

NATALIA

I TAKE A SWIG OF VODKA FROM THE BOTTLE, STARING DOWN NESS AS she comes back into the house. "What?"

"I know that's vodka."

"You can read the damn label, that's not impressive."

"So," she starts to tick off fingers, "you just got dropped off by a Darkling, who says you had a phone call with Tony, and you've been missing for two days. What's going on?"

I eye the half-empty bottle, then chug until my lungs are burning. There's only about another mouthful, so I fight through it like a winner, trickling the last dribbles into my mouth.

I toss the bottle into the rubbish bin. "Nothing."

"That doesn't work on me, babe." Ness holds a finger up, the other hand balled on her hip. "Who was that Darkling?"

Sighing, I turn my back on her to splay sweaty, thick fingers on the cheap, flecking countertop. "His name," I take a deep breath, hanging my head, "is Callahan. Yes, he's a Darkling. Two days ago, I saved his life. Me, an heiress, saved the life of a fucking Dark Seraphinus."

"What?" Ness's voice is a shrill squeal cutting the air and piercing my ear drums.

One side of my features screws up as I flinch. "I didn't know. I got coffee, I walked out, boom, smite, man on the ground bleeding out of his eyes, nose, mouth, and a hole in his stomach." I turn, one hand on my hip the other gesturing at the floor. "He wasn't moving, eyes closed, I didn't realize what he was."

"By the Mother!" Ness shakes her head. "And?"

"I saw him on the way in, he had sunglasses on, sitting outside, drinking coffee." I throw both hands in the air. "He was cute, saw him dying, I just–it was just save a life from a Lighter."

"The Mother, your mother, and my mother are going to hang us by our toes, beat us with sticks, then strip our marks when they hear about this."

I sneer. "They aren't going to hear about this. It's that simple. We pretend like none of this ever happened."

Ness shoves her fingers in her hair, grabbing at the long, glossy strands of black. "They were here, two of them, in our driveway. You got out of their car. I have his phone number."

"What?" I gape at her. "You didn't!"

"I did to get him to leave after I saw his eyes. Hopefully no one saw anything too, you know, Darkling about them. It's night. Our chances are pretty good, I didn't realize until he was up close, when I looked harder. Freaky how much they appear human."

Scoffing I say, "If you don't see their eyes."

Ness runs her hands the rest of the way through her long, loose hair, then drops the shinny locks to let her arms rest at her sides. "What about the last two days?"

"Oh, Callahan is some kind of in charge guy, the kind with servants, although he calls them vassals, and he's got a great home. That gorgeous palace right outside the city? Yeah, that's his place. Pretty sure that's what all the living taxes we pay have bought."

"Uh, yeah, do you not pay attention to the tax forms? Callahan Barraco is the Seraphinus that owns Narwal."

I make a face of disgust. "Great, he's the Darkling that owns our city and the one we shell out fifty percent of our earnings to for the rights to live in his city."

"More important question. Why do you know where he lives?"

I roll my eyes, crossing my arms and recap the interesting day I had.

She frowns. "Why the fuck didn't you fight back?"

"There are dozens and dozens of Darklings in that place. One I can handle, maybe two, but not that many. I thought my chances were better if I behaved. Thought he'd just, you know, let me go." I gesture around our dismal kitchen. "Then he offered me a contract with him."

Ness blinks a few times, face pulled long with surprise, her features stretching. "What the Mother have you done? A Darkling, a freaking fucked Dark Seraphinus, offered you a contract to serve him? You didn't take that did you?"

"No."

"Good, because the Mother only knows what the Magia on a whole would do to you if they found out you were working for a Darkling. We're supposed to kill Seraphinus, not save them or work for them."

"Yeah, but do you know why?"

Ness rocks back like she got slapped in the face. "What?"

"Why do we kill them? The Magia were originally supposed to be part of their elite world, a bridge between the Light and Dark."

"Sure, then they set that bridge on fire. We decided to take those ashes, rebuild ourselves, and we protect those that can't protect themselves from those assholes."

I shake my head. "No one ever tells you why we stopped being their alliance. Burned bridge, slammed door, we get stupid metaphors yet no real history."

"Babe." Ness frowns, stepping closer.

"You're the history nut. You literally get off on it, but not even you can find the truth. That's sketchy. They're hiding something."

Her features soften. "What has gotten into you?"

Rolling my shoulders, I drop my arms. "No, nothing, he wasn't a monster. Aside from the minor imprisonment, which, honestly–" I hold a hand up, ticking the positives off on my fingers. "A, the waterfall shower with hot water for like runes, B, a massive bed that felt like I was sleeping on a cloud. C, he's sexy to stare at. And, D, best of all, when they did feed me, it was delicious."

Both of us glance around at our kitchen. There is a cabinet that the door is hanging at an angle. The yellowing countertops that are chipped. The rundown, beat-up linoleum tile is peeling at the corners. The rest of the house isn't much better, everything second-hand, old, falling apart. Our hot water heater lasts for seven fractions of a rune. After that, the water turns blistering cold.

Ness flicks my shoulder. "Yeah? And? They live like gods, we knew that. They own everything in this world, and just deign to allow us," she gestures between us, "and humans to live in it."

"Well, it was nice to pretend I could live like a god, okay? Plus, not kidding, that man," I fan my face, rolling my eyes.

"Yeah, I saw, he's dreamy, but he's a Darkling."

"And Tony," I lift my hand to flip off the space between us. "The fucker set me up. He asked me to dinner. Turns out it's for his mom, which means he probably won't show, although I have to. Mother, it was humiliating. Callahan made me have the call on speaker. The smug ass sat there listening to Tony be...well Tony."

I reach out gripping the air like I'm strangling the life from something with a thin neck. Baring my teeth, I groan before dropping my hands, staring at Ness.

The bottle of vodka is kicking in, the world warming into a fuzz around me just when I need it the most. Tony, and anything related to him, makes me crazy.

Ness tries to smile, grabbing me by the upper arms, then leans over slightly to compensate the height difference for direct eye contact. "It's going to be okay. Marry Tony, give him a couple kids, then..." She sighs.

"There is no 'then', that's it. It's all arranged by the Assembly. I have no say in the matter."

"I know. I don't need the recap." She moves toward the yellowing refrigerating unit. "You need more vodka."

"The cherry on top?" I laugh, "Callahan says I got myself involved in whatever he's into, telling me that killing the Lighter is going to draw Light and Dark to me, and depending on the side it would be if they wanted to kill me or enslave me. Oh, he also thinks I'm a Light Seraphim—not Seraphinus, because those are fucking different by the way."

"Yeah, Seraphim are from Seraphinus and human relations."

I glare. "How do you know that? Callahan had to tell me."

"I read. You should try it." Ness pulls a bottle of vodka out of the freezer. "Here, take this, finish it, go to bed."

"Sure, great, that's super helpful, *Vanessa*."

"You know what's helpful? Covering for you at work, so you still have a job and telling the Darkling to fuck off so he didn't hang around and get us in trouble. I'm giving you vodka to help you sleep the nightmare off that is your life and being supportive of my friend."

I accept the bottle, blurry eyes on the floor, toeing at a square of the stick-on flooring that is peeling up. "Sorry."

"Eh, I get to meet a guy I like, fall in love, and do what I want. I don't have to marry my sister's ex, so we're square."

Gripping the bottle, I curl my lip. I whisper, "She'd know what to do."

"Um, no." Ness struggles against a laugh. "You idolized her way more than she deserved. She wouldn't have known how to deal with this any more than you do."

I slump against the counter, toying with the bottle of vodka in my hands. "She would have done it better."

Ness steps next to me then smacks me in the back of the head.

Rubbing the spot, I glare at her. "Thanks for that."

"Here to help," Ness laughs. "You're a thousand times better than little Miss Pretended-To-Be-Perfect."

"Sure," I shrug one shoulder, eyeing the vodka, tossing it between my hands. "But not really. She should have passed initiation."

Ness puts her arm around me, squeezing. "There's nothing you can do about it. I mean, if you want to take a ride on the Darkling just once, I've got his number. I swear I won't say a word." She pretends to seal her lips by running a finger over them as they press together.

"You know," I say with a slow smile, "That is not a bad idea. Maybe you can set that up as my bachelorette party."

"How's next Night's day looking?" Ness snickers. "I'll message him to let you sit on his face."

I lift the bottle. "Cheers to that," I say. Then, knowing Ness, I add quickly, "Don't actually do it."

CHAPTER 8
CALLAHAN
1ST THORN'S DAY, HEATWAVE, 4049 6TH MILLENNIUM

A<small>FTER</small> I <small>DROPPED</small> N<small>ATALIA OFF</small>, I <small>DROVE AWAY LEAVING MY</small> contact information with the dark-haired woman. I'm not done with Natalia, though. She is going to be useful.

There are far too many rumors about what happened swirling in my world. Too many are searching for the one who killed the Light fuck that morning, so ever since I left, I've had someone watching Natalia. Several of my strongest contracted have rotated through shifts on surveillance with instructions to protect her. If someone else were to locate her, I want her both alive and within my reach.

It is a mild annoyance to go jumping through hoops to get her to agree to a contract. However, a Light Seraphim that could take down a Seraphinus without proper training, and willing to save my life is worth playing a game for. It would not be the stupidest prize I've ever won.

I know where she'll be tonight. I made arrangements. Tonight, I will be watching over her.

I opt for the motorcycle, speeding down the parkway, cutting between cars to weave through the traffic. Horns blare. It's mildly irritating. I just ignore it. I have plans with no time to deal with humans.

I park at the back of the lot where I can keep my eyes on the door as well as have a good overview of the parking lot. My watch indicates it's closing in on Thistle rune, so I kill the power on the bike, settling in to wait.

Leaving the helmet on, I scan the lot, watching cars park. Bodies come and go, then I see a small figure getting out of a black car in a black dress. I check her over. Natalia, with her hair shorter, wavy, and so blonde it's white. Tony was right. As loathe as I am to agree with something vile, it suits her better.

A man gets out of a nearby lifted truck, in a dress shirt and pants. He scowls at her, hands on his hips. They have an exchange that seems as tense as the phone call. She claims she's going to union with him, yet there is something broken about their inter-actions. Whatever they mean to each other, I'm certain I can use that to my advantage. I just need to understand it first.

Leaning forward, arms crossed over the fuel tank, I strum my fingers as they go back and forth. Tony isn't small. He doesn't look soft, and he isn't a visually vulgar specimen of humanity either. For some reason, that irks me, but I shrug it off. A human isn't even close to comparable to me. I will not be jealous of one.

Tony leans forward, arms crossed. Natalia points to her hair. Tony points to her feet in flat shoes. She throws her hands up. He grabs her wrist, pulling her behind him to the door without another word.

I get off the bike, secure my helmet, and push sunglasses on to peer around. By hiding my eyes, I can pass for human. That still doesn't mean a human can compare to me in any facet.

The hostess smiles at me as I enter the restaurant. "Hi! How can I help you?"

I incline my head. "A couple just came in, blonde woman, black dress," I hold my hand up to indicate Natalia's height at my upper chest level.

The woman cuts her eyes to the side, chewing her lip. "I'm sorry, sir, are you part of a party that is already here?"

"No."

"Then unfortunately, I don't know what you're talking about. If you'd like a table–"

I slide my glasses down the bridge of my nose to stare over the lenses at her. "Don't piss me off, human."

She goes pale and grabs a menu. "Right this way, sir, will you be joining them?" Her voice is almost an octave higher with fear.

"No, I want to be nearby."

She sets me at a table across the way from their booth. I choose to sit with my back to the table to avoid detection. To the side is another occupied table with an annoying couple arguing over when to have children.

Natalia was concerned about her ability to have children. It came up during our negotiations, as well as during the phone call I heard. She didn't seem to want children. There was no sense of a maternal drive or cooing about the idea of being a mother.

I hadn't heard the word Magia in centuries. It was a term I learned as a boy during history lessons, and that was it. I had to pull out books I'd long forgotten to review their existence. I had been under the impression that Magia were extinct.

Natalia had dropped the title heiress, something to indicate her ancestor was one of the first, a ruling faction that worked between the Dark and the Light before they revolted in search of more power. Like all living things, greed is a common trait.

The Magia overstepped, wanting to rule over the Light and Dark instead of functioning as a counterweight to balance the two. It was the second time in history that Light and Dark worked together, having a common enemy and something the Magia hadn't foreseen.

The fools had been eradicated, at least mostly. They were destroyed then cast out for their ambitions to be worms to die in the dust. Apparently, they are trying to regain what was lost by selective breeding for the last two millennium or so. It's working. Natalia packs a punch, so much so that I mistook her for a Light Seraphim.

I order bourbon, listening, waiting. There seems to be nothing besides the quick, hissed bickering between the two next to me, so I glance over my shoulder to check on my lightning bug, then face forward again after a quick scan. Tony and Natalia are sitting across from each other staring at menus without speaking.

I check my watch again, contemplating how long I have before the Dark following me would take notice of Natalia. The rumors are rampant, a lot of talk about being the one to either kill it or bring it to heel were being offered up. Most of the talk reported to me has included purple hair, so it's helpful she changed the color.

Massimo drops in the seat next to me, turning his head away. "Convenient seat."

I take a drink. "Effective."

"You sure about this?"

I sent Massimo to engage with the Light, to draw one here as a scare tactic. "You've been questioning me a lot lately," I say. "I'm beginning to lose my patience."

"Stick your head up a pig's ass then. I'm not a standard contract."

I grin. "No, my friend, you are far more indebted."

"You're barely healed, picking this fight is something I am advising against."

I lean back, stretching out my torso, "I'm healed."

Massimo grunts, then steals my drink, throwing it back. "You're a proper bastard for this setup, using others to do your dirty work."

Shrugging, I stare straight ahead. "She needs to change her mind. It's one Light fuck. She handled one herself. I can manage that half dead. She'll survive."

"Others may not."

"Others aren't my concern, and I'll try to make sure Tony is a casualty."

Massimo sighs, a reminder that he is above all else, my conscience in most situations. Now isn't a time for me to develop one though. I have a use for Natalia, everything else be damned.

Massimo tenses as the perky hostess sits another nearby. "Here's your menu."

I toy with the ice in the bottom of my glass, spinning it around in a lazy fashion. I give it a moment, then look. Marius gives me a salute. Jacques shrugs, pushing his long blond hair back.

I face forward. "Fuck."

Massimo chuckles. "I did advise against this soirée."

"Shut up."

"Did you even try to hide on your way here?"

"I wasn't this obvious," I sneer under my breath, giving Massimo a dirty look. "This wasn't me. This is something else. Maybe this is your fault."

He slumps lower, crossing his arms. "No. I was after a Light."

"Then coincidentally, we are here waiting for a show that was going to happen even if we didn't set one up."

"Then I'm going to need another drink before this mess starts," Massimo lifts his chin, searching around. He hunches back down, lowers his voice. "Sterling and Jezabelle too. Damnit, Cal."

This was not me. This is a free-for-all that I walked into. I take a glance around. Natalia in the corner of her booth. Tony is next to her. Jezabelle sits at the far end of the room, her blonde hair in a high ponytail. Sterling resides in the corner, inclining his head. I curl my lip, outright groaning at Telra to Marius's back.

Telra holds my gaze, grinning at me like she's the cat that ate a canary. She winks, eyes dropping toward her chest to direct my eyes lower. I follow her line of sight to her breasts on display in a low-cut black top, hating myself for falling for that trick.

I sit right, staring at the wall, heart starting to pump harder.

Every contender is here, all of them here for what's mine. "This is going to be a problem."

"Problem? No, this is going to be a fucked mess."

"When this starts, get Natalia out of here quick."

"I've got your back," Massimo says, "you watch your front though."

The waiter stops by as I scowl at Chlem being seated at the table in front of us. "Can I get you anything else?"

Massimo points at my empty glass, "Two. Bring them, then you'll want to find a new job," he says, pulling his glasses down to show his eyes.

"Shit," the waiter curses under his breath. "I kind of liked this one."

"Enough to die for?"

"I'll be right back." He nods, turns, and leaves.

I cut my eyes to Massimo. "Really?"

"Seems like a nice kid." Massimo shrugs.

Two drinks are delivered in a hurry, the kid forcing a smile. "It's on the house, guys." He knocks on the table, then disappears.

"See, nice kid." Massimo grins, taking a drink.

CHAPTER 9
CALLAHAN

WE SIP ON THE LIQUOR WHILE I FIGHT TAKING ANOTHER LOOK towards Natalia. The room goes quieter as the couple at the table next to me departs. The only ones talking are Natalia and hers.

Natalia's voice is thin. "The Harvest season is fine, but why this Harvest?"

Tony scoffs. "It's just time, Nat. Time for us to get married, start trying to have kids. We'll need a few to make sure that there's one that can make the cut. This way we have time. We don't have to rush, put so much pressure on ourselves."

Natalia groans. "I'm not ready for that. Any of this. We still need time to work on this."

"Getting married is working on it. We get married, you quit that stupid job–"

"It's not stupid," her voice lifts, cutting off his irritating words. "I'm not quitting either, even if we get married, if we have kids."

"When, Nat. When we have kids. We have to do this. Stop being dramatic. I'm a good man."

They fall silent.

The only noise in the room is when I drain my drink, the ice chinking against the glass. I set it down. It's the only move I make.

The first to move is always the first to lose. Patience pays in a game like this.

Tony mutters, voice low. "Their eyes. They're Darklings. All of them."

"Let's just go," Natalia says. "Call your mom, have her meet us somewhere else."

Marius stands, always the impatient one. "You're not going anywhere, sweetheart."

Natalia's voice is strong as she answers. "Why? We were just trying to eat dinner. We aren't looking for a fight."

The slight pulse of electricity fills the air.

Massimo has his head ducked, fighting a grin. He wags it back and forth, then lifts eyes crinkled at the corners to me. This is about to go sideways in a way I hadn't planned for. Putting both hands on the table, I tense, ready to push off.

The zaps grow in frequency and length, an announcement of what is to come.

Chlem calls out, "The rest of you can go home now. I'll be taking her with me."

Jezabelle's voice is full of a sneer, "Not happening."

"You'll be the first to die if you get in my way."

The ground rumbles, the ice in my glass dancing. There's a moment of calm where my heart beats once, then the crack of a smite. Blinding illumination fills the room as I call on my magic. The Light blisters my skin, pain spreading across the surface of my body.

My magic hisses, wrapping thicker around me, taking most of the hit to protect me. The boom renders my hearing useless while chaos blossoms as the Light walks into the room.

I shove to my feet and spin, eyes searching for Natalia. Instead, I stare at a grouping of melrags conjured by Jezabelle, a shadow beast.

The melrags snarl and snap their long, curved teeth, silvery drool dripping from their jowls. While melrag bites are nasty, their venom icy pain, their claws are the bigger threat. They are razor sharp able to slice through skin and bone.

I eye them and they lunge.

Massimo steps next to me, blasting one, catching another by the throat, toppling from momentum. He yells over the din, "Get her and go!"

Scanning the players locking in battle, I reach for the hilt tucked into the back of my jeans. I pull it free, adjusting my grip. My magic races up the hilt, winding around and through it, forming a flaming blade as another melrag fixates on me.

I hadn't planned on having to get this dirty. If I had, I would have worn something else. I like this shirt.

My shoulders roll, my magic shredding through bone and muscles, forming wings. The melrag screeches, rushing at me. I parry the claws, side stepping it while using its trajectory to hurl it against the wall. I slice at its back, getting hit from the side by something else. Hitting the ground, I roll with the other body, jerk my head up, tendrils of black racing over me.

"Got your back," Massimo laughs, crouching to launch at Marius.

Tony's bellow cuts through the air. "Nat!"

The beating mass in my chest stutters. This whole thing is for naught if Natalia gets taken or killed. I fend off a melrag, throwing it at Telra. She screams as I turn away, searching the room.

Sterling holds a karambit to Natalia's throat, dragging her backward. Her eyes meet mine, panic evident in her features. One of her hands reaches toward me like she knows I'm going to save her.

I run, ducking a blast of Dark magic to grab her hand. With one sharp yank I pull her from Sterling's grip, my magic forcing him backward at the same time. She yelps, crashing against my chest as I raise my weapon, the blade flaming to life.

"Back off."

Sterling pulls a second karambit from his back, flipping them in his hands. He takes an aggressive stance, lifting his hands with an arrogant smirk. "Not this time, Cal."

I curl back one side of my mouth, staring him down. He's taller than me with a broad forehead and wide nose. His thick, twisted locks are pulled back today. "You came prepared."

"She's coming with me."

"Fuck no," Natalia says, stepping towards him to jut a hand against his chest. A burst of white Light emits from her palm, sending Sterling flying backward through a wall.

A grin steals my lips as I spin her away from the attack of another melrag, turning my back on Sterling. It claws, snarling, so I lift my blade. Natalia stumbles away as I counter, cleaving the melrag in half. The creature disappears with a yelp, dissolving into dust, a fine rain of ash filtering through the air.

I glance for Natalia as the Light bears down on me swinging a golden blade radiating with a brilliant glow. Narrowing my eyes against the Light, I sneer, maneuvering in defense until the I get an opportunity to swing back. I drop, kick its legs out, and then stand.

Light flashes, a feminine scream ripping through the air from somewhere.

I get shoved from behind, pitching forward to the floor.

Metal rings against metal, Massimo engaging the Light. "You're fucking distracted. Get...her...an' go," he pants, struggling to block and deviate the Light's strikes.

The ground shakes as I turn away. Another melrag lurches at me, so I drive my blade through it, shadows wicking to nothing-ness as it screeches one last time. The world shakes, the remaining melrags screeching and howling as they tuck tail and run. Every-thing stops, faces swiveling with wide eyes.

Chlem stands in the middle of the room, his short sword tip embedded into the ground. I bare my teeth, snarling a curse under my breath. He lifts his blazing purple gaze straight at me, his magic swirling in glowing purple and shadows.

This has gone from bad to worse to straight fucked. The ground begins to crack, radiating from the blade. Others around me are disengaging, running from the beast being called forth by one of its own. He's a Draco, smorgonkin, and an idiot, calling forth a smoragon in this enclosed space.

I whip around, desperate to locate my prize. She's across the room, Tony pulling her in close as the room rumbles. I snarl, taking one step toward her.

The world tips beneath my feet. I scramble to avoid going with the ground pitching toward the center of the room, the flooring crackling with fine lines of separation. I spring forward, grabbing the edge of the broken piece of concrete and tile trying to dump me into the crater, leveraging myself over the edge before it slides into the black hole created by the incoming smoragon.

I roll across the remaining part of the floor, coming to a stop and looking up in time to watch the smoragon burst into the room. It roars, whipping its head back and forth on its long neck, glistening black and glittering with purple plumes of smoke burst around it. It stumbles to the side, and its breath blasts into the wall, shattering windows.

Too deteriorated to hold its own weight, the building groans, sliding and shuddering apart. I take one look at Natalia, sprinting to her, and throw myself at her, tackling her and Tony to the ground. I throw my wings up to block the crumbling debris falling around us, protecting us from the building collapsing down.

"Oh, my Mother," Natalia whimpers. "Your wings are on fire."

Ignoring the ignorance of her remark, I shove up with a grunt, forcing the debris off us. Batting and stretching my wings, I stand, offering my hand to Natalia.

Tony bares his teeth, throwing his hand toward me. "Fuck off."

"No!" Natalia shoves his hand in another direction, sending

the shock wave to the side of me. It breezes by as I consider taking the head off the impudent man.

The ground trembles, and I almost topple. At my back the earth-shattering roar of the smoragon leaves my ears ringing. I glance behind me, the air rushing past my body as the smoragon inhales, its long neck arching and chest scales spreading, exposing thin flesh illuminated from within in a purplish glow.

"Fuck." I drop flat, letting the burst of energy going straight over me.

The smoragon tramples over a few steps, each one rattling tons of marble and concrete. I get my feet under me, grabbing Natalia, yanking her from rubble.

A hand closes around my leg and wrenches.

I let go of my prize to catch myself before my face hits the ground. A whizz of purple streaks straight at her as I lift my head. "No," I yell, fear widening my eyes.

She crosses her arms in front of her, bracing. Light bursts in an arc, blinding me. I squeeze my eyes shut, turning away. The beating in my chest skips, the pulse in my neck spiking with a painful jab. Opening my eyes, I stare at fractured rubble, unable to lift my head.

There is no way she survived that. There are Seraphinus who couldn't handle that. There's no plausible way a Seraphim did.

Tony grapples for footing, climbing over me. I growl, smacking at him with a wing to send him elsewhere. The weight disappears off my back and I stand, taking a few steps.

Natalia stumbles away over the uneven ground.

She took a full impact and is managing to walk—or at least limp—away. She is everything I could hope for.

I grin, ducking the smoragon's tail whipping through the air. I shove my hilt into the waist of my jeans and run straight for her. Tony helps Natalia, half carrying her away.

As I run toward them, Massimo tackles them to the ground, so I change directions, leaping over broken rubble into the parking lot. Throwing a leg over my bike, I kick it to life, peeling out and heading for them. Massimo is on top of Tony, punching him in the face as I come to a halt by them.

The smoragon pulls back to attack again, so I push the kick-stand down with my foot and jump into the air. Beating my wings, I lift to face it. I cross my arms, throwing up a shield to block its attack. The force knocks me back, almost blowing me out of the sky, but I grunt, muscles flexing, wings catching me.

Its breath is dying, the force lifting, so I throw my arms back, unleashing my magic, Dark rippling through the air to meet the smoragon's. The breath catches fire, flames racing into the beast to explode within. The beast howls and thrashes, falling to the side. It won't stay down long. Not even that would kill it. I've just pissed it off.

I drop to the ground, surveying the chaos. Telra takes off. Marius and the others are still skirmishing.

As I land, Tony gapes from the ground, blood leaking from his mouth, "What kind of Seraphinus are you?"

I turn to Natalia. Extending a hand, I say, "This is your last chance."

"Don't fucking touch her," Tony says, struggling against Massimo.

Massimo flips him over, his hand curling in the front of his shirt. "If you want her to survive, she comes with us."

I hold Natalia's wide gaze, her eyes glazed over. "The deal has changed," I tell her. "If I save you, it's an immediate agreement to the new contract."

She bobs her head, one trembling hand lifting.

"Nat, don't!" Tony struggles against Massimo and his Dark, raising his voice. "What are you doing? Nat? Nat, fucking look at me!"

Her eyes never leave mine, bright silver flickering back and forth.

"We don't need this—them," Tony yells. "You're strong enough! We can take that thing."

That is irritating. He'd see her dead trying to take on the beast.

Massimo shoves off Tony to stand. "You're either delusional or ignorant, either way she'd never last against that. I can't even take one on my own."

The smaragon roars and someone else screams, probably Jezabelle. It is time to move.

"This little chat is over." I throw my leg over the bike, toeing up the kick stand as I hold my hand to her again. "I'm leaving with or without you. Make your choice."

Tony screams, reaching for her. "Don't you dare!"

She puts her hand in mine. I close my fingers, dragging her into my lap. She pulls the skirt of her dress up to get her leg over the bike while I slip an arm around her waist, helping her situate.

The smoragon snarls, sending a burst of purple that streaks past us. Sterling slams into the side of a nearby car.

He gets an arm under him, picking his head up to bare his teeth at me. The white is brilliant against his warm, golden-brown skin.

I pucker my lips at him in return. He's lean and lanky, my only true competitor. I like him enough I'd extend help if I thought he needed it. That was a love tap at best. He can handle a smoragon, so I move my intentions back to the more pressing issue of Tony.

He takes a step forward. "Nat, stop! They'll kill you for this."

I grab the handlebars, securing her in my lap between my arms. She's trembling, straddling the bike backwards to face me. She's mine. Safe between me and the handlebars.

She belongs to me.

"Stop, don't do this."

Massimo shoves Tony back. "She's made her choice. She's no longer your concern."

"That's my future wife you winged fuck. Don't touch her.

What did you do to her? Nat! Snap out of it. They're Darklings, Nat."

I turn the bike's front wheel, revving the engine. Balancing, I pick my foot off the ground as I take off with my prize. She leans into me, her arms circling my torso. She's shaking, her legs tensing, trying to tighten as I make the turn onto the main road. Her small hands clench at my back, nails digging into muscle.

As soon as I can, I'll put the contract in my skin. She survived the smoragon's direct hit. There are numerous ways I can think of to use her. I'm never letting go.

My knee almost skims the road as I take the on-ramp to the parkway. Using my wing as a pivot, I keep my knee and the bike from dragging the road, gritting my teeth against the riptide sensation feeding through my magic into my shoulder.

I pull the bike back upright and accelerate. This isn't the most conducive way to ride with her, but it keeps my wings free. I know she's safe in front of me as opposed to at my back. I'll deal with the blind spot.

"Oh, Mother!" She screams, her voice warbling. "It's following."

It was rather stupid of her to believe it was going to be as simple as leaving it behind. Chelm wasn't going to give up. They all saw what she's capable of. As strong as she is, that would be enough for any of them to pursue, but even more delectable, the Light is an effective weapon against the Dark. Every player that was in that room is drooling, but she's in my lap, soon to be my contracted.

They can salivate while they fuck themselves blind. She's mine.

I weave through traffic. Humans seem to be doing their best to be as aggravating and as in my way as possible. They honk. I should bring the smoragon down on them for my amusement. They'd run scared. It'd be worth a chuckle.

Natalia screams, one hand moving from me. Weight settles on

the back of my bike with precision and balance. I don't have to look behind me to know who it is.

Massimo yells with humor, "Just me, Light Bug. Don't go blowing holes in me."

Her hand rests against my back again. "Oh, my fucking Mother, what is happening?"

"Breathe, Little Light. Cal will take care of it. Take Fifth," Massimo yells, as he lifts off the bike.

I cut between two cars to skip over a lane for the upcoming exit, horns blaring. Fifth will lead to March which ends in a desolated section of buildings. Massimo, my right hand, directing me somewhere I can spread my wings to fight back without hindrance.

Ignoring traffic, I cut up the shoulder. Overhead are roars and explosions, Massimo no doubt pressing his luck with the beast. I crank the accelerator, sliding through the intersection not waiting for the lights to give me right of way. My Dark streaks forward to stop a vehicle from hitting us. The car crumples and spins out.

I don't pay heed or stop. I don't need Massimo getting himself killed. That would be an annoyance worse than humanity as a species.

Natalia screams, nails digging into my back, her body pressing closer. Her head knocks against the side of mine in her attempt to get closer, as if that is doing either of us any good.

"Natalia, stop," I yell over the rush of wind, trying to compensate for the jerk I made when she headbutted me.

Keeping the bike steady, I head for March Street.

CHAPTER 10
NATALIA

THE WHIRLWIND RIDE COMES TO A STOP IN AN ABANDONED SECTION of town, the bike's engine stalling out. I'm shaking. No matter how I tense or try to control my quivering muscles, there's too much adrenaline coursing through me. I cling to Callahan, my fingers digging into the hard muscles of his back for dear life, the world still moving around me despite us sitting still.

Any number of times he almost laid the bike down, or almost collided with another vehicle. He'd survive, but I might not. Ki or not, some things aren't healable, and I have no helmet.

Massimo about gave me heart failure when he landed on the back of the bike, dark blue-green skin, black horns curling back from his temples like a ram in his true shadow form. How he managed to land soft and graceful with as massive and bulky he is, and how Callahan managed to not lose balance and crash with all the extra weight, is unknown.

I'm so far in over my head.

I accepted his contract.

'What was I thinking?'

Accepting the deal was a split-second decision because it buys me time before I have to deal with Tony and the thought of having children with him. Besides, there is a dragon of tar and smoke that breathes purple, and I barely survived its attack. I almost didn't get my shield up, and even throwing every bit of my Ki behind my block, it hurt.

He glances up and around. Other than his wings on fire—which had to be hurting him even though he didn't seem to notice at all—he is still in human form unlike Massimo. There's a roar overhead.

He flips the visor of the helmet up to meet my eyes. "Get out of sight and stay out of sight. Massimo will find you to take you away from here."

I stare, not daring to blink or my eyes may not open. "What are you going to do?"

"Kill it. I just don't want or need to be distracted trying to protect you at the same time."

Beneath my fingers, his muscles flex, the corners of his jaw bunching tight as he frowns, staring up again as a massive roar is emitted. An explosion detonates, the air vibrating in my chest. "Um," I manage, my voice a hair above a breath, "I don't think I can let go."

He reaches around himself, grabbing my wrists to pry them away from his back. Forcing my elbows to bend, he presses my hands between his, holding my gaze. "Take a deep breath and get up." His tone is tight, almost angry.

My legs are bent up, hiked over his thighs, the skirt of my dress shoved up to my waist. Quaking, I swallow, finding his calm in his gaze.

I nod, sliding my hands from his, and I pull one leg over the bike. My knee buckles on my support leg. I flail, managing to stay upright as I stumble away from the bike. I get upright, blinking at the vacant bike.

I drop my head back, peering into the sky, to see two figures battling with the dragon. My heart races as a plume of purple erupts in shimmering heat from the beast, engulfing Callahan and his already burning wings.

Massimo drops from the sky, wings wrapped around his body as he pelts toward the ground. A dozen feet up, he spreads his large dark wings of leather, which catch him, slowing his landing.

Massimo chuckles as his feet touch the ground, shakings his head. "Come on, Light Bug." He reaches a hand that is elongated with thick, curved black claws instead of fingers.

I shrink a step away, then find a resolve within me. He might look different, but he's given me no reason to not trust him. I reach out, his talons clicking as they close around my wrist.

"Don't even think about it," he says, tugging me closer.

I open my mouth, about to protest innocence. A blade embeds in his shoulder, the force knocking him off center. His grip loosens, and I am ripped from away from him as several of those shadowy, four-legged creatures tackle him to the ground.

"Massimo!" I scream as the creatures begin to rip into him.

A hand closes around my throat from behind, the grip on my arm tightening to the point of pain. A female voice hisses in my ear, "Don't fight and I won't have to hurt you."

I stumble to keep my feet beneath me as I'm dragged backward. Massimo wrestles with and kicks at the beasts. They snarl and snap in return, biting and clawing. It's a blur of shadows and movement my eyes cannot follow.

Callahan hits the ground, cleaving one of the beasts in two as Massimo struggles to his feet. He turns toward me, "Natalia!"

Purple blasts down on him, so he throws an arm up, one burning wing lifting to protect him. Black tendrils wrap around him in a hazy dome, thickening to blot him out of sight. I catch a glimpse of him down on one knee, forearm over his head before he's gone from sight.

I dig my heels in and square my shoulders. We jerk to a halt as I clench my abdominal muscles, fighting against her. Slamming my elbow into the woman, I use my other hand twisting her wrist to break the grip cutting off my air flow.

Hissing, my mysterious assailant recoils, letting me spin, layering my palms, then pushing forward into her stomach. The Ki burns through me, a flash of light accenting the burst of power.

Her eyes grow wide as she stumbles a few paces back. At least she's still in human form, her blonde ponytail swinging. Darklings in shifted form scare the burning afters out of me.

With a set jaw and narrow gaze, my attacker stops herself in a low crouch. "I told you not to fight. You're going to need to learn to take orders better."

She leaps forward, diving through the air. We crash to the ground. I topple while she is on top of me, hands wrapping around my throat. Pressure behind my eyes builds. My lungs burn, demanding air.

I grab her face, angular, sharp features, pinched with concentrated rage. Baring my teeth, I force Ki into my hands, glowing bright like molten metal.

Light glimmers through the woman, illuminating from her eyes so I dig deeper, push harder. My mind is going fuzzy, but the woman's grip is loosening, going limp as pinpricks glisten through her skin.

She rips away, screaming. I roll to my knees as something strong collides into me, claws ripping into my side. A shrill scream tears my throat as I curl into a ball, arms over my head for protection. I draw on my Ki, the sacred geometry along my spine burning to life. Everything goes bright white around me, and I pant, eyes blurred from unshed tears.

Hands grab at me, sharp pointed nails scratching across my flesh. I kick, instinct taking over, muscle memory recalling defensive maneuvers. Upright, I block punches with open palms backed with Ki to take the hit, the resulting contact nothing more than dull thuds echoing in my forearms.

The woman glares, attacking with ferocity. Her fists are

covered in inky Dark, her whole body swathed by shadows. The magic hisses at each contact with my Ki. I take an opportunity to spin in close, slamming my elbow into her face.

I pant, the woman on the ground, yet still stirring, getting up. "Fucking Mother," I yell, kicking at her. "What does it take to put you down?"

The woman skitters away, giving me a second to breathe, drawing in ribbons of much needed air through my nose until I feel my lungs might explode. It would be easier if she attacked with her magic. I could take it and use it against her. For an unknown reason, she's holding back.

Massimo dances and slashes at the beasts, dipping in and out of sight over the mysterious woman's shoulder. Overhead, the ear-splitting screams and roars remind me Callahan is busy fighting a dragon. I'm exhausted, sluggish muscles straining against use, but I'm on my own.

I lift my hands, eyeing the woman. Magia aren't human, but we can't match Seraphinus in a fair fight for long.

She stalks closer, grinning, fingers elongating into black, skeletal talons. "Have you had enough? All you have to do is submit."

"Massimo," I scream. "Get out of here."

He hurls a beast away, whipping to face me. "What?"

The woman is a few steps away, so I back up, keeping distance between us. "Go help Callahan."

He roars, laughing while he blocks and throws another beast to the side. "Because I'm not already doing something?"

"Get out of here!"

I bend my arms in front of me, crossing them over my chest. The tips of my middle fingers press against my thumbs, opposite hands at opposite shoulders. I close my eyes. The marks down my back ignite, blazing with agony.

"Massimo, now!"

His eyes go wide, and he lurches back, wings beating, as he

rises into the air. The woman swings. I throw my arms away from my torso, releasing the Ki. The world goes bright white, blinding me as the magic shreds through me like a thousand razor blades yanked from my body.

A scream of blazing pain erupts from the release. It may come from the other woman, maybe it was me. The world comes back as blurs of shadows and muted colors in the settling evening of the world. I sway, tipping over sideways, but catching myself, panting on one knee.

Before me stretches charred earth. Nothing but the desolate ground remains, the beasts and woman gone. I slump, my knees folding, and my butt hits the dirt. My body pulsates and quivers, so I lay flat, staring overhead at Callahan battling the dragon still.

I took on a Seraphinus and I'm exhausted. I can't imagine the strength he has to handle a dragon. An explosion of purple flames that glitters too bright causes my eyes to water and narrow.

Someone lands next to me. I peer through one eye at Massimo grinning down on me, pearly white teeth glimmering starkly against his dark, marbled, teal skin. "Are you hurt?"

"Kind of." I stick a hand up, and he grabs it, hoisting me to my feet. "Now what?"

Above there's a shrill screech. Massimo and I both tilt our faces up to the source. My heart skips, unsure if Callahan is all right.

The dragon is falling from the sky. Massimo curses, grabbing me close to force me to into a crouch, his black wings blocking out everything.

The ground shakes, the whole world stirs with the impact, then Massimo is standing, letting go of me. He shakes off dust and rubble, rubbing at his face. A grimace flickers across his face as he stretches a wing.

With his head tipped back, he mutters, "He could have been nicer about that."

I gape at the dragon laying still nearby, smoking like the

remains of a fire tend to do, several buildings destroyed beneath it. Callahan descends, wings pulsing in steady beats as he hits the ground. He straightens his shirt, slicks back the longer strands of his raven hair from his face and turns to me.

Cursing in awe, I ask, "Did you really kill that thing and *not* break a sweat?"

"Yes," he smirks, his wings of fire retracting into his back. He extends a hand. "Now you belong to me."

CHAPTER II
CALLAHAN

Natalia stares at me.

I stare right back, eyes stretching, face pulling tight. She is going to fight. I like that. She's strong. My conviction of the notion wavered as Jezabelle had tried to steal her away. She was limp, not fighting. Turns out all she needed was a push.

She crosses her arms.

I narrow my eyes. It is easier for her to refuse now that the beasts and players aren't bearing down on her. She needs a reminder.

I wiggle my fingers, raising an eyebrow. "There are other smoragons, and I will drop you in a nest if you test me."

She sighs and throws her hands up. "I didn't say anything."

I press my hand forward further. Natalia huffs as she takes it.

I jerk my chin at Massimo. "You're on clean-up."

He inclines his head, then leaps into the air, spreading his wings and taking off. I pull Natalia in close until she's pressed against me. I turn my mouth against her ear. "When I give a command, you follow it. I don't repeat myself."

One of her small, warm hands rests on my abdomen. She nods. "You're going to have to forgive me. I'm not used to orders."

"Get used to them," I whisper, my nose brushing against the silky strands of her hair. "I have plans for you."

She shivers, sucking in a breath before pushing away from me, face to the ground. Clearing her throat, she turns her back to me. "Right, using me and all."

I take her hand, glancing around for my bike. The back wheel is peeking from under a broken brick wall. I pull her to it, letting go to lift the slab, grunting as I heave the debris away from the motorcycle. Hoisting it onto the wheels by the handlebars, I inspect for any serious damage.

Deciding it's still useable, I throw a leg over it, then look to Natalia. "Get on."

Natalia nods, head turned, and then she pulls her skirt up, sliding behind me. She reaches around me, her hands resting on the fuel tank. The proximity of her is brushing against my senses, even though she's not touching me.

My Dark stirs, itching for her touch. It whispers in my head, *"Fix it."*

I frown at her hand placement. It doesn't strike my fancy either. That's going to change. I always get what I want.

Kicking the bike to life, I twist the throttle to rev the engine into a dull roar. I push off, moving through broken pieces of buildings, the air full of dust. I hit the main road and accelerate. The others on the road are nothing but a hazard to my ability to move. Street signs, lights, and speed limits are mere suggestions as far as I'm concerned.

I dodge vehicles as I speed along, heading for home. By the time I'm pulling into my underground garage, Natalia has her arms wrapped tight around me, her face pressed against my back. I grin as I shut off the engine, kicking down the stand.

She lets go, slipping off the bike.

I mirror the act, then head for the door, calling over my shoulder. "Come."

"I'm not a dog," she says with ice. "If you want me to follow you, then say that."

I stop, the muscles in my shoulders tensing. A ripple tears through my gut, as I clench my jaw. I don't take orders. I fight for my life twelve days a year to ensure it. I growl, then continue walking away.

She trails behind me as we head upstairs, through my home into my office. The first time I had her brought to this room I was puzzled, contemplating how to proceed. This time, I have perfect clarity.

I point to a chair, stepping around the desk. "Sit."

She drops down in it with a loud exhale. Ignoring that subtle sign of a tantrum, I open the top drawer of my desk, slipping a piece of contract parchment from it onto the middle of my desk. My fingertips press to the surface, the beige page smooth.

Magic seeps from beneath my skin, tendrils of fine shadows seep across the page, sinking into the pores of the paper to bleed together, coalescing into stains across the page in a fine scrawl. Words of what I want, everything she will give to me, and in return, what I offer.

With the contract written in detail, I spin the page, sliding it closer to her and lifting my gaze. "Sign it."

Natalia frowns, a crease developing between her eyebrows. Her white-blonde hair is shoulder length, a bit wavy about her face. Her bright eyes glisten like silver, shifting back and forth over the contract. She looks to me. "Do I get to read this first at least?"

"No. You already accepted. Now sign it."

"Yeah, all right, sure," she rolls her eyes. "But how the fuck am I supposed to know what I'm doing if I don't read it?"

"Follow orders, don't do anything obviously stupid, and the rest you'll learn."

"Pen?"

Her ignorance is outstanding. "Use your magic. It's more binding."

She shakes her head, lifting a hand to rub her fingertips together. "That's not how my magic works."

"Then you'll bleed and use your blood," I shrug, crossing my arms. Ink isn't going to work. I need her essence on the contract, inescapable and undeniably binding.

She frowns at her fingers, the tip of her middle finger beginning to glow. I tense, my magic snarling at the glittering bright gleam. She presses it to the bottom of the page, signing in thin, neat curves. She's untrained, sloppy, and clumsy with her magic.

If this is the best the Magia have, there's no threat to me or my kind from them. Tony is an ignorant fool. He thought Natalia could fight a smoragon. Maybe in a few years after proper training, she might, but not today. While the Magia might be breeding power, they don't know how to wield it.

When she is finished, I pull the page closer, resting my palm in the middle of the contract. My magic leaks free, tendrils of black signing my name. I wipe the contract parchment clean, drawing the words into the palm of my hand, then smear them across my forearm.

The words twist, righting themselves in my skin, spiraling around my forearm, ending with her name in glistening silver. It's odd to my eyes. The Light never was something that agreed with me, and of the two other contracts I wear, they are with fellow Dark. Their names are spelled out in magic as black as mine.

"Dude," Natalia says, lifting her own arm, my contract mirrored in her flesh. "What is this?"

"Your contract."

She inspects it, then sighs. "Great, a slave branding. Lovely." Her eyes roll at the ceiling. "That's more than gross." She drops back in the chair, wincing as she crosses her arm over her stomach to wrap a hand around her side. "Now what?"

I barely contain my glee, extending an open palm. "Ring."

She blinks at me. "What?"

I grin wider. "Your future union is void. Give me your ring."

She sits up, frowning. "That wasn't part of the deal."

"I told you it was a new deal." My chest swells with fulfilled greed. "The ring, Natalia."

She worms the ring off her finger. She holds it in her other palm. "I'll just put it somewhere."

"Give me the ring, Natalia," I growl, my euphoria slipping as she fights.

"I'm going to need this when this," she lifts her arm with the contract, "is over."

I lean forward on the desk, both hands flat on the surface. "You won't."

She scoffs. "Pretty sure in ten years–"

"It's not ten years," I say, my voice full of fire and ash, possessive passion overcoming my words. "It's not even twenty years."

Her face goes lax. "What?" she whispers. Blinking, she begins to harden, her features twisting with fury. "How long?"

"As long as you're alive," I tell her, staring into her eyes without remorse. She took a full hit from a smoragon. She glows brighter than either sun. She's going to have use beyond my imagination, and she's mine.

"Are you fucking kidding me? I have a life, obligations to the Magia."

I stand, lips pulled to one side. "I know all about your Magia. One less breeder is in my kind's best interest. Although truth be told, your kind doesn't bear much of a threat to me."

Her mouth opens, jaw hanging lower for a heartbeat, then she closes it. She repeats the motion a couple of times before scowling. "What are you talking about?"

I extend my hand as the door to my study opens. Massimo shifted to human form slips in. We exchange glances, then I return my attentions to Natalia.

"Give me the ring," I command again, knowing her contract

must be searing her skin for ignoring the order. "I don't like repeating myself. I suggest you avoid making me."

It is for the best I kept the rules about what she can't do to a minimum, rather highlighting what I expect her to do. I'd crafted the contract knowing she isn't going to know the rules, that she likely will push the boundaries if there are any to poke at. She is making me regret it though.

"Fine." She throws the ring at me. It hits me in the chest and falls to the desk with a clatter. "It's yours."

Just like you, I think while my Dark purrs.

I stifle my chuckle, pluck the ring off the desk, and toss it in the trash, turning to Massimo. "Get her to her room. She stays there until I decide."

It's a dismal power play, but I need her to understand I am in charge. Sending her to her room will be the least invasive way for her to comprehend that fact. It would also be the least damaging.

On occasion, I've had to break those I've claimed, shatter their will then rebuild them. It is taxing, yet a necessary step in those cases. I'm hoping she's smart enough to cave willingly, but given how she's glaring with disgust, I'm going to presume things will be more difficult than I prefer.

"All right, Little Light Bug." Massimo grabs her under the arm and lifts.

She hisses and swats at him. "Ow, let go, I'll walk, or..." She turns to me with snark, "...should I get on my knees and crawl? Not sure about proper protocol."

I stare, my mind playing out the image of Natalia on her knees crawling toward me. My eyes travel over her, enjoying the mental pictures as much as I'm annoyed by them.

I clench my jaw at the red ribbons of ripped skin visible in her side. "You're hurt."

She flips me off, staring at Massimo. "Where am I going?"

I take a step around the desk. "Nowhere until I get you medical attention."

Natalia inhales and swells, leaning into her yell directed at Massimo. "Where am I going?"

"Sit down." I raise my voice, reaching for her.

She turns with putrid rage written all over her, smacking at my hand. "Do I look like I need your help?"

"Yes, you're bleeding. Sit." I try to grasp her shoulder, but she recoils a half step, staying out of my reach.

Natalia tips her head back and laughs. She quiets, standing with her head tipped back. Light shines through the tears in her flesh. It dims and fades, leaving behind thin slivers of healed skin beneath the open cuts of her dress.

Lifting her head, she meets my eyes and flips her middle finger at me. "I took this deal because I thought it would buy me time before I had to deal with Tony and children but don't make the mistake of thinking I needed you."

My lips peel apart in horror. I have no idea what she is or is capable of, and I've tethered her to me for life.

'And I thought Chlem summoning a smoragon was the sideways part of this evening.'

She still has not obeyed my orders, so I withdraw them before the contract enacts punishment. "You're excused."

Massimo sighs. "Come on." He gestures to the door with a bow. "I'll show you to your room."

Watching them leave, I drop into my chair, rubbing a hand down my face. Controlling Natalia is going to be difficult, contract or not. Training her is only going to compromise my dominance further, yet I know it will be necessary. I'm going to have to play dirty. Nevertheless, I had been right about one thing; Natalia is going to be useful.

CHAPTER 12
NATALIA
1ST NIGHT'S DAY, HEATWAVE, 4049 6TH MILLENNIUM

BEING LOCKED UP SUCKS BIG, HAIRY BALLS. IT'S BOREDOM AND restlessness. It is anxiety closing in the walls closer and closer with each ticking fraction of a rune slipping by in dull waiting. The mind is its own worst enemy.

I'm trapped in a pretty cage with no idea what comes next. Never for a moment, not the smallest fraction of a rune, did I ever consider that he'd force me to sign a contract for life.

I can't not stare at it. It's on my arm like twelve thin black wavy lines circling around my forearm. I can't make heads or tails of it, the script fine and illegible. It looks to be living ink across my skin, shifting fluidly on my flesh the way glitter glints and sparkles in the light. Trying to focus on the words is like trying to nail down smoke.

There seems to be impossibly about a million words, and it changes each time I make any attempts to focus on it. The only clear part is his signature at the end of the rings of words circling around my arm.

Callahan Matteo Barraco.

I guess it's better than Anthony Michael Washington. At least

Callahan didn't pretend to be nice or to care about me. I won't have to hear about children like I'm a baby factory.

Hopefully. I can't imagine that a Darkling wants to force me to give him children.

My left hand is lighter, the barren skin at the base of my ring finger irritated, sending messages to my brain telling me something is missing. The weight and encasement of the ring were something I had grown accustomed to. A sense of nakedness settles on me without it, and there is nothing to distract me from fixating on it.

It's not as if I *liked* wearing it. It just became common practice. The change is uncomfortable. I only wanted to delay things, never imagining that my life would be forfeited. My heart skips as I wonder if I'll ever see Ness again.

To distract myself, I stretch, moving through flowing poses to build stabilizing strength and flexibility. Being small, I learned there are other ways I must operate to win fights rather than brute strength. Smarter, not harder, is how I succeed. I find leverage points, shift momentum, often relying on speed and agility.

The door opens, and someone enters as I am balancing in a headstand. I open my eyes to an upside Massimo in the doorway. He frowns down at me.

I allow my eyes to close again, concentrating on staying straight, legs in the air, toes pointed. He'll talk when he wants to, and I'm not going to until he does.

He chuckles. "You are going to be a handful, aren't you?"

I smile, shifting my weight to one arm, giving him the finger while remaining upside-down. Wobbling, I return my weight to both arms before lowering bent legs in opposite directions. "What do you want? Has the man in charge decided?"

Callahan's voice is sharp. "Yes."

My eyes pop open, and I stare at black boots, horror sliding through my gut. "Do I have to call you "Master"? Please tell me I don't, that's just...I'll cut out my tongue first."

Massimo smiles, crossing his arms, and leaning against the doorframe, leaving Callahan to be the one standing in front of me. "You shouldn't antagonize him."

"I'm not. I'm being serious. I'm not referring to him in that way." I extend my legs out into a full split. "Owning people is illegal, morally wrong, plain disgusting, I could go on, but you seem like a smart man, you know the rest."

"I don't care what you call me," Callahan says, from outside my view. "I do own you, and you'll do what you're told."

"Oh, fabulous." I roll my eyes "So, what am I supposed to be doing, Sir Dickhead?"

"That title will be unacceptable," Callahan says with worn patience, but Massimo winks at me. "For now, I need to train you."

I close my eyes again. "Seems redundant."

"Your use of magic is rudimentary and crude. You're probably full of bad habits that will get me, or yourself, killed. I can't rely on poor results."

I drop one leg down behind me, then the other as I arch into a backbend. "Sure. How is this working?"

"Massimo is going to start training you. You will answer to him as if you were answering to me."

I hum, bending my knees, dropping my body to the floor, legs and arms bent under me. "Great."

Callahan shuffles closer, placing his feet on either side of my head, and I stare up into his face glaring down. "The next time I see you, I expect you to give me your attention."

I force a wide grin. "You have my attention, so I'm not sure what you're referring to, Sir Jacks Off A Lot."

His eyes narrow. "I expect you to be vertical."

"Oh?" I push up into a handstand. My arms burn with effort,

but I tighten my core to help draw me straighter, ensuring my toes are point so that I am straight.

"Don't push me," he says in a low, tight voice.

Massimo strangles a cough like stifled laughter in the background.

"I haven't touched you." I chuckle, wobbling. "Don't make me laugh. This is harder than it looks."

"Natalia."

"What? I'm vertical, aren't I? Or am I leaning?" Muscles are starting to tremble, but I'm not going to give.

His feet adjust, his stance opening.

I grit my teeth, straining to maintain the handstand.

There's an audible smirk from Callahan. "I can stand here longer than you can hold out."

"Eh," I wince. "Maybe. Let's see how good your patience is."

He makes no response.

My muscles are starting to twinge in angry protest. The burn through my shoulders intensifies. I'm going to need help, so I exhale and center my core, drawing on Ki to fortify my strength.

Runes seem to pass. I dig deeper, the marks down my vertebra igniting as I call on too much Ki. It stings, adding to the discomfort, even as the Ki helps to ease the burning ache in my muscles. I focus on breathing to distract from the effort and discomfort.

Black tendrils seep from beneath Callahan's feet, crawling up my arms. My limbs are starting to shake, my elbows threatening to give as the Dark wicks away the effects of my Ki. They weave around my forearms, stretching higher and lacing together until my skin is obscured in black coils.

I clench my core muscles, the marks blazing down my back. Light shines beneath his magic, the pain lessening. The shadows turn a deep blue, my magic coming through as pinpricks, like stars in a moonless sky. If it weren't inducing a dull agony, it would be gorgeous.

The Dark climbs higher, wrapping over my shoulders,

spreading its burn. The tendrils close around my neck, restricting my airway but not closing it off. I close my eyes against tears, channeling Ki through my body in quick bursts of energy to compensate for the lack of oxygen.

The ability to breathe returns, and I pant, struggling to hold the handstand while fending off his magic. Every muscle, tendon, and ligament is tensed, searing with exhaustion and twitching with spasms, warning me I won't be able to hold this for much longer.

Desperate to prove I'm not weak, I accumulate Ki then send it through my body in a massive push of magic. It shreds my pulsing and aching muscles, a searing slice that cuts through my skin. My scream catches in the back of my throat, but his Dark breaks free of me like flesh peeling off bone in stringy strips.

It echoes my strangled screech, withdrawing. Callahan grunts and takes half a step back.

An arm wraps around my legs, wrenching me off my hands. I yelp in shock, my knees bending over the arm, squeezing tight as it lifts me higher. I hang there, fingertips brushing the floor, seeking purchase. My body is too tired for me to pretend to fight back much beyond the feeble attempt to reach the floor.

"You're going to learn," he says, his voice full of simmering heat that lifts the little hairs down my spine. "One way or another. You can make this easy on yourself, or I can break you."

"Put me down, asshole."

"I don't take orders. I give them. The next time, you'll stand on your feet and look me in the eye when I'm talking to you. You're going to start showing respect, or things are going to get harder than they need to be."

I laugh. "I never do anything the easy way. The Assembly hated training me. My father got so fed up he quit trying to even talk to me. Tony is always complaining." I shake my head. "Bring it, bitch boy. You're not the first to try to make me into something else."

"You signed a contract. Do what you're told to do. It's simple."

"Yeah, I signed something." I sneer at his boots. "I have no idea what it said, so you can't really fault me for not following directions."

The way I'm dangling, he must have his arm held out level, away from his body. The deltoid must be bearing my weight, but he shows no sign of struggling. I lift my chin, staring up his body.

It's taut and flat, with narrow hips and long legs. The man is insufferable, but I admire his attractive build and strength. Not that I should be drawn to him. He's a Darkling.

Without warning, he drops me. I greet the floor with a smack, groaning at the pain lancing through the primary contact points of my head and shoulder. It helps break the enticing captivation he holds. "Mother, asshole—excuse me, Sir Asshole."

"Do what you're told. Don't piss me off. You stay where I put you, and you don't cause trouble for me. Now get up."

I roll to my knees, giving him a two-finger salute. "Sir, yes, Sir."

Callahan stares down at me with livid blazing across his face. He turns to Massimo, waving a hand at me and snarling. "She's your problem for now."

Massimo crosses his arms. "Did I piss you off? I've been against this from the beginning."

"She needs to be trained, and I'm running out of time. I'm going to Narthik after the Council hearing. I expect her useable when I return." Callahan steps past Massimo and out of the room.

"That idea is stupider than the first," he calls after Callahan, a hand to the side of his mouth. Massimo turns back to me and steps forward, offering a hand. "All right, Little Light, clock is ticking."

I smack his hand away and stand, trying not to wince. The effort that took was more than I've exerted in a few years. Between the fighting yesterday and my charade of defiance, my body is pissed. My muscles are like old rubber bands, loose with no snap left. "When's the end?"

He smiles on a sigh. "Six days. I have six days to teach you how to properly handle yourself."

I cross my arms, jutting a hip. "I can handle myself just fine, thank you very much."

"I'm not talking just in a fight," Massimo says, sitting on the edge of the bed. "You signed a contract."

"I have no idea what it even says," I argue, curling a lip and turning my face away. "All I got was a fuck off and sign on the dotted line."

He leans forward, elbows resting on his thighs as his hands dangle between his legs. "Easy, Little Light. I'm not the puppet master pulling your strings."

"As good as." I shake my head.

"You made a deal with Callahan, and you need to accept and honor it. He's going easy on you, but you're testing his patience. He's not known for kindness."

I scoff. "Of course not. He's a Darkling. You both are."

He snarls, and gets his feet, tensing as he takes a half lurch at me. "The Dark isn't evil."

Frozen in shock, my eyes travel down him with caution, raising an eyebrow in skepticism. "You look evil right now. All menacing," I say, flicking my hand at him. "Like you're about to tear my throat out."

He grins, but it's wicked, like a predator trying to taunt its meal into false security. "Little Light, don't tempt me. My magic is salivating over destroying you."

I take a step back, pulse racing.

Under pain of death by dragon along with the hope that I'd have time before being a baby machine, this seemed like a good idea. When I needed protection, I saw no reason not to trust them to keep me alive, but standing in this room alone, squared up to a Darkling, I believe I made an error.

Massimo straightens, tension disappearing from him. "Natalia."

"Tallie," I correct him in reflex.

He smiles, sitting on the edge of the bed again. "You are safe with me and from me. You belong to Callahan."

"Work for."

His expression morphs to empathy. "You signed a contract. You're Callahan's property."

"That's gross."

"You tried to use him. He beat you at your own game. Deal with the consequences."

I scowl. "I'm not fighting, even if I think it's sick that he considers me property."

"We're all property. Every contract he holds is a soul he owns."

I frown.

"We all sign and accept it. You need to as well."

"I'm trying."

"You're fighting. Every time you open that mouth, you talk back. You don't want to do what you're told, which breaks your contract."

"Fine. So, I'm having a hard time adjusting. Can you blame me? I'm not running, and I signed the stupid deal." I lift my forearm covered in the contract, rotating it back and forth. "I sold my soul, lost my whole life when I expected to lose years. I think I've been pretty fucking nice about it so far."

Massimo crosses his arms and stretches his legs. "I'd hate to see when you're not being nice."

I grin, face down, kicking at the floor. "I had to learn to be rough and tough."

"Mean isn't the same as tough."

"Let's put it another way. I had to learn how to stand up for myself and not get pushed around because everyone thought I was given things because I'm an heiress and not because I earned them."

Massimo smiles. "You're here because of the abilities you've shown. Lose the attitude. You're not proving anything with it."

I scoff. "Sorry, it's part of the personality now. Spend too much time pretending to be something, and you wind up becoming it." I step closer to him, leaning one shoulder against the post of the bed and cross my arms. "I'll work on keeping my mouth shut. How's that?"

"Better." He rolls his shoulders back. "We'll run with that for now and move on."

"Brilliant. What stupid idea is next?"

CHAPTER 13

NATALIA

2ND EVERGREEN'S DAY, HEATWAVE, 4049 6TH MILLENNIUM

THE NEXT DAYS ARE BRUTAL. I HEAL WOUNDS AS FAST AS MASSIMO can inflict them, broken bones, split skin, internal bleeding, and more. Once Massimo went too far, and I thought I'd die. The world went out. My heart barely beat for fractions of a rune as I tried to send waves of Ki through me. I half believe it was sheer stubbornness that kept me going, a life force all its own sustaining me rather than admitting he'd bested me.

I got a half-rune break after that incident, then he went right back to kicking my ass.

In all fairness, he's haggard as he limps into my room to collect me this morning. Perching on the edge of my bed, he winces, moving slow and favoring one side for his weight. I watch from the floor, still stretching in preparation for what's to come.

He slumps, grunting and scowling at me.

"What?" I ask, popping up. "I'm ready."

He holds his hands up. "I'm taking this morning off."

Frowning, I cock my head. "Is that an option? Aren't you under orders? And I say you, but I mean we."

Chuckling, he holds hands up, showing me his palms. "Yes, but I've spent days trying to kill you, and I don't heal the same."

I cock my hip, hand on it, and hold a finger up. "Tying to kill me?"

Massimo snickers. "Yes. Thought I did once. Thought Cal would shred me to pieces for it."

I glare with rage. "Trying to fucking kill me? I thought you were training me?"

He shrugs, resting against the corner post of the bed frame. "Experience is the best teacher."

"Oh, fucking Mother," I say, throwing my hands in the air. "I wasn't trying to kill you. If I'd known that was on the table, I would have."

He smirks. "Feels like you were."

"I barely tapped my Ki." I giggle. "I didn't even invoke my sacred geometry."

He raises his eyebrows. "Your geometry?"

I bend my arm overhead to point down my back. "My markings?"

Massimo shoves up with one arm, wincing, holding the other against his stomach. "Let me see. I didn't realize there was any importance to them. They aren't something Seraphinus use, and humans do stupid things to their bodies of clay."

I turn around, lifting my shirt. "There's a total of forty-seven. Complete the training, you get all of them, and they're as much a bitch to earn as they are to get embedded in the skin." I tap a finger against the vertebra at the base of my neck. "Worst part, the open eye. It's the first one, showing you can connect to your Ki."

"This is what you meant about earning things?"

A soft knock resounds in the room. I drop my shirt and turn to him, glancing at Callahan leaning against the door frame. I try to think back, counting the days and realize I've had six blissful days of freedom that are now over.

I curl my lip at him, meeting Massimo's eyes. "Yes. Most Magia don't earn all forty-seven. Some can only get a few, like Ness. She managed to earn the first few, enough to heal and shield, then quit. A lot of people think I can't perform. They think I got my marks because of my bloodline, but I didn't. I fucking earned them the hard way."

Callahan tilts his head. "The hard way?"

I cross my arms. "They made it harder for me. You think experience is the best teacher? Figure out why I'm so good at healing."

Massimo bobs his head, keeping his arm against his stomach. "They made it worse because you're female."

I lift an eyebrow. "I'm a baby machine. Come here," I press my hand into his chest, then shuffle him back to the bed. "Sit."

He plops onto the mattress with zero resistance.

I kick his foot out of the way to stand between his legs. I press my hands to both sides of his shoulder. "Don't move."

I inhale deep, aligning my spine, centering my core to draw on my Ki. I send it through him in little pulses. A low guttural noise emits from his chest, causing me to grin with my tongue between my teeth. I shouldn't enjoy this, but for the hundred times he broke something and all the pain he inflicted, I'd be lying if I said I wasn't. Besides, I know what Ki rippling through a wound feels like. I've experienced it so many, many times. It's not so bad.

"Shut up, you big baby, I'm going slow."

"Feels weird. Like–" A snap of sinew cuts his words off, and he groans.

I shift my hands lower to the center of his chest and between his shoulder blades, no longer concentrating on his shoulder. "Stay still." I take a deep breath, closing my eyes and aligning. "Seriously, don't move," I warn him.

"Whatever you say." He chuckles.

I force Ki into him in a steady stream. It courses through me into him, a drawing sensation, that pulses in time with my heart. Little pits of resistance give way until my Ki flows easy and even. I draw away, breaking the connection to cease the stream of magic.

He stands and stretches, rolls his shoulder with a grin. "You healed me?"

I shrug, hugging myself. That was so far against the rules I've damn near circled all the way back. Then again, I saved the life of a Darkling and signed a contract with him too. I'm breaking every Magia law in existence. "Yeah."

"I feel bad for almost killing you."

I almost smile. "Honestly, I thought you had for a moment. Didn't know if I could fix that one."

Callahan scowls, stepping closer. "What?"

Massimo laughs. "You said train her." His grin fades as Callahan swells. Massimo puts his hands up. "I treated her like everyone else."

"She's not like everyone else," Callahan growls, his face tense.

I give Massimo an eye roll but keep my mouth shut. I'd promised that much. Taking a few steps backward, I stay out of whatever this is, but Massimo doesn't back down.

"No," he says, "she's harder to kill than everyone else. Short of instantaneous death, maybe impossible given how she heals. I stressed her to see what she was capable of, and she claims she wasn't trying hard, so I failed."

Callahan turns to me, and I take up a defensive position, staring back into his black eyes. Biting my lower lip, I remain silent like a good little vassal.

His eyes narrow a fraction. "Were you trying hard?"

"Not to die? Sure." I drop my hands and cross my arms. "To try and kill him? No."

He grips his fists and steps toward me. If I don't move, he's on course to collide, so I shuffle back until I'm pressed against the wall.

Callahan towers over me with murder in his eyes. "Why not?"

Startled, I blink. "You're joking right?"

"What is the point if you hold back? Pull punches? When you fight, you fight to kill. You don't do me any good if you won't commit."

As much as I want to defend my choices, I rest my hands on

the wall, fingertips to the paint. Staring back as blank as I can manage, I nod. "Sure. Fine."

His chin lifts, head cocked to stare down his nose at me. He lifts an eyebrow, then turns away. "At least you taught her one thing," he says facing Massimo. "I want to see what she's capable of. I'll meet you in a quarter rune."

When Callahan is gone, I flip off the empty doorway then turn to Massimo. "He's not serious."

"He is. Thanks for healing me, or it would have been an easy fight, and he would have been cranky."

Shrugging, I glance at the floor and then sweep my gaze out the window. "Well, shit. What happens if one of us does kill the other?"

He gives a halfhearted smile. "If I kill you, he'll kill me."

The gardens beyond the pane are filling with light as the suns reach further into the sky. "Why? What does he want to use me for?"

Massimo shakes his head. "That's your business. Contracts are personal. That is between you and him, not for me to say. I have my own contract." He lifts his right hand. The same four lines of scrawled scripture that Callahan wears on his. The words are hazed, like squiggled runes of another language.

I drop my eyes to the contract on my forearm. His is larger lettering, barely anything compared to the lines dancing across my skin. I grip around my arm and the script. "I thought you two were friends."

Massimo smiles. "My contract is a lot more vague, less explicit, which leaves it open to interpretation. It's a double edge. I get a lot more freedom, but also much more responsibility. I'd say it's friendship."

"Right-hand man?"

"Yes."

"And why does he need a right-hand man?"

"You have so much to learn." Massimo smiles. "Come on, Little Light, we need a warmup."

CHAPTER 14
CALLAHAN

I CHANGE OUT OF THE FORMAL ATTIRE, TRYING TO GET comfortable. At least Natalia was on her feet, not doing weird things with her body that distract me. I'm on edge around her, hyper-aware of everything. I've always been protective of mine, it's part of having contracts, but Natalia is elevating that sense.

I want her. It's almost a need for her that's growing. I remind myself she belongs to me. I have what I need, which is the end of the matter. Clear, concise thought is necessary. Distractions will get me killed.

Picking up my phone, the screen illuminates to display another three missed calls from the unknown number. Scowling, I check the time, then call the unknown number.

A female's scream crackles through the speaker. "About time pretty boy."

I pull the phone from my ear to glare at it, then return it to my ear. "Who is this?"

"Where's Tallie, you gorgeous, Darkling creep?"

My mind whirs and clicks, logic piecing things together. "I see. You are the friend."

"I want to talk to Tallie."

"No."

"No? What does that mean, asshole? Yes, now, if she's even still alive, put her on the phone."

I comb fingers through my hair, heading for the door of my chambers. "Natalia is alive. You failed to change her mind, but a smoragon did. She belongs to me."

"Hey, asshole, you can't own Tallie. That's not okay. What the fuck is a smoragon? The dragon that was in the city last week?"

I shake my head and hang up. The Magia are idiots, breeding ignorance. I slide the phone into a pocket, ignoring the rings as the woman calls back a few more times before giving up.

I reach the open courtyard at the back of my home where Natalia and Massimo are already present. They sit on a stone bench at the edge of the lawn, Natalia laughing as Massimo speaks and gestures with his hands.

She seems relaxed with him, easy-going, different than the way she glares at me.

Natalia is shaking her head while Massimo tips forward, roaring with laughter. At least they are getting along. That will be helpful in coming events.

My phone is ringing again. I answer it, "Stop calling me."

There's a soft giggle. "But I miss you so," the voice purrs.

My eyes narrow, lips pinching tight. I should have checked who was calling. "Telra."

"Hello, Cal. It's so nice to hear your voice after that nasty business."

"What business?"

Her voice carries a smile, "The smoragon and Light Seraphim. I was so worried."

Clamping my jaw, I breathe in through my nose. I believe Telra was worried about me like I believe I shouldn't have ended our relationship. I don't. I threw a melrag at her in the scuffle. I'd assumed she'd have gotten the point. "What do you want?"

"I think I'd make a beautiful queen," she sighs in a wistful, almost dreamy voice. "What do you think?"

"You are beautiful," I admit, humming a bit as Natalia stands, puts her hands in the air, and throws herself forward into a handstand. The woman seems to like being upside-down.

"Don't tease me," Telra grins through the phone. "I could be your *King*, or I could be *your* Queen."

Natalia's arms bend and give, her knees bending and tucking into her chest as she rolls then stands. She catches me watching, the smile fading from her lips. She turns her back, jerking her head. Massimo tilts around her to look at me.

Telra sighs. "Are you there? Are you remembering? We could work together, you know."

"I'm not interested," I say in a firm tone, eyeing Natalia. My Light bug is waiting on me.

"Hmph," she pouts. "One Light Seraphim doesn't change things that much."

"Yes, that's why you all showed up," I scoff. "Everyone in that room knew otherwise."

She laughs. "Think about it. I'd love to be your Queen."

I disconnect the call without answering, heading to meet Natalia and Massimo. I sit next to Massimo and jerk my head. "Go, and don't hold back."

She huffs and rolls her eyes. Her demeanor has shifted as rigid and edged as a knife. There's no more smiles or laughter. I'll ignore that.

Keeping her back to me, she moves to the middle of the field.

Massimo pats me on the shoulder. "She'll get there."

"It's already better. I don't know how you managed to get her to keep her mouth shut, but I want to."

Chuckling, my friend shakes his head. "I pointed out she played a game and lost."

"So did I."

"Nicely," Massimo says with a grin. "Do you really want to watch me fight to kill?"

"Have you been?" I turn burning fury on him.

Massimo nods. "Yes, I treated her the same. She appreciates it."

"Then yes," I grind out, gripping the edge of the stone bench, wrapping my fingers under the lip to squeeze something solid. "I need to know what I have."

"What we are guessing we have is fairly accurate."

"Guess and fairly aren't words I'm comfortable with. It's like guessing if a woman had an orgasm. If I have to ask, it didn't happen." Massimo stands. I swallow my nerves, my heart rate picking up as my voice goes hoarse. "Don't kill my Light source."

Massimo chuckles as he heads for Natalia. He says something low that I can't make out, she glances back at me.

She turns to Massimo again, voice loud enough for me to understand when she asks, "You're sure I'm supposed to try to kill you? Any tricks I know are fair game?"

"Yes."

She rolls her shoulders, "One hundred percent positive you can stop me? Because if I kill you, I'm stuck with him." She jerks her thumb at me.

"Try it," Massimo laughs.

She nods, takes a step back, leaning on her heel, "You're healed? Fair playing ground?"

"It's not. You're at severe disadvantage, Little Light," Massimo squares up. He lifts clenched fists.

Natalia mirrors his motion with open hands. "If by disadvantage you mean you Darklings are stronger, faster, and harder to inflict physical damage on, then yes."

Grinning, Massimo attacks. Natalia does a lot of defensive maneuvering, and they shuffle around. They move, standing face-to-face, exchanging strikes and blocks in a back-and-forth exchange.

Massimo gets a clean strike in to her face.

Clenching my jaw, I resist the urge to stop this. It shouldn't exist at all when they stand on level ground engaged in sanctified combat. They both agreed to the fight, and I need to know she can handle herself. I have no business interrupting an agreed combat. It's a desire I squash.

I can't afford a liability this late in the game. It's stupid to be bringing someone on this far in, but Natalia is a rare circumstance. I may have infinite uses for her.

She whips back to face Massimo while the markings on her spine glow white through her shirt. She blocks, strikes, then does a backflip, landing and lifting her hands.

Massimo steps, punching the air, and sending black streaks to her. I wait, holding my breath, but Natalia doesn't move. It hits her, and she twists, whimpering in pain.

I clamp down on the slab beneath me to hold myself in place. I'd expected ten times better. I'm not thrilled at watching Massimo inflict pain on my lightning bug. The woman hadn't even formed a shield with ample time.

It's pathetic. This ends now. The ideas I have turn to smoke. I'll keep Natalia to feed from, the only use she'll have for me.

Prying my stiff fingers loose from the concrete, broken pieces break loose, falling to the ground. I stand, not wanting to watch her bleed, knowing she will with so little ability.

Natalia's eyes meet mine as she lifts. Her eyes are solid black, the skin around them appearing bruised. Her features are twisted into something nasty, making me pause.

As she turns to Massimo, she holds a palm out, fingers splayed. A blast of shadowy Dark magic hurtles back to him.

I curl my lip knowing the attack is a waste of energy. Massimo has plenty of time to form a shield and does.

I take a step forward. What I thought she is capable of is different than what she is showing she is. I've seen enough. I've recalculated my plans.

Her blast cleaves straight through Massimo's block. The magic creating his shield acts as if it is not there at all, her attack cutting through it and into him with zero hinderance. My jaw drops.

Massimo crumples. Natalia stands up, putting her hands together. She waits, as do I. Massimo doesn't stir.

Natalia curses, rushing to him. She rolls him, pressing a knee into his chest and slapping a glimmering hand down onto his forehead.

Massimo jerks.

Natalia hisses through bared teeth. "Don't fucking move, dumbass, or I might kill you for real."

I walk over to Natalia and Massimo, a pulse of Light flickering in her hand. She pulls back, and Massimo blinks up at her. "What the fuck was that, Little Light Bug? Was that Dark?"

Standing, she shrugs. "You two are fucking dumb. I'm not Light. I'm not Dark. I'm both, and while I can't generate Dark, I can manipulate it if you give it to me. It fucking hurts, though." She rubs the back of her neck. "Mark forty-seven if you care to know."

Pulling her hand away, I brush strands of her hair away to expose the marking. "I want to know more about those." I realize I'm holding her hand in mine. It's so small, her skin soft. I release her, taking a step away. "Can all Magia generate Light and manipulate Dark?"

Natalia winces. "No. Magia typically can't generate, just absorb the magic of another and send it back."

"These marks?" I hook a finger under the collar of her shirt to try and steal a glance down her back, "They allow you to do that?"

She laughs. "No, Mother, they just—no, it's not like I got the mark, so the mark lets me do this thing." Her wrist flicks in a dismissive fashion.

"Then what do they do?" I cross my arms, forcing my face into a scowl.

She sighs, "I hate that question."

"I don't care. Answer it."

"No, I hate that question because I don't know how to answer it." Her eyes roll to the top of her head as she stares at the sky, "Um, so, the process? You master a skill. I had to focus the Ki, harness it, then perform the task without the sacred geometry. Once a Magia does that they have earned the right to the mark."

Crossing her arms, she rubs her hands up and down like she's trying to warm herself, wincing and glancing around. "The mark itself is a son of a bitch with an involved process to get it inked. After you wear the geometry, it," her face screws up as she wiggles a level hand back and forth, "helps? It's like, the mark helps you link to Ki for that purpose? Like paving a path with stone makes it easier to walk, but no, the mark doesn't just let you *do* anything. It's me. I did it." She winces again, looking at Massimo. "Sorry, dude. You asked for it though."

Massimo rolls up, then stands. "Where has that been all this time?"

I hold a hand to him, glaring at her. "You baited him in. Let him hit you."

She rubs the side of her face. "I'm small. I'm used to getting the shit kicked out of me. I just found ways to use it to my advantage."

I frown, then shift my gaze to Massimo. She's like me. In a way. Maybe that's why she saved me, some part of me had called to the like in her.

Like calls to like. *Similis*. It's a connection on a subconscious level that can alter actions without being aware of why.

Pulling my phone out, I tap on the unsaved number to connect a call, then toss the phone to Natalia. "Talk to your friend so she stops calling me." I jerk my chin at Massimo, turning away.

Together we move further away, out of range for Natalia to understand this conversation. Not that she's paying attention. Her face is lit up and she's grinning ear to ear. I frown as her expression flitters to something less joyful, cradling the phone against her ear.

Massimo puts a hand on my shoulder. "Satisfied? Or do I need to get my ass kicked again?"

"No," I shrug him off.

"No to which?"

"She's coming with us."

Massimo curls his lip. "You're jumping from one bad decision to another. You can't bring her to Ilbuio. They'll kill her. Fuck, *it* might kill her."

I rub my mouth, then drop my hands on my hips. "We don't let them kill her, and she's strong enough to survive the city. I want her by my side."

"She's Light," he says tersely.

"Which is precisely why," I glare. "She's my contracted. I'm allowed to bring her with me."

Massimo shakes his head, rubbing the back of his neck. "She's starting to ask questions."

I shrug. "Let her."

"Should I be answering?"

I watch Natalia sit, smiling but shaking her head. I'm going to need her trust. "No. I will."

"If you're set on this, then we have an accelerated timetable on her."

"Yes," I drawl, "Gathering Shadows is barely more than a week away."

"You know damn well we don't have enough days left for this."

"I've made up my mind."

He grumbles, shaking his head. "How'd the Council go?"

I flash teeth. "Fine."

"And the search?"

"I didn't find another codex."

Massimo nods. "I'll look into it more."

"Fine. I'm taking Natalia. She needs to look like a queen, and I need to know more about her."

I walk to Natalia, stopping in front of her, crouching and holding out a hand.

She ducks her chin, "I have to go, babe. The master is back." She lifts her head, wrinkling her nose as she obviously fights a grin. "Yeah, that is not happening…no…no!" Natalia laughs hard.

Grabbing the phone away, I press the speaker to my ear. Natalia's eyes grow wide, and she reaches for the device. I roll my shoulder back to keep my possession, catching the woman on the other end of the phone saying, "…really a face you should sit on."

I smirk. Exactly what my cock is thinking. The comment is only going to encourage it. "Interesting. I'm hanging up now."

"Oh shit."

Ending the call, I stand, slipping my phone into the pocket of my jeans. "Come," I hold my hand out.

Her eyes drop, her cheeks pink as she sets her hand in mine. "I have no idea what you heard."

"No?"

"All right, I have an idea of what you may have heard, but that's all Ness."

That is disappointing. I pull her to her feet, tugging her close to me. "Just Ness?"

Natalia tips her head back to meet my eyes. The tip of her tongue wets her lips. The movement draws my gaze. I'm tempted to find out what she tastes like.

"Yes."

I release her and step back. "You're coming with me."

She opens her mouth, then cocks her jaw, narrows her eyes, sighs, and relaxes. Her head bobs in agreement.

Massimo is right, ten days isn't enough. I need to do things differently, so I tell her, "You can ask."

"Where?"

"You need clothes."

"I have clothes, which I'm not asking too many questions about."

104

I knew she was going to accept my contract before she did. I knew she was going to be here, that she'd need them. I'd sized her up, made the arrangements, choosing the room she'd stay in with care, ensuring she'd be close to me, and that she would have everything she needed.

"You need other clothes. A week from now you're coming with me to Ilbuio."

Her eyes widen at the name of the Dark capital. That is good, she knows what it is. It's a start.

I take her chin in my hand, making sure to hold eye contact. "I need you to look a certain way when you're at my side."

Natalia throws her hands up. "I traded one dickhead for the next. Whatever, you own me, right? Dress me however you want."

"If I decide, you may not like what I pick." My eyes travel down her body. "How much of you I chose to put on display."

She scoffs. "How about I go naked?" Something sparks to life in her eyes, bright and dangerous. She steps closer, almost against me. "If you want a distraction, it could work."

I need her to wear a tarp that hides her out of sight for her not to be distracting. "I can't afford to be distracted."

She gives me a wicked grin. "I'll make sure I distract others then."

I sidestep her, wrapping my hand around her wrist instead. "We're going now."

I need away from the topic before I lose my self-control. Thoughts of her naked, picturing what that might look like are pinging in my mind. She's a distraction, one my cock is only too happy to indulge in.

Imagining her nude is hard to stop. The concept of other eyes roaming her flesh irritates me, though. There would be too many, and too many with ideas on what to do with her. She is already going to be a beacon, drawing others like moths to a flame.

She follows in my grip without fighting. "So, I'm just going to ask, why Ilbuio?"

I hesitate. There is so much she doesn't know. While there are certain things she doesn't need to know, I need to prepare her. "You walked into the middle of a war."

"Brilliant," she says on a soft laugh. "Because I never do anything the easy way."

A pang twinges my gut. She has no idea what is coming. What I'm doing to her isn't fair, but the world doesn't give allowances to be fair. I'm going to use her in the games, and if she can survive that, I'll keep her for my use in the contest.

I've vetted and prepped all my contracted for what is coming. I've been on the contenders list for nearly three centuries. Everyone has advance warning. Not Natalia, though. She doesn't have a clue what I'm going to do with her or what she's going to face.

I glance over my shoulder at her, frowning in remorse. I'm not used to guilt, but it's an undeniable rock settling in my gut as I stare into her wide gray eyes. "If this was easy, I wouldn't need you, and you wouldn't be here."

CHAPTER 15
NATALIA

CALLAHAN'S WORDS BURN. HE IS HONEST TO A FAULT. I'M HERE because he wants to use me, and I was attempting to flirt with him.

'Stupid, party of one. Check, please.'

He appears human, so long as I don't look at his eyes. That makes remembering he's a Dark Seraphinus more difficult. I squeeze my hands into fists, then relax them. I don't need silly fantasies in my head.

I press my lips, following him to the underground garage. I groan in silence as he drops my wrist while standing next to the motorcycle. He picks up a helmet, slipping it on my head with tender care, before flipping the visor down with a flick of his pointer. Surprisingly, the helmet fits like a glove.

I slip onto the bike behind him, wrapping my arms around his waist, my palms clammy as they rest against the tank in front of him. He kicks the stand up, walks it out of the parking spot, and turns the key. The engine flares to life, and he takes off, the front wheel lifting, causing me to almost slip off.

Squeaking, I tighten my arms, gripping him by the waist.

Falling off at these speeds won't kill me, but the last ride was full of potential. This one is starting off on the wrong foot. His muscles flex beneath me, bunching smoothly like liquid steel.

I shriek at him, grabbing tighter as he moves through an intersection that he does not have the right of way for. "Fucking Mother."

Horns blare from the cross-traffic, tires squealing. Callahan doesn't seem to notice or care. Seraphinus are top of the food chain, owning the world, all the land and people in it, people like me. They don't follow rules or human law. They do what they want.

Callahan clearly does what he wants, although I don't know how high in the pyramid of power he sits.

I should probably figure that out. I need to know what I am tethered to for life, what I got myself involved in. If his home is any indication, including the people reporting to him, he is fairly high.

He stops the bike, and I take a breath to get my frazzled nerves under control, still holding tight.

He laughs, the sound muffled from beneath his helmet. "You can let go now, Lightning Bug."

I release my death grip and get off the bike to glance around. The street is familiar, full of designer and expensive stores. Ness and I would walk here every year on Mother's Day when the shops were done up for the holidays, drinking hot chocolate, and window shopping for all the things we'd never be able to afford.

This is going to be an interesting experience if nothing else. I set the helmet on the bike as he turns to me. He runs fingers through his dark hair, before sliding sunglasses on. With his eyes obscured, I can't tell what he is, the same way I failed to register he was a Darkling when I saved his life. It's a strange thing, knowing what he is capable of versus how he looks.

"How does this work? I just, pick a dress?"

"Gathering Shadows lasts twelve days. You'll want at least that many."

"Twelve?" I gape. "I have to find twelve dresses?"

He leans his backside on the bike, crossing his legs in front of him and then his arms. "I'll be keeping you with me for a while." He grins full of wicked humor. "Your whole life in fact. You'll want more than twelve."

I close my eyes, rubbing the skin between the brows. "Do your kind not re-wear anything?"

"I expect you to represent certain abilities I have, including wealth. I own various cities on this continent and the next. I don't need other Dark seeing any weakness, perceived or otherwise because you wear something twice."

"Mother," I breathe. "You lot are narcissistic assholes."

Callahan scowls. "You're a display, Lightning Bug, I need you to look good. It makes me look good."

I throw my hands up. "Arm candy. Got it."

He chuckles and stands. "You'll be making a statement, but you are far from decoration. Your contract includes protection of me."

Scoffing, I turn, start walking, scanning shop fronts for where to begin my search. "You killed a freaking dragon. If we're in a position where you need me to protect you, you're screwed."

He falls in step next to me. "Tony seemed rather insistent that you could handle it. It's called a smoragon, by the way, not a dragon."

"I really don't care what it's called." I stop, eyeing a store. "And don't say that name, it puts me in a bad mood. I start twitching unless I have vodka."

Callahan moves to the door, opening it and jerking his head. I move inside as he follows. "You were going to union with him."

"And now I need a drink."

"You wanted to use me to avoid that. Why?"

I scan the merchandise on display. "What's the dress code for this thing?"

"Expensive. Why?"

"So I know what I'm looking for."

One of his eyebrows lifts as he stares me down. "You're intentionally being obtuse. Why were you intending to union with him? Why did you attempt to use me to avoid the situation, and only temporarily?"

"Yeah, well, contract for life terminated that little setup, so moot point," I say, heading further between racks.

My forearm burns. I clench my teeth, stopping to glance down at the contract. The lines are raised, edged in red. It happened the first night too. I assumed it was skin irritation resulting from being branded at the time.

Callahan steps next to me. "You have to answer to me. The contract is warning you that you're in contempt."

"That's fabulous and bullshit." I clench a fist, then unfurl my fingers to go searching for dresses. The burn increases and I round on him. "All right, back off, I'll tell you. You don't even know what you're asking, okay? Let me just—" I let out a heavy sigh "—figure out how to tell you."

He gives me an amused look, a smile toying with the corners of his mouth. "I'm not doing it. The contract is. Until you comply it will continue to get worse. If you disregard it long enough it will kill you."

My eyes stretch open. "Wait, what?" I glare, holding my forearm aloft for viewing. "This thing is going to kill me?"

He laughs, shaking his head. "Eventually. I didn't give you many rules. I didn't want you dead for pushing boundaries."

"Really? Couldn't tell. It's like a thousand words. Not that I can read any of it."

"I was very explicit in what I was demanding of you." He slips his sunglasses to the top of his head and checks his watch. "Answer me or it gets worse."

I huff and start checking dresses. "Fucking Mother, how do I explain this?" I shake my head, turning dizzy at the options. "The Magia, the Assembly–" I stop, frowning.

Taking a deep breath, I try again. "The Assembly wants the Swans, that's me, and the Washingtons, that's Tony, to mix. They decide which families have the ability to breed, then set it up based upon available children, how long ago they were mixed, and whatever other criteria they use to preserve our bloodlines."

"You were set up to marry Tony because of bloodlines."

I smile despite nothing being funny. It is sad, horrifying, so many things, but not entertaining. "There were three of us–three Swans," I say, meeting his gaze. "There was my sister Natasha, me, and my younger brother Nicholas. Two Washingtons, Tony and his sister, Sarah. There were options, no big deal."

"It would sound as much."

I sigh, "Sasha, as everyone called Natasha, was the golden girl. Did everything right. A perfect little Magia. She was gorgeous, always knew the right thing to say. The Mother reincarnated." I brush hair out of my face. "She was stronger than me too."

Turning and moving to inspect other dresses, I go on. "Sasha grew up believing she'd marry Tony. They were perfect together. They never fought, I mean, they had disagreements, but they were great together, totally in love. She and Tony had their whole life planned out. They knew the day they'd get married and when they'd start having kids. It was chiseled in stone. All that was left was for them to check the box off after they'd done it."

I lean against a rack, frowning at Callahan's expensive shoes. "Sasha should have survived initiation. It doesn't make sense. She'd already mastered healing. She should have been fine. I still don't understand. You don't start training and earning your marks until after initiation, but you pick things up growing up around it–Ki. Sasha had done enough to earn her first twelve marks before she ever went through initiation. I know what initiation is, she should have made it through, but she didn't."

Running my hands down my face, I puff up my cheeks and eye a vibrant fuchsia dress. That would stand out in Ilbuio, the Dark capital, home of shadows and all things Dark.

Another one next to it catches my eye. "Exactly how distracting should I be?"

He tenses, inhaling sharply. I glance over, following his line of sight back to the dress that had caught my attention. It's more gauzy material, appearing to be completely sheer, hardly qualifying for the word "dress".

"Dude?"

"Buy it."

I'll need to see if it fits, or if they even have my size. I skim the rack, pick one up, and drape it over my arm. "It was fine. There was still Nick and Sarah. Nicky stepped up. He got to know Sarah. They had a thing. I think it was more duty, although they seemed to like each other. Nick said he was happy. It was fine."

"What happened?"

"Initiation," I sigh. "He started. He got to the part where you can't turn back, and right before he took that step, he changed his mind. He wanted to back out." I stop, closing my stinging eyes. "The Assembly tried to force him."

The memories of that night haunt me in slumber often. Nick's pleas of fear, the way he sounded begging. I had fought, tried to defend him, physically challenging the Assembly members. They'd made me pay for it later, but it didn't matter anymore. Nick was dead.

"He didn't need to be a practicing member to mix the bloodlines, so I didn't understand why it mattered. He didn't survive initiation either. The day after we burned him and put his spirit to rest my father told me I was marrying Tony."

I avoid eye contact with him, stepping through racks with him at my heels, picking up other dresses to try on. "You heard him calling me Nat? That's what he called Sasha, the only one who did. Then he started calling me Nat. He kept trying to make me like her, the dresses, the way I should act, talk, look, the things I should be interested in, just everything. I get it. He loved her, really loved her, but…" I trail off, shrugging.

"You're not her."

"She really was perfect." I smile at dust in the air. "Seriously, perfect, with a capital P. Me? I never do anything the easy way," I admit, lifting my eyes to his steady gaze.

He smiles with closed lips. "You tried to use me to avoid him temporarily."

"Yeah, temporarily. That worked out great," I lift the arm marked with the contract. "So, thanks for that." I flip him off.

He wraps his hand around mine. "That is a habit you need to break. Doing that in front of the wrong company will force me to do something I don't want to."

I pull free, scoffing. "I figured out how to act for Tony. I can figure out how to act for you. Right now, you're getting the real me, so deal with it, Sir Fuckface."

"You intended to go through with the union and producing children with Tony."

"Eventually. I felt like I had to, but I wanted more time before doing it though, so," I wave a hand at him, "you. I'm going to go try things on now if master allows it."

Without waiting for him to respond, I head for the dressing rooms. I hang the multitudes of gowns on the hooks, staring at them. Lifting my arm, I inspect the contract, having returned to its normal state. It shifts, his signature sliding under the surface of my skin like something has been added to it.

Scowling, I drop my arm. Figuring out how high Callahan is in the pyramid is taking a back seat to figuring a way out of the contract.

I try on dress after dress, moving from store to store. I do my best to pick out things that are sexy, sticking with dark, muted colors, mostly blacks, but there's a silver dress I fall in love with.

Then there are shoes, lingerie which is awkward to pick out, but at least Callahan makes himself scarce for those moments. I pick out makeup, a sugar scrub that smells heavenly and lotions, everything I can think of to primp and pamper. If I'm going to be arm candy, then I'm going to be the best damn-looking candy I can possibly be. Besides, I get to be expensive and extravagant on Callahan's coin.

CHAPTER 16
CALLAHAN

NATALIA IS WILTING BEFORE MY EYES, SHOULDERS SLUMPING. SHE IS becoming a lot less picky as we move from store to store. I check my watch and then our surroundings.

The leaked knowledge that I'm a contender is annoying. There could be an attack at any moment. At least I have Natalia with me to help if necessary.

Runes have ticked passed. I'm getting tired of being on my feet. I turn to her as we move down the paved walkway. Everything is set to be delivered to my estate and the suns are sinking low, the sky turning to a dusty turquoise.

"Are you hungry?" I ask.

She nods.

I steer her back to the bike. She follows, one pace behind me and off to the side. I hold out my hand, and she rests hers in it. That's a good sign. She's starting to learn.

I pull her next to me, then drop her hand. While she has a contract, technically a vassal, I want her at my side, not bowing her head at my heels.

Learning what she is capable of this morning has given me perspective, and I've spent all day sorting data and weighing options as I escorted her shop to shop. My mind is made up, the devised plan for my little lightning bug solidifying. I want an equal, a partner.

We walk in silence to where I parked, and I pick up the helmet. I slip it over her head, securing it in place. She's drooping, shoulders slumped as if she's gone limp and yet still upright somehow.

I flip the visor up to see her eyes, they gray dull and hazey. They flicker to mine, and I tilt my head, eyebrows pulling together.

"Are you all right, Lightning Bug?" I ask, trying to smile.

She shrugs. "Bzzt, flash. That's what those things do, right?"

I grin for real. "Or smite. Think you can figure out how to smite for me?"

Natalia stares at me in contempt. "I'm Magia, not Seraphinus. No smiting." She reaches up and flips the visor down.

Chuckling, I get on the bike, and she slides behind me. She wraps her arms around my torso this time without encouragement, her helmet resting between my shoulders.

I kick the stand up and fire the bike to life. As I walk it back, a car slams on its brakes, tires screeching as they lock up against pavement. I flex, one wing bursting free and into the front end of the oncoming vehicle to stop it from colliding with us. The horn blares, steam hisses, and my magic retracts. I frown at the inevitable hole in my shirt while coils of Dark wrap protectively around me as I drive away.

The helmet rocks side-to-side between my shoulder blades. Natalia is shaking, but it's not jittery fear, more like laughing. I think she calls me an asshole, but it's hard to hear between her helmet and the air rushing.

Her mouth is going to be a problem. No one else under contract would dare, but I'm not wearing those contracts either. They aren't as consequential as the woman behind me. With her, I'm going to win the contest.

She'll be my queen.

My magic jolts me with a surge of energy as much as the thought rudely wakes me like static shock. I grip the throttle, accelerating to drag my mind to something else. Regardless of what she claims to be, my little lightning bug carries the Light within her, and I am Dark.

She's alluring, but my enemy. My contract is a dangerous game, although most games I play are.

Telra is trying to make a deal for a reason. We had our falling out after she took Chelm's spot on the contender list three years ago. She knows what it means for me to have control over a Light Seraphim. Even if Natalia isn't a Seraphim, she has the ability to call Light. That is enough.

I park, shutting off the engine, and she slips away. I get sunglasses on and take her hand, leading her inside.

The host greets me with a wide smile, showing crooked teeth.

"Two," I say.

The boy bobs his head. "It's about a three-quarter rune wait. Can I get a name?"

I reach up, drawing my sunglasses down to display my murderous glare without hindrance. His eyes grow wide as I push the glasses back in place.

"Right. I'm so sorry," the boy says, his voice frantic. He searches the podium. "Give me five—one fraction of a rune." He holds a finger up and walks away.

I lean against the stand, my lips pulled to one side in irritation. Too many humans clog this world. I'm waiting because of them. If I wasn't so relaxed and at leisure, I might kill a few to speed things along.

The host returns to say, "This way."

The boy turns and I begin to follow, but someone lacking intelligence speaks out. "Oh, come on!" A man gripes behind me, lifting his voice over the din. "I've been waiting fifty fractions and they just walked in."

The small entryway packed full goes quiet.

Natalia puts a hand in the middle of my back then shoves me forward. "You go," she says with a worn voice, which tightens and lifts, "And you shut the fuck up."

The host has turned back, eyes flickering. He is stuck in time, frozen like he's ready to take another step, unable to make up his mind. He's smarter.

I take a step toward him.

"Yeah, better walk away."

Natalia laughs. "You really don't want to do this."

"Shut up. I was talking to your douchebag boyfriend."

"Um, baby," a female voice says, "I think, um, maybe we should just wait."

I turn, eyeing the man. He's bulky, probably lumbers with so many muscles bulging. I cross my arms and incline my head. "I'm going to recommend you grovel for forgiveness, and I'll let this go because I'm not in the mood for a fight."

"He's sorry," Natalia says, turning to the man and inclining toward him, adding force to her voice. "Right? You're sorry?"

"No, I'm not sorry," he responds with a sneer. "You probably suck cock to get whatever you want."

My lips twitch to one side, my eyes pinching as I consider. In languor, I step closer, stretching my shoulders back, my neck to the side. "Shut your mouth, Clay Pot."

The man laughs, and a woman grabs his arm. She tries to cut between us. "He's sorry, really, sir. It's—he's hungry, and he gets cranky when he's hungry." She does her best to smile. "And he's sorry."

I use a finger to slide the sunglasses along the bridge of my nose to expose my eyes for clear sight.

The woman goes pale, trembling. "Please, sir, he meant no disrespect."

The man jerks away from the woman, moving closer to me in some lapse of judgment. "Oh, you're one of those fucks? This is

118

what everyone's so afraid of? You?" His face scrunches on one side as he sizes me up. "You don't look tough."

My gaze cuts to Natalia, gauging how she's going to take this. She thinks the Magia are about protecting humans from my kind, but I'm not letting this go either. Seraphinus haven't been on this world longer than the animated clay vessels, however, we rule it for obvious reasons. When humans forget, I like to get my claws bloody.

Natalia puts her hands up while shaking her head. "You can't help stupid. Just don't kill him and we're square."

Reaching out, I grab the man by the throat, hesitating as I weigh if it's worth putting Natalia down to prove the point, and decide it's not. I don't want to fight her. More accurately, I don't want her to have cause to fight me.

I slam him to the ground in one swift motion. There are gasps and people moving away, the male spluttering and wheezing.

"Don't piss me off," I growl, dropping on one knee, tightening my hand around the man's fragile neck. "You're going to thank her for your life, human."

He has the audacity to laugh. "You just proved she sucks your dick to get ahead in life. Must be some good shit, buddy."

"Oh, Mother." Natalia storms over and grabs me by the shoulder, her fingers like steel intruding into my muscles. She leans over me. "A, not sucking anything. B, you moron, everyone knows not to piss off a Seraphinus. Do you have a death wish?"

I turn to her. "Go sit down." I jerk my head to the side.

She tenses, and her eyes drop to the contract on her arm. "Fucking Mother." She throws her hands up and turns, walking away.

I check over my shoulder to ensure she's following the host away, noting the direction they move before returning my attentions to the insolent, ignorant irritant. "I'm not killing you, because of her, but I'm not letting this disrespect go, either." I retract my hand, balancing on the balls of my feet. "You answer to us, you bow to us, and respect is owed."

Black tendrils slip from beneath my fingertips, my magic seething out of me. It's writhing with rage, demanding repayment. I pull on its reins. I'm not going to let it loose. Using magic won't teach this human anything.

I grab the front of his shirt, and the idiot tries to punch me. His blow glances off the side of my face as I freeze in shock. The contact is there, although it lacks enough force to affect me in any manner.

Humans are fragile and weak, the contact harmless and without sting. I wind back and return the blow. It might sink through his minuscule logic receptors that I and my kind are that much better.

Bone crunching beneath my fist gives me an elated feeling. I so enjoy this. I just needed the incentive to move. The man is limp, and I let go to stand.

I turn, walking away to find Natalia.

When I drop into the booth across from her, she glares over a menu. "Did you kill him?"

"No."

"I hate you for making me walk away."

I pick up the second menu. The Dark in me coils tighter with greedy need, desiring her. "If I believed you, I'd add a rule against it in the contract."

"Yeah, I noticed that earlier, watching it move. What the burning afters? You can add to it whenever you want?"

There is so much I must teach her. "I can change the contract any time I want."

"What did you add?"

She still can't read the contract. That's a bad sign. "You are not allowed to talk to Tony."

She doesn't comment, so I check her face over the menu. She's frowning at me, but there's no malice to her features.

The waitress stops by, her ears back and eyes wide. "Hi. Hello. I'm, um, my name is Amy, I'll be helping–taking care of you," she says, swallowing. The pen and pad are shaking in her hands as she prepares to write. "Can I start you-you off with something to drink?"

"Relax, Amy. He's not going to kill you."

"Um..." The waitress gets closer to tears.

Natalia points to herself. "I'll keep you alive even if the kitchen screws up his food. Promise."

I lift my eyebrows, but don't contradict her.

"O-okay."

"Can I get a glass of vodka? Like, straight vodka, full glass, no ice, please?"

"Er, um," the waitress blinks, then answers in a strangled confusion. "Yeah, and...?" She points the pen in her hand at me.

"Bourbon, neat."

She leaves, and we exist in silence as we have so much today. I drop the menu, scanning the room for potential threats.

When our drinks are delivered, Natalia picks up her glass, starting to chug. The waitress and I stare as she inhales the vodka until it's gone in a single gulp without a pause to breathe.

"Um," the waitress says, then asks, "should I get you another one?"

Natalia bobs her head. "Yes, along with a water, no ice as well."

The waitress leaves, and I offer Natalia a look of impressed confusion, narrowing one eye.

She does a double take then tilts her head. "Oh, was that against the rules?"

She damn well knows it wasn't by the contract on her arm. I shake my head. "I can carry you out, put you on the front of the bike again."

Struggling against a laugh, she turns her face away. "Yeah, that's not going to be necessary."

"You can handle that much alcohol?"

She grins wider, meeting my gaze. "Magia," she points to her chest, and I take the opportunity to stare at her breasts. "That's like a shot for a human. I'll process that in ten fractions, have a buzz for half-a-rune, then be sober again before we walk out of here."

The Magia are a footnote from my boyhood lesson days. They weren't considered to pose any serious threat, and they were also denoted as destroyed. It seems they've been rebuilding right under our noses and do in fact carry potential threat.

"Do your kind often kill Seraphinus?"

Her mouth pinches, then she picks up the menu, hiding behind it. "Sometimes, when your kind are assholes."

My fingers twitch at the insult, but I let it go. I wonder about the few contracted that have gone missing. I assumed they'd been killed by Light, but I was ignorant of the menace in my city.

I need to know more about them, about her. "Tell me about your marks."

The menu drops to the table. Her features pull inward in a scowl.

I stare back, raising my eyebrows.

Sighing, she twists her face to the side, lower jaw cocked.

I wait. The contract will ensure her compliance. I won't show weakness by begging.

"All right, fine," she snaps, setting crossed arms on the table and leans forward. "I've already broken every other Magia law, so sure, why not. There are forty-seven of them. Each one is earned individually. Each is a badge of honor. Anyone who earns all forty-seven is said to have hit 'Pinnacle', meaning the individual has the epitome of control over their Ki."

She continues with her explanation, going through all the marks one by one and how to earn them, until the last marks. She starts talking less, getting vague. I don't press the issue. I'm getting more information than I can digest.

I'm dizzy, trying to grasp the various concepts and foreign

knowledge. She mentions the process of getting them ingrained in her skin, glossing over details. There must be more than a jar of jade ink and a needle involved.

"The last, number forty-seven, is the ability to take in magic as well as send it back. It's the reason I fought so hard to hit pinnacle. I wanted to be able to do that."

"All forty-seven were necessary? Couldn't you pick which ones you want?"

"No," she says. "That's not how it works."

"Why not?"

Her mouth opens, she freezes, then closes her mouth. "You know, I don't have a fucking clue. I assume because they form a bridge, but I have first-hand knowledge that they aren't required." She rests her elbow on the table, propping her chin and hums. "That's typical with the Magia. The Assembly speaks and no one can question it. That's how it is, and that's the way it is." She rolls her eyes.

Dinner slips by. She's smiling, glowing. I cock my head, peering at her. She acts like a Seraphim yet claims she isn't. It's hard to deny the way the Light weaves over her skin, the lace-like patterns visible in the dim light of the restaurant.

It's not right either. The Light presents the same as Dark, in tendrils and ropes, not a pretty swirling pattern. I have no idea what she is.

"You said Magia aren't able to call the Light. Could your siblings?"

She stares, then shakes her head. "No."

"Did it develop after you earned marks?"

"No, why?"

I frown, strumming my fingers on the table, the tendrils of black reaching out toward her in a preemptive defense against the Light, like a warning to back off. "You're glowing."

She holds her hands up to check them. "Oh, shit, that's new."

She rubs her hands together, then looks again, as if she thought she could rub away the fine silver web.

"It's a natural defense. Your magic is responding to mine." I lower my eyes to where the shadows are leaking from my hand. "It's a way of protecting yourself from me."

She laughs. "Where was that when I was signing a contract to sell my life?"

"You were on high alert. You haven't been relaxed around me before for your magic to kick in a subconscious guard."

"Ki doesn't do anything on a subconscious level. It requires focus." She's talking to her hands, moving them, and then she checks down the front of her shirt. "Damn, it's everywhere."

I hum, curious about what that will look like. My Dark is intrigued too. That's dangerous. "Let's go."

I walk behind her toward the door, watching for any faltered steps or wobbling. There is none.

Outside, the air is sweet and cool now that night has descended. Natalia's glow is brilliant, even in the dim flood lights lining the sidewalk.

She stops, turns, and gapes at me. "It's like fucking star light or something. What the burning afters is this shit?" She shows me her glittering hands. "Is this permanent?"

I chuckle at her demeanor, taking her hands in mine, making the Light shine brighter still. "I don't know. Your magic may eventually deem me trustworthy. As I'm Dark, it's not likely."

"So, I'm just going to glow for the rest of my life?"

I shrug. "Around the Dark, I suspect yes."

She starts to turn away, then whips back to face me, horror chiseled in her face. "What about in Ilbuio?"

I grin. She will burn bright, the only Light in the Dark. It will reinforce me with her at my side. A source of power to one such as me. "You'll be my own little star," I say, putting an arm around her shoulders. "Come on."

I steer her a few steps closer to the bike, but a shadowy man steps in front of us, his face obscured by the backlighting. "Nat, is that you?"

"Tony?" She hisses. "Ah, shit."

"What?" Tony asks, taking a step closer. "What's going on?"

My little star stays silent, biting her lips between her teeth and turning to me. She's a quick learner. I squeeze her against me in reassurance that I will indeed handle this for her. She will never have to deal with this fucking waste of space ever again. That's my job now.

Tony takes another step, reaching for her. "You need to come home. You took off with the Darkling. My mom, your mom, and the whole Assembly is fucking furious."

She tries to take a step back, so I flex to keep her at my side where I want her. Putting a hand up to stop him, I feed venom into my voice. "You need to leave. Turn around, walk away. She belongs to me."

"What?" Tony lets out a soft laugh and glances around, shoving a hand through his hair. "Are you fucking mad? This is him, isn't it?" He leans closer, peering at me. "The same one? Nat, come on, take my hand." He reaches again.

I step between them, crossing my arms. "Natalia, get on the bike."

She walks away, going around a nearby parked car to get to the bike. Tony turns, but I grab him, moving us to switch sides, positioning myself between them. I watch her sit down on the bike and put her helmet on, then turn my attentions back to him. "You need to stay away from what's mine."

"I don't know what's going on, or what you've done to her, but they'll kill her for this. Do you understand me? When they find her, and they will, they'll kill her. Just let her go."

"No," I tell him, turning away.

Tony grabs me by the arm. "I'll let you live, but I'm taking Nat."

I almost dissolve into giggles. "You'll let me live? What a ridiculous notion, clay monkey."

"You're not hearing me, buddy. Nat's coming home with me. We all go home alive, and I'll figure out a way to convince the Assembly you're some powerful Seraphinus that was controlling her to save her life. Just let her go."

I eye Natalia on my bike. There are greater threats to her life than the Magia, whether I keep her or let her go.

The magic within me snarls at the idea of releasing her. *'No. Mine.'*

She is mine, and I have uses for her. Her name is in my skin, and the contract says I will protect her, but it's inconsequential. I'm never going to let go or allow her to be taken from me. I'm not sure how difficult she'll become if I kill this human, though. I don't have time for difficulties.

I shrug, half turning back towards Tony. "Run back to your pathetic leaders–your Assembly–and tell them I *am* powerful. I *am* controlling her. I *am* keeping her, and there's not a damned thing you or yours can do about it. You have two choices, let go or I kill you."

"Good luck," Tony chuckles, grip tightening. "Take your best shot."

My lips curve. "You would like it if I used my magic, wouldn't you? You could throw it back at me. You have the same marks and ability to use the Ki as Natalia does? I won't, though. I will rip you to pieces with my claws and wings, burn you to ashes, then piss on your remains."

"How the fuck?" He lifts his voice, focusing beyond me. "Nat, you fucking traitor. You're going to die for betraying your own kind."

Breaking free of his grasp, I turn into a swing. It catches him off guard, and it's not strictly following the rules of engagement, but he threatened mine. It's a gray area, however deserving.

He stumbles with a hand to his face. I'll grant Magia are more durable than humans. That same swing decimated the jaw of a clay pot a rune ago.

"Threaten mine again and it will be the last thing you do," I say. "You've made your point. I do not care. Annoy me enough and I'll wipe out your infectious colony in my free time for fun."

"Nat wouldn't let you. That's her family, her friends."

"She wouldn't get a choice in it. Natalia, *Tallie*," I stress, "belongs to me. She is mine, and she's never been yours. Had you and your kind been more favorable, you may have been able to possess her, but your actions gave her to me, and now that I have sunk my claws in her, she's always going to be mine. Tell your Assembly whatever you'd like on her decisions, coerced or freely, but know that it's because of you that she accepted my offer."

"Nat!" Tony yells, swinging at me.

Blocking, I swing back, catching him in the gut. He coughs, gagging as he doubles over.

I lean closer, my voice low. "Call her Nat one more time and I'll rip your tongue out for it. We'll see if you can heal that."

I shove Tony with as much force as I can muster, sending him flying into the distance before turning and walking away. When I settle on the bike, Natalia shifts in against me. She trembles as her arms wrap around my waist, the helmet pressing against my back.

I rest a hand over her arm, using the other to direct the handlebars as I walk the bike backward. She'll be okay as soon as I get her away from that monster. He had his chance. He failed to keep her. It had been easy for me to give Natalia an escape, as well as to make sure she stays. It's something Tony isn't capable of.

I turn the engine over, taking off, but going slow so she doesn't get scared. Still, her arms stay wrapped around me tight. She needs to get used to touching me, but I like the way she is holding on. I like the way she feels.

CHAPTER 17
NATALIA
2ND THISTLE'S DAY, HEATWAVE, 4049 6TH MILLENNIUM

WAKING UP IN THIS INCREDIBLE BED, SUNK DEEP INTO A MATTRESS that should be too good to really exist, I sigh at the ceiling before rolling over to stare out the window. Tony had called me a traitor. He's right. I've betrayed the Magia with all the things I've told Callahan or Massimo. I avoided certain things, but I've shared enough to show the weaknesses of the Magia.

I saved his life. I healed Massimo. I accepted a contract. I reveled our secrets. I've broken every law possible.

Callahan and Tony had words last night. I don't know what was said. Through the helmet all I could make out were facial expressions, no words breaking through barrier of the protective equipment, but Tony took a few hits.

Throwing back the covers, I get up, stepping into leggings and a sports bra. I slip on a loose shirt that hangs off one shoulder. Gathering the hem, I tie a balled-up knot to secure it tightly around my waist, a slice of skin on display.

I don't know what day of the week it is anymore. Hope's day, Bloom's day, Evergreen's? It doesn't matter. I don't have a job to get to, or people to see, or things to do. All that exists in my life now is doing whatever Callahan deems.

I step into the early morning air, the day already hot and humid. The Warmwave season is starting, the temperature cranking up as the world moves out of the Blooming season. The seasons of Harvest, then Decay will follow. The world will go cold and curl in on itself, the larger orange sun will be absent through Snowdrop, returning in the season of Cloudburst.

I stop, puffing up my cheeks to blow out a breath. I'm getting ahead of myself. In a matter of days, I'll be going to Ilbuio, and there is no telling what that will bring. The Dark capital is notoriously dangerous, seeping and simmering with the Dark and all its brutal magic. Humans know to stay away, even the Magia teach to avoid the Dark's cathedral buildings.

At least I'm not glowing right now. It had been beautiful, delicate strings of glimmering Light weaving and swirling over my skin, but it freaked me out. Ki requires focus, centering, intentional use. It doesn't just appear, crawling across skin as a protection.

I drop into a semi half-split, starting to stretch. Holding, I wait for muscles to release, sinking deeper, then switch sides. I go back and forth a few times, loosening tension, before moving on to other positions.

I miss music and Ness.

We'd crank the music, go through stretching and core strengthening work outs, all while talking about everything. Even if it was just me complaining, venting, or sometimes even crying over Tony and everything that led to the engagement. After last night, I desperately want to talk to Ness.

I go through stretches then tuck and roll, using the momentum to carry my body into a handstand. I drop one leg overhead to the ground. The other follows, pulling me upright again, and I come face-to-face with Callahan.

He crosses his arms, scowling. His black tee-shirt and sweats do nothing to hide the strength rolling off him. "Do you like being upside down?"

"I don't mind it," I reply, taking a half-step away to put distance between us. I'm not sure how much I trust him. "It can come in handy in a fight."

His head tilts to the side, "How?"

I sigh, checking the distance between us, then put my hands up. "Swing."

He shifts one foot back, lifts fists, and swings. I block, noting the easy force he's using, and nod. "Again."

He swings, I push back, he counters. I flip, kicking my legs over my head. Backflip completed, I stand a few paces from him, and lift my hands.

He motions me back to him. "Now for real."

I walk to him, lifting hands. He swings. I block, then counter. He grabs my wrist, tugging me off balance. I go with the momentum, rolling past him in the tuck-and-roll to a handstand and then over, on my feet, spinning around.

He's on me in a blink, so I do my best to divert his swings with open palms, keeping up the increasing pace. I spin, kicking him in the face as I throw myself through an aerial, then I'm on my feet, hands up.

Callahan rubs his jaw as he stalks forward. "Stop holding back."

I fend him off, blocking his punches with open palms and forearms, gritting my teeth, and forcing Ki through my limbs to absorb the blows. We shuffle. I do a spin kick to his face. He swings, and I attempt to backflip out of the way.

His hand closes around my ankle, and I'm yanked in the opposite direction, back into him, hanging upside down, my leg in his grasp. I clench my abdomen muscles to curl up to him slightly and laugh. He scowls, then jerks me upward.

"Shit," I squeak, flying through the air.

His arm wraps around my waist, jerking me into him, pinning me upside down against his torso, my butt to his chest. My knees bend over his shoulder, my heels digging into his back.

Panting, I wait, vulnerability leaving my stomach fluttering with butterflies.

I laugh again. "All right, now what?"

His free hand lifts, curling around my throat, his voice low and silky. "If I had a blade, it would be easy to gut you, slit your throat, any number of ways to kill you."

"But you don't."

His hand shifts, cupping my jaw. "I could break your neck, get my claws out to play. It would be so easy to rip your throat out."

"Sure, but..." I tense my legs, squeezing his torso, reaching around his thighs, and throw myself upward. He grunts as I yank his weight off center.

As we fall, I get one leg over his head and land on top of him, kneeling upright over his head. I smirk, "And now, if I had a blade, it would be easy to slit your throat." On his back, he scowls up at me, his face between my legs. My feet are still pinned beneath him, so I imagine that glare is due to discomfort, but I giggle. "Guess I can tell Ness I sat on your face now."

The words come out unbidden, no filter between brain and mouth. Hearing them shocks me, and his eyes darken so they reflect no light. Large warm hands settle on my thighs. "I think she intended a different meaning," he says in a low, husky voice

"She said sit on your face." I clear my throat, my eyes stuck on his mouth. "She didn't specify with or without clothes or results. I think this qualifies."

"No," he says, voice tense but his lips curl on one side, the shadow of a dimple forming at the corner. "How much do you know about Seraphinus?"

"Um..." I breathe out. His large warm hands are still on my legs, his head between my bent knees, and his body pinned beneath me. The warmth of his breath is seeping through the thin, stretchy material of my leggings, distracting me from his words. "What?"

"What do you know of my kind? The Seraphinus."

I've never been so aware of my skin. I've never had a man's head between my legs before either, and he's asking about knowledge.

I lift my head to stare straight ahead. "There's Light and Dark, but that's just what kind of magic they use. They evolved from the original gods, with myths that say you were created by the gods or your kind were created by two Ancients. No one really knows, right? You're hard to kill. Live for centuries, and..." I close my eyes, head tipping back, trying to recall anything else.

His hands squeeze. "What else?"

"You mean besides that whole, you lot own everything, and have no qualms killing humans, well, really each other either?" I force a wide, fake smile down at him.

"The Seraphinus weren't created by the gods. They aren't a union between gods and Ancients. We were made by two Ancients. The Dark was made by Mallafic. The Light was crafted by Beenin. What else do you think you know?"

"There's a Dark King, a Light Queen, and a Council made up of both sides that functions to govern you."

"The Dark is ruled by the Dark King. The Light is ruled by the Light Queen. Don't assume those titles change with the gender of the holder. They are honorific titles dedicated to our origins. The Dark King refers to Mallafic. The Light Queen refers to Beenin. The Council has elected members. They're chosen at random by lottery and serve for a decade to keep things fair. Six Dark and six Light sit on the Council at any given time, and they govern conflict between the two factions but do not rule over either side. What else?"

"Dark and Light hate each other, and I mean you lot really hate the other lot." I wrinkle my nose at him. "No idea why, but I don't think the two sides are currently at war, or at least, as much as you two quit fighting."

"Mm," his chest rumbles beneath me. "Yes, we do hate each

132

other. That links to our origins as much as our laws and what we are. On a very base level, our magics are enemies. The Light are self-righteous, arrogant, annoyingly deceitful fucks. The Dark may seem less dignified, but we are honest and fair. Go on."

"There's a capital of Dark and Light. We're taught to avoid them."

"Ilbuio is the heart of the Dark. Izul is the capital of the Light. Anything else?"

I tip my head back, staring at the delicate blue sky. "Not really. The Magia Assembly is based off your Council."

"Makes sense, the Magia were the Council between Dark and Light." He stares up at me, and then adds. "I'm telling you this because the Dark King is dying, and it's going to bring conflict."

"Is this what I walked into?"

"Yes."

"How?"

Callahan smiles, one side of his mouth pulling back. "You saved my life."

"And you're continuing to make me regret that." I sigh, leaning forward on my hands on either side of his head. "Why exactly did that involve me?"

"The Dark Throne is not inherited. There is a list of five contenders for the throne. I am one of them."

My eyes open wider at him. "So, what, you're an heir? Like a prince?"

He lifts his eyebrows. "No. Not a prince. Marius is the son of the King, so closest to that term, which comes with perks and certain abilities, but prince implies heir. The Dark doesn't have heirs, only inheritors."

"Okay..."

"He's on the list for the right to fight for the Dark Throne, but not because he's the King's son. The Gathering Shadows Ceremonies in Ilbuio are games designed to set the contenders' list.

The King decides the games, as well as how one wins. The five of us who both survive and score highest are put on the list. You'll be walking into a war zone when you step into Ilbuio."

I shift, my feet numb, and I'm getting nauseous. Moving away from him, I spin to sit in the grass, knees bent with my head hanging low. "Mother."

Callahan settles next to me. "You need to understand what you're walking into. The Light fuck came after me because I'm a contender. Light is after disrupting the exchange of the Dark Throne. They'll take any opportunity to destroy the Dark, and Dark is going to be fighting itself."

I curl into a ball, wrapping my arms around my knees to make myself smaller. "I put myself on the board as a player by saving you."

"You're a wild card. Light will kill you for saving Dark, and saving a contender is worse. Dark is going to hunt you to use you."

I lift my forearm, indicating our contract.

"While I have good standing that will protect you from other Dark by our laws, but it puts you in a worse position with the Light. There are laws against me, the Dark, forcing you, the Light, into servitude, and the Light is prejudice against the Dark. Even without coercion, the mere act of accepting my contract will flare their indignation."

I scoff. "Pretty sure you coerced me."

He tucks a piece of loose hair behind my ear. "I would have saved you either way, but I'll admit I did use the situation and your ignorance to my advantage."

I glance his way, but move on, frowning at Massimo approaching.

He stops a few paces away. "I see you found her."

I perk up. "Found me?"

Callahan leans back on his hands. "Yes. You left your room."

Running a hand over the contract, I inspect it for a rule against leaving my room. It's still illegible to me though. "Was I not supposed to?"

"No."

"The contract let me."

He smiles. "You don't have many rules."

I throw my hands up. "I don't even know what this thing says. How am I supposed to follow the rules when I don't even know them?"

Massimo crosses his arms. "You're all right, Light Bug. We were concerned about what you might do after your evening. When you weren't in your rooms, we wanted to locate you."

I cock my head, confusion claiming me. "What?"

"We didn't know if you'd go back to the Magia."

Jutting my head forward and widening my eyes, I blink at him like he's an idiot trying to explain something he doesn't even understand. "I'm going to guess that's against the contract, but are you fucking stupid? Tony said they're going to kill me, and I believe him. I know the Magia. I'm not that fucking dumb. Why would I go anywhere near them?"

"We don't know much about the Magia, or even you, Little Light," Massimo drops to sit on the ground cross-legged. "It could have been a scare tactic. Come back now, or they kill you. Some would go thinking they could save themselves."

I shake my head, recalling the Assembly's response when I interfered with Nicky's initiation. Groaning, I drop my face into my hands. "A, going back would be going back to Tony, which, just no. B, I'm assuming you two would come after me if I did go back, and that's if the contract didn't kill me first. I'll take my chances against the Magia before I try to take you two on."

Callahan chuckles. "Smart choice. It would have been easy to bring you back and I'd change your contract significantly for my benefit."

I roll my eyes. "It wouldn't be that easy."

Massimo laughs. "You may have a chance against me, but Cal would put you down like a mutt."

I cut my eyes to Callahan, who grins. "It would be easy."

"I was doing okay."

His grin grows. "I wasn't trying."

"What happened to don't hold back?" I ask with a raised eyebrow.

Massimo leans forward, "Cal always holds back, even with me. You'll see him let loose during the games at some point though. It's usually after he gets fed up. He gets lazy."

Frowning at my hands in my lap, I realize even in the bright morning faint silver threads have formed over my skin again. I didn't notice when it happened, I'm not calling it, nor channeling Ki. "Seriously," I gripe, lifting my hands to show Callahan. "What is this?"

He shifts closer, reaching out toward me. "Defense." He puts his hand close to mine, hovering, not quite touching, yet I can feel it on the edge of my senses. Black opaque tendrils wrap around his hand as my Light burns brighter. "Your magic is learning."

I drop my hand, and the black tendrils soften, more translucent. "Magic doesn't learn. I learn, and channel Ki. That's my magic."

"Little Light," Massimo says. "That isn't the Magia and Ki, it's the Light, and Light learns. The Light and the Dark are both entities that exist within us—the Seraphinus or Seraphim in your case. It's a living, symbiotic entity within us. It learns and grows, like a muscle."

I smile at Thomas approaching. "Hi."

He inclines his head, his eyes lowering. "Ms. Tallie." He shifts his focus to Callahan. "Sir, someone came to deliver a message for Natalia."

Callahan sits up, frowning. "Who?"

"They didn't give a name. It was an older gentleman, human from what I could tell."

He leans back. "Message?"

Thomas bobs his head. "Return to the fold and all sins will be forgiven. Do as you have been instructed without further delay, or Vanessa will die."

CHAPTER 18
NATALIA

I'm on my feet. "Nope. I'll take on whoever I have to. Do whatever I have to, to–"

"Sit down," Callahan says.

I flip him off, which causes Thomas to blanche. Ignoring the contract searing at my refusal of an order, I talk to Thomas. "You said older. Beard? Bald? Eye color? Anything you know."

A hand wraps around the front of my shin then pulls. My knee gives, and I fall into Callahan's lap. "I said 'sit', Natalia. You're going to have to start to learn–"

"I get time, right? That's enough for me to work with," I say, heart hammering even as I try to reclaim my feet.

"Go," Callahan growls over my shoulder. Thomas about-faces and leaves.

I struggle, squirming against Callahan as his arms clamp around me. "Damnit," I curse, "this isn't about leaving or breaking your contract. This is about Nessy."

"Stop," he says. "Now."

"Fuck you. I can't just let her die. I'll come back."

Callahan sighs, shifting and pulling a phone out of his pocket. He holds it up for me to see him calling an unknown number. His thumb taps against the screen initiating the call, then a second time to put it on speaker.

It rings twice before it is picked up. "Tallie or the dickwad?"

"Ness," I say, then Callahan's hand covers my mouth.

"Vanessa, go home."

"I am home, put Tallie back on the phone."

"She's listening. Someone is coming to collect you."

Massimo stands, stretching as he smiles. "That's me." Dark blue leather wings spread from his back as he jumps into the air, taking off.

Ness's voice comes through the phone, tense and tight. "What's going on?"

I can't get a word out with Callahan's hand clamped tight.

He answers her in a calm voice. "Natalia is staying with me, and the Magia are displeased."

Ness makes a slight 'eh' sound through the phone. "Not surprised." She sighs, then says, "Ah, shit. Tony in his stupid jacked-up truck just pulled up. What is going on? Should I be worried about something here?"

"Do you have a back door?"

"Yeah."

"Use it."

I manage to pry his hand from my mouth. "That special bottle of vodka I have in the freezer that you promised me you'd never touch?"

"Uh, I'm not going back for vodka." Ness laughs. "I don't care how much that bottle cost."

"It's Ki-cha."

There's a pause. I can make out her sharp inhale, then she's yelling through the speaker. "Are you fucking kidding me? Ki-cha, as in the real deal, fucking Ki-cha? You've had a bottle of fucking Ki-cha in our freezer for the last six years?"

"Told you not to drink it," I snicker.

"What the fuck? I could have drunk that at any point. Oh great, he's knocking. Why is Tony here? Why the fuck didn't you tell me what was really in this fucking bottle?"

I shrug, relaxing back into Callahan. He lifts, shifting me in his lap, his arm easing but remaining around me.

"All right, fucking Ki-cha acquired, and, oh look, a full bottle of Grassel. Sure, I'll need this too," Ness says. Her voice drops. "Ah, fuck, he's looking through the windows. Someone tell me what is happening before I lose my shit and cry."

"Back door, now," Callahan orders her, then asks, "What the fuck is Ki-cha?"

"Ask Tal," Ness says softly through the phone. "Out the back door, now what?"

Callahan rubs his jaw. "What options do you have?"

"Um, other people's yards?"

He flips the phone to check his watch. "My man should be there soon. Is there any chance you can fight him?"

Ness releases a soft, hysterical laugh. "He's Pinnacle."

"No," I whisper, shaking my head. "She can't fight him. He'd kill her. Ki-cha, babe, use it if you have to."

"Oh?" Her voice is full of a smile as she asks, "We're okay with killing Tony now?"

Callahan smirks. "Yes. What is Ki-cha?"

I shake my head. "Later. Look, you said Tony was looking through the front–"

"Oh, fuck me sideways," Ness hisses, then yells, "Hi, Tony." There's a lot of static like the phone was dropped or shoved in a pocket.

Ness's muffled voice still wafts through the speaker still and I grip my fists, that white glimmering lace shining brighter as my heart thumps heavier. "What's up? I'm just–you know, double-fisting day-drinking because Tallie skipped out on me... What? No, no I haven't heard from her just the things around about some Darkling... Oh, yeah, yeah that's bad."

Callahan's mouth finds my ear. "Little Star, if you burn any brighter my magic is going to get pissed off and eat you."

Ness rambles on. "Oh, no way does Tallie betray the Magia. She's all about the Magia... What? No, everyone questions things, but she's never questioned that... Hey, oh, this one's mine, how about you take a drink from this one?"

I drop my eyes to my fists that are nothing but balls of bright light, the insides of my wrists glowing so my flesh shines orange. Unfurling my fingers, I take a shaky breath to whisper, my voice brittle with panic. "I'm not doing this."

"Relax. Take a deep breath. Massimo will be there soon. He'll bring her back here. She'll be safe. I'll find a use for her and give her a contract."

The Light is dimming, my hands glowing from within materializing from the Light. They shake as I stare.

Ness keeps talking, her voice getting louder, a little more stressed as she forces a laugh. "Yup, that's true, Tallie can be stubborn, so stubborn, but no way does she just hop on a bike and take off with a Darkling of her own free will."

Tony's dull roar makes its way through the phone. "I saw it, twice. That fucking Darkling bitch said it was because of me, so now you're coming with me. I need answers and we're going to get her back."

Callahan rumbles with a muted chuckle, turning his head toward me, his curved lips brushing against the shell of my ear. "No."

"Ah, shit, you know, didn't want to have to do this, but this is getting too weird and I'm not–er, yeah, that, uh, wrong number."

The phone blasts static, then Tony's voice comes through crystal clear. "Tallie's Sexy Darkling? What the fuck is this? How long was this going on?"

"Okay, yeah, funny story–" The call ends.

Callahan tosses the phone to the side, then his hands cover

mine. "Massimo will be there soon. He can handle that clay pot. Deep breaths, Little Star, deep breaths and don't shine too bright."

"Oh, Mother," I whisper, grabbing his fingers tight. "If something happens to Ness because of me, because I did this..."

His arms press tight, his nose nuzzling the side of my neck. "Calm down and breathe."

Tendrils of his Dark are crawling over my glowing flesh, twisting, and wrapping up my arms. It's a soft kiss of cool slithering against my skin.

"Shit," I say in a weak breathless voice. "Are you going to kill me?"

"No," his lips whisper against the thin skin of my throat. "My magic is curious and hungry. It wants to play, but I won't let it hurt you."

Inhaling through my nose, I take a deep breath and bob my head. The shadows shift to a deep midnight blue as the Light emitting from me becomes brighter beneath his magic.

"Close your eyes. Take a deep breath. Calm down."

I lay my head back on his shoulder, focusing on breathing. I hold it for a few fractions, ribcage fully expanded, then exhale.

"Your magic is wild right now. It's going to react to your emotions in unpredictable ways. You need to be careful. You're surrounded by Dark that is going to react to your Light on instinct."

I nod, head rocking against his shoulder. "What is happening to me? Ki doesn't act this way."

"This isn't Ki. This is the Light. How old are you?"

"Twenty-nine."

"When do you turn thirty?"

"Third Hope's day in Snowdrop."

Callahan stays silent, his heart steady against my back. I'm in his lap, our fingers laced together. That should scare me. He's a Darkling. My whole life I've been warned they are the enemy, dangerous. I trained to kill Seraphinus, but sitting here, cuddled against him, his thumb caressing over the bone of my wrist, I get a sense of comfort.

The Light and Dark are enemies, yet his magic isn't hurting me. I breathe deep, my eyes closing as I relax into his solid build. For the first time in a long time, I'm trusting someone can handle what I can't.

The thumps of my heart increase in pressure, each pulse striking harder than the last as my anxiety rises. I'm trusting him and it is terrifying.

Something heavy hits the ground and Ness laughs. "Mother."

Ripping away from Callahan, I open my eyes, up. "Ness?"

She laughs, getting up on shaking legs. "That was a ride. Good thing I'm not afraid of heights. What the burning afters is going on?" She lifts a bottle of vodka.

I stop short as Massimo steps away from Ness, wings pulling into his back. "Which one is that?"

"Not the Ki-cha, which, bitch, what the fuck?"

"It was for an emergency. Did you use it?"

Ness gives an exaggerated grimace. "May have killed your boyfriend?"

Massimo cuts in, a hand on Ness's shoulder, turning her to him a bit. "Was that in the bottle? Ki-cha? What is Ki-cha?"

Rolling her eyes, Ness says, "He's been asking me what was in the bottle the whole way here."

Wrinkling my nose, I say, "Ki-cha. It's uh, it's good for emergencies, a little hard to make."

Ness laughs. "You know I didn't make it. You get to tell them."

Callahan steps next to me. "Yes, enlighten us."

I laugh. "I'm sorry I didn't get to see it go off, like, deeply depressed. I've been dying to see what it would do."

Ness points at her face, "About blew my head off. Definitely singed my face. Do I even have eyebrows?"

The thick black arches of hair are pristine above her wide set eyes aside from the small white scar that runs through her left brow. I grin. "You're good," I say, before shaking my head and facing Callahan. "Basically, Ki-cha is blood."

Ness lifts the bottle. "Blood after a forty-seven day fast, you crazy woman. When did you fast forty-seven days and I miss it? How is that even possible? How did you even manage that to begin with and seriously, how did I not know? Where the fuck was I?"

Staring her in the eyes, I wait for her to figure it out. "You were there."

Ness leans in, opening her eyes wider. "No, like, really?"

Sighing, I tip my head to the sky, staving off the memories. "Right after what happened with Nicky. I was over halfway there already, thought it might come in handy if, you know, I pissed them off again."

Ness cracks the vodka bottle open and hands it to me. "Cheers, babe, because I threw that to get Tony to back off right before this sexy Darkling over here dropped down to save me. It was glorious, you should be sorry you missed it." Her brown eyes glaze over, her face going lax.

Callahan lifts his chin at Massimo as I start to chug. "What happened?"

Massimo gives a weak smile. "I saw the flash and thought she smited the bastard." He points at Ness.

Turning to me, Callahan lifts his eyebrows. "I thought smiting wasn't an option?"

"That was the Ki-cha," I say. "That was a one-time special. I'm never going to make it another forty-seven days without food ever again in my life."

Ness laughs, taking the bottle. "That wasn't a special. That was a nightmare I wasn't sure you'd survive."

Callahan narrows his eyes, jaw clenching. "Explain."

Ness pauses, bottle lifted to her lips. "Oh, Tallie here almost died a few years ago. Yeah, she pissed off the Assembly real good, so they hit her with a Ki blocker to prevent her from healing while they whipped the shit out of her. Joke was on them 'cause apparently my girl here was still healing, but they kept going until she couldn't heal anymore–drained of Ki. Then they left her to me to try and keep her alive. Eventually, the Assembly let her mom come heal her, but, yeah, first night I thought for sure she was going to die."

Wincing, I keep my eyes on the ground, reaching for the bottle. That isn't accurate. My mother gave me the reversal for the Ki blocker, but I had to heal myself. I didn't tell Ness at the time to keep her safe. It's never occurred to me to go back and explain it.

I do my best to force a laugh. "On the bright side, Ki-cha."

Callahan's voice is deep and raw. "Why didn't you heal her?"

Stiffening, Ness blinks. "Ki blocker? I didn't have an antidote so any Ki I fed into her just, like, dissolved or something. That's how I know they dosed her. I tried. A lot."

I wipe my mouth on the back of my hand, passing the bottle back to Ness as I sigh. "Good times with the Magia."

"I have no idea why you didn't run sooner for the shit they've put you through."

"Stupidity?" I fake another laugh, feigning innocence. I don't want her to know the truth, that I was concerned about them doing exactly what they did. It was terrifying to think they'd go after her.

Ness thinks, mouth pinched off to one side, then shakes her head. "No, not stupidity. I know what it is. Sheer stubbornness because you won't back down from anything, so, no," she holds up a finger, "no that's about right then, stupidity. You should have run a long, long time ago and never looked back."

"Yeah, you're probably right," I upend the bottle to pour vodka down my throat.

Ness turns to Massimo. "We're gonna need more of those," she gestures at the bottle, then turns to Callahan. "Or are you the man in charge?"

He inclines his head. "I am."

"Great, like twenty-four more of those." Ness steps forward and spins, putting an arm around my shoulders. "I've heard about this place, now I want to see it."

Ness pries the bottle away from my grip, lifting it to check how much is left before pulling me toward the house.

I snicker, moving away from Massimo and Callahan. "You're going to freak out. We say they live like gods, but you have no idea."

CHAPTER 19

CALLAHAN

NATALIA IS A DISRUPTION IN MY LIFE OF MASSIVE PROPORTIONS. I'VE never encountered this in the three-hundred-and-eighty-seven years I've walked this world. Limerence is taking root within me, and the Gathering Shadows Ceremonies are looming on the horizon. My head isn't clear or focused, plus I'm grappling with control of myself and my magic.

She's developing Light in an unprecedented manner, almost as if the Light in her is growing rapidly in reaction to my Dark. This is dangerous. There's never been a documented case of Light and Dark existing together outside of short periods of time. I have no idea what will happen.

My knowledge of the Light is limited. It's borderline insanity for me to believe I can train it. I don't have any other recourse to take. No Light is going to aid me.

She had glowed brighter than ever before as she lost herself to panic over the other woman. I should learn her name. I'd offered to find a use for her, and a contract. It is clear Natalia was willing to die for her. A weakness to her would be a weakness to me.

The way she'd shone coupled with how my magic reacted on an inadvertent level tells me I made the right decision. Natalia is going to be a weapon I can wield, so long as I don't consume her first. My magic drools with hunger every time I'm near her, although I can feel something else weaving in the Dark, a providence developing.

I walk through my greenhouse, along the rows of my botanical garden. Up one aisle and down the other. Some of my trees I've nurtured for over two centuries now, keeping them alive, growing and molding them to my fancy.

Stopping in front of my oldest tree, the very first seedling I grew, I try to force a smile at it. "Hello, old friend."

They are more my friends than most other living creatures. I keep contracts, plenty of bodies, and I tend to them all, but none are friends. In this life, interpersonal relationships are as likely to get me killed as they are to offer assistance. Massimo is the exception, although there's a fine line to his contract and our friendship that we walk, which can be taxing at times. Instead, I talk to my trees, confiding in them my secrets. I help them grow, and in return, they stay with me so I'm never truly alone.

The solemn silence presses in around me. I sigh, tucking my hands in my front pockets. "She says she is Magia, and I believe her, but she's more than any other I can trace in history." I rock on the balls of my feet. "I am going to be able to use her, feed from her, but I don't want to hurt her. I have this need for her, and it's not just to use her. I need to keep her safe, it's a draw to the like in her." I smile, lips twisting, "She can pull in Dark, using it the way I can eat Light."

The tree trunk is thick, split, with a dead branch twisting around the living part where green leaves flourish up top. It took a long time to create, decades in fact. Other than repotting, root care, and trims, I've left it to survive as is.

"I'm afraid of her," I whisper. "Of what my magic will do to her, what she could do to me if I can't train her, and I have no idea how to train Light. Her magic is starting to develop, barely coming to the surface, yet already knowing me as an enemy."

I need her to trust me so that her magic will trust I am going to use it, but not consume it. I could suck the Light from her, eat it all to feed to my magic, but she can provide so much more than that single act would.

"Natalia is going to need freedom and room to grow. I need to let her," I say, stopping to frowning.

I already knew that. Still, it's more than that. I want her to have that freedom, to be an equal at my side. I inhale sharp, a pulse in my temple from my magic.

My mind and magic whisper together. Tantalizing ideas of her naked under me whimpering and writhing, shining with that fine silver lace.

"She is tempting. Beautiful, and has a fight to her, a strength."

Natalia will be a weapon under the right circumstances, like the Gathering Shadows, but she is still a woman. I need to respect that and her, so her magic will learn to trust me, maybe even like me.

Reaching out, I stroke a leaf between my thumb and forefinger before turning away. I walk through my home in a slow gate. I need Natalia to be comfortable, to give her magic time to trust me. That means spending time around her.

Maybe it's *similis*. Maybe it's lust. Either way, the feeling of adronitis grips me. I *want* to spend time with her.

As I approach her rooms, poppy music blasts at a significant decibel, two women shrieking with laughter over the blaring song. I stop in the open doorway, pulling my ears back and wincing at the volume. Natalia and her friend are on the bed, both with half empty, opaque bottles of vodka in their hands.

I'd sent for a case of the Drossamier, the best I could buy to indulge my little star. Hearing about her life helps me understand her compulsion for the substance, but that life is over.

My mouth pulls down and to the side as I grimace. The Magia abusing her, the sick relationship with Tony, those things are over, but she may long for those days as she serves me.

149

They scream over the music, pointing fingers and chugging alcohol. I should have refused the drinks. I need Natalia's attention, need her prepared, but something inside of me caved.

"I like it," my Dark tells me. *"It's different, new."*

"Different how?"

"It's weird. It's warm and sassy. It thinks it's funny." My dark hisses, but it lacks malice.

Her friend lifts the bottle, her lips in the shape of an O, about to take a drink, she stops, frowning. "Babe, you're glowing again, and I mean, literally, not just, like, happy to not be dealing with the Magia anymore."

Natalia glances down at herself and then to me in the doorway. "Mother, why?" she asks like a child whining over candy, lifting a hand to me. "Why does this happen? Isn't there an off switch?"

I smile, halfway to a laugh. I'm a bit dazed at the volume of the music and women, but step into the room. "No. The Light is part of you, and your magic is growing, barely in infancy gauging on how it's acting."

"Oh," friend croons. "Infancy, reason number thirty-seven. You don't have to be a baby machine."

Natalia laughs, lifting her bottle to take a drink. "Mother, I think you skipped a few numbers but how'd we miss that one on the list?"

"Negative two, I'm never collecting on that bet."

"What bet?"

"That Tony screams Natasha when he comes, then cries after sex with you for the first time," friend says through laughter. When the words have been forced out, she tips her head back, bursting with more laughter.

Natalia rolls her eyes, and they land on mine. "Yeah, we'll never know."

A scowl steals over me at the idea of someone else touching her. Moving closer I sit on the bed, kicking my legs out straight, resting my back on the pillows along the headboard. I request the vodka by extending my hand. She gives it over, and I take a drink, curling my lip. It's not my favorite liquor.

Friend calms down and grins. "Guess we'll never know if he's compensating with that stupid lift kit and mud tires on that freaking pavement princess truck either."

Natalia giggles, putting a hand over her mouth. "I can answer that."

Friend's eyes grow wide, and my temper stirs.

Friend's humor crashes, turning to distress. "Actually what? Tell me you did not!"

"I never told you all the times I walked in on him and Sasha going at it?"

The jaw on Friend drops. "What? No! No, you did not! What? No!"

Tipping over, Natalia laughs hard enough that she starts gasping for air. "It was so many times. They fucked like rabbits. The first time was right after their graduation. I went downstairs to tell them to turn down what they were watching and boom," she throws out a hand, "on the couch, Tony's bare ass. Sasha fell off. I saw his dick flopping. It was great, and by great, I mean I thought about using Ki to burn my eyesight out."

Friend screams with laughter. "What did you do?"

"Turned around and walked back upstairs, but I walked in on them screwing again and again. I felt like it was some weird curse." Natalia sits up, glancing at me, glimmering brightly, her magic warning mine creeping towards her, searching, hungry and curious. She reaches out, grabs the bottle back, doing a quick shot, then offers it back to me.

As I accept it, she turns back to her friend. "I walked in on them in the community boat house, our pool house, the front porch swing at Jessie's parents, the freaking library, everywhere and every time I turned around. I saw his dick more times than I want to admit."

Friend as she shudders. "Ew."

"It's bent, and I'm not talking like that upward curve. No, I mean," she draws a sideways bend. "That's generous. He's definitely compensating. It's more like..." She draws a much smaller bend, like a four-inch ninety degree turn in the air.

Friend chokes on vodka, while I take a drink to hide my own grin. It wasn't like anyone could help what the gods gave them, but I'm glad I get a laugh at his expense. The treatment of Natalia at his hands is irritating at best. He deserves a warped cock.

Natalia holds up a hand and ticks up fingers as she lists off points. "A, no idea how he managed to get that thing straight enough to go in, and B, can't imagine how that thing ever worked or C, how Sasha actually enjoyed it."

Friend takes a drink. "If this wasn't good vodka, I'd throw up at trying to figure out answers to any of those questions."

I incline my head. "Feel free, I can afford to buy you plenty more."

"That," Friend peels a finger back from her grip around the neck of her bottle to point at me, her gaze on Natalia. "Sit on his face."

Laughing, I tip my head back, humor echoing from my chest. Natalia twists, grabs a pillow, and swings it, smacking Friend in the face. "Stop."

Friend glares. "Bitch, you spilled vodka."

"Bitch, that man owns me," Natalia snaps back, lifting her forearm. "Stop making it weird."

"It's already weird when you say he owns you."

Natalia hugs the pillow, leaning over it. "Fine, but I already sat on his face, so stop saying it."

Friend's eyes grow wide as I chuckle. "Technically, yes, although I doubt it was in the manner you meant." I take a drink to stop from remarking on my consent to try again in the way she had intended.

Blinking, Friend tilts her head, eyes moving to Natalia. "How did you manage...? If ever there was a woman that could screw up sitting on a face, it would be you."

"I did raise that point." I say, turning to Natalia. "I believe I was right."

She shrugs. "She didn't specify how I was supposed to sit on your face, just that I was to sit on your face, which I did. Can we change the subject now? Are you really going to let her stay here?"

My eyes move to Friend. To renege on the offer would be a form of lying, something the Dark is staunchly opposed to. "Yes."

Friend perks up. "What? Wait, I get to stay?"

"You'll get a contract," I say, relinquishing the bottle to Natalia. "You'll be expected to comply with rules and act accordingly. Refusal of the contract or any termination of said contract will result in the expulsion of yourself from these premises at best."

"Oh, you're all sexy when you're a hard ass." Friend laughs. "So, what's this contract?"

I slide off the bed and stretch my arms over my head, the muscles down my spine and through my chest and abdomen pulling taut. "That depends on your skill set. Tomorrow morning, courtyard, Sun rune. We'll see what you have to offer me." I meet Natalia's stunned gaze. "Be there too. We need to strengthen your magic."

She sits straighter. "I want to turn this thing off, not make it stronger."

"That *thing*," I say, twisting the word, "is you, your magic. It's going to grow, whether you want it to or not, and it's why you have a contract."

Natalia nods, staring down at the bed between us. Her face is soft, her features drawing in. I get a pang through my mind, my magic communicating something I don't understand.

My chest aches at her expression, and I try to smile. "You'll like being able to use it."

She bobs her head, still not looking at me. I leave, shrugging off the dejection, as I retire to my rooms for the evening.

Locked inside, I draw the curtains, switching off the electrical lights to submerge myself in complete darkness. I exhale, soaking it in, head tipped back to savor the dark before sitting on the edge of my bed.

I close my eyes, wanting to fall into the nothingness of true darkness. Even without light, faux or real, I can see everything crystal clear. An advantage the Dark has over the Light, but right now, I want to float in the dark.

The inky black seeps behind my eyes and through my skin, the blackness soothing my raging insides and calming my mind. It leaves me chilled, my flesh tingling, while reinvigorating my magic and anything akin to a soul I have.

Natalia's Light comes to mind, like a star burning bright in the shadows. I sit up, pulling my clothes off, and dropping my shirt next to me on the bed. I settle back, wrapping a hand around my pulsing and growing cock. The weight of Natalia on my chest, her legs spread before my face from this morning come back, but this time she's naked.

Tightening my hand, I stroke, breathing out hard through my nose. My cock isn't bent, it hardens straight, throbbing with blood flow. Natalia would like it. Pleasure courses through me, a mental picture of her glowing behind my closed eyes, the way she would taste lingering on my tongue in a phantom desire.

I stroke faster, breathing harder. The next time she sits on my face I'd make sure she enjoyed it. She'd come for me. She'd call my name. I grip the shirt in my other hand, shoving it over the head of my cock as reach release, my balls tightening, pleasure ripping through my abdomen.

Laying there, muscles relaxed, I breathe in through my nose, heart racing, and half unconscious. Bliss rolls through me. I give in to it, listing in the lingering rush of the orgasm. Finding a jolt of motivation, I sit up, throw the shirt aside and pull myself into the middle of my bed. I collapse face down in pillows, passing out.

CHAPTER 20

NATALIA

2ND THORN'S DAY, HEATWAVE, 4049 6TH MILLENNIUM

I BOUNCE BACK AND FORTH BETWEEN LEFT AND RIGHT HALF-SPLITS, watching Ness twitch and fuss. She's inches taller than me, her hips wider and her chest larger, but she needed clothes. I have plenty to spare, so I provided her with attire. The outfit is comical, like an adult in children's clothes. The leggings are too short, even worn low on, and the shirt hem is too high. Worse, the fabric looks painted on tight, about to split at the seams.

Ducking my head, I struggle to swallow my giggle. She throws up her hands, groaning. "I'm going to do one split that will end up with me splitting out of these clothes."

I offer an encouraging smile, "It might help your case."

She tentatively starts trying to get down into splits, easing into it with leg stretches. The leggings pull but hold. "What am I even doing here?"

"You know why you're here."

"Yes, the Magia were going to kill me if you didn't go back, so your Darklings came and saved my ass, *hard*. Now there I'm here though, what am I doing in this yard? I don't have any kind of skill."

I slide into a full split. "You have skills."

"Comic relief? Bait? The expendable one in the group?" Ness glances up over my shoulder. "Oh, hi."

"When," Callahan starts with a terse tone, "someone comes to me for a contract and tries to sell themselves, they usually high-light better options."

She scoffs. "Hey, I'm all for being here and, you know, staying alive. I'm really appreciative. I'll grovel, beg, kiss your shoes, whatever makes you Darklings happy. I'm not above that, I just really don't know what I can offer you."

I lean forward, grass tickling my nose. "Shut up, babe. You can heal, you've read every history book there is, and you can talk to anyone like they're your friend in thirty fractions of a rune. You're great with other people." I roll, lifting myself up on forearms, getting my hips over my shoulders before drawing my legs together then arching my back. Bending my knees and lowering my feet to my head, I sink into the position, muscles pulling taut.

There's a deep, booming laugh, then Massimo asks, "Are you trying to bend into a pretzel?"

Ness scoffs. "Your form sucks." She moves in my peripheral vision, getting into the same pose.

"Do Magia not have bones?" Massimo asks. He sighs when neither of us answer. "Serious question, ladies."

"We do." Ness lowers her feet to the ground, practically forming a circle with her body.

I grunt, "Show-off."

Walking her feet out, Ness pushes off on her hands, then stands. "Form. Yours sucks."

I straighten my legs, lifting to my hands, put one foot down, then the other. "If you spent half the time you do on form trying to master your Ki, you'd hit Pinnacle."

Pointing at the ground, Ness rolls her eyes. "That gives me wild, hot sex. Ki gives me headaches, disappointment, and bruises."

Smiling, I shake my head. Turning to Callahan I put hands on my hips. I lift my eyebrows, asking him without words.

He jerks his head at Ness, eyes on Massimo. "Figure out what she can do." His eyes flicker to me. "You're with me." He extends his hand.

A thrill runs through me while I try not to grin too wide as I put mine in his. The elation dies as the fine silver Light over my skin shines brighter. Black tendrils seep from his skin, curling around me, and his fingers close around mine.

He draws me away while Massimo puts his hands up, open palms. "All right, little one, hands up. We're going to see what you've got."

I follow Callahan as he walks backward, our hands linked together. He stops and pulls me closer, his eyes on mine, an inch between us. The black shadows seep from him, curling and twisting toward me.

I lift my free hand, weaving fingers through the strands. They dance away from my touch, but remain, tasting the air around me.

He chuckles. "You need to learn. Your magic is going to grow, and you need to control it." His hand squeezes mine. "Look at me. You need to control it."

"Yeah, got it. This is what you need me for, isn't it?"

Callahan frowns. "I am going to use you, your magic. Yes, it's going to be easier for me if you control it to do that, but, no, this is more than me wanting to use you. You need to stop denying what you are. The Light is an entity that coexists in you. If you don't learn to live with it, to control it or communicate with it, your Light will run wild. It will strangle your life. It will kill you."

I nod, breathless. No one other than Ness ever did something for me that didn't benefit them. Callahan isn't either, but it's close, closer than anyone else.

Letting go of my hand, he puts both of his up, palms to me. "Put your hands against mine, close without touching me." I do as he commands, he nods. "I don't know what Ki is, but right now, I want you to pretend like you don't either. Push the Light out."

"How?"

"How do you use Ki?"

"Thought I was supposed to pretend like I didn't know right now."

"Little Star, don't test me." His voice is a dangerous whisper. "I don't want you using Ki. I want you to control the Light."

I drop my eyes from his to his chest, the intensity of his gaze giving me weird tingles in parts of my body. "I center myself, drawing the Ki to meld it for what I need."

"How did you learn to do that?"

I tip my chin up, licking my lips. "I started to figure out how to center myself, aligning, and feeling the Ki."

He nods. "Feel the Light. I don't know what it feels like, but I can tell you about the Dark. The Dark is chilling shadows. It's emptiness, hollow, echoes and ringing, silent, isolation. It's the still and quiet, where nightmares collect and lurk, the weight of sleep and death."

My chest aches, meeting his eyes. "It sounds awful."

A slow smile steals over his face. "What does the Light feel like?"

"No clue, but I'm hoping it's better than you make the Dark sound."

"Close your eyes."

I narrow my eyes, then close them in a relaxed state.

His fingers slide between mine, strong and cool. "Feel me?"

I breathe out slow, nodding. I'd have to be dead to not feel him. My scalp tingles, my abdomen aches as it fills with tension, and my lungs constrict.

Something about this man is drawing me in and making me lower my defenses. It's not safe to trust others. Plus, if something seems too easy, there's usually a reason for it, and trusting Callahan is easy.

Cold slithers around my wrists. I gasp.

"And you felt that? The Dark?"

"Yes," I whisper.

"Tell me what the Light feels like now."

I frown, my eyebrows drawing together to form the wrinkle steadily developing as a permanent line between them. Searching, I attempt to feel something, focusing on my skin, where the Light twists together. The warmth of the sun, the sense of him hovering a breath away, but there's nothing else.

Shaking my head, I say, "I don't know."

"It's there, you just need to find it. Feel it." His voice is low, soft.

Scrunching my eyes shut, the cold wraps tighter around my wrists, slinking like a caress of a gentle breeze. "I don't feel anything."

"Try harder."

The way he describes the Dark sounds like loneliness and fear. That means Light is the opposite: comfort, peace, things I don't know. Frustrated I groan, hanging my head. "It doesn't feel like anything. There's nothing there."

"What does Ki feel like?"

"Calm, like straightening your spine, aligning your hips and shoulders into perfect posture, then sinking into a deep stretch."

He hums. "Does the stretching help you connect to your Ki?"

"Yes."

He keeps talking in that low, soft tone. "Can you feel it now? Without centering?"

I open my eyes, lifting them to his. Frowning, I blink. "No? No one has ever asked that before. I was raised as Magia, knowing about Ki and the ability to harness and draw power from it. I just know it's there."

"You need to accept the Light. It's there. Stop refusing what you are. It's part of you."

I shift, widening my stance, but not pulling away. Black

tendrils are wrapping around him like they are trying to protect him. "Am I hurting you?"

"It's warning you to back off. It can sense you, the Light. It's not threatened, just letting the Light know it's there, watching."

"You can feel it?"

"Yes. It knows you're weak, learning. It's curious and hungry, but I'm keeping it under control. You're safe with me."

I breathe deep, holding tight to his last words. Callahan is a stranger, but he's beautiful and honest. He's protecting me from his magic, as well as the Magia and Tony. He sent Massimo for Ness. He's going to keep her, finding what she can offer him, so he can give her a contract.

A glow starts in my chest, warmth spreading through my veins. He wants to use me. He said so, but he didn't pretend. This is different from the Magia who wanted me to breed for them, who didn't want to train me or for me to question things.

My voice is soft, broken. "If I ask you something, will you answer me?" I take a breath, eyes stinging.

"Yes."

"Would you tell me the truth?"

He chuckles, "The Dark has an honor code. Lying breaks that code. I will always be honest with you even when you may prefer I'm not."

I squeeze my eyes shut, heat blooming in my core. "Cal," I manage in a soft whisper.

His hands tighten, and I open my eyes, staring at him in a blurred haze. His head leans closer. "I'm here."

Hope threatens to break free of its cage where I'd locked it away, shoved it down deep in a pit in my soul. Hope that I could be more than a mother, more than a tool, more than what I have been expected to be my whole life. Hope that maybe someone would see me, not my bloodline, my marks, my sister, but me.

The world glows, and it's coming from me. I lift my eyes to his, even as he squints back. The hazy white ring is gone from his eyes. Tendrils of shadows, thick and opaque, constrict around him, multiplying and growing angry, licking out toward me. They dissolve as they meet the glow emitting from me, but he isn't moving away even if I am his enemy.

'He'll stay.'

I burn bright and hot. The world goes white around us, and his hands slip from mine, his presence ripped away as the brilliance reaches a crescendo then bursts.

"Cal?" I blink, the world returning in muted, dirty colors. As my eyes adjust, I refocus on Callahan. He is on the ground, flung feet away, laying in the grass on his side, but he's twisted, shoved up on the arm beneath him. I hurry over. "Cal?"

He sticks his free arm out, palm to me, fingers splayed. "Stop, Natalia."

I halt in my tracks, but Massimo runs past me, kneeling to grab Callahan's shoulder. He shrugs away to stand with his back to me.

Massimo follows him up, crossing his arms and scowling. "You're going to get yourself killed."

"I'm fine."

"We don't know how to train Light, and it hates us." The muscles in Massimo's neck stand out as he leans into his roar. "There's no reasoning with it, and she just threw you across the lawn." He flings an arm out, pointing into the distance.

I dig my big toe into the grass. "I didn't mean to."

"You did it. Your magic did, the Light." Massimo rounds on me, growling, teeth bared in rage. "You're not trained. You can't control it, and it's going to be pissed around our Dark. You're a danger to yourself and us. You're going to either kill him or get him killed."

I shrink in on myself, slinking back a step and hanging my head. Wrapping arms around my stomach, I fight the urge to wither away to nothing. There isn't anything to say except maybe he is right.

The Light glowing in me dies under the weight of Massimo's glare. He curls his lip at me then turns back to Callahan, who has his back to me. His shoulders are tense, fists clenched at his side while the Dark oozes from him, surrounding him in a shadowy aura.

Our magics are enemies, and he owns my life. Whatever I thought in the moment is gone, my glow with it. It shrinks, filtering beneath my skin so not even its silver web glistens over me.

CHAPTER 21

CALLAHAN

I WAS WRONG. I HAVE BEEN SO VERY WRONG. NATALIA'S MAGIC ISN'T manifesting. It isn't starting to develop. Her Light is matured.

I grip my fists, struggling to control my magic. It had been fooled. The way her Light blasted me halfway across the yard pissed it off. It doesn't want to listen to me right now, so I'm grappling at restraining it.

My Dark is ravenous, drooling, struggling to reach out toward her. It wants to taste that power, drink it and consume it. That much strength is delicious.

Lifting my chin, I call out, "Go do something else. Stretch. I don't care. Get further away from me."

Her voice carries on the breeze, small and quiet. "I'm sorry."

The Dark in me is hissing, wanting to extinguish her Light. "I'm fine but get away from me before my magic eats you."

They recede, the fury of my magic dwindling. I turn to Massimo.

He curls his lip. "You're not going to stop."

I shake my head. I had not been prepared for that. I was foolish enough to believe the Light was beginning to flicker to life.

Instead, it was hiding out of sight, barely sticking its head out of the sand to cover her in a delicate warning of what was buried, a sign that it acknowledged the Dark, but didn't care enough to come out to play. Like an idiot, I talked Natalia into unburying it, dragging it out into the open, and it let me know it isn't pleased with me and my Dark.

Rubbing the back of my neck, I laugh. "No, I'm not stopping."

"It was one thing when she was barely illuminating, the Light flickering like little sparks and we thought she was developing, that we could teach the Light to accept us. But that?" Massimo points to where I had been thrown from. "Your plan is madness knowing she has that much power. Light will burn out the Dark until there is nowhere for it to exist on instinct, and her magic just told you to fuck off."

I scrub my hand down my face to clear away my scowl, stretching my shoulders to ease tension from my neck. "That's what killed the Light fuck. What we've been guessing at. It would have sensed my Dark. It would have known it was fighting its own kind. It still did it." I turn around, eyes searching for my little star.

"It might have been protecting her because she wasn't aware of any of that when she picked the fight. It might have been a fight or flight instinct where it chose to fight, even if it fought itself to stay alive."

I flex my shoulder blades toward each other, grinning. "Does it really matter? It was willing to save Dark to save itself. That's exactly what I need from it."

Massimo stares at me with frost in his gaze. "You have gone insane."

"Possibly. It's been there the whole time. It comes out to ward away the Dark, but it's not fighting, and Natalia isn't either."

"Your fucking point?"

"Her Light is matured, and it still isn't treating me like a real threat. It's not, *not* trusting me already. If I manage to train her, help control her Light? It'll trust me."

He sighs. "You'll be the next Dark King for sure."

Scoffing, I drop to a crouch on the balls of my feet, elbows on my thighs.

The quiet stretches between us as I wrangle my Dark under control. Soon enough it would taste her. What happened would have to be good enough for now. I need her to be able to control the Light first or we'll rip each other apart. Her magic made that clear.

Taking a breath, I stand. "What did you get from Friend?"

"Friend?" Massimo cocks his head, face screwing up with confusion. "Tallie's friend Vanessa?"

"I forgot her name."

Massimo widens his eyes. "You're an asshole." He rubs his hands together. "Not much. It was less than half a rune before Tallie sent you flying."

"Go find a use for Vanessa," I say, eyeing the two women at the far end of the yard, moving their bodies into weird positions. That must be a Magia thing, although the quip about hot sex is giving me all kinds of ideas.

"You aren't seriously going to piss her magic off again right now."

I smile, winking. "It could be fun if I did."

"If you have a fetish for pain." Massimo drops his aggressive stance. "After all these years I tend to believe you do."

"Mm," I chuckle. "Hard to argue. Maybe I did for a while, but it didn't last."

Massimo exhales harshly, scratching where his jaw and neck meet as he stares down the women. "What the fuck were you thinking bringing this nightmare into our lives?"

I snicker. "Things were getting boring."

Grumbling under his breath, he turns his face away. "He damn well knows boring is better. There's less chance of dying."

Knocking a closed fist against his shoulder, I say, "There are only days left for me to work with her, get her to control her magic, get her ready for—ah, fuck," I check my watch. "Amelia is coming today."

Massimo shakes his head. "I don't have time for a tailor to stick me with pins. I'm busy finding a use for Vanessa and getting ready to leave."

I give him a stony stare. "I need you looking pretty."

Massimo puts his hands up. "I'll find time. Maybe I can have the conversation portion of the interview while Amelia does her thing."

I pat him on the shoulder as I move toward the women, both upside-down, laughing about something. Vanessa topples, but Natalia stays.

I lean forward, reaching the backside of my arm around her legs, rolling my shoulder to force her lower body downward and behind me.

My other hand slips to her back, lifting her torso. I cradle her like that pressed against me. "Talia."

The Light traces over her, bright silver reacting to being close to me and my Dark again. She blinks at me, her eyes wide, the same color as her magic. "Yes, Master?"

The woman is going to make me crazy if my magic doesn't do the job first. It is snarling at me, demanding to be set free while she hangs limp in my arms.

I put her on her feet. "Did you feel the Light?"

Her eyes lower, her lashes fanning against her cheekbones. "I think so?"

"Good."

"Are we doing that again?"

"No," I say, taking a step back. The Dark is seeping free of me, reaching out in search of her Light. I do my best to rein it in, but it hisses at me, pushing closer to her. It doesn't always listen to me, which is what makes this so dangerous. "I can't handle that."

Her eyes lift to mine and her mouth makes an adorable little pucker even as she breathes out, "Oh."

I smile. "You didn't hurt me, but my magic is pissed. Do that to me again right now, and I'd lose control of it." I jerk my chin at Vanessa. "You, go see Massimo. You two aren't done."

She slumps away muttering. "Stupid... Fucking pointless... My ass is going to get thrown out so hard."

I return my attentions to Natalia, eyebrows pulling together. "Does she have a use?"

Natalia's face pinches. "Yeah, my friend, and I can be a lot more ornery."

Stepping closer, I lean my head down toward her ear. "Little Star," I snake an arm around her waist, jerking her against me. "There are easy ways to do things, and there are hard ways. If you want to be difficult, I can make things very, very hard."

She clears her throat, her face down, her voice strained. "I like hard things."

"Not as hard as I'll make it." I use my free hand to tip her chin up so I can look her in the eye.

"Hard is the best," she manages. Her eyes are shining, her face pink, lips sucked between her teeth. She's fending off laughter.

I stare down at her in shock. I go back through the words, breathe out sharp through my nose. If she wants to play, I'll play. "I will make something so hard you'll scream."

Natalia snorts through her nose. "You were trying a bit too much on that one." She steps back giggling. "What do you want me doing?"

"You'll be busy with Amelia for most of the day. In your free time, I need you to figure out how to connect to the Light, feel it." I hover my hand over her as I draw it down her arm. "I thought you were developing. You aren't, at least I hope you aren't, or I may have more than I bargained for."

She rolls her eyes. "I'll work on it."

"Learn to feel it. Figure out what it feels like, how to connect to it, the way your stretching connects you to your Ki."

She nods, chewing on her lower lip. "Okay." As I turn away, she asks, "Do you have a guitar somewhere?"

I glance over my shoulder. "No."

She nods. "Okay."

I walk away. I have things to do, including finding a guitar.

CHAPTER 22
NATALIA

AMELIA IS A FOUR-FOOT WOMAN WITH DARK HAIR AND A THICK, rough dialect from the northern part of the continent. From what I can tell, she's human, although I learned a lesson on assuming with Thomas.

I've been stuck with pins more times than I can count or care to, and I'm only now realizing how many dresses Callahan bought for me as I try on one after the other.

Ness gasps. "Holy shit."

I glance down and wince. "I look ridiculous."

She drops her jaw. "Uh, no."

I smooth the tule skirt down, eyes on Amelia as she pins the length for the hem. It's the last dress, although the first dress I picked out with Callahan that is sheer tule. I turn back to Ness, who steps further into the room, leaning with one knee up on the wall next to the door.

I grimace. "How bad is it?"

Ness flips me off. "You're hot."

Grinning, I shake my head. "I'm not unattractive, but I am not a dress kind of girl and this dress?"

"I'm not sure that's a dress." Ness laughs. "I think you're wrapped in tulle, and I can see nip." She points.

My face flames as I lay an arm over my breasts. "I'll put something on under it when I actually wear it."

"No," Amelia stands up. "No under. I make dress fit, put something under then it will be wrong."

Widening my eyes, I say, "No, really, I've got this strappy black–"

"No," Amelia says. "Done now. Go change."

Removing the gown without getting stabbed or disturbing the pins is a tricky feat, but I do my best before getting back into my leggings and loose shirt. As with all the others, I hand the gown over to Amelia.

Amelia collects everything up and leaves, looking like a toddler carrying laundry for a six-foot grown woman. I'm not that big, but it's comical. Amelia somehow makes the feat look effortless, though.

Gaping after her, Ness and I giggle, then she turns to me. "What did I miss?"

I grin, then exaggerate a grimace, drawing one side of my mouth over and down. "Cal's taking me to Ilbuio." Walking to the bed, I throw myself on it, facedown to cuddle a pillow beneath me. "There's this thing there. I have to go. The dresses are because I'm arm candy."

"Back to the 'you're hot' thing." Ness laughs, coming over to lay down next to me, propped on bent arms.

"Not like Sasha." I pick at a piece of lint on the duvet.

"Shut up." Ness shoves my shoulder. "You've always been twice as pretty. Don't forget, she was always jealous of your skills."

I shake my head. "How'd it go with Massimo?"

Ness groans and flops flat on her back, staring at the ceiling. "I have zero usability. I couldn't do a damn thing he asked of me."

"Did you remind him you can heal?"

"Fucking Mother." Ness sits up to gape at nothing, mouth

open. "He stabbed himself. The man straight up stabbed himself through the arm and had me heal him. I was so stunned I just stood there watching him bleed for a fraction, too freaked out to focus. He says you're better and faster."

I can imagine her standing there stunned. I can't blame her for it either, I would have done the same. "Who does that?" I curl my lip. "Still, two healers are better than one."

"Babe, I don't know. Judging by how he talked to me, I'd say that isn't something he's interested in."

Studying her, I shake my head, dropping it to hang. "Callahan says you'll get a contract. All we need to do is to come up with something for you to do."

Bursting into a hysterical laughter, Ness says, "I'm average. Perfectly freaking average, at everything, which is kind of cool. I can do anything averagely but, that's it. Maybe I can offer to suck dick."

My eye twitches. "Freaking really? Maybe try something else before you start dropping to your knees."

"Jealous?" Ness winks. "Hoping he'll let you instead?"

I sit back on my heels, grab the pillow, and smack her in the face. "Stop."

The thought isn't new. It has crossed my mind in fleeting passes, but the contract around my forearm puts a stop to those ideas quick when they do come up. Callahan is achingly beautiful with a face I'd love to sit on. It would be a great first face sitting experience.

Ness sits up, legs crossed. "I'm so screwed."

There's a knock on the door and we both turn to Callahan standing in the doorway. He's got an acoustic guitar in one hand by the neck.

I sit up, blinking. "I thought...?"

He steps over, offering it to me without responding. Accepting it, I cross my legs, situating the instrument in my lap and running my hands over it. He said he didn't have a guitar, but here he is, handing one over. I furrow my brow in confusion. He doesn't lie, so he didn't have one, but now he does.

Plucking at the strings, I cut my eyes to Ness. "Any requests?"

Callahan answers. "What's your favorite?"

I look at him and suck in a breath, holding it. There's a song I both love and hate. It hurts my heart, beautiful in the way broken things tend to be.

Ness scoffs. "That's easy. 'I'll Stay' by Dark Marrow."

He leans against the post of the bed, eyes on mine. "Can you play it?"

Clearing my throat, I push the stray hair from my face, and bob my head. "I can, but I need a warmup." I point to Ness. "Your pick first."

"'Taste of Sugar'."

I snicker. "Dark Marrow tonight it is." I start strumming. Ness is singing the lyrics, but when I roll from 'The Taste of Sugar' into 'Through The Shredder', I start singing with her. We grin at each other through 'Beautiful Mistake', then I shift and settle.

"All right, 'I'll Stay'," I say, nodding at Cal. "In a very acoustic version, pun intended." I point at the guitar.

Clearing my throat again, I get comfortable and strum. Ness shakes her head, laying down, tucking her hands under her head.

My fingers find the right strings, and I close my eyes. This time, when I sing, I sing alone.

"*I'm so tired and cold*
So alone
So old

"*My heart's in pieces*
My body, it aches
I feel like I'm shattered
Broken, and battered

172

Still searching, for home

"Lover, I know
You're scared I'll leave you alone
But I'll fight when I feel like dying
Just trust in me
I won't let go
Just hold onto me
Hold onto me
And I'll stay

"There's a light on at home
But you're not here to hold
This is getting so old
This fight is dragging on
And I can't breathe
when you're gone

"I'm so scared, I'm all alone
All I want is to find my home
But I won't give in
I won't let go
Darling you know
I'll fight when I feel like dying
Just trust in me
I won't let go
Just hold onto me
Hold onto me
And I'll stay

"Just hold onto me
Hold onto me
And I'll stay

"All I've wanted
was a home
All I've needed
was a home

"And you're home

"So take my hand and don't let go
Because Lover, I know
You're scared I'll leave you alone
But I'll fight when I feel like dying
I'll take on everything
If you'll trust in me
And be my home
You don't have to be alone
I won't let go
Just hold onto me
Hold onto me
And I'll stay

"Darling, you know
I'll be your star that guides you home
And fight when I feel like dying
Lover, I know
You're scared I'll leave you all alone
But I'll keep you close
I won't let go
Be my home
And I'll stay"

I PLUCK THE LAST CHORDS AND FALL STILL, THE QUIET SETTLING IN
the room like the weight of a death shroud. My heart is pumping,

steady with heavy pressure. After a moment, I open my eyes to find Callahan watching me, frowning.

"Right," Ness sits up. "How about something a little less slit your wrists, now? Oh, what about Taylor James? Hers are always fun."

I force my lips to curve and nod. "Sure."

I get a couple notes out then there's another knock. We all look to Massimo, who takes up the whole doorway with his bulky, ripped build. The scar down the side of his face crunches as he screws up his face. "I could try to be a little more delicate with this, but fuck it, I'm just going to go ahead and say this and move on because I have things to do. She's useless."

I glare. "Ness isn't useless."

Callahan sighs, frowning at Ness. "Give me something."

"I will literally scrub toilets if I have to," she says with wide eyes. "Like, I am not picky. I'm not Tallie. I won't survive a fight against the Assembly, and I get the feeling Tallie's not going to be able to come back to stop them."

"No, she won't," Callahan says. "I also don't have time to wipe the lot of you out right now. You must have some kind of skill, a job?"

Ness lifts her eyebrows. "Sure, customer service, sales. I know a bit about motorcycles and other small engines, but Tallie can fix an engine," she jerks a thumb at me. "I can heal, better than what I showed today because, dude, that freaked me out."

Massimo shrugs. "If that freaked you out, you're not going to be useful when there's a reason to heal us."

"I can sing decently." She chews on her lower lip. "I was a history major in college. I thought I could get a tour job or something, travel the world. That worked out peachy as you can tell."

Rubbing a hand over his face, Callahan moves away from the post of the bed. "Anything else?"

"I mean, if I'm really reaching, I minored in dead languages for my second-degree education. That's totally useless, though. They're dead, as in, not used."

Callahan lifts his face to Massimo, who raises his eyebrows and cocks his head. They stare at each other, and then they both pivot in slow motion toward Ness. "What languages do you know?"

"Finch, Quesform, Seraphin are the dead languages, but I am fluent in Brish too."

Callahan inclines his head. "I do have a use for you. Come with me."

Rolling off the bed, Ness stands up. "I think it would have been easier if you two would just say 'these are things we need, here's a list, pick something you can do'."

"You talk too much," he mutters, exiting the room.

I blink after them as Ness disappears next, leaving me alone with Massimo. "That's a good thing, right?"

He smiles. "Yes, Light Bug, it is. She'll get a contract if she can stop talking long enough to sign it. Do you need anything?"

"No."

"Then I have about eight more things to take care of before I get to go to bed." He inclines his head. "Notify Thomas if you need anything."

I brush my fingers along the strings and rets, over the lines of the body of the guitar. It's sleek dark wood, polished so it almost has become reflective.

Strumming, I hum a few notes and sing.

"I'm so scared
I'm all alone
All I want is to find my home"

The Light glimmers in my fingers, illuminating brighter as I switch notes.

"But I'll fight when I feel like dying
I'll take on everything
If you'll trust in me
And be my home"

Lifting my hand, I scowl at it, annoyed with the Light dimming away. There is no Dark around me right now to draw it forth, but now I know what does.

CHAPTER 23
CALLAHAN

"Sit." I direct Vanessa to the chair across from me on the opposite side of my desk. She sits in a hurry, staring at me. She's remarkably quiet for her character. "Seraphin. You can read it, write it, speak it?"

She nods. "Mostly. I have an old textbook I'll want before I say one hundred percent because it's a dead language, so not used. Ergo, I'm not exactly fluent because well, to be fluent in a language you need to use it."

I set a blank page for a fresh contract on the desk. I instruct my magic on what I want, and it picks up a pen, scrawling the words. I slip the page over to her, my Dark offering the pen.

Binding is not an important factor in this agreement as this won't be a worn contract. She is going to behave without threat from me. All I have to do is throw her out, and she knows it. She knows I know it. She's not stupid, I'll grant her that.

Natalia would be difficult for a while, although I could break her if I had to. The corner of my mouth twitches with disdain. I don't want my little star broken. The thought of a mindless Natalia irks me.

I am demanding compliance and submission, but not strict

obedience. I want her mind intact, the spark in her eye. The uses she serves are better suited to someone capable of logic and rational thought.

"What is this?" Vanessa asks, taking the pen.

"A pen."

"Oh, good one. No, the contract." Her eyes are on the page. "Is this just normal paper?"

"*Ligan pagin.*" I say, amusing her curiosity.

She exaggerates a frown, head tipped to the side. "What is that? Living page?"

"Yes." I lower into the chair, resting into comfort. The fact that she could translate the term is a good sign that she will be able to fulfill this task. "Contracts must be written on *ligan pagin* or they aren't rooted in magic, and they are useless."

"Neat."

"This is your contract. It is an agreement to my terms in exchange for my protection. I will protect you as one of my own, including but not limited to other Seraphinus, Seraphim, the Magia, and any attacks against me, including things like signs of disrespect or general offense."

"What do you want from me?" She crosses her arms and leans on the desk.

One side of my mouth curls. "Does it really matter?"

"No." She pulls the page closer and frowns at it. "I am going to need to know what I'm doing, so sort of, actually, yes."

Natalia had those same concerns. Whereas her contract was extensive for obligated actions and limited restriction, Friend's is rules of compliance with little required action. It would be best for her to understand the arrangement.

I settle my elbows on the armrests and press my fingertips together. "Sign the contract and I will tell you. It has a clause that this information will not reach Natalia. Should you speak to her about this matter, you will be in contempt of the contract. Contempt results in expulsion. Once you tell her something you aren't able to unsay it, which means if you break this rule, you will die."

Vanessa's warm brown skin goes a bit paler. Her eyes are large, stretching wider as she gapes at me. They are set across a small nose, one of her eyebrows marred by a scar. Overall, she's a pretty female.

She nods, dropping her eyes to the desk. She fiddles with the pen, chewing her lower lip as she sets the pen down. "Hiding things from Tallie doesn't work out well."

I make a note of her warning. "You're here because I can use you, and because I want to use Natalia. She is rather fond of you."

Friend snorts through her nose. "I'm the only real family she has. Her mother..." She rolls her eyes. "She's on the Assemlby, did you know that?"

"No."

"Yeah. She was part of the whole 'almost kill Natalia for acting out bit' before she healed her."

I stare with putrid rage, black tendrils of my Dark wrapping around my fingers. One day, when I have time, I will exterminate that nest of cockroaches. They are in my city, breeding, and now that they are crawling out into the world and exposing themselves, I know they exist. I'll cleanse my city and wring the life from all of them for what they've done to my little star.

Taking a deep breath, I flex my hands open, forcing them to relax. She's mine now, the past is the past. Still, when I have time, I'll root them from my land.

Vanessa stares around aim, surveying the room. "Yeah, and her father? That man hasn't spoken to her in years. He will straight ignore her or walk out of a room. Sasha and Nick didn't survive initiation, but I'm not going down that road. Tallie's been pushed, pulled, punched, stepped on, coerced, but no matter what, she has me."

"Mm." I flex my ears back, studying her down my nose.

My Dark snarls, wanting blood for blood. *'Natalia is ours. We protect ours.'*

I send an agreement to it, then focus on Friend. "Loyal of you."

"Eh," she laughs. "So, you want to know what use I have? Natalia. I'll keep my babe together for you to use her, and I'll be happy about it because you already seem to be treating her better than the Magia ever did."

I take a deep breath. "Seraphin."

"Yeah. Why do you need me for that?" She holds her hands up, still holding the pen in one. "Not complaining, I need a use, happy to comply, but don't your kind still use your language?"

"A little, but not commonly. Some magic requires spells, the language comes up, and yes, I know a fair amount, but I don't have enough time, and this frees Massimo for other tasks." I gesture a hand at her before resting my fingers together in a steeple again.

She nods. "Great. What do you need me to do?"

I pull open the top drawer of my desk, slipping a thin book from within to rest it next to the contract. The hardcover is wrapped in living black skin that ripples with scales that click open. They emit a hiss of air and then snap shut.

"What the ever-loving nightmare is that?" She shies away with mock horror, or perhaps it's genuine. It's overly exaggerated, so I'm not sure.

The aromas of decay and death hang in the air, increasing a bit more each time the tiny scales click open. I shift to lean on one arm, deliberating on how much information to share. "A Dark Codex."

She hums, eyeing it with disgust. "You know, I love books. I love everything about them, but that thing..."

"There are seven in total. That is only one. You're going to translate it."

"Why?"

"I don't like being questioned. The less you know, the less likely you are to say anything I don't want you to."

She nods, flipping the pen through her fingers, "Yeah, got it. What am I looking for?"

That is a difficult question. The Dark Contest will likely be within a year or several. Soon is all anyone knows for sure. It's set the Dark on edge and the Light bolstering to strike when the exchange happens.

The texts are ancient, created at the beginnings of the Seraphinus. I can use the magic contained within the Dark Codex for an advantage. I already have, and if they hold what the rumors claim them too, there's even more magic I can exploit just waiting for proper translations.

"Translate it. The entire codex. Every word in it. I want it in common language. You don't need to look for anything specific."

She pulls the contract toward her, presses the pen to it, then sighs and pulls back. "My babe is going to ask. I'm not joking, lying to her, and hiding things? It'll piss her off. She forgives a lot, but not lying, so..." She clears her throat. "Can I get an amendment on this contract that I can tell her I'm translating a book? Just, something about you learning new magic or something?"

It's not a lie, her attempt at a false reason, but I'll not share that. I don't want Natalia involved in this. I don't want her anywhere near this. She carries the Light, and the Light isn't going to react kindly to the Codex. It also shouldn't be granted the secrets of the Dark.

"Curious that you're willing to lie to her for me."

Friend grins wide. "Buddy, I'm hearing you loud and clear. I am here," she says, pointing to the contract, "because of Natalia. So, two things. I'm dead if I don't accept. That's pretty clear and straightforward. The second isn't so much. I get the feeling you care about her, and the last thing I want is to cause problems for her here because the alternatives seem bad or worse, like she goes back to Tony and the Magia or ends up hurt or dead. Am I right?"

I smile. "You may be more intelligent than I have given you credit for."

"It happens." She shrugs.

I lay my hand on the page, adjusting the contract. "Amended. You may say limited, vague words about what you are doing for me." I shrug. "I also added an amendment that when possible and present, you keep Natalia in an acceptable condition for my use. Failure to comply results in immediate contempt of the contract."

"And death." She sighs. "Yeah, got it. Anything else I should know?"

"The contract exists as long as I need you to use Natalia. Hers is for the expanse of her life, which means you may be tied to me for the remainder of hers and therefore yours. However, if I no longer have use of Natalia or she dies, your contract will be void as well."

She shrugs and signs the contract. She sets the pen down then shoves the page at me. "Whatever. My babe could do worse, and I can't go back unless she comes with me."

I pick the book up. "Natalia is not to see a word within this book."

"Can I ask why? Why am I being forced to keep this a secret?"

I lean my head to the side, stretching my neck. "The Light doesn't deserve to be involved, and she's Light. I'd prefer her to not see the Codex at all."

"Part of the contract?"

"An order which you are obliged to follow per the contract."

"Oh, I have an order clause? Neat. Something I should have known, by the way." She takes the book from me, scowls, and drops it. "Ew."

"Get used to it. You're excused."

"Oh, that book?" She glares at the one on my desk. "The one I mentioned? I'm going to need that from my home, or a copy."

"Tell Thomas. He can get you anything you need and tell Natalia Sun Rune in the courtyard."

She picks up the book, shivering. "Ick, this thing is so gross."

She walks out still blathering useless words. I watch her go, then slip the contract from the desk to file it away. The woman would free up my valuable time for business or locating another Codex while not taxing Massimo. He doesn't have time for translating and I won't trust anyone else in my world with the job, contracted or otherwise.

A use is a use, and it would make Natalia happy, and compliant, to have her friend.

There is another reason for the contract though. If Natalia ever steps out of line too far, I have leverage. She can glow as bright as she wants. It won't matter. My little star is going to be wound in a web so tight she'll never see freedom again.

CHAPTER 24

NATALIA

3RD THORN'S DAY, HEATWAVE, 4049 6TH MILLENNIUM

THE DAYS SLID PAST. I SPEND SO MUCH OF IT WITH CALLAHAN working on harnessing the Light. Knowing how to draw it forward makes it easier, and regardless of Massimo watching like a hawk, I manage to control the Light enough to not unleash fury on Callahan again.

We leave for Ilbuio in the morning, and my endorphins are running high. Needing to calm down, I grab the guitar, settling on the bed.

I pluck strings, chewing on my lower lip.

> "*Each day I wake*
> *every step I take*
> *I'm preparing for combat*
> *And I really don't want that...*"

Silver threads twist around my hands and fingers. The end of the bed dips, and I stop, glancing up to meet Callahan's steady gaze. He tilts his head, turning, then sliding up to lay with his head near my bent knee. "You don't have to stop."

"If you're here, you need something." I lean over the body of the guitar, arms resting on it. "So, what's up, Master?"

He reaches up and runs a hand down his face, trying to hide his smile. "Ilbuio and Gathering Shadows, that's what's coming. We will arrive tomorrow in time for the selection ceremony and the welcoming dinner. The games officially start on Moon's day." He settles, tucking an arm behind his head. He breathes out his nose, and his eyes close, his eyebrows pinching together.

"A war zone. Right," I whisper. Staring down at him, I fight the urge to trace fingers over his strong jaw.

"It's more than that, Little Star." His teeth clench, the muscles at the corners of his jaws bunch, then relax. "You need to watch your words and your tone. When I tell you to do something, do not roll your eyes, do not flip me off, and most definitely do not give me that cute sass."

I grin. "I'll try to be a good little vassal and keep my lips firmly pressed shut."

A smile steals across his face. "I need you to behave or I will have to deal with you."

"Deal with?"

His head twists toward me, eyes opening as he grins wide. "Punish. If I let you go, it will show weakness, a soft spot."

"I have to keep my mouth shut." I slide my hand down the neck of the guitar, the steel wrapped strings rough beneath my fingers.

He shifts, rolling over, sitting up. "It's Dark, Ilbuio, and will be full of Dark Seraphinus. You'll glow, and every eye is going to be on you. They'll hate you, want you dead."

I nod, turning eyes to the guitar. I take a deep breath. "I'll manage."

His hands reach out, taking my face between them to lift my chin and hold my gaze. "It's twisted games." He winces. "They're designed to hurt, to kill, and every single one of them has a price. Not even the winners win."

I swallow, licking my lips. His eyes drop to them, lingering long enough to give me a tingle in my stomach before they lift. "Okay."

A corner of his mouth pulls back, his head tilting to the side ever so slightly. "I'm going to keep you with me, on my arm, next to me. You'll share my chambers, and you'll be my partner in the games. You'll be with me all the time, within reach where I can keep my eyes on you. I won't let anyone take you from me, and I will protect you when I can."

I smile. "As long as I keep my mouth shut, right?"

"I'll still protect you from them, just not from me."

"Lovely."

He snickers. "I almost can't wait until you don't, so I get to put you in your place."

"Exactly what are you going to do to put me in my place?"

"If I told you, it would ruin the surprise." His gaze crawls lower, eyes sparkling with danger. More of his Dark slithers to the surface. "Isn't anticipation half the fun?"

My skin is on fire, begging for the cool kiss of his touch, to feel the Dark against my flesh to caress the burn away. "Personally, I like the satisfaction of the act itself."

He chuckles, a deep breath caught in the back of his throat fighting to get out. "You win. I don't know how to come back to that one without trying too hard." He lets go of my face, resting his elbows on his knees, the humor fading from his tone. "I can't prepare you for what's coming, but I need you to at least understand it will be brutal."

Turning my head to the side, I stare out at the night through the window. The sky is a thick blanket of blackish green and the deepest ocean blues, littered with pricks of silver stars. Anything that can rattle him must be horrid. "This is what you want to use me for?"

"I want to use you. There is no 'use you for'. I have uses for you, yes. However, there is no specific use that you are going to fulfill. There is no, 'I use you for this thing and then I'm done'. I am never going to be done."

His words are a deep gravel, rumbling from his chest. Nodding, I sigh, returning to the strings, plucking a few, positioning my hand on the neck to strum a few chords.

"Each day I wake,
every step I take
I'm preparing for combat
And I really don't want that...

I stare at him, shifting on the neck, strumming.

"A battle ground of trauma
And bloodshed without sound
The way the demons pull me down
It sucks me low like an undertow
But it's all in my head
please tell me it's just in my head
I'm so scared this is real
the demons stalking me..."

He's watching at ease, face relaxed. I give him a smile, then slide my fingers to along the neck to the next note.

"Do I have to face the combat?
Because I don't want that
But I'm preparing for combat
And I don't want to do that
But maybe I do, what if I do?

"Nothing comes easy, and everything goes
Everything I do, I do the hard way
So I'll set myself on fire, just to keep the demons at bay
This fortitude is taxing, and every little thing can be so distracting
I can't find the glow at the end of the tunnel

"So I burn myself out trying to be my own light
When everything inside feels so alone, it's so hard to fight
But here I am facing the dark
I'm preparing for combat and I claim to not want that
But just maybe I do

"I'm so tired
Every day is a fight, and in the night I can't sleep
Afraid of the dark, I wake and I stand
It's haunting me, my demon brigade
I'm too much of a coward to let go
To face the dark six feet beneath
So I'm preparing for combat
Because maybe I could want that

"Claws tear me apart, here in the dark
And I'm so afraid, they're laughing at me
I can't get it to go out, that dim spark in me
But everyone dies, it's just a matter of time
Could I hold on, could I face another day
Could I face my demons in combat
Do I really want to want that
There are no rules here, to their warfare

And I remind myself, everyone's dying
it's a matter how fast,
It's a brutal fight, but I'll meet my demons on a battlefield
Every day I wake, every step I take
I'm preparing for combat,
but I really think I want that"

I let my head hang as I strum the last few notes.

"Natalia," he says, reaching out and brushing loose strands of hair from my face, one finger drawing over my cheek bone to tuck the hair behind my ear. "What I'm about to do to you, to use you for, is cruel."

I tip my head back, laughing to stop myself from crying. "At least you're honest about it. The Assembly wanted to use me, pretending like it was righteous or just a duty or some shit. Tony, too."

Callahan shakes his head. "I'm going to amend the contract that you're never to say that name again."

I set the guitar aside. "Can I ask you something?"

"Yes."

"The Magia, they tell us we are supposed to kill your kind. I get why, you lot are assholes, doing whatever you want, creating a lot of a collateral damage, but turn back the clock?" I draw circles with a finger in the air.

"I'm going to choose to overlook what you said about me and play along. What do you want to know?"

"The bridge that burned, the peace that dissolved and threw us out, what was it?"

His spine straightens, something strange flickering across his face.

I go on. "The Assembly says we were part of a peace accord that went up in flames. Literally, that's what we're told. Not even with Ness's obsession with history can she even find the answer. What really happened?"

Callahan stares at me like I asked why the grass is purple, then breaks into a grin, tipping his head back to laugh. "The Magia were created to be the Council between Light and Dark, but they got ballsy. They attempted to take control over the Dark and the Light. It's the only time that Light and Dark truly had peace because we shared a common enemy."

"The Magia."

"Yes. They're breeding for power in a pathetic attempt to regain control." He jerks his chin toward me in a head nod. "I'd say it's working."

"Oh."

He shrugs. "It was one of the reasons your contract is for the duration of your life. I wasn't about to let them keep you or breed you. There's not a single Magia noted in history that seems to be as powerful as you beyond the first imbued. I'm not handing that kind of power to an entity that wants to kill me."

I rest back against the pillows, crossing my arms over my stomach. Uncrossing my legs and bending my knees up, I frown. "And here I thought this was just about using me."

"A pleasant side effect." He chuckles. "It didn't change anything."

"Life," I say, holding my forearm with the contract up.

"It's a lineage contract, actually, and no, it helped to solidify my decision, but that isn't the reason your contract is for life."

"What was?" I hold my breath, waiting to see if he would answer.

He shrugs. "If I continue to win at Gathering Shadows, that brings me to the contest. Winning the contest makes me the next Dark King. I am never going to run out of uses for you."

I scowl. "What happens if you lose Gathering Shadows or the contest?"

"Typically, losing results in death." His words hang in the air, my heart skipping in painful clunks. "The objective would be to not die, which is why I'm going to use you. If I survive, which I plan to do, I'll be the Dark King, and I will need something powerful enough to stay the King."

Holding a finger up, I tilt my head. "Question. If you die...?"

He stares at me, a sadness creeping across his face.

Realizations seeps in. "I die too?"

A half-cocked smile smears across his face, the most adorable expression of ashamed pride. "I did warn you?" His eyebrows lift as he turns up the charm. "And that the objective is to not die?"

I laugh. "Oh, well, that makes it better then."

CHAPTER 25
CALLAHAN
3RD NIGHT'S DAY, HEATWAVE, 4049 6TH MILLENNIUM

ILBUIO LOOMS ON THE HORIZON, THE BLACK GLASS AND STONE CITY spiraling beneath clouds of ash. Even at a distance the light of the suns is dimming, the city scaling into the sky. There's a hazy, gray fog closing in, partially obscuring the buildings twisting and connecting as a mountainous landscape. The Dark lives on its own terms, connected to this world by the Dark throne at the very heart of the capital.

I stare at it from the backseat window of the car, frowning even as Natalia sleeps on my shoulder. I turn away from it to Massimo, shying from Natalia's glow with narrowed eyes.

My friend smiles, "She's only going to get brighter."

"I'm aware," I answer in a tight voice. "I don't need you talking to me like I'm stupid in Ilbuio. Act like I'm in charge for once."

I give Massimo room to breathe and move. We've had our fights and growing pains as we learned things the hard way. He's one of the three contracts I wear. His, Natalia's, and my oldest contract passed down from my father as a linage contract.

Unlike the one passed down and the first contract I wore, Massimo's contract was the first worn contract I ever wrote and signed. Like Natalia, he's tethered for life. Our agreement has shifted over the years, yet it's simple. He answers to me, but the rest is "we" rather than "he". *We* respect the contract. *We* protect each other, he acts in *our* best interests. For all intents and purposes, he and I are a unit, two acting as one to survive in this world.

He sneers. "I don't need you telling me how to act. Save it for our Light bug when she wakes up."

My hand cups the side of her head, my face turning to hers, lips brushing her forehead. My little star glimmers silver, even in sleep. Inhaling deep, I smile against her temple. "She's going to be a handful."

"That shouldn't make you grin like that. It should scare you."

Natalia is going to sass me, talk back, probably swear at me and I'm going to have to put her in her place. The upside to that headache is that no one is going to push me this year. Not when I have a Light source at my side.

I shrug my free shoulder, taking care to not disturb her. "I can handle her, but I'm betting she behaves more than you think she will."

He cocks his head back to stare down his nose at me. "You think?"

I snicker. "She said she would, and I said more than you think, not that I think she's going to behave."

Massimo grins. "Fair enough. I'm almost looking forward to the games this year. It was fun stretching my wings and claws with that smoragon. I want to pay Clem back for summoning that cursed thing, and Marius for the cheap shot he took when the building was coming down."

I haven't told him yet. We haven't discussed it. I assumed he'd realized why I was bringing my little star. I lift my eyebrow. "Mass."

He chuckles, but the mirth dies as he meets my gaze. He gapes, widening his eyes. "No."

"I decide, not you."

"No," he snarls, jabbing a finger at me. "You're out of your gods damned skull if you think I'm trusting her with your life."

Natalia stirs. I bare my teeth, annoyed he woke her. After our conversation last night, combined with her haggard appearance this morning over breakfast, I suspect she'd gotten little rest through the evening. The stress I caused was unavoidable. I needed her to understand what comes next as much as she could.

I drag her into my lap, pressing her face into my neck. "Go back to sleep, Little Star."

"She's the gods damned Light, you fool."

"I know she carries the Light, that is precisely why I'll be using her."

"You're playing with fire."

I drop my chin and give him a long look. "That's exactly what I do. I eat Light and create fire. Thought you knew that by now."

"Fuck!"

Natalia mumbles as Massimo glares. She yawns, shuddering before picking her head up. "Hm?" Upright, she blinks at me, then scans around us. "Why are we yelling?"

Massimo turns his face to the window then back, baring his teeth. "Cal has lost his mind."

"Oh. How about we slap an 'out of order' sticker on his forehead then?" She shrugs, slipping off my lap to settle between Massimo and me. "When we get there, I kick his ass out, and you and I go home."

I shake my head. "No, you aren't going anywhere, and I'm not out of order," I say tersely, scowling at Massimo.

He sneers. "You cannot be serious. Bringing her was bad enough."

I narrow my eyes, "Why did you think I was bringing her?"

He roars, "There is no fucking way I'm allowing her to be your partner in the games."

"You don't allow me to do anything," I reply, an edged warning to the words. "You aren't in control. You do as you are told, and, if you forget your place again, I'll rewrite your contract."

Natalia frowns and flips me off, then turns to Massimo. "Why?"

Scoffing, I say, "Do that again, and I'll break that finger. You need to-" She slaps a hand over my mouth, causing my eyes try to pop out of my skull from the rage and shock building within me.

'She did not just do that.'

My Dark laughs as my temper flares.

She twists toward Massimo. "Why?"

"He's about to rip your arm off for that," Massimo gestures at the hand over my lower face, even as I'm reaching for it.

I wrap my fingers around her wrist, twisting it to free my mouth, bones snapping. A soft whimper releases from her as I fling her hand away. It was too much force, but she'll heal in fractions.

"Never do that again," I snarl, adding the clause to her contract.

Cradling her wrist against her stomach, she hunches over it. Her head is inclined forward, eyes shut, lips pressed hard enough together to lose their color. The Light over her has intensified, stinging my eyes.

I breathe out my nose, guilt stirring and my magic petulant. "Talia," I start, trying for a soft tone.

Her eyes snap open as her face whips toward mine, something furious in her eyes. "Go fuck yourself with whatever you're about to say, then jump off a cliff." She twists to face Massimo. "Why don't you want me to be his partner?"

He chuckles. "That." He lifts a finger, drawings a circle. "You don't listen. You don't follow orders. You're the Light, and you have no idea what you'll face in the games. I don't trust you not to get him killed."

"He just broke my wrist."

195

"You slapped a hand over his mouth like you're in charge. You aren't."

"Neither are you."

Massimo tenses, eyes flaring open as fury contorts his features. "Little Light–"

"Second of all," she lifts her voice, "the contract isn't going to let me hurt him or me to let him get hurt."

"It would take a fraction of a fraction of a rune for him to die. The contract can't do anything about it. It's not even enough time for it to realize the breach or warn you, and then the contract will be void given the holder is deceased."

Silence permeates the backseat, then she laughs. "Fucking awesome. Fuck that though, I don't care. If he dies, then what? He said I will be dead, too. If I'm not, then what? I'm out on my ass and I have to go back to Tony? No thanks on both counts, dude."

I fight my grin at Massimo's perplexed expression, then grab her jaw, twisting her face toward mine. "I didn't intend to break bones, but you need to behave. Every one is going to be watching you. I can't have you disobeying or acting out."

If I can't keep her in line, I could lose everything. Dark law states that a contracted can challenge the contractor. If she did that and won, she could legally kill me and take over everything I am and have. It's why several lineages are as large as they are and why I have everything I do.

Worse, if she steps out of line far enough to portray that I am weak, I could be disgraced. I'd lose every contract and be thrown out of Dark society, left on my own, exposed without King or Council protections.

"Dude," she sighs, raising an eyebrow but smiling. "I so regret saving your life."

I grip tighter. "Have you healed?"

Her eyes roll, complete with the sassiest flutter of her lashes and flinch of her features I could ever imagine. "Yes, Master." She twists the term with vinegar.

"That," I jerk her face closer to mine. "That attitude stops right now. We'll be in Ilbuio in half-a-rune, and you gave me your word you'd behave."

"I will. I don't need you to keep reminding me."

Sneering, I drag her into my lap again, wrapping a hand around the base of her jaw. "Until you start showing respect and knowing your place, I'll be reminding you how I want you to act."

"Ugh." She relaxes, head tipping back. "Mother, I swear, when we get there, I'll be the best little vassal you own."

"Promise?" I chuckle.

"No, because when I make a promise, I don't break it. I mean, I'm going to try, I really will, but I won't make a promise I can't keep, and I still don't know all the rules."

"Keep your mouth shut, don't give me cute sass, and do what I tell you. It's that simple."

"I'm saying I'll do my best. That's as much as you're going to get."

Massimo shifts, eyeing Natalia. "Then promise me something, Light Bug, because he's not going to change his mind, and I'm not happy about this. Promise you'll watch his back and keep him alive. You protect him with your life, and you help him win the games."

She leans her back against the door panel and sighs. "I promise I'll do everything I can. You might not trust the Light, but I'm not the Light."

Bobbing his head, Massimo faces the window. "All right, Lightning Bug. Don't forget, though, if he dies, you die with him. I promise you that."

She shrugs, shifting lower, the corners of her pink lips twitching. "It'll be better than going back to being a baby machine."

Sliding my arm between her and the door, I roll her body into mine, tendrils of my magic slipping over her, wrapping around her in a protective web. Her face lands in the crook of my shoulder and she nuzzles into me.

My arms tighten, as does my chest. Dark strands of my magic lash tighter and thicker. It soaks up the Light, pulsing with appeasement as it feeds. Contracting a Light source is by far the best choice I've made in a long time. No longer do I have to search out Light Seraphinus or Seraphim. I have my little star to provide me with sustenance.

She goes limp with sleep as Ilbuio looms closer on the horizon. Tension coils through me, anxiety laced in my magic as it prepares for battle. Despite the inherent peril of the coming days, for the first time in centuries, I'm not worried about my life in the games. I'll be fine.

Natalia is a partner who can stand at my side, who could take a hit and survive, and who would be able to handle what I couldn't. It's strange and inexplicable, but I know it would break me if my little star went out.

CHAPTER 26
NATALIA

F INGERS STROKE THE SIDE OF MY FACE, ACCOMPANIED BY A SLITHER of cool against my skin.

Callahan's voice is a deep rumble. "Talia."

Light is evident behind my closed eyelids, getting brighter as I drift into consciousness. My lips curve and my toes curl as he cups the side of my face. I don't know what is happening, but I like it.

Turning his face toward mine, his lips brush my forehead. "Wake up."

I don't want to. I'm tired, so I try to delve back into sleep. My forearm burns, and I twitch, complaining, "Ow."

With consciousness comes coherent logic. I'm cuddling with the man who claims to own me, branded me with a contract and his name on my arm, and broke my wrist very recently. This is wrong, yet I'm so comfortable I can't bring myself to move. Morally revolting doesn't always override physical desire.

"You have to obey my orders," he chuckles, using the back of his knuckles to caress my jawbone. "You need to wake up. We'll be in the city gates soon. I want you cognizant when we get out of the car."

Groaning, I push my face further into his neck. Inhaling deep his scent of bourbon and honey, I relax, then pull my face away and blink, the glimmer of Light over my skin harsh in the dim car. Beyond the windows the world has grown dim, a white-gray sky peeking from beneath thick, murky, slate clouds.

Turning in Callahan's lap, I press my hands and the tip of my nose to the passenger window, my breath creating little patches of fog as I stare at Ilbuio. The jagged steeple rooftops are built at the base of sharp mountains. They start at the riverbank, rising, lifting higher and higher, echoing their natural background.

We drive over a long bridge, a mist closing in and filling the air. I strain my eyes against the window to see the black water, smooth as glass. The vehicle slows as we pass through wrought iron gates, open between massive stone pillars, and I lose my breath as the illumination of the world goes dim within the city walls.

The narrow and twisting road is rough and full of bumps as it curves through the buildings, a steep grade upward toward a gothic cathedral. Its face houses a massive inset circle filled with decorative metalwork and glass, intricate and beautiful. I gape, mouth open, the steam from my breath obscures it from sight.

Peeling my skin from the glass, I turn to Callahan. "This is Ilbuio?" I jab my finger against the window, nail tapping the smooth, hard surface.

"Yes." He hums, gazing out the window.

"Wow," I whisper and go back to staring at the building. It's wide and tall, its towers topped in sharp points reaching into the sky, with arching stone-enclosed bridges connecting it to other buildings, creating sprawling, intricate architecture that I could spend runes staring at. Ness would be squealing. "Everyone talks about Ilbuio being dangerous and dreary." I frown at the foggy haze clinging to the shingles and allies. "But it's gorgeous."

Massimo chuckles. "I suppose it has a charm to it."

200

I bob my head, then lift my hands, sighing at them. "Fucking really? It's brighter and there's *more*."

Callahan's hand closes around one of mine, his other arm giving me a little squeeze. "Yes, you're going to glow, Little Star," he says, chuckling. "Your Light is going to be furious at being surrounded by the Dark, and the Dark is going to be just as furious at the Light."

At my back, Massimo scoffs. "Every powerful Dark Seraphinus in existence will be in Ilbuio for the games, and they're going to be ready to tear your throat out at the first opportunity because you're Light." His voice twists into a sneer. "Not to mention most would love a chance to make Callahan take a hit. It's just another reason this is a bad—no, it's fucking worse than bad—decision."

"That's enough, Mass. You behave too," Callahan says, keeping his gaze on me. "He's right, though. Everyone will be searching you for a weak spot. They'll want you dead because you are the Light."

I stare at the headliner. "Great. This is getting better and better."

He takes my face between his hands, staring into my soul. "Do not trust anyone, ever. You stay at my side, or with Massimo, because if you aren't with us, you're in trouble."

My blood pressure is rising, my heart clunking at its usual pace, but harder, berating my ribcage like it could smash its way out to hide from this mess. I breathe out long and slow, my eyes staying on Callahan's. He holds my gaze, his thumb running over my lips, and the world stops.

Dark stubble fills the lower half of his narrow face with its square cut jaw. A crease mars his low, prominent brow between the thick, black eyebrows at the top of his thin nose. I see every detail of his handsome face down to the faint creases in his tawny skin. He takes up my whole sight, blocking out all else.

Everything crashes around me as the car pulls to an abrupt stop, jerking us. Callahan tosses me off his lap and into the seat

201

next to Massimo, his voice terse as he repeats, "Behave, Little Star."

I blink, a bit dazed as his door is opened. Callahan slips out, standing and speaking to someone I can't see.

Massimo clears his throat, speaking low. "Breathe, Light Bug. If you ever aren't sure what to do, follow my lead and keep your mouth shut."

"Mhm," I bob my head.

He chuckles. "You need to get out of the car now."

"Shit," I whisper. "You know, until now this has all just been an idea, not really real."

One of his large hands gives me an encouraging squeeze on my shoulder. "Count to three then do it. Don't think."

Callahan stands off to the side, the door open, and his hand extends into view, waiting, demanding to be taken.

'One.'

I breathe in through my nose.

'Two.'

I hold it, and my heart skips a beat.

'Three.'

I reach for his hand, knowing he'll hold tight. The glittering magic over my skin shimmers brighter as we touch, settling when his fingers close around mine. Quivering, but determined, I slide out of the car, setting one high-heeled encased foot down on worn slate cobblestones.

Callahan helps to draw me out of the vehicle and takes a step to the side, tucking me in close to him for safety or to give Massimo room to follow. I don't know which. The Light grows brighter, but a few strands of Callahan's magic reach out and twist around my arm, caressing in gentle reassurance and the Light dims.

I focus on the massive building. Up close, the stones seem darker, sleek shades between gray and black, but the grand decorative window spanning the front of the cathedral is so much more impressive. His face turns to my head, his mouth above my ear as he whispers, "Welcome to the Dark Palace, Little Star."

Forcing myself to take a breath and swallow my nerves, I bob my head but press my lips together. Around the grand entrance, bodies are still, faces turning to me. The weight of dozens of eyes settles on me. They glare, malice radiating from the Darklings, Dark magic coiling tight around all of them.

Something inside of me screams in fear, ordering me to run. Instinct rings in alarm that everyone present will rip me to pieces. I squeeze Callahan's hand as hard as I am capable of, my knuckles aching, my fingers burning with the exertion.

A man approaches, medium build and height, thick black hair slicked over to one side. His eyes crinkle as his face splits into a grin.

He shakes with laughter as he stops before us. "On behalf of my father, the Dark King, welcome to the Gathering of Shadows, Callahan." His eyes slide to mine, a fleck of brilliant red in one. "Hello, again."

Refraining from speaking, I stare him down, unsure if we have crossed paths. I know that day at The Gardens with Tony there were several Darklings present, although I wasn't focused on their faces. The only one I can clearly recall is the woman I fought and killed.

Callahan emits the tell-tale hitch of breath that accompanies a smirk. "Marius."

Marius smiles at me, his rat-like features full of malice. Dark entangles around him, thrashing at the presence of my glow. "Curious that you'd dare to bring your new pet."

Every ounce of strength I have is funneled into smashing Callahan's hand in mine. I bite down on my tongue and press my lips, remaining silent like a good vassal. I gave my word I'd try.

"A weapon is more useful when it's present for use."

That red marring flickers as Marius surveys me. He's clean shaved, his face cut with sharp features that sneer at me. "Your usual lodgings are available for your use, unless you'd like to request alternate chambers this year?" His gaze leaves me, shifting to face Callahan.

"The same will be fine."

"Would you like someone to show you the way?"

Callahan chuckles, "I know where they are."

"You really should," Marius says with a smug grin. "Someone will fetch your belongings and deliver them." He sidesteps and gestures toward what I mistook to be a cathedral. His gaze moves to my other side, narrowing as it slides over me. "Massimo."

"Marius," he answers in a tight voice.

Pivoting, Marius walks away, and Callahan leans over, "Little Star, breathe."

I let out a breath I had been holding without thought.

"Good, and know if you squeeze any harder, you'll be healing my bones next." I do my best to unfurl my fingers, as he chuckles, pulling me forward and up the wide carved steps.

Those standing nearby flinch and glare as we pass. Massimo surpasses us with elongated strides to open the decorative door, metal twisted over wood. He holds it for Callahan and me to move through. On the other side, Massimo slips to our backs, following as a shadow.

Dark presses in around me, leaving my skin puckering with goosebumps. My chest has too much pressure, and a soft whine starts in my mind. I grit my teeth as the silver Light emitting from me increases. "Damnit."

Callahan cuts his gaze to me in a sharp look, eyebrow raised. I suck my lips between my teeth, turning my eyes up and away to avoid being chastised.

The ceilings are vaulted, intricate stonework everywhere my eyes land. The walls hold stone torches to illuminate the corridors. I try to remember each and every turn, stairwell, and hallway. We pass through one of the bridges, the arched floor connecting between the main building to the next tower.

Massimo opens another door, this one much smaller and plain, ushering us inside. It's an open room, two couches across a low table. Two doorways leading to other areas obscured from sight on the back and side wall.

Callahan drags me inside before dropping my hand. "Mass."

The door clicks shut, and Massimo steps next to us. "Sir?"

"Cut the shit. No one else is around."

Rubbing his mouth, Massimo snickers. "What am I doing?"

"Pick a room." Callahan checks his watch. "Commencement is in a few runes. I don't need you until then, and I want to relax for the last bit of free time I have."

Massimo bobs his head to the side, glances between the doorways, then enters one, shutting the door. I stare at it, a bit dazed and overwhelmed, the world spinning a bit.

Callahan says, "You're with me."

"Hm," I hum, eyes fixed on Massimo's door.

"Little Star?" His voice is a husky whisper, worming through the cocoon I'm spun in. It's like the Light has bundled me up, sealing me away for safe keeping. "Talia." My name is sharper.

Prying myself out of the trance, I turn to him. "Yes, Master- Owner- Boss thing?"

Giving me a half-cocked smile, he jerks his head to the open doorway. "Come on."

He steps into the room as I follow. A bed, a dresser, a small table, and another door that's a bathroom. My eyes move back to the bed. It's a big bed, but it's the only one.

Flopping down on his back, Callahan laces fingers behind his head. I search the room for some hidden mattress and clear my throat. "Am I sleeping on the couch?"

"No."

"You expect me to sleep with you?"

"Yes."

"Not what I expected when you said I'd be sharing chambers."

He closes his eyes, at ease. "The Dark is a dangerous place for the Light. I won't allow you to be beyond my reach."

I shift, hugging myself. "Look, dude, uh, Callahan–"

"Cal is fine," he says with a wide grin. "I will be a gentleman, but you will need to accept while we are in Ilbuio you will spend every second at my side."

"I can take care of myself."

"I take care of you. You let me use you. That's the contract."

"Great, well, I got a nap on the way here, so I'm going to..." I twist to the door.

He snaps fingers and points next to him. "You are going to lay down right here next to me where I can keep an eye on you while we wait for our things to be delivered."

I grit my teeth, taking a few hesitant steps to the end of the bed, knowing the contract will ensure my compliance if I attempt to refuse. Still, I drag my feet even if there is nothing I can do except accept this. We barely know each other, making this arrangement more awkward than Tony kissing me.

Laying on my back next to Callahan, I focus on my breathing instead of him. I begin to relax, tension melting from muscles, and my eyes slip closed. He shifts, his fingers lacing into mine. His magic slithers like two cool twin snakes around my wrist, and I pretend it's the contract that keeps me from pulling away.

There is no way this doesn't end in disaster. As much as I want Callahan to be my home, to stay, it's a reverie.

CHAPTER 27

CALLAHAN

I KNOCK ON THE BEDROOM DOOR WITH A SINGLE KNUCKLE. "TALIA."

My little star is inside under orders to get ready. I check my watch again. The Gathering of Shadows Commencement Ceremony is about to start. My nerves are balling together, tightening my chest. I want my Light source, and I want to get this over with.

There's no answer from within, and I glance at Massimo, then check my watch again. There's nowhere for her to have gone, no way in or out but the door I'm standing in front of. There's no way anyone or thing could have gotten to her. Still, anxiety starts to crush my lungs.

I dragged the Light into the very heart of the Dark. I have no idea if this is going to work, or if the Dark is going to suffocate the Light.

My Dark is cranky at my lack of belief in her strength, but I worry about her.

Knocking with two knuckles this time, I lift my voice. "Natalia."

The door swings open, and I breathe out, my eyes traveling down her body encased in tight silver material. Her loose hair is hanging straight, ending at her collar bones, white against pale skin. She glitters like a jewel under the sun, but her eyes and lips are coated with dark makeup.

My cock throbs as I linger on the exposed expanse of her chest, the sides of her breasts on tantalizing display. She's too bright, glistening in the shadows, but I want to peel that dress from her and taste her. My Dark wants to see her bare, every stretch of skin glowing. I yank on it to keep it under control as it begins slipping from beneath my skin in long tendrils in search of her.

I extend my hand. Words of compliment flicker across my tongue but never make it beyond my lips, my Dark and cock too much in control of my mind to form a proper statement.

She balls her fists before flexing her hands and accepting it. There's a twitch to her eyes, a tug on the corners of her mouth that betray her masque of tranquility. Smiling, I draw her into the common room, facing Massimo. With a nod, he strides to the door, opening it.

Her high heels echo around us as we move through the palace. Nearing the top floor, the corridors fill with others, all turning toward us. Natalia presses closer as I move her hand to the crook of my arm to keep her against my side. There isn't one face that doesn't twist with fury or disgust, and the Dark within them surfaces, warning the Light shining from my little star.

When we reach the center of the palace, I pull Natalia into the throne room where the festivities will begin. At one end is the top arch of the massive stained glass and iron work window on the face of the palace overlooking the city. The other end holds the throne, lacking its tenant. I draw Natalia to a corner near the window to wait for this to start.

Whispers are low, everyone on edge as we wait. Natalia shifts, her hand in my elbow trembling.

I survey the room, turning my head to bring my mouth closer to her ear to keep my voice low. "Breathe," I tell her.

Chlem catches my eye, curling his lip. He's short and stocky. I know from experience he packs a punch, maybe the physically strongest of all of us.

There are plenty of unfamiliar faces, those who are replacing contestants that didn't survive last year or new contractors starting out on their own. The new ones are always interesting. Every Dark Seraphinus knows about the games and how they work, but there's something the experience lends that they lack, setting them apart.

I single out the others I know are on the contender's list with me. My gaze lingers on Marius, who relies on stealth and intelligence. Sterling talks to his usual partner, a half-cocked grin of arrogance pulling his face when our eyes meet.

He inclines his head to me, so I return the gesture in respect. His locks are pulled back, his black clothes tailored to his long, lean body. We've struggled against each other several times, always exchanging wins. The best games are when we are on a team together. He's brilliant and wicked.

Jezabelle was a contender. She died at the hands of my little star for trying to steal her away. It leaves an open slot on the list now, although there's nothing set in stone until the games are over this year. Anyone of us could be knocked out of our position, and death is always a possibility. One little mistake can make all the difference.

As more filter into the room, Telra walks through the crowd, head held high. My eyes follow her, the black dress she's wearing hugging curves I've traced a thousand times. My old lover is as dangerous as she is beautiful, a definite wild card.

For about half a decade, we were involved, and therefore allies in the games as much as we were capable of. Our involvement predated her being a contender, though. When she ranked on the list, I took the opportunity to disengage, having been dissatisfied with our relationship for some time.

She catches me watching her, and smiles, lifting a hand. A finger rests on her round chin, then she trails her hand down her neck and lower, following the exposed skin of her deep cut dress. This time, I hold her gaze, not playing along.

The low buzz of the room ceases, our Dark King entering. Dark warriors flank him as he is helped forward by Eloise, a petite woman, whose lineage is bound to serve the Dark Throne for their ability to heal.

With the King situated on his throne, the games are about to start. I twist my head toward Natalia, the top of her head level with my mouth because of the heels. I keep my voice low. "When they call my name, you stay here with Massimo."

She squeezes my arm in acknowledgement.

The King sits on the throne, Eloise backing away with her head low. His pale skin has a gray tone, the skin wrinkled. He's looking worse than ever.

He rests his cane before him and snaps his fingers. "I welcome to Ilbuio all the fresh blood and those who have lived long enough to return." He coughs. "In accordance with our laws, the Gathering of Shadows Ceremonies are to determine who should be your next Dark King. Every contractor who has proven enough strength to garner contracted is entered into the games. You are warranted one who contracts their life to yours for assistance, proving not only your strength but that of those you control."

Eloise steps forward, rolling apart two rods to expose the length of a scroll. "When I call your name, present to our Dark King, and name your partner. Once a choice is made, it will be recorded for this year's games. You are allowed only one. The choice cannot be altered once selected, and should your partner be destroyed you are not permitted another."

Players are called. They step forward, bow, and name their partners. I grind my teeth, waiting. All the others on the contender's list are summoned before I'm called forth. A fleeting moment of self-doubt sings through me as I bow to my King. Snarling at my magic for its doubt in Natalia, I lift my chin stating, "I name Natalia Swan as my partner."

Eloise's eyes grow wide, and the room explodes with whispers. She clears her throat, glancing over my shoulder. "Callahan, are you enlisting the Light as your partner?"

"Yes."

Her mouth pinches, her hand withdrawing her hand from the scroll as she twists to our King. "Will this be allowed?"

My fingers curl in loose fists. "There is no rule against using the Light. She is my contracted."

The King's face doubles in wrinkles as he smiles. "If she is contracted, she is a viable partner. Callahan is correct, the rules allow it. If he wishes to be sent to the afters, so be it."

Bobbing her head, Eloise puts a hand to the scroll. "My apologies. Can you repeat the name? I'm more familiar with Massimo Verta."

I smile. "Natalia Swan."

"So be it. Natalia Swan is the selected partner of Callahan Barraco."

Inclining to my King in respect once more, I turn then stride through the crowd back to my little star. She blinks at me, and I offer her my hand as another name is called. I smile as she takes it, pivoting into place at her side to rest her fingers in the bend of my arm.

Massimo never flinches, but he snarls under his breath, "I'm fucking pissed at you."

I shrug. He knew it was coming. We'd discussed it. He even made Natalia promise to watch my back. There should have been no surprise for him, so I don't care to amuse his feelings.

CHAPTER 28
NATALIA

WHEN CALLAHAN DECLARED ME HIS PARTNER, EVERY DARKLING snarled. I swallowed hard and glanced at Massimo for reassurance. His face had twisted like there was a vulgar taste on his tongue he couldn't be rid of.

It's been stuck like that for the last couple of runes. I'm not comprehending why he's so disgusted with me being Callahan's partner, but the reaction from around the room told me he's not the only one.

So many names were called, it felt like hundreds. Everyone who stepped forward was a Darkling. As far as I can tell, I'm the only one present who isn't. I don't know what I suspected, maybe humans serving the Seraphinus perhaps, or at least some Seraphim, but every single one of them has the full black eye. Men and women of all heights, builds, and skin tones stepped forward one after the other and provided another name. I'd lost count of how many were enlisted.

I shudder, standing silent, off to the side like a good little vassal. From what I can tell, this is some kind of reception. There are drinks and music while they all mingle. Callahan is off somewhere, leaving me in Massimo's care. Everyone else is giving me a wide berth.

"Psst," I hiss.

His jaw muscles bunch. His face twists to me, and I can feel the rage rolling off him. "Shut your mouth, Light."

I roll my eyes. "Why are you suddenly so against me?"

"You're going to get him killed."

"Because I have some kind of Light magic?"

Massimo curls his lip and faces forward.

"I promised you."

"You really don't–" he stops and tenses, fists shaking at his side. "The Light doesn't save the Dark. You're ignorant, unprepared, and I have a difficult time in the games with more strength, magic, and experience." He takes a deep breath and stretches his hands open. "They're going to come for you. *All of them.* You don't stand a chance. It's going to leave him on his own and exposed after you're dead."

I fight a giggle. "You know my whole life I've been trained to kill Seraphinus."

He snarls under his breath, making no further response.

A woman stalks toward us, the way a model glides along a catwalk. Massimo's shoulder twitches as she stops in front of us. She's taller than me, with a diamond shaped face and prominent cheekbones. Her eyes crinkle at the corners as she smiles. "Hello darling."

Massimo grunts. "Telra."

"How are you?" She waves a flute full of bubbling fluid.

Jerking his head, Massimo says, "He's over there."

Telra turns and wrinkles her nose, "Oh, how silly of me." She laughs softly, tipping her head back. Her free hand presses to the expanse of exposed skin of her chest. "Well, I'm here now. Tell me, how have things been?"

"Busy."

"Has he missed me?"

Massimo grins. "Why would I know?"

She waves a hand, moving to take a drink, then hesitates, lowering the glass. "I know propriety and I know what goes on behind closed doors. I have my own contracts."

"You do."

"So," she draws the word out, eyebrows lifting with exaggerated intrigue, "has he been missing me?"

Massimo shrugs, rolling his shoulders back. "He's been busy."

Telra turns her gaze on me. I keep my face blank, staring back. "I can see he has his hands full. Hello, Light whore."

My ears pull back as I force a smile, digging my thumbnail into the tip of my index finger. "Hi."

Staring down her nose at me, she scoffs, then returns her attentions to Massimo as she tosses her black hair. "I'm terribly afraid he won't survive this year with that thing as a partner. Not even my darling Cal is that capable."

"You should discuss that with him."

Telra laughs, that kind dainty chortle that accompanies an elegant, beautiful woman. "I plan to. Oh, I will hate to see him dead. It will be an absolute waste."

The opinions of my abilities are bleak, goading my temper, so I bite down on my lips, refraining from an outburst.

Callahan approaches, lips pulled back on one side. He stops at Telra's side. "What are you doing, baby?"

"I was coming for you, but stopped to say hello to Mass."

Callahan lifts a single brow in humor. "I see."

"Yes, and now that I have your attentions, I want a dance." Telra shoves her flute at me.

I jerk my head back, then scowl, taking the glass for her. Telra puts her hand in the air. Callahan takes it, leading her away.

I mutter, "Guess I'll just hold onto this then."

Massimo sighs, rubbing the side of his nose. "Yes, Lightning Bug, that's what vassals do."

"Who was that?"

"Telra."

"I'm assuming his girlfriend?"

He sneers. "Jealous?"

"No," I lie, throwing back the contents of the glass, because I need alcohol to deal with the fact that I'm seething green with envy of the woman. She's drop-dead gorgeous, and Callahan sees it. A blind man would somehow be able to sniff out those incredible curves and pretty face.

I shouldn't care what Callahan does or with who. Picturing that feeling as a cockroach, I imagine smashing it, impaling it beneath my stiletto heel.

We return to standing in silence, and I fiddle with the glass in sheer boredom. The last dribble spins in the bottom as I roll the flute in gentle circles until I am dizzy, and the world goes fuzzy. I lift my eyes, squinting at the blur of life before me in color, like an out of focus oil painting.

It's sweltering inside my skin, perspiration collecting at my nape. The wooziness isn't from watching spirals. "Um, Mass," I manage, my tongue sticking to the roof of my mouth. "Something's wrong."

He glances over at me. "What?"

I stare into the glass, the world swaying. "I don't feel well."

Squaring up to me, Massimo tenses and frowns. Setting his palm on my shoulder, his fingers dig into me with ferocity. "Stop that."

"What?"

He plucks the glass from my stiff fingers, sniffing at it. He growls, setting the glass on the floor and scanning the room. "Damnit, Little Light."

Shaking my head, I wobble, reaching out for him to keep myself upright. "I'll be okay," I mumble with clumsy lips.

His words are a hash snarl, "That glass reeks of abricin. It's fucking deadly. How could you not smell that?" He grips my shoulders, holding me steady, while the world twirls in brilliant hues around us. "Gods damn you to the burning afters."

My stomach lurches, but I swallow the bile. "It-It's poi-son?"

"Yes, and even a drop is lethal. The gods and Telra only know how much you've ingested. You'll be dead by morning and Cal will be without a partner."

A giggle bursts out of me. It shouldn't be funny, because he's furious, his fingers digging like weapons into my arms. A wave of nausea hits me, terminating my humor. "Mother, I need to lie down."

"You can't," he says. "We can't do anything without Cal's say so, and he's busy with Telra. She'll likely keep him busy, too."

My stomach churns and separates like worms knotting and slithering slime. I close my eyes, reaching for Ki. "Mass, I'm going to be sick."

"Don't. Don't fucking do it. It'll make this worse."

I sway, and he yanks me in tight, holding me pinned to him under his arm. "Fuck."

I shiver against him. He's blissful warmth. I don't know when my blood switched from boiling to ice.

My abdomen clenches as stomach flip-flopping in my gut. I try to ignore the creeping desire to regurgitate the contents of my stomach to the floor. Breathing slow, eyes closed, I focus on collecting Ki.

Callahan's terse snarl penetrates the fog. "What is going on?"

"She drank what Telra handed her. It was laced with abricin."

"You let her drink it?" Callahan's voice is a razor of fury. "She's fucking ignorant. She doesn't know any better."

"Which is why I advised against this."

There's a low growl. My stomach heaves a few times, lurching noxious air into the back of my throat. My knees buckle. Massimo grunts, his arm flexing tighter to keep me from sliding to the floor.

"Talia," Callahan says. "Can you heal this?"

I shake my head. "No, I–" I nearly throw up again, shuddering.

"Take her to the room."

Massimo grunts. "Breaking her neck would be kinder."

"No. Telra broke the rules. She needs to die by the poison, or I'm out a partner with no recourse. I won't get recourse for killing my own partner, and that's giving Tel leniency."

I grit my teeth, head swimming, bile burning my throat and lungs. The poison is destroying me as I try to center, reaching for Ki again.

This isn't a wound that I can shove Ki through to seal closed, but I need the Ki to keep me alive. I need to focus, but my mind is a heavy fog, hard to traverse.

I'm jostled, then swung into arms, floating through the world. Nauseous, I want to curl up and die. This is so much worse than what the Magia give during initiation. I'm not sure I'll survive. I'm also not certain I want to with the way my head is spinning, and my tongue is like a block of sand in my mouth.

I made Massimo a promise. I hold tight to that thought, managing a deep breath to gather my Ki and send in quick pulses through my body. As quick as the poison works, I need to counter it. I waited far too long to start, but I grit my teeth, digging deep for resilience. I've been here before, and I'll take great joy in proving Massimo wrong.

I'm dropped, hitting solid ground, and groaning at the pain lancing through my skull.

"Damnit," Massimo curses, fingers pressing against my forehead. "Thought you'd be out already."

"Asshole," I whisper, inflaming my raw throat.

He sighs, picking me up again. This time he deposits me with care onto something softer. "Just relax. There's nothing I can do to help you, but it'll be over soon."

I half strangle on a laugh that's lodged in my throat. Conserving my energy, I don't respond to tell him he's stupid.

Instead, I return to channeling Ki through me in a constant stream.

My insides want to come out of me. Whether or not it's allowed, I roll to the side, hurling out what my body is rejecting. It splatters. I shudder, collapsing back.

Massimo's whisper breaks through the haze. "I'm to blame, Little Light Bug. I should have been watching you. Fuck." He growls in the back of his throat. "I was too pissed to want to take care of you. Now you're dying, and it's my fault Cal's going to face the games alone."

The Ki burns through my throbbing body, a cold sweat overcoming me. My joints ache, my muscles hurt, like a fever settling in. I pray to the Mother, struggling the breathe. Losing reality, I sink into bitter agony.

THE SHROUD OF DEATH IS LIFTING.

Massimo scoffs. "Gods, she's either too fucking stubborn to die or Telra laced it with something to drag this out."

Callahan answers, his voice raw and deep, "The latter. Stubborn or not, my star is going to die." He sighs, his voice deepening to a snarl. "When she does, I'm going to break your fucking wings and I'll make sure this time they can't heal."

"I don't–"

"You were supposed to be watching her, you fucking waste of Dark."

"This is on me. I'm not disputing. I'll submit to whatever you deem fit, but breaking my wings is going to make me a lot less useful."

"You're right. Your wings are too valuable to me. I'll cut your dick off."

"Not like it gets much use anyways."

Every beat of my heart pulses agony through my body, so I keep pushing Ki, shivering, and drenched in sweat. An eternity of misery rolls by in ten billion ticking fractions, then shatters, gone in a flash. My mind slips into conscious awareness.

I send a few more waves of Ki through me, whimpering at the searing pain rippling through my ravaged body until there's no resistance, the results of the poison subsided.

"Mother," I groan, flailing for something to grab to pull myself up.

Callahan curses, calling a shortened version of my name. I don't know where that came from, but since it's not Nat or Natalia, I'm fine with it.

A large hand grabs mine, yanking it. "Talia?"

Sitting, I manage to peel eyelids over dry eyes, like sandpaper against sensitive skin. Narrowing my eyes, I peer at Massimo and Callahan gaping at me slack jawed. "Water," I rasp. "Need water."

Massimo is on his feet. Callahan kneels before me, his red-tinged-tawny skin a bit pale. He takes my hands between his. "Talia?"

A tumbler of water dangles in my vision, and I snatch it. Chugging it, I try to swallow too much at once, my throat screaming in a deep throb. I choke it down anyway. Massimo takes the glass, fills it from a pitcher, and offers it back.

I shake my head, reaching for the whole pitcher. He hands it over, and I guzzle until the contents are secure in my stomach. Wiping my mouth and licking my lips, I frown, then shudder. "What the bitter fucking afters was that?"

Callahan grabs my chin, forcing me to meet his black eyes. "Abricin, and it's deadly. There's no antidote, there's no known survivor. It's pungent though, easy to avoid."

I frown, "I didn't smell a damn thing but alcohol."

He lifts a flute toward my nose, "Inhale."

I do and shrug. "Nothing."

Scrubbing a hand down his face, he sighs. "Must be because you have human senses."

I eye the glass in Massimo's hand. "Can I have that?"

He smiles with tight features and pressed lips, almost chagrin as he offers it. "I'll get you as much as you want, Light Bug."

I drain the glass, handing it and the pitcher back to him. "I'm good."

Callahan stands, frowning. "You said you couldn't heal it."

"I can't," I say, wincing. "I can't just "heal" it. All I can do is channel Ki and hope to keep up with repairing the damage as fast as the poison creates damage. It's how you pass initiation to begin training, by the way. Whatever the burning afters that was, was way, way worse."

He sighs, scrubbing his face with both hands, and then rubbing the back of his neck, staring down at me with something between fury and admiration. He checks his watch then turns to Massimo with hands on his hips.

"Breakfast is in two runes." Callahan slips his arms around me, lifting then cradling me against his chest to carry me into the room we're sharing. He kicks the door shut and sighs. "What can I do for you?"

I shake my head. "I want a bottle of vodka, a hot shower, a full body massage, and like, three weeks of sleep."

"The shower you can have, and I can give you about two runes of sleep."

"I'll take what I can get."

He carries me into the bathroom, lowering me to my feet before leaving me there. I crank the heat on the shower to boiling, scrubbing the sweat and aches away. I wrap in a towel and peek out the door to find an empty room. With a sigh of relief, I find a loose shirt and leggings, then bundle my hair to dry.

Stumbling on trembling legs, I set my sights on the bed. The door opens, Callahan entering and kicking the door closed behind him. "Talia?" He extends a bottle of vodka.

"Mother love you," I manage in a husky voice, reaching out for it.

He steps forward, grabbing me against him and lifting me off the floor with one arm. I squeak, legs clinging to his hips. Taking the last couple of steps to the bed, he sets me on the edge, passing the liquor to me.

I crack the lid, chugging as he frowns at me. Pausing to catch my breath, I swipe at my mouth. "You're either trying out telekinesis or you want to say something."

"No one survives abricin."

"Magia," I say, pointing a finger at myself. "Poison doesn't work on us. Well, ha, I mean it works. The effects will set in, and that was worse than I imagine the burning afters will be like, but I'll survive."

Sinking onto the mattress next to me, he hangs his head. Wagging it side to side, he lays back, exhaling. "Anything else I should be aware you're capable of?"

"You're going to learn sooner or later I didn't need you to survive the dragon, and Mass is going to realize I'm a lot more capable than he thinks."

He sits and smiles with half his face. "Done?"

The bottle is half empty, so I upend it down my throat until I've polished off the last drop, then chuck it to the floor. "Now I am."

Jerking his head, he says, "Lay down."

I crawl up the bed and collapse, face down. He settles next to me, and one large warm hand runs under my shirt, up my back. My muscles twitch and quiver. "Um."

"Shower, vodka, massage," he says, dragging a thumb down the long muscle along my spine, "then sleep."

I had been joking, sort of, but I am not going to complain. My body feels like it got beat with a bag of hot coals. Drooping into the mattress, I relax, fading into sleep under the catharsis of his strong his hands. A girl could get used to this.

221

CHAPTER 29
NATALIA
3RD MOON'S DAY, HEATWAVE, 4049 6TH MILLENNIUM

THE NEXT MORNING, I DRESS IN BLACK WITH A SMOKY EYE AND SIX-inch heels. I'm ready to murder a Darkling, and I want my attire to match my mood.

I avoid Callahan's gaze. Last night, or maybe it was this morning, his hands were everywhere on my body. Now the warmth of embarrassment flushes across my face and chest when I so much as glance towards him.

He pulls a chair out for me at a long table filled with Darklings, helping me down into it. Massimo sits on one side while Callahan claims the other, pinning me between them. I breathe out, a sense of security settling in me.

I scan the faces up and down the table, my eyes lingering on Telra. The blaze of Light over my skin sparkles brighter. I grip my fists, clenching the silky material of my dress in both hands, bunching it tighter and tighter until my fingers tingle with numbness.

She turns her face toward me, her eyes widening. I resist the urge to flip her off, instead narrowing my eyes. She knows what she did, and I want her to know that I know as well.

Callahan leans closer, his mouth skimming the shell of my ear. "Little Star."

Clearing my throat, I tip my head back, concentrating on the carved stone creating the decorative ceilings. "*Mhm?*"

He chuckles, stroking the back of his knuckles along my forearm. "You'll have the chance for payback."

"Will I? I didn't know if you'd be okay with that."

Tucking a loose strand of hair from my chignon behind my ear, he says, "In the games you have free rein. No one but me is off-limits."

"So, if I kill your girlfriend you aren't going to get all pissy?"

Callahan keeps his eyes forward, a grin smeared across his face. "No. Right now, though, behave." He flicks my wrist under the table.

Food is served on silver dishware, and I drool at the fruit and nut bread, clearing the plate in record time. My eyes slide to Callahan's, salivating over his half-full dish.

Massimo chuckles, exchanging his for mine. "That was like watching a ravenous melrag down a corpse."

I groan, shoving food into my mouth, gobbling it down without even tasting it. "I'd eat a corpse if it was all that was available right now."

There's nothing left, yet my stomach is still rumbling, clenching tight with hunger. The space under my tongue prickles, like tiny needles jabbing my flesh to draw forth salivation. Callahan swaps the empty plate for his, and I inhale everything he's passed on.

I'm tempted to lift the plate to lick the crumbs away, but I'm saved by another course being served. Eggs and bacon. Mine is gone in about two fractions.

Massimo exchanges our plates without ever touching his. "How you manage to eat your body weight every time you consume food is mildly impressive."

I bob my head to the side, chewing bacon. "Magia. Our food

bills are extensive. Presently, it's because of the Ki expenditure last night. It's like coal to fuel a fire."

When the food is gone and the plates cleared, the room falls silent. Every head twists to the Dark King. His mouth curls, a wicked gleam to him. "Let the games begin, Eloise."

Eloise stands. "As is tradition, to honor the twelve days there are twelve sacrifices. Each draws a straw," she says, holding up a glass canister crammed full of yellow stalks.

Moving along the table, she offers the jar to some Darklings, but not others. Her nose is rounded, and her hair stuck between blonde and brunette. The dainty features match her petite build. She peers at me with curiosity, no animosity to her expression as Callahan draws from the jar.

I lift an eyebrow, and she moves on, passing over me and Massimo. At the head of the table, she sets aside the empty vessel, folding her hands before her. "Players, please reveal your selection."

Callahan snaps the stalk in half in one hand, a misty blood red haze hissing out. He curls his lip, dropping it on the table. His is not the only crimson smoke rising, although not every broken straw releases the fog.

"Chosen, please stand."

Chairs scrape, various Darklings rising to their feet, including Callahan. My ears tickle, recalling the word sacrifice. More than a dozen are standing, though. I count twenty-four as Eloise smiles. "Chosen, please bring your partners to the arena hypogeum. The rest of you can enjoy your morning or view the fights."

Chairs scrap against stone while others move, and Callahan offers me his hand. I take it, then he drags me from the room, shoulders up, movements stiff.

We're back at our suit in a hurry, Callahan shoving me inside. "Change. Dress for a fight."

"Tell me what is happening."

Guiding me into our shared room with a hand on my lower back, he says, "It's a game."

"I heard the word sacrifice. What kind of game is this?"

"One that decides if we live or die, so change, and don't pull punches."

I gape, recoiling with mouth ajar. "Excuse me, has every Darkling here lost their mind?"

He's pulling at the buttons of his dress shirt. "Stop staring, take off the gown, then put on something you can do the flips and bends in that you love so much."

I reach around myself, fumbling for the zipper. "You know games are supposed to be fun, right?"

He snickers. "Were you expecting card games?"

Without answering, I grab clothes, throwing them on the bed before wiggling out of my dress. I'm trying to ignore him as I change, both because I want a good hard look at him and because I'm not sure I'm comfortable with him getting a good hard look at me. His ex-girlfriend makes me feel flat and shapeless.

Stealing a few glances, I notice he's got black markings on his back, several intersecting circles with jagged rune like characters and dagger-like designs decorating the inner lip of the largest ring. He turns to face me, catching me staring as he works a plain, black t-shirt over his head. My face flames and I turn my back to finish changing.

In stretchy black pants, with my sports bra peeking from under the off-the-shoulder shirt, I focus on him. He's in all black, appearing even more menacing in grunge clothes than the tailored, polished attire.

Stepping to me, he takes my face between his hands, meeting my gaze. "Twelve die. There's no way around it. Survive, that's all you have to do. I'll take care of the rest."

I frown. "You're pretty much saying you're going to murder someone."

"Would you prefer to die?"

225

"No." I snicker, "Although if you would've asked me last night, I might have said yes."

"Then I'm going to murder someone." He steps back, taking my hand as he does to tug me out of the room where Massimo is waiting.

He has his head tipped back, face at ease, hands in his front pockets. The bulging muscles even appear slender and limp, but when he turns his eyes on me, my blood runs cold. "Light Bug, you promised."

I force a smile. "Sure did."

Callahan says, "Talia will do well."

It's lovely that he has confidence in me, even though I'm about to throw up my nerves. "Yeah, all I promised was to keep you alive. I did not promise results that deserve that kind of belief."

Shaking his head, but smiling, Callahan walks me out the door and through the palace.

The Dark Palace would be so much more fascinating if I weren't lingering on the precipice of the afters. Ness would love this, the architecture and history, and while it's not what I enjoy, I am in awe of the stonework.

When we stop at a cross-section of halls, Callahan turns to Massimo. They exchange glances, then Massimo turns left, disappearing into the shadowed corridor.

I peer after him. "Guess that was bye?"

Callahan squeezes my hand in a tight pulse. "He'll be watching."

"So, don't break my promise?" I turn to him with a wide, faux grin.

He yanks me in, torso-to-torso, his eyes drinking me in. "I don't care if you do. I need you to survive. Promise me that, Little Star."

"Jeez," I say, fear tingling across my skin. "You're really worried about this aren't you?"

"That's an order. Promise me you will survive."

I frown. "Is a forced promise worth anything?"

"You don't break your promises. All I need to do is get you to say it, then you'll feel obligated."

"I mean," I grin, "that was the plan, right? To not die?" The contract is flaring on my forearm, beginning to sting. I'll do what he says, but I'm going to make him wait.

His lips press against my forehead. "Little Star, behave, which means follow orders. Now promise me."

Rolling my eyes, I step back. "Promise I'll try to survive." I wink. "It's pretty much instinctual."

THERE WAS SOME PUSHING AND SHOVING, ANOTHER DRAWING, AND then Callahan pulls me away. "We're last."

"Is that good?"

He flexes his shoulders and stretches his neck. "Doesn't matter. Do you want to watch until then? See what's coming?"

"I'm operating under the delusion that I know what I'm doing. There's no need to go shaking my self-confidence."

Offering his hand, his eyes crinkle with his grin. "All right, then we have time to kill."

"Thought we were killing a Darkling."

"That's later." He draws me down a narrow hall, checks around the corner, then slips us into a small room that I can only summarize as a jail cell. "For now, I want you to not absorb Dark and send it back, and if possible, don't heal until after we're out of the arena."

I lift my eyebrow. "I thought I wasn't supposed to be pulling punches."

"You're not," he taps the end of my nose. "Full swings and go

227

for blood, but they don't know what you're capable of, and I don't want them to just yet."

I rub the frown away, smoothing the crease between my eyebrows at the top of my nose. "Why?"

"Let them underestimate you and me. Let them see you as weak. They'll be more susceptible when you need an advantage."

I bob my head, everything pulling taut in me with nerves. "Right. How does this shit work then?"

He smiles. "We go in the arena, you stay alive, and I kill someone."

"This is downright barbaric."

"This is Gathering Shadows. It's designed to make you bleed, to test your strengths. The Dark is strictly meritocratic. These games determine who will compete to be the next Dark King."

I scoff. "You compete to compete? What if you aren't interested in being King?"

His lips press, pulling in a tight grimace. "It isn't optional. The strongest must be King. If you refuse to play, someone else will kill you so they survive."

"Sure," I shrug. "But don't show up."

He tips his head back, laughing from deep in his chest. "Not an option. You have to play, or you get contracted. If you're a contractor like me, you get your freedom, but you play the games."

There's an explosion overhead, dust raining down. Callahan tugs me against him, wrapping his arm around my waist. I bury my face in his chest, squeezing my eyes shut and holding my breath, waiting for the air to clear. The cool skim of his magic wraps around my forearms and waist.

"This is awful."

He vibrates with a low rumble. "It's not so bad. Twelve days a year I fight for my life and the rest of the time I do whatever I want. It's better than servitude so long as I don't mind getting my claws bloody." Another groundbreaking detonation goes off, and he says, "Hiro must be struggling."

CHAPTER 30
CALLAHAN

Hiro and his partner, Thames, survived. I breathe easier knowing that. I like Hiro, he's a good man, as much a friend as I can have. Being a contractor means I fight fellow contractors to the death every year. It doesn't lead to much camaraderie.

I stand next to Natalia at the gate, waiting for our fight to begin. She's shifting and dancing in place, so I smile at her. "Relax, Little Star, I don't know these players, so either they're weak or new. Either way, one of them is dying."

She bobs her head and stretches, legs straight, face pressed to her knees. It gives me a distraction from what's coming with ideas of what I'd rather be doing. Once I get us through the games, I'll have all the time I want to play out those fantasies.

The metal gate scrapes and drags, chains rattling as it's hoisted to grant entrance into the arena. At the other end, two walk into the open field, both shifted.

Natalia squawks, miss-stepping, and halting. "What the ever-loving Mother?"

I grimace, putting my hand to her lower back and leading her into the arena. "We're allowed to shift in the arena."

"Shift? As in shadow mode?"

With humor, I cut my eyes to her. "Shadow mode?"

"Darklings change into their shadow-selves with wings and claws and sharp teeth," she says, holding two fingers at her lips, pointed downward like fangs. "And they get faster, stronger, and– oh fuck me."

I grin at the offer. "Later. Right now, we have other activities planned."

Her face flushes pink as she sucks her lips between her teeth.

Our opponents are Lycans, humanoid structures twisted with wolflike attributes. I don't know their names. I didn't care to remember them from the drawing. Knowing names makes this harder to deal with.

It's one of them or me, or worse, my little star.

My magic stretches, wrapping around me in tight coils and expanding outward. It's heavy, full of Natalia's Light. Her magic hasn't realized mine has been feeding on her, or it doesn't care. My assumption is the first because the Light is no friend of the Dark.

I stop, Natalia halting with me in front of the men. They snarl, ignoring me and focusing on her. She's a lovely distraction, the perfect bait. They'll go after her, leaving me free to rip a head off.

A horn blares, and they lunge at her. She swears, tackled to the ground. Blood flings through the air as she shrieks. I growl, my fingers elongating, my bones breaking and snapping as my talons come out.

Light blasts, causing both beasts to retract a half-step. I lurch behind one, grabbing it by the jaw, claws sinking into flesh.

Idiots. They should've gone for me. This would have taken longer.

I twist, flesh and muscles rip, bones crunching and breaking. I toss the head to the side, snarling at the other. It gapes as the horn sounds, ending the game at the sacrifice.

It snarls, pointing one long, curved talon. "That was already dead."

I turn to Natalia on the ground, her stomach ripped open. "Talia." I hesitate, my magic lashing in rage. "Are you dead?"

She chokes, gurgling on wet. "Ma-may-be? Not su-sure."

I shake my head at the remaining opponent. "She's alive." I shift my hand, talons disappearing as I peer down at her. Her stomach is ripped open, innards ripped out, her torso a gory mess. I drop to a knee next to her, commanding her under my breath, "If you can, wait."

Eloise rushes toward us. She drops to her knees, hands laying over Natalia's destroyed abdomen. Her eyes closing as Dark surges out of Eloise over Natalia's torn and tattered flesh.

Holding my breath, I wait. I have faith in Eloise, even though Natalia would have healed herself faster.

She giggles, "Mother, that tickles."

Breathing again, I sigh. Natalia's shirt is stained and ripped, but healed skin is visible through the tears. She's fine.

Eloise pulls back. "Far be it from me to question you, Cal, but I'm inclined to believe I'm going to have my hands full trying to keep this thing alive for you."

"She may surprise you."

Natalia sits, hands to her stomach. "Damnit, you could have warned me. I was so not ready when that horn blew."

Shrugging, I stand, offering my hand. "You survived."

She smacks at my hand, getting up on her own.

"Talia," I snarl.

She tenses, glances around and winces. "I missed," she says, grabbing my hand.

I drag her out of the arena seething. When we are out of sight, I slam her against the wall in the corridor leading down to the cellars. "Never do that again."

"Sorry, Master-Owner-Boss."

I snort through my nose, grabbing her jaw by the underside, tipping her head back. "Are you fully healed? Never mind, don't bother answering. Heal yourself."

Her Light pulses a few times, then she nods. "I'm healed."

"Good." I step away. "We're going to collect Mass."

"Excellent." She catches up to me, skipping to my side and falling in step. "That's it? We're done?"

"For the moment," I chuckle. "I've never had an easier time ripping someone's head off." I rub my jaw, trying not to grin too wide.

"Dude, give me a warning next time."

I cut my eyes to her. "You did well."

"I got tackled and damn near ripped in half."

"Now everyone thinks you're weak, easy prey."

She shudders. "An accurate statement if there ever was one."

"You're not. I suspected they'd go after you, but they ignored me. I've never had that happen before."

She stops, hands on her hips. "Did you really…" she hesitates, "use me as bait? Is that what I am, fucking bait?"

"This time," I shrug. "They were idiots. Don't expect that again. No one with a brain turns their back to me."

"You, sir, are an asshole," she says, humor in her voice.

No one is around, so I tolerate it. "You're hard to kill. I was counting on that."

"It still hurts."

I twitch, recalling her shrill shriek piercing the air. "It's going to." The confession is ripped out of my core in a harsh whisper. Pivoting into her, I lift her against me. As much as I want to protect her, wrap her in my Dark and shield her, I won't. I can't.

She wraps her legs around my hips while her eyes stretch open to stare at me in shock. "What'd I do?"

"I'm going to do whatever I have to in order to survive, including using you or hurting you. You have one obligation beyond serving my needs, and that's to survive. Do you understand me?" I dig my fingers into her thighs, pressing her against me with all the strength I can muster, desiring to keep her safe.

"You're going to bleed, you're going to scream, and sooner or later you're going to kill for me."

Her head drops to my shoulder as she sighs. "I regret that I ever signed your contract."

"No," I snicker. "That's against the rules of our game." Setting her on her feet, I slip my fingers in hers. "Come on, Little Star, Mass is waiting."

She skips next to me, swinging my hand. "Lovely. I'm sure he'll be thrilled with my performance." The words imply an eye roll.

"He should be. They didn't so much as look at me."

CHAPTER 31
NATALIA
4TH STAR'S DAY, HEATWAVE, 4049 6TH MILLENNIUM

THE PLATES FROM BREAKFAST ARE CLEARED AWAY. YESTERDAY afternoon there was another game, but Callahan didn't draw our involvement, so I was spared another round of claws. This morning there are a few empty seats, the table full of tension as we all wait for our King to speak.

"Let's see how well you all can get along after trying to tear each other's throats out yesterday." He coughs on a laugh. "Eloise."

She stands, moving around the table with a deck of cards. Callahan draws the top card, setting it on the table after a quick glance.

I shift, frowning at the skirt of my dress, tracing the lace with a finger until Eloise has returned to the King's side. Her voice lifts. "Teams of five will play against each other in grab ball. Reds stand and collect."

Ten players form a group off to the side.

"Blues...Greens...Yellows..."

Callahan stands. I take his offered hand, following him to a group of Darklings. They sneer at me, shuffling a step away.

One is Marius, who shakes his head, crossing his arms. "Just my luck, dead weight."

I press my lips, while Callahan chuckles.

Eloise calls several more groupings together, then silence rings. She turns to face us, "You have half a rune to get acquainted with your team members, strategize, and report to the arena."

One of the men holds his hands up, "I'm new here. These are my first games, so I'll introduce myself. I'm Mattingly, and my partner," he jerks his head, to the man next to him, "is William."

A pair of women smile, introduced as Beatrice and Cat. Marius's partner is Jacques, and the final pair is Traver and Lyra.

Callahan nods, "I'm Cal. This is Tallie."

I smile at the way he gives my name, while they all give me glares of disgust.

Marius shakes his head, saying, "I won't be saving the Light."

There are echoes of agreement, which ceases my smile.

Callahan narrows his eyes. "She's my contracted."

Traver glances at Lyra, then crosses his arms. "I don't care if it signed a contract. It's the Light."

Mattingly's eyes cut left and right in quick twitches, then he caves in on himself. "We're going to need to work together, aren't we?"

Callahan shrugs. "We don't have to. I can get my partner across the line first and leave you to fend for yourselves, or I can help you. It's your choice."

"Fine," Marius drawls, his thin lips turning up at the corners. "See you there."

We all shuffle off to our respective rooms to change into suitable attire, converging in the dank alleys beneath the arena.

MATTINGLY'S CHEEKS PUFF UP AS WE WAIT AT THE GATE. "CAN someone explain the rules?"

236

I'm relieved he asked because Callahan went over it with me, resulting in my head spinning with little to no understanding taking place. These things are called games, although that's like claiming sink holes are swimming pools.

Travers bobs his head. "Grab the ball, carry it across the line."

Marius holds a finger up. "Only one at a time can cross the line with the ball. Once over the line, you sit and wait for the rest of your team to do the same."

Callahan adds, "Once all your surviving team has crossed to the safe space, the game ends. The winning team is awarded points per life."

In the room, Callahan had gone over the rules, and then indulged me with what he wants: Me, across the line first. Massimo wasn't happy, as it will leave Callahan alone to get across the line. He argued against sending me first, but in the end, we both answer to Callahan with no choice other than to do as he says.

Mattingly scratches behind his ear, "Are we trading off or just —" As the gate begins to lift, he grumbles. "Someone tell me what to do, and I'll do it."

Marius sneers, walking into the arena with his partner, deigning to call over his shoulder. "Win."

"Shouldn't we shift? We're stronger that way."

Callahan hangs his head, shaking with laughter, not offering any further advice to help the Darkling.

We line up in the middle of the field facing the opposition. They all fixate on me, tussling and pushing at each other like all ten of them are trying to occupy the spot in front of me. It's not a good start, but at least none of them are shifted.

"You're dead, Light Bug."

Unlike when Massimo uses that nickname, there's nothing cute about it.

"I'm going to rip your wings off, Light whore."

I square my shoulders, cutting my eyes to Callahan with unease.

"He won't be able to protect you from all of us."

Biting my tongue, I tip my head back, staring at the open sky in search of sunlight. I have an overwhelming craving to see the suns, but the cloud coverage ranges in shades of gray, no trace of either sun visible. This place is suffocating me.

The horn blares. This time I know what it means, feigning back as two lunge at me. I spring over, feet over hands to keep clear, then upright. I strike the air with an open palm, sending a shock force through the air to repel another attack. I dodge a punch, tuck and roll past two more opponents, then start running for the other end.

My feet are ripped from beneath me, Dark wrapped around my legs, and I fall toward my face, getting hands out to catch myself. Callahan still wants me to refrain from absorbing the Dark or healing for now, so I send Ki through me to detangle from the magic around my ankles instead of pulling it in.

I flip to my back as something collides onto me, bearing me into the sandy dirt. Weight and pressure collapse my lungs, so I stick out a hand, sending Ki through my arm and into whoever is kneeling on my chest. They fly back. I flip, feet over head to propel myself upright and spin.

The horn blows. Everyone stops, so I follow their lead, panting a bit. Callahan is snarling at Marius in the safe space with the ball under his arm.

He spins it on the tip of one finger shrugging. "You said it was my choice. I chose this." Marius tosses the ball toward the middle of the field.

Callahan finds my gaze and jerks his head away from the end of the field. We all reset. The horn sounds, the opposing team launching at me. Dark magic ensnares them, Callahan growling. More Dark stretches out, several breaking free. I fend off magic with shields of Ki. The horn sounds.

Jacques is in the safe space, laughing with Marius.

My insides quiver with rage. The other team isn't interested in playing the game, and my team is using it to their advantage. They're using me.

We repeat the same sequence six more times, Callahan trying to rip Darklings to pieces to protect me. Two lay dead, I think. They're in the dirt, unmoving, and no one trying to help them. Callahan is shaking and snarling, glaring at the other end where the rest of our team is lounging with wide grins.

I nudge him with an elbow and shake my head. A Darkling from the other team knocks shoulders with Callahan on his way to reset at the line, muttering about betraying the Dark.

He scowls. "When the horn sounds, grab the ball and run, Talia."

We set, the horn blows. I flip over magic, tuck and roll, grab the ball, then blast someone with Ki. Callahan is close, engaging two, while I stare down six.

I drop kick the ball toward the safe space and prepare to fight. Steadily, one swing and step at a time, I approach the safe space.

Callahan rushes toward the line, grabbing the ball up. "Talia."

I duck, blasting my attacker to turn toward him. He's standing on the edge with the ball in hand. One step and he would be safe. He's poised on the edge, but not going over, refusing because he was going to push me to safety first.

My heart races as I stretch my arm out, my hand shaking. Callahan moves to toss the ball to me, and I release Ki. It knocks him off-kilter, and as he recoils, he steps over the line.

The horn blows.

Everyone stares, mouths hanging open. There is a hush that descends on the field, everyone frozen and silent.

Everyone except Callahan. "Natalia!"

"Yes, boss?" I bat my eyelashes.

"What the fuck were you thinking?"

I struggle against a laugh. It's only going to piss him off more, but I lift my hands, palms up and lingering by my shoulders as I shrug. "I promised Mass."

He looks ready to burst with rage.

Mattingly chortles, coming to stand next to him. "She committed suicide to save you. Light saving Dark." He rubs his jaw in consideration. "Weird. Kind of feel bad for hanging you out to dry."

Ignoring the other Darkling, Callahan throws the ball to the middle of the field, and I head to follow.

"Talia."

I freeze, glance over my shoulder to meet his blazing gaze.

"Stop pulling your punches."

I wince, not sure how I feel about killing. It's an odd flavor. I've killed before in defense of others too weak to help themselves, but never out-and-out murder. A game isn't why I was trained.

His voice is low and razor sharp. "They will kill you. Don't hold back anymore. I'm giving you free rein," he says, fists clenched at his sides.

Facing him, my head shies to the side, excitement skittering through me like a puppy trying to find traction on a slick floor. I wouldn't mind seeing what I'm capable of. "You sure about that?"

Jacques laughs. "Free rein to die?"

From behind me someone yells, "Stop talking and get set."

Callahan's gaze never waivers. "Get your ass across this line immediately. That's an order."

I give a mock curtsy before blowing him a kiss. He gave me free rein, and I'm going to take full advantage. "Thanks, Owner-Boss-Master, didn't know that was the name of the game."

Marius joins Mattingly on Callahan's other side. "She's awfully chipper for someone about to die."

"Me, die?" I poke my chest, back peddling. "I'm going to play a game. Games are fun, right?"

Traver toes the line, face full of humor. "The only thing that's kept you alive will be sitting on this sideline. I do applaud you sacrificing yourself for the Dark, though. Didn't think the Light would ever do that."

"Oh, honey," I say, like I'm talking to a child. "I'm not the Light."

They all sneer, but Callahan smirks. "Go. You're allowed to do whatever it takes."

Laughing, I jog to the middle of the field, facing the other team. There's seven staring me down, but I grin.

I have free rein. Callahan said so.

The horn blares. The Darklings fan out, moving to flank and surround me. I get a running start, kicking the ball as hard as I can toward my safe space. It's sailing toward the end of the field until Dark magic grabs it, crumpling and deflating it before throwing it toward their end of the field.

"Well, that's just rude," I say. "Now I'm going to have to run all the way over there to get it."

They all grin and chuckle, one leering. "It's time you were snuffed out, Light."

I dodge stringy black tendrils from one, drop and spin kick another. "Can't we just play the game?"

Backflipping, I avoid the reach of another attack, kicking the Darkling behind me. Centering, I draw Ki, then rush at one of them.

Leverage, body weight, and momentum are my friends, so I use every one of them. I throw myself into a forward handspring, launching myself at him legs first. My legs wrap around his neck, and I spin, dragging him down. I land crouched on my feet, palm at his head to finish him with a wave of Ki.

Lifting my eyes to the others, I laugh. "One of you could have carried that ball across your finish line by now."

Dashing at another, I flip hands over head, pushing off with a wave of Ki for assistance to bound over one. He turns and swings. I block, feign, ducking an attack to hit back.

Dark sinks into my side and I recoil, whimpering as the icy

241

magic stabs through me. I draw it in, baring my teeth at the female Darkling it's emitting from. "That really stings!"

She sneers. I send her magic right back to her. Her shield ripples, unable to fight itself, and she crumples.

I pant, grinning at the remaining five. "No one is going for the ball? Really? No one?" My forearm burns. I glance at it. I haven't obeyed his order to cross over the line. I need to hurry up, the clock is ticking. "Isn't that the point of this?"

They hesitate, looking at each other. "What was that?"

"Mallar's shield was useless."

I stifle my giggle, hands up. "Don't you all lose if you kill me?"

One grins wide, shrugging. "It's worth a loss to put out the Light."

CHAPTER 32

CALLAHAN

Watching Natalia fight Massimo was damn near laughable. I thought she was weak, incapable. Standing in the safe space, my toes against the line, I watch her climb Warryl like he's her personal jungle gym, then take him down. Next is Mallar with her own magic. My little star keeps cracking jokes and grinning like she's having fun.

I might be in love.

Marius asks, "Did the Light bug just channel the Dark?"

Natalia is a rush of Light, throwing her body around, flipping, spinning, and taking down the players one-by-one. I had no idea how much she's been holding back despite me telling her not to.

Traver let's out a low whistle. "All right, Cal. I'm impressed."

Three are left standing. They exchange glances, taking a step away. Natalia cocks her head, then her eyes stretch to take up her whole face as the remaining opposition shifts.

"Ah, fuck me." She gapes, and then laughs. "Er...not really an offer though."

I grind my teeth. Two Shadowbeasts and a Venominx close around her. Her Light flares as the Dark converges on her. Shifted, the players are faster and stronger. Clenching my fingers and jaw, I work to restrain my magic squirming for freedom to interfere and save her.

I can't help. She did this to herself. I hope it hurts, but I'm concerned she won't survive. Pain I'll tolerate. Death is unacceptable.

She keeps fighting. One of the beasts sinks their talons into her side. Her scream splits the air and I clamp down tighter on my jaw and magic.

The shadow beast rips free, blood slinging as his magic wraps around her, another shrill shriek rendering my ears ringing.

I might not be okay with my little star being hurt.

Mattingly sighs. "She did better than I expected."

"Yes," Beatrice says, with a curt hum, then she shrugs, voice chipper. "Oh well, one less glowing whore in the world."

Natalia's eyes are black, filled with the Dark, while her brilliant glow intensifies. I squint, eyes watering to maintain watching as she rams her palm upward into the Faeling's face. It crumples, knees folding as the body goes limp. She yanks free of the strands, doubled over and glowering at the last two.

Retreating from them, she bares her teeth. They pursue in haste, bearing down on her.

Marius chuckles. "She's still fighting. I like that."

My skin crawls with the implication, but I'll worry about his interest another time. I'm focused on my little star, refusing to so much as blink. She flashes, brilliant silver illuminating her, then she's upright and swinging.

Light flashes, the shadow beast flung across the field.

Mattingly scoffs. "How? She's got to be half dead."

She healed. I know it. They don't need to.

The Venominx pounces, taking her down, claws sinking into her torso. Her scream leaves me sickened. "Fucking Mother, that hurts! Stop poking holes in me."

Beatrice laughs. "It was a good show while it lasted, but

Jaboko's got her pinned. There's no way she survives both wounds."

I resist the urge to break something, reminding my Dark we both forfeit our lives if we help.

Dazzling bright bursts from Natalia. Jaboko flips backward, lands on his feet, and lunges back at her as she flips to her feet. Venominxes are tricky like that, their catlike nature lending both agility and the ability to always land on their feet.

The beast is sprinting across the field, as Jaboko struggles with Natalia. She rolls them, landing on top. Dark tendrils wrap around her, twisting from her as she slams her fist into his face, shadows racing down her arm into Jaboko.

She's rolling to her feet. Her head whips around. "Anyone know where the fuck the ball is?"

"Damn," Mattingly mutters, rubbing his face. "Thought she was done for sure."

She faces the beast, hitting the air in front of her, and the world goes white.

I blink spots away. She's running, dead sprinting toward the other end. The beast is following, reaching out with his magic, tendrils racing through the air. She's blind to the attack, and the Dark pierces through her.

She falls forward, the magic dragging her back to the Faeling. "Oh, come on. You could have just let me get the ball and I would have come running right back at you."

Marius chuckles, "Tarim will finish her."

I grin. Tarim gave her the Dark. She'll use it against him. "No."

Natalia kicks and squirms, screaming, "Dude, you're supposed to be going after the ball. Didn't anyone explain the rules to you?"

Traver's laughs. "She's sassy."

I should have been more specific about what free rein meant.

Tarim is grappling, trying to get a solid swing in. Natalia takes his legs out, and they continue the fight on the ground. Breaking free, she rolls backward, throwing her legs over her head, reclaiming her feet. Her eyes are black, her face contorted, and she extends her hand, shadowy Dark tendrils erupting from her palm.

They lash out, needle-like barbs sinking into Tarim, slipping past his shield as if he never called one. He roars, hitting back, his magic streaking into her, then right back at him, until they are woven together with too many strands to count.

"You really should have just played the game," she taunts him with a laugh. She glows, some of the Dark turning shining blue, and Tarim's sharp yell is cut short.

The Dark dissolves, fading away with Tarim's death. She doubles over, hands on her knees as the horn blares, signaling the end of the game.

I take one step toward her, and Marius moves in front of me, arms crossed. "That's not a Light Seraphim."

Flashing teeth, I sidestep him. "No."

"What is she, Cal?"

I step in front of her, limping on stiff knees. "Talia."

She lifts her head, raising her forearm. "This thing is pissed."

The words of her contract are red-edged and puffy. My ears pull back. I'd given her an order she wasn't able to comply with. Reaching out, I run my hand over it, my magic wrapping the seared flesh. "I rescind the order."

"Asshole."

"I also rescind your free rein."

"Whatever." She stands, groans and doubles over, a hand to her abdomen.

I glance for Eloise, but she's busy. There are others much closer to slipping into the afters She will prioritize by those that need the most assistance.

The display of prowess she put on was more than enough to tip off everyone watching. No one is going to believe she is a Light Seraphim. "Heal, Talia."

Her eyes close as she inhales through her cute button nose,

nostrils flaring. She glimmers, her Light pulsing, then she looks up at me. "Um, I'm almost afraid to ask, but you're not going to wring my neck now, are you?"

"I should," I say, offering my hand, "but I won't."

Natalia slips her shaking hand in mine. "Great. Tell me I'm done. I'm done for the day."

Eloise is racing forward, so I hold my hand up, shaking my head. "Natalia is fine."

She slows, brow drawn with confusion. "How?"

My lips twist, chest swelling with pride. "Natalia heals quickly."

Eloise scowls. "Faster than I can heal her?"

"Yes."

Marius is at my shoulder, his partner, Jacques, hovering. Marius's narrows his eyes at Natalia, asking, "What is she?"

"Mine."

He narrows his eyes. "By right of royal, I demand to know what you brought into Ilbuio."

Damn him. It's an unfair advantage he has to make me share my secrets for his benefit. "Natalia is Magia."

Eloise frowns. "You would disgrace yourself by lying?"

I bristle with indignation. "No. How dare you?"

"Magia are useless. Everyone knows that."

Natalia laughs, doubling over in hysterics.

I raise an eyebrow at her antics, then face Eloise. "We assume so, yes, but she is Magia, and far from useless."

Natalia chortles, upright. "Why the fuck do you all think we're so weak? Your kind made us."

Marius crosses his arms, tilting his face toward her. "Which is why we know what you aren't capable of. You're mostly human."

Eloise steps closer. "Magia weren't capable of controlling either Light or Dark. I wasn't aware they still existed at all."

Natalia hums, pressing her lips and turning away.

I shrug. "They're breeding for power."

Marius curls his lip. "It appears to be working. We should discuss this with my father after the games."

I incline my head to him. "If he desires, I will comply. Talia," I squeeze her hand in mine. "We are going."

MASSIMO MAKES A FIST. NATALIA BUMPS HERS AGAINST IT grinning. He smiles, showing off perfect teeth too white against his cool, deep brown skin. "Good job, Little Light."

I push Natalia toward our bedroom. "Go change."

She bobs her head. "How am I dressing?"

"Formal."

She disappears into our room as I turn to Massimo, baring my teeth. "You're too important to kill, but I'm tempted to carry out my threat to cut your dick off."

Massimo crosses his arms, staring me down without remorse. "Why?"

"She hit me to knock me over that line."

"I saw." He shrugs. "Everyone saw. I think half the audience about died in shock."

I scoff, one hand on my hip, the other dragging down my features. "Our team too. I don't care about that. I care that she did it because of the promise she made you."

His eyebrows raise, boredom weighting the rest of his face. "Your point?"

My fingers curl. "I wanted her across the line. Safe."

"Did you make that clear to her?"

I scowl, head tilting, asking if he's stupid without words.

"Then she disobeyed you, so I'm not sure why you're yelling at me."

"Because it's your fucking fault."

248

Massimo sighs, dropping his hands to his hips. "She did what I would have. You're the contractor. Your life is more important. In fact, you wouldn't have hesitated if it was me, you would have crossed the line on your own."

"She's not you."

"No, she's harder to kill than me. You're treating her differently. Stop it."

Natalia steps out of the bedroom in a black dress. It's a second skin of soft fabric that stretches tight against her, highlighting her subtle curves. The choice she made has long sleeves, the hem ending two inches past her butt. There's no possible way she's wearing anything beneath, or it would be visible.

'Great, that's going to torment me.'

'I like it,' my Dark whispers back. *'Let me touch it.'*

She steps past me. I cut my eyes to her back, the marks down her back on display, the dress open from shoulders to the top of her ass, confirming my suspicions that all that is in my way of seeing her on display is that flimsy fabric that would be so easy to tear.

I turn to her as she grabs the bottle of bourbon and starts chugging. Her eyes find mine, holding my gaze as she downs the bottle. Grimacing, she sets the empty container to the side, then shudders. "A, that's so gross. I want vodka. And B, I agree with Mass. Stop treating me different."

My Dark turns giddy. *"That's cute."*

"No, its not. They are banding together and turning on me. Damnit."

Sneering, I point a finger, waving it between them. "You two need to remember I don't take orders. I give them."

Natalia struggles against a laugh. "Cal."

"You are different, like it or not, I don't care. I can replace him." I jerk my head at Massimo. "Not you. A Light fuck is never going to submit to a contract or serve the Dark. You say Magia aren't commonly Light, so both of you need to remember who is in charge here and do what the fuck I say, when the fuck I say, without a fucking word of pushback." I inhale to catch my breath, unsure of when I started yelling.

Massimo frowns, turning his face away. "That's the point. We serve you, which means giving our life for yours."

Natalia crosses her arms, leaning against the table to stick her legs out, crossed at the ankles. "Look, Master-Owner-Boss, it's easier for me to keep myself alive than to try to keep you and me alive simultaneously."

Amused, I lift my eyebrow. "Thought you didn't do anything the easy way?"

She opens her mouth, hesitates, then bursts into laughter. "Fair point. Fine, when I fuck that up, would you like to die? Or should I?"

My eyes narrow in my annoyance, jaw set. I'm trying to ignore the fact that I can make out her hard nipples beneath the pathetic excuse for coverage. My Dark is making zero effort to do the same.

She shrugs. "I don't take the easy way out, but I'm not stupid either. You contracted me to do this, so let me do it."

Massimo chuckles. "She's right. You named her your partner. You can't have her sit on the sidelines."

This is a nightmare. I don't know where the sudden sense of camaraderie came from. It's my worst afters when they decide to stand against me. I shove a hand through my hair. "When I tell you to do something, do it, or I'll let my contract tear you apart. That goes for both of you."

Massimo shrugs. Natalia rolls her eyes. They're going to ruin me if this keeps up.

Natalia picks up an unopened bottle from the mix of options, checking the label. She then inspects other available choices, shrugs, and picks one, cracking its lid.

I step forward, snagging it from her grasp, setting it aside. "Mass, go get vodka."

The door snaps shut as he leaves to comply. I grab Natalia by her narrow hips and yank her against me. My magic purrs, twisting away from me to slither over her. She tips her head back, and I rub my hands up her ribs then down over her hips, feeling along her to confirm my suspicions. Nothing.

She's going to be the most abhorrent test of self-control. One I want to fail.

"Little Star," I grind out. "Behave."

"I did."

I grab her dainty neck, fingers wrapping around the base of her jaw. Dark seeps from my skin, tendrils twisting around her throat. My Dark is salivating and humming with greed as it soaks in her Light.

I want her just like this, wound tight in my Dark and a bit breathless. The pulse point in her neck beneath my hand speeds up. "I expected you to cross before me, and allow me to reiterate, the only one in a game that is off limits is me. *Me*. I am off limits, as in, if you attack me again, I suggest you run. Run as fast as you can and pray to whatever gods you want for mercy, because I will have none."

CHAPTER 33
NATALIA

I'M WAITING ON THE COUCH WHEN MASSIMO RETURNS WITH TWO bottles of vodka, as well as a bourbon to replace the one I managed to gag down.

He extends one vodka to me and winks. "Don't listen to him. You promised me."

Callahan steps out of our shared room, scowling. "Mass, I will fucking break something on you. Quit it."

Snickering, Massimo deposits the two other bottles on the drink table. "She can heal me."

"She'll be under order to not, and I will change your contract if you push this, and when we go home, I'll stick you on dish duty."

"It'll be a vacation."

Callahan rubs the side of his jaw and sighs. I take the opportunity to crack the lid on my new bottle, but Callahan plucks it from my grasp. "You already drank an entire bottle of hundred-year-old bourbon."

"But you sent him to get me vodka," I pout.

"Yes." He extends his free hand. "We have free time until the second round." He checks his watch. "That's two runes."

Massimo asks, "What do you want me doing?"

I shrug. "You have free time until we reconvene. I'm taking Natalia, this," he holds the vodka up, "and I'm disappearing for a bit to relax."

Sliding his hands into his front pockets, Massimo rolls to the balls of his feet and stretches his shoulders back. "Understood."

Callahan wiggles fingers at me, so I slip my hand into his. He leads me out of the room, through corridors of stone and intricate ceilings. I keep quiet, not sure of protocol, if I'm allowed to speak or if I'm supposed to be acting as a good vassal.

He stops at a window, shoving one side, the decorative glass structure rotating, and he pulls me through the opening onto a small stone path before shoving it back into place.

The foliage lining the stones is thick and the path narrow, so I trail a step behind him, even though he maintains his grip on me until we come to an open, round clearing in the lush garden. At the far end, a massive, twisted tree grows.

The bark is black, and sapphire illumination glitters from the cracks of the skin. Mesmerized, I pull free of Callahan, stepping toward it.

"Hysterium," he says, following. "It grows from Dark, feeding off it."

"A tree that grows from Dark?"

"A vine, technically."

I eye the gorgeous entity. The trunks are interweaving, thick and warped. "Looks like a tree, but like, a million years old."

"It's older. About four million, I think. It's the largest one in existence, but Ilbuio is full of Dark for it to feed from."

"It's beautiful."

He hums, staring at it with soft features.

I step closer, tilting my head back to take in the massive top end. Vine-like branches are full of purply-blue flowers, and thin chords that end in elongated crystals dangle overhead. I reach toward one, and it turns black, Dark coiling around it in tendrils of smoke.

253

I pull back, not wanting to hurt it. "Guess it doesn't like me either."

Callahan chuckles. "You're the Light."

I hug myself, nodding. "Yeah, I got it. Dark doesn't like me. Ever since we got here, I've felt wrong."

He steps behind me, bending his arm around me to offer the bottle, his other hand brushing the back of his knuckles down my arm. "I wondered if the Dark would try to extinguish you. It sounds like it's trying."

"Great. Thanks." I rip the vodka from his grip, twisting the cap.

His hand land on my shoulders, squeezing, followed by his thumbs dragging through tense muscles along my spine. "I was betting you were strong enough to withstand it."

"You were gambling with my life? Nice." I start chugging.

He kisses the back of my head. "It was a safe bet. Your Light is strong."

Taking a breather from the bottle, I lick my lips. I'm not certain where this affection came from, the soft touches of his hands and mouth. It scares me.

Clearing my throat, I ask, "This is what you do with your free time? Stare at vines?"

It's a safer topic for my alcohol-soaked brain to follow than the butterflies in my stomach. Callahan is wicked temptation with his handsome face and pouty lips.

He sighs, moving away to a stone bench nearby, dropping onto it. Fatigue rolls off him, his back hunched so he rests his elbows on his knees. His hands wrap around the back of his neck as he hangs his head.

I step to him, my heels clacking against the stone in the dreary ambiance. Offering the vodka, I say, "Drink. It helps."

Lifting his face, he asks, "Helps what?"

"Everything. Tired? Drink. Stressed? Drink. Anxiety? Headache? Have to rip heads off and fight for your life? Drink."

"Have to marry your sister's ex?"

I shrug. "Drink."

He shakes his head. "Are you dependent on liquor?"

"Are you asking me if I'm an alcoholic?" I shrug. "Alcohol is technically a solution."

The ghost of a smile pulls one side of his lips back. "Yes, I stare at vines." He snags the bottle. "And trees."

I twist to plop next to him, basking in the glorious hysterium. "I mean, it's awe-inspiring. You should get one for your place."

He takes another drink before returning the bottle. "I've tried. Well, I've tried to add one to my collection. I've been unsuccessful."

I cut my eyes to him. "Your collection?"

"I have collected fifty-seven different species trees."

"You're joking."

"No. I've tried to cultivate hysterium, even in the garden, but it dies every time." He sighs. "I don't know why. No one really knows why it grows some places and not others. It's the only known plant that feeds on Dark, but that's really all we know about it. It's as much a mystery today as it was to the Ancients."

He's staring at it with longing, an open honesty to his voice. "Really?" I point at the hysterium. "Trees? Well, at least plants. That's your thing?"

He glowers at me. "What's wrong with trees?"

"Nothing," I laugh. "It's just, I don't know, I expected skulls of the dead, or maybe a serious weapons collection."

He cocks his jaw, eyes narrowing with disgust, then he turns away. "I have those things too," he drawls, tone snide. "Generations worth."

I nudge him. "You surprised me."

"Because the Dark isn't supposed to–"

"Don't go dragging Light and Dark into this. They have nothing to do with it."

He stares at me with a peculiar frown.

255

"What?" I shrug, taking a drink. "I just never pictured you as a botanist."

He chuckles. "All right, you might have the Light, but you aren't Light."

"I have been telling you that. Only said it a thousand times."

I finish the vodka, the world fuzzy on the edge of my brain. Kicking my heels off, I bend my knees, curling in half to cuddling against him. "Can I ask you something?"

His arm drapes over me, his Dark slithering and twisting around me. "Anything."

"What are the markings on your back? Are they like mine for using Dark?"

Callahan tenses, his breathing stilling. "No."

The word is clipped. I give up on expecting any further response, turning my attentions back to the hysterium. It appears to have three gnarled trunks that spread out and wrap together, each trunk made from dozens of bunches, each formed by smaller vines twisting together. It's gigantic, creating a canopy of the dangling violet petals and crystals hanging and glinting in the fog.

It's damn romantic. That realization makes me want to puke.

Callahan's voice jerks me back to my senses. "It's a protection spell."

I jerk away, lifting my eyes to his. "Spells aren't real. Witchcraft is made up nonsense."

He flashes teeth. "It's not common knowledge. As far as I'm aware, it's an edge I have over the competition, but the marks are a spell."

My mouth is hanging open, so I close it. I lean my back into him, rough stone beneath my bare feet. "I'm going to need a bit more than that."

"No, you *want* more than that."

"Sure." I tip my head back against his shoulder.

"It's old magic. The kind that grew wild when the Ancients roamed the world."

"How do you know it? Or did someone else do that to you?"

"Little Star." The nickname carries a warning.

I pout, whining, "I'm curious."

He relaxes, pulling me into his lap. Half-drunk, I'm happy to snuggle in with my head on his shoulder, eyes slipping closed. He's warm, opposed to his Dark curling around me, wrapping me up in him. "I've already told you more than I ever intended to, but Vanessa mentioned you don't react well when someone hides things from you."

"Nope," I say. "Just...put it in my contract that I can't ever repeat it or whatever."

"I have something. An old something."

"That book Ness says I'm not allowed to see?" He mutters about contempt, so I nudge him with my elbow. "Stop it."

A deep rumble shakes his chest. "You're aware I hold your contract and I'm in charge, right?"

"Sure," I say with a yawn.

"What did she say? She might have put herself in contempt."

"She told me," I say with vehemence, "not to ever go in her room, to always knock, that she was using a dead language to translate this mysterious book so you could learn new magic." I fight to quash the fury rising in my chest. "She told me to never ask about it, that I was to never have anything to do with, that you didn't even want me so much as in the same room as what she was working on, and that, that was all she was saying, and she only did it to avoid contempt."

He hums.

"If you hurt Ness, I hurt you."

Callahan squeezes me. "That will put you in contempt. Behave."

"This old book that I'm not allowed to see or know about, what is it?"

"You expect me to tell you despite being aware I don't want you to have this information?"

"I'm asking you to."

"This isn't for the Light."

"You just said I'm not the Light."

He laughs, then presses his lips against my temple. "It's a holy text of the Dark, and your Light isn't going to care what I say. Stay away from it."

I nod against him. "Will do. How does it work? The spell."

His voice twists. "So you can kill me?"

I pick my head up, blinking sticky eyelids at him. "Dude," I frown. "I'm not going to kill you."

He peers with disbelief etched into his face. "Light burns out the Dark until it no longer exists."

I grin. "Not Light, so, I promise."

He taps the end of my nose. I startle, crossing my eyes trying to see the tip. "It's protection, that's all I'm saying."

"Fine." I snuggle in, shuddering with a full body yawn. "I'm still promising not to kill you."

His fingers brush my hair away from my face. "It's my magic. It's more complicated, a lot more. When I cast the spell, I almost killed myself."

My fingers curl into his shirt, "Don't do that. I kind of like you."

"Little Star," he says with a rumble, mouth curving against me.

"Why'd you almost send yourself to the afters?"

"The spell, it consumed damn near all my magic. I knew the risks and took precautions. Secluded myself. Massimo was the only one to know. I knew I'd need protection if I survived, so I needed him with me. It took several seasons for me to recover enough to be comfortable that I'd be able to protect myself, even longer until my magic returned to full strength."

My limbs are heavy, and I'm comfortable, falling down the rabbit hole. Giving in to another yawn, I press my face into the side of his neck.

"It's how I survived the smite. The one you retaliated to on my behalf."

"Oh."

"Thank you." His voice is so quiet I almost miss it. "I wasn't aware it was coming. In such a public place with so much noise and movement, I didn't even notice the charge building, so I never shielded."

I open my eyes, shifting to meet his gaze. "I really did save your life."

"Yes." The right side of his lips hitches up. "I didn't even know what happened until I came to in my bedroom and was informed of the events."

He's breathtaking. I reach out tracing his smile. "It's only because I thought you were a hot guy who needed help."

In jest, he nips at my fingertips. I grin with my tongue between my teeth as he chuckles. "I was."

Snorting through my nose, I worm into him again. He strokes his fingers through my hair, and I shiver in pleasure, closing my eyes, enjoying this moment. My Darkling might be wicked, but he's beautiful and honest.

CHAPTER 34
NATALIA
4TH BLOOM'S DAY, HEATWAVE, 4049 6TH MILLENNIUM

BREATHING HARD, I STARE AT CAL. HE'S OUT OF BREATH TOO, BUT grinning. His hair is a mess. My muscles are rubbery. "That was fun."

Chuckling, he shakes his head, taking a few steps away.

He turns, surveying the massive creature we took down. Cal had called it something. I don't remember what. I was trying to keep him alive while helping to kill it before it killed us.

Days have gone by with us fighting for our lives and engaging in twisted games. It's getting easier. We are sinking into a rhythm that works, communicating with mere glances and head nods. Falling in sync has made us a stronger pair, better equipped to work together.

From beneath its corpse, something wiggles free. It's a miniature version of the beast, with wings of black velvet tucked against its body. It yips, wagging a tail with a cute tuft of lime green hair, somewhere between wolf and dragon. Stumbling forward, it yips, spinning in circles as it chases its tail, biting at it.

The strings of my heart are tugged. The beast had drooled green acid and breathed putrid smog that choked me, burning my lungs, but this is a baby. It stops, neon green eyes that glimmer fixing on me.

It crouches, butt in the air, tail wagging. My eyes sting. The beast wasn't trying to kill us.

I wipe at my nose, blinking away the stinging. "It was protecting its baby."

I kneel, sitting back on my heels and holding out a hand. It stumbles and flops toward me, stopping short to growl.

I wrinkle my nose, snapping fingers. "Come here."

It sits back on hind legs, snarling.

"No one's gonna hurt you."

It watches, head tilting and ears flopping in adorableness as I inch forward.

"Talia." Cal crouches next to me on the balls of his feet. He grabs my hands. "Seowolves are deadly, even this young they're venomous."

"Well, it's a good thing I'm immune to being poisoned to death." I laugh, pulling my hands free, crawling to it.

As it tries to run, I grab it by its scruff, lifting. It's hanging limp in my grip, paws curling in toward its body, whining. I pull it close, cuddling it against my chest with it on its back. Taking care to not put too much pressure on its wings, I smile. "Hi, little one. It's okay, I'm not going to hurt you."

Cal sighs, "Put it down before it kills you."

Grinning, I roll my eyes at it. "You're not gonna hurt me, are you?" I lower my face closer to it, it licks my nose, leaving slobber behind. "Yeah, you're a good–" I check its stomach "–boy. You're a good boy."

"Talia." He runs a hand down his face.

I glance at him. "What?"

He shakes his head. "No."

"Come on, it's a baby. Look how cute he is. Besides, think about it as a pet. If we raise it? Train it? It's a badass security system for you."

261

He eyes me, then drops his sight to the creature. "Fair point. Come on." Cal stands.

We walk to the arena gate, but the guards shift, blocking our exit. "A beast still lives." The woman grins.

I freeze, my eyes lowering to the baby cuddled in my arms. It stares up at me, long, forked black tongue flopping out, head tipped back like it's having fun going for a ride without a care in this world.

Cal reaches out to scoop the pup out of my grasp in one large hand. I remain motionless, arms cradling emptiness against my chest, my heart squeezing.

It was a baby, not even mean.

He lifts it up, pulling it from my view. My arms drop to my sides. I dare not to even breathe. It was cute and sweet, with floppy ears. The warmth from the creature fades from my skin.

There's a couple of whimpers, a yipe, then silence. I don't move. I don't do anything except fight back tears.

The guards relax, stepping aside to allow us to leave. Cal walks past me. I blink at his back, screaming in my mind for my body to move.

It jerks forward like a puppet manipulated by clunky strings. I inhale sharp through my nose and straighten my spine as I follow Cal back to our chambers. I walk, unseeing into the shared bedroom, sitting on the edge of the bed.

The mattress dips, Cal's weight settling next to me. "Little Star, look at me."

I blink, my lashes clumping together. "It was helpless and adorable."

His hands cup my face, thumbs wiping over my cheek bones. Concern flitters across his face, his thick dark eyebrows pulling together. Sighing out his nose, he presses his forehead to mine. "You'll be okay."

"But it isn't. It was just a baby. It–"

"Sh." He pulls me into his lap, cradling me against him. "I made it quick."

His strength and magic envelope me as I sob. "I hate them. All of them, and these stupid games, and you."

Holding me tighter, he presses his lips to my forehead.

"H-how do you do this?" I lean away, meeting his black eyes.

A bereft haze claims his features, his eyes half closing as he look away and swallows hard. "Welcome to the Dark, Little Star."

I DRESS FOR DINNER, BARELY MANAGING LIPSTICK AND MASCARA. MY chest aches. For the first time in my life, I'm not hungry. My tongue has a sour taste in my mouth, and there's a bottomless pit threatening to eat my Ki deep within my core.

The twisted trials are awful, but until now waking up with Cal and the little moments we share when we escape the games and others have been enough to gloss over the pains. He's done this for centuries, but the way he looked at me, lost and fractured, had penetrated deep into my heart. It hurts him too.

Cal keeps my fingers gripped tight, giving me gentle squeezes. I move in a daze, exhausted from days on end of pain and death. There are more and more empty seats at the table every time we sit down for a meal, making my heart hurt.

The first course is served. I frown at the shiny metal dome over my plate. No one else is given one.

With trembling fingers, I raise it up. Red fluid is congealed, coating the bottom of the shallow dish, and what is in the middle isn't food.

I slam the lid, but too late, the image of the young pup's severed head is seared in my brain. My hands slip into my lap as I stare at the dome.

Cal lifts it, sighs, then rests the cover back into place. "Take mine."

"Please don't make me."

He nods.

I stare at my reflection in the polished silver, trying to dig that sight from my brain as everyone else eats.

The second course is delivered, and again I get a silver-domed plate. Peeking beneath the lid, I catch sight of a vibrant green tuft of hair. I drop the lid, slumping back in my seat. I didn't want to eat, not sure if I'd even get food down or keep it down, but I would have preferred force feeding myself to this.

I sit, straight backed and silent, trying to focus on the carved decoration in the edge of the table.

On the third course, I lift the lid and the body flops out, tiny legs with massive paws that once held promise for the pup to grow big and strong. It's too big for me to cover, the body sprawling from beneath the metal dome. I retch, and Cal reaches for my hand beneath the table.

I pull free. He did this. He killed it.

Cal rests his hand on my thigh instead. It stays there through the course, even when dessert is served. The silver platter set in front of me is a tall crystal cup with a decorative stem. It's full of layered creamy substances topped with a green eyeball, hazed with death, like a cherry on top.

I pick up the spoon to push the body part out of sight into the whipped cream before setting the silverware aside.

When it is cleared away and after dinner drinks are served, I get nothing. Slumping lower in my seat, I breathe out in relief that I'll be spared from further courses of dismembered pup.

The table falls silent as we all wait for the King to decide what comes next. Some nights there are games, other evenings, we are granted the time to do as we please.

The Dark King calls out. "Did you enjoy dinner, Light?"

Cal squeezes my leg. Without looking at the King, I respond, not able to muster fury or hatred. "No offense to your chef, but I found it completely inedible."

Massimo coughs next to me, covering his mouth with a closed fist.

I continue to scan the decorative ceiling as the King answers, "How unfortunate. Please, allow me to make this indiscretion right."

Without transferring my gaze, I twist my face in his general direction. "Your concern is touching, but I'm fine, thank you."

"I insist." His voice hardens.

Fingers snap. There is movement elsewhere, something dragging across the stone flooring, then everything goes still.

The Dark King's voice echoes around the room. "Stand up and open the box."

Cal tenses. Massimo curses under his breath. I twiddle my thumbs still staring at the massive balustrades supporting the arched ceilings as my heart rate picks up and sweat beads along the hairline. Tonight is focused on me and me alone.

I turn my eyes on the King, his face full of wicked glee. I sigh, too broken to even try to twist a smile of hatred. Next to me a whispered breath from Cal orders me to comply with the demand.

Standing, Cal's hand slips from my thigh, and I walk around the table, my heels clicking against the stone as I approach the box. I squeeze my fingers then flex my hands open, frowning at the present.

It's a few feet wide square, wrapped with a big blood-red bow. There is not a shred of me that believes this is a gift.

As I reach for the ribbon, the King says, "Stop. I think your petulance has irked me."

I let my hand fall, and for one fraction, I pretend he'll rescind the gift so I can sit down. I almost laugh at myself for even thinking such a thing. My arms hang limp at my side as I wait.

"Smile, Lightning Bug, you're too pretty to frown."

I twist my lips with vinegar and fire. Telling a woman to smile is like asking to be bit, no matter her mood.

"No, I don't think that's enough. I've offered you a gift, and your sourness wounds me."

Pivoting on my heels, I sneer. "Then I'll sit down, and you can keep your gift."

There's a collective gasp of shock from the table.

The King scowls. "Marius, my boy, help the lightning bug see reason."

A chair scrapes against the floor. "Yes, father."

Marius moves in front of me, and he leers at me, the flick of red in his eye shifting with his pupils as he inspects my body. He reaches out and tips my chin up with a finger, sliding along the underside of my jaw to wrap his hand around my throat.

Dark slithers around my neck even as his fingers dig in. "Smile."

Squaring my shoulders, I force my lips to curl, baring my teeth in warning the way predators do.

He pulls me a step into him and spins us, so we face everyone sitting at the table.

His nose nuzzles my ear. "Isn't that so much better? You're so much prettier when you smile."

His Dark is crawling over my chest and shoulders, sliding beneath the fabric of my dress. Not even Cal is so brazen with my body, and he owns me. Flicking my gaze to the wall behind the spectators, I avoid looking at Cal and Massimo as I center, drawing on my Ki, waiting.

We stand there, all eyes on us as his magic slips over my skin. I quiver, tensing against shaking at the repugnant touch of his magic. It's too much like a caress of my skin, stirring abhorrence at being touched without permission. Disgust is boiling in my gut, like angry acid at the violation.

His free hand slips one of the straps of my dress down my shoulder, his hand following it to drag along my arm. The brush of his lips against the top of my shoulder leaves the tiny hairs along my spine tingling with warning.

"How vulgar that the Light infected something so beautiful." His hand travels back up my arm, then his fingers trail across my chest, tracing the edge of the low v-neck to stop between my breasts.

I clamp my jaw, and decide I'm done behaving. Cal will be furious with me later, but I'm done being nice. If the Dark wants to play a game, then I'll play. We will see who wins.

Drawing air through my nose, I close my eyes. His Dark is all over me, and I drink it in.

His mouth opens against my neck, warm and wet. It lingers, then he sinks his teeth into me.

Pulling back as I jerk, he chuckles. "What would you do if I decided to have you, right here, right now for everyone to watch?"

"As you disgust me, I believe that would be referred to as rape, and I advise you reconsider."

He grins against my ear, his voice staying a throaty whisper. "Cal is watching."

"Everyone is." I keep my eyes closed, ignoring the way they burn from humiliation. Everyone is watching him touch me, running his hands and magic over my body. They're doing nothing to stop this sick display, and it feeds my rage and revolution alike.

He slips fingers under the edge of my dress, the pads of his fingers rough against the thin skin of my breast. "Do you think he would save you? He wouldn't."

Attempting to remain cavalier, I force a smirk, but there's nothing I can do to stop trembling in his grasp. Instead, I focus on absorbing his Dark to meld his magic to my use with Ki. "I don't need him to save me."

His hand grabs at the fabric on my thigh, starting to bunch it up with his fingers, working to drag it higher and higher.

I lift my voice. "I am advising against this."

"Or what?" He snickers in my ear, getting the skirt hiked high enough that he can push it out of the way, his hand against the bare skin of my leg. He pins the dress with his wrist to draw a circle over my thigh with his thumb.

"You're crossing a line."

He laughs, fingers settling against my inner thigh, sharp pointed nails scraping over my skin.

I slam my elbow back into his side, his nails sinking into my thigh as he growls in response. My leg stings, pulsing with heat.

He retracts his fingers, recoiling a half-step. "That was stupid, Little Light."

I grit my teeth and open my eyes, turning to face him with a wide grin. "Stupid was giving me your magic."

He takes a step away, horror alive in his features as I lift a hand, Dark coiling around my fingers and wrist, stretching along my forearm. I give it a look of consideration before facing him.

"I'm not the Light. I'm Magia, and I don't need Callahan for a fucking thing."

He stumbles in an attempt to flee from me as I reach out with the cold fury of the Dark, thick, black tendrils racing forward. He throws up a block, but his own magic cleaves right through it, wrapping around his neck. I yank him back to me, sending more Dark to wrap up his legs, forcing him to his knees before me.

Snarling, he blasts me with magic.

I flinch and grit my teeth, absorbing it as I wince at the singe it leaves radiating through my core, then bare my teeth. "The next time you want to touch a woman, I suggest you have her consent."

"You can't–" he pants "–do this."

"Who is going to stop me?" I twist his words. "Your father? He isn't going to save you."

"Bitch," Marius manages. "You'll die for this."

I smile down at him struggling on his knees, wrapped in tendrils of Dark like a furious puppet on strings fighting his puppet master. "You think you're capable of killing me? Really? I could send you to the afters without effort."

There's so much Dark built up inside of me, demanding to be unleashed. It sings with fury at the way he touched me, an ache that the pup didn't deserve to die. That they'd kill it for game then feed it to me was sickening.

I slap my palm to his forehead, forging my rage with the Dark as I ram it back into him. "Consent is important, asshole."

He snarls, skin shifting to a marbled black and blood red, bones breaking, but the change reverts as he goes limp. Dark and blood alike dribbling out of the orifices in his head like oozing ichor.

The Dark is ebbing out of me slower, so I step from his body, releasing the last of it. There's absolute silence in the room as I face the table. My inner thigh is stinging, throbbing and wet from where Marius managed to pierce me with his nails.

Spinning on my stiletto heels, I stare down the King. His displeasure is evident in every crease and wrinkle of his face, but I grin. "Your move."

CHAPTER 35
NATALIA

THE KING GLARES. "WE'LL FINISH OUR GAME, BUT SINCE YOU decided to throw a tantrum, you'll get the choice—Callahan can pay for your indiscretion, or you can face twice the challenge."

I cock my jaw, giving him all the airs of mock consideration. My contract includes protection of Cal, so deflecting a punishment will put me in contempt. Besides, I earned this, albeit acting in self-defense. I'm not going to run scared or try to avoid it.

"You know what?" I force a laugh. "I'm having so much fun. Fuck it. I'll double down."

Wood scrapes against stone as the King slides from his seat to stand. He's taller than I realized, carrying himself with dignified superiority as he stalks toward me, his cane tapping the floor in an eerie pattern of sound.

Up close, I can see the same red mark in his eye that Marius has, the only bright thing to his skin and features. "Give me your hand."

With an eye roll, I stick out my hand. His wraps his fingers around my wrist, his hand blurring and shifting to deep red-and-black marbled skin with red tipped claws.

"My son already pierced your skin, infecting you. Another dose will only add to my amusement," he purrs, thin lips spreading with cruel mirth. His four fingers wrapping around me dig into the sensitive, thin skin of my wrist. "I could tell you what my lineage is capable of, my special little skill, but that would ruin the surprise." He chuckles low as he withdraws, leaving behind bloody imprints of his claws.

Frowning at them, I shrug, letting my arm hang at my side. "It sounds like I'll be having a blast. I can't wait."

The King hesitates, shoulders tensing, then he begins to move again. Eloise helps him into his chair, setting his cane aside as she stares at me with a grim expression. I wait, the King taking a long drink from his silver chalice. He eyes me, watching, no doubt giving whatever he injected me with in his nails time to manifest.

My thigh is stinging, so I send a few pulses of Ki through me to close the wound. The room begins to warm. My head thickens, an odd rhythm to the squelch of my heart in my ears.

I draw Ki, centering to prepare to fend off poison, but other than warm, I feel no signs of erosion.

I glance around, catching sight of Tony leaning against a pillar nearby. I jerk, putting a hand to my chest. "The fuck are you doing here? Ah, shit." I wince, bracing for the contract to lash out, but nothing happens.

He makes no answer.

My skin tickles, like something on the edge of my peripheral senses is watching me. I twist my back to Tony, instead staring into gray eyes that mirror my own. I suck in a breath, my voice hoarse. "You?"

Sasha smiles with closed lips, her dainty and perfect features muted with melancholy. "Little sister, you don't look so good. You're a bit pale, and I do mean paler than usual."

I blink, heart racing. It's been so long since I've seen her. Words fail me, clogged in my throat.

Clicking her tongue, Sasha shakes her head. Her golden curls flounce around her head, big and loose and perfect. "I won't fix this for you, and you know you can't handle this on your own. You're not as good as I am, not as smart, not as quick, nor even as pretty." She giggles. "Oh, dear sister, whatever have you gotten yourself into? Didn't you listen?"

"Don't go too deep," I whisper. "Keep your head above water by staying where you can stand."

My sister bobs her head, clasping hands before her. "That's right! You didn't teach Nicky the way I taught you, though. You didn't help him. You weren't ever able to, too weak."

I snarl, recoiling, snapping at the air like a rabid animal. "Leave him out of this."

"How can I after what you did?" She checks her nails. "Or I suppose that is, what you didn't do." Her eyes are full of malice as they find mine.

"It wasn't just me." I point a finger, venom in my words as I shout. "It was your job too, and you failed him as much as I did."

"Do you think Cal could ever care about you? You're weak, too tender-hearted, too soft for someone with his strength. He's just using you, and you can't go home. You'll never be as good as me, it's why you'll never be as loved as I am."

I frown at the contract. Sasha wouldn't know I left the Magia. Cal changed my contract to prevent me from talking to Tony. It never seared me in contempt for speaking to Tony.

'Sasha is dead. This little chat isn't real.'

My eyes flicker to the King as he watches with a tug on the corner of his mouth. "Oh, that's fucking great. I'm hallucinating now, is that it? Thanks. This is going to be so much fun. When's the second half of this starting?"

He lowers his cup, dangling it from his fingertips. "Open the box."

I roll my eyes, pivoting toward the box. Instead, I find my

father staring at me with repulsion. Shaking his head with hands on his hips, he mutters, "You're an absolutely disgusting failure, the wrong children died."

Chortling, I flip him off. "I know for a fact this isn't real. You'd think my own mind would know how to properly hallucinate something to make it seem real."

Batting at the air, I walk through my father. He vanishes in a swirl of colored fog that spreads out and around me. I flounder, lost, until the clouds part to revel a giant present with a blood-red bow.

I yank the ribbon, tugging it free. The air is warm and humid, sweat prickling out of my pores to roll in beads down my body. I close my eyes, standing on a beach, basking in the suns. Ness laughs at something nearby, and a salted breeze wafts a cool relief across my hot flesh.

Shuddering, I brush away the memory. It's not a pleasant one, containing a moment I believed I wouldn't survive. I had been terrified to the core, frozen by fear and helpless to do anything to save myself.

I open my eyes to a deep red ribbon shimmering in my hand. Frowning, I wonder where it came from. It rises and falls, dancing and twisting like a snake performing a ballet. Releasing it, I rub my eyes, the world around me engulfed in a haze of pastel pinks that shimmer gold.

A voice floats through the haze. "Open the lid."

An enormous box sits before me, glowing under a mysterious spotlight. With shaking hands, I reach out, popping the top, pulling it off to the side, then peering into the cavern within. As I loom over the opening, hissing smoke billows out of the box in violet and blue plumes tinged with stars and confetti.

I blink at the thing rising from the box, its multiple heads on long bodies of slick, shimmering black scales. Fine black tongues dart from fanged mouths to taste the air. I squeal with joy, reaching out toward the bobbing and weaving serpent heads. "Fun noddles! Oh, if Ness were here, she'd love you."

Trying to stroke one, it recoils, hissing and striking with speed, sinking its fangs into my hand. I jerk away, sucking in a breath as I shake my hand, pulling it closer to my chest for protection, merely succeeding in drawing the thing closer, the teeth sunk into me. "Ah, fuck, you're real and that hurts. Let go!"

I shake my hand, and the serpent dissolves to ash. A burn rolls up my arm, warning me of the injection of some venom or other. I try to center to draw on Ki, but I wobble. The world spins, the air colorful and glittering. I stumble a few steps, then scream as more serpent heads streak forward, fangs pierce into me.

Laughter echoes around me in the pretty mist. I swat at the heads of the snakes, and they turn to dust, filtering into the air as glitter.

I spin around, the burn igniting to a full inferno in my blood, scalding my innards. Sasha. Tony. My father. They're watching with disdain.

More heads are rising from the mist, licking the air, following the scent of blood. I try to blast them with Ki, but I can't focus enough to draw it. They attack, and I flounder, whimpering and falling over. Twisting, I land on my elbow, pain lancing up my limb.

The thing strikes again, long fangs piercing my flesh to bury deep within me. I shriek at the flare of searing pain.

Tony crouches next to me, snickering. "You really thought you were too good for me? I had the best. You were just sloppy seconds."

I kick while trying to crawl away, yelling at him. "You have a four-inch bent dick, so you don't get to say shit. Now shut up." I grab at heads to yank them free, but they decompose beneath my touch, scales flittering away.

An agonizing burn is rolling through my muscles as I force

them to work. Cal kneels in front of me, staring down his nose. I glare back. "The fuck do you want?"

Shaking his head, face to the floor, he sighs. "I wanted to use you, and this is the best you can do?"

"Yeah, well, fuck you too then. This isn't exactly–Fucking Mother," I scream as several more heads find purchase in my flesh.

I sit up, right through Cal, and he dissipates into a swirl of colorful haze. My body is turning to lead, my muscles turning to flexible fire as boiling blood pulses through me.

I can't breathe. The world swirls as colorful fog. A black beast, like a snake with front legs, materializes before my blurry eyes from the glittering plumes of purple and pinks.

Two more heads sprout, racing out to sink into me, one in the side of my neck. I try to scream, but it fizzles in my throat. Whimpering, I scramble to rip it out. I fling it into the mist as it begins to decay even as two more sprout from the body, twisting to life.

Tony sits cross-legged next to me, shaking his head and resting back on his hands. "Nat."

"Fuck you," I sob. "I'm not her."

"Baby," he chuckles. "If you would have just tried harder you could have been as good as Sasha."

I'm too busy pulling heads out too flip him off again or listen to him tell me how worthless and pathetic I am compared to Sasha. Even as I pull one out, two more sink in. I shake, sobbing and snarling all at once. "Shut up, just shut up, you fucking useless, piss poor excuse of a man."

Cal is on my other side, shaking his head and chuckling. "Am I a piss poor excuse of a man?" He rubs a hand down his face. "He's right. I used to think you could handle yourself. I thought I could use you. How wrong I was."

I turn, his image blurred by unshed tears. My heart rolls over in my chest then stops. Tony I can handle, even ignore, but not Cal. Trying to stomach his horrendous opinions of me breaks something in me. It shatters like a mirror, the world churning into bleak, sparkling grays.

Cal, my beautiful, wicked promise of hope disappears. I fall back, everything going black. Pain overtakes my senses, every nerve throbbing with agony.

There is no more point in trying or fighting. I'm not capable of much.

Laying there, more fangs split my skin as the fire burns hotter. I can't even scream.

My heart stutters, rolling. There's nothing but an endless nothingness full of pain and horror unfurling before me.

Tony's starts blathering again. "You wondered why I couldn't ever love you?"

A deep voice growls at me, clouded in deep bass and heavy drums. *'But it's all in my head, please tell me it's just in my head, I'm so scared this is real, the demons that are stalking me.'*

I take one shaking breath. The next line whispers out of me by sheer will. "I'll set myself on fire, just to keep the demons at bay."

Forcing air into my lungs, I grip at the cold stone beneath me. My nails scratch the surface as I tense my abdomen and clench my jaw. Pressing my shoulders back, my core snaps into place. Ki rushes through me.

More fangs cut into me, yet it isn't just whatever venom it has drawing me to the afters that is blazing alive within me.

Sasha laughs. "Baby sister, you're never going to survive. You never were as good as me."

Tony grunts. "Nat, you're a mess. You're always doing things the hard way. Always making problems. There's no point in pretending like you can handle this. Why can't you just be like Sasha? Why, Nat? I wanted her. I loved her. You're not even close. How could you think I could ever want you?"

Light burns in my chest. "Shut up you fucking annoying bastard," I pant. "Ness is right, I'm better. I've always been a thousand times better, and she couldn't ever do what I can."

I send a massive wave of Ki through my body. It shreds my muscles, and crackles in my bones. I relish it.

A scream rips from my chest as I dig deeper, clarity returning. I hold onto Ness and all the times she told me I am gorgeous, strong, and capable. Every word she's said to keep my broken pieces together replays in my mind. The world goes white behind my closed eyelids as an explosion reverberates from my chest.

CHAPTER 36
CALLAHAN

SHE SAW TONY IN HER NIGHTMARES. THAT IS THE SKILL OF Basileus, the Dark King and his lineage's ability. Those infected see their worst fears. It doesn't make too much sense, but bent dick says enough. Perhaps it's the fear of returning to him to breed for the Magia.

Quaking with fury, I sit there glaring at her body. I'd kill her for this if she wasn't already dead.

Watching her talk to air was mildly irritating at worst. She didn't reveal any great secrets, but it was comedy at her expense.

She stood there, staring as the shadow serpent crawled out of the box. That was mortifying. She didn't move, even reaching for it while babbling nonsense. I know why. The venom of Nightmares distort reality. As immune to dying from poison as she may be, the toxin isn't designed to kill.

It wasn't killing her. That was the shadow serpent sinking fangs into her, and she was too high to do a damn thing about it.

I sat here, watching her pull heads out of her body as our contract set my arm on fire, warning me of a breach of my duties, that I am in contempt. It won't kill me, like hers would kill her for disobedience. Still, it's searing pain like knives dragging through living tissue. It worsens, trying to get my attentions so that I perform, but I can't take care of her.

Getting involved would kill both of us, and she is dead anyway. She'd been struck too many times, and she isn't illuminating brighter. Her Light isn't pulsing. She isn't exhibiting any of the typical signs of healing.

If she'd been clear headed, she could have dealt with the shadow serpent in fractions of a rune and been done with this twisted little game. Getting dosed twice ensured her fate.

I clench my fists and jaw, trying not to react. My magic is writhing out of me in angry lashes, destroying everything nearby it can find. Those closest move away while I stay motionless, wanting to look away yet unable to tear my eyes away from the disaster.

She mumbles and drops flat on her back, her Light dimming, almost out. My chest caves in like ten tons of weight crushed my ribs.

Stupid, stubborn woman.

She should have let me take the hit. I would have with enthusiasm. Natalia is mine to protect and she hadn't earned this. None of it. The young seowolf being served up to her, the way Marius violated her, or being fed to a shadow serpent dosed on nightmare.

Marius has infected me on more than one occasion. Others of the same race too. I've been dosed on nightmare more than I care to admit. It's an experience that should be reserved for the darkest, most agonizing afters there are.

Adding a shadow serpent to the hallucinations, with warped reality that fixates on the deepest fears is undefinable abhorrence. She isn't just going to die. She is going to die in terror.

I stare, grinding my teeth and fight against my Dark. If I lose control, if it takes over, I'll shift. As it is, it's gnawing at my will, my fingers breaking and elongating before returning to humanesque.

Whimpering, Natalia twitches in the throes of death as shadow serpent heads continue to attack her body. The fine silver lace over her goes out, and I hang my head, staring at my shaking hands, pale from the loss of blood flow. They ache and burn as I try to force them tighter.

The Dark will snuff out the Light until it no longer exists. It's instinct. I should have known her demise was only a matter of time the moment I decided to bring her.

"Mass warned us..." My Dark screams, furiously turning on me to send lances of pain through my skull.

The King laughs. "A loss for Callahan. Someone mark it."

As if that point against me in the games mattered. I'd lost everything when her Light went out. My partner, my Light source, my weapon, and any shred of heart I might have grown. My future queen lies dead thirty feet from me, dying while I'd sat here, watching, useless.

I bare my teeth, fighting my magic. It's screaming, trying to reach out for my little star, desperate to save her from being consumed, trying to make me answer it's desires.

My eyes lock on the contract, waiting to watch it fade from my skin. No one is talking or laughing anymore. The jeers and taunts had been frequent, but death has a somber effect on everyone, even if only temporarily.

"Leave it," the King barks, then laughs. "Let it eat the body first. It deserves a last meal for snuffing out the Light."

Silence descends again, interrupted only by the soft hissing of the shadow serpent. I focus tight, sore eyes on the contract, trying to breath.

Massimo whispers, his voice a hushed awe. "Cal."

I ignore him, then there are other gasps. Lifting my chin, I glance over the table to Natalia's body. Her torso glimmers orange with flickering lights that crawl over her.

My Dark shifts with curiosity. *"Firelight?"*

I blink. It gets brighter, a quiet hum filling the air. Firelight is a rarer Light Seraphinus skill.

Massimo lurches to his feet. "Run!" He twists, knocking his chair over as he bolts away.

I scowl over my shoulder at him dashing from the room. I'll worry about disobedience later, turning back to Natalia. She glows brighter.

Her voice rips through the air. "Shut up, you fucking annoying bastard. Ness is right. I'm better. I've always been a thousand times better, and she couldn't ever do what I can."

The air charges, the hum building louder with quickening zaps. Little flashes of vibrant blue electricity pulse in the air.

My jaw drops. My heart beats once.

"Run," my Dark whispers. *"Now, lazy host!"*

I jump to my feet, my chair toppling with a bang. I turn and run, knocking into others as everyone realizes what is coming. The sizzle of electricity intensifies, the air zapping my skin. It tingles over me as I shove out of the room then throw myself behind the wall for protection.

Someone stumbles, falling into me. I push them further into the hall as the crack of the smite booms like a thunder, rattling and shaking the palace. I sway with the rumbling ground, dropping low into a crouch to curl against the wall, ducking my head, and covering it with a hand.

Bright light illuminates the hall, emitted from the strike Natalia called.

Others not blocked from the Light, either too close or still trying to get clear, sizzle with screams. The brightness goes out, leaving phosphenes in my vision. I stare at nothing before me, bright spots slipping and sliding around my view, my eyes wide and my heart racing.

That wasn't just a smite. Whatever it was, it rocked this palace to its foundations, vibrating my bones. My little star is more powerful than I'd ever realized. It almost terrifies me.

Almost. I'll grin about that later.

Several heartbeats later I move, crawling my way the few feet up the wall, muscles quelling as I sneak a peek around the corner.

A breathless male voice asks behind me, "What the fuck was that?"

I turn to him over my shoulder. He's young, younger than me, maybe in his second century. It's hard to judge age, we all look like a midlife human. "Smite."

The man nods, the skin above his wide nose wrinkling. "Heard of 'em, never been around one."

"Don't. They hurt." I scan the room. The wreckage of the tables and chairs is scattered around the room. There's no sign of the shadow serpent.

"You're Callahan, right?"

I curl my lip, annoyed by this conversation. "Yes."

"My father was Leopold Baron."

I push my eyebrows together as I consider. "I know the man."

"My father died last Decay season. Said I should find you before Gathering Shadows. I stopped by your estate recently but was told to fuck off. I know I'm not much of a fighter, but I'm smart. My father said I shouldn't fight, to instead ask you for a contract. He said you'd be the next Dark King. He was right, I'm not strong enough to survive this. I've been lucky so far."

Scowling, I whip my face toward him. "Do you mind? Natalia just smited the shadow serpent to the burning afters. I'm trying to figure out if she's alive."

The man nods. "Yeah, right. She was your vassal."

Vassal. I laugh. Natalia is a force, a weapon, and she has a contract, but she stands at my side.

I step into the hall's threshold, others clamoring at my back, none daring to enter before me. Natalia is on her feet, stumbling with the Light laced over her skin. She stops, taking one shoe than the other off, holding them by the thin heels in one hand, gathering her skirt up in the other. When she walks, she weaves, unsteady on her feet over to the remnants of the bar.

She stops, dropping her dress, crouching to shift through broken glass. Plucking up a bottle, checks the label and shrugs. She unscrews the cap, before tipping it up to chug.

I gape, feet rooted. When the bottle is empty, she drops it, the glass tinkering as it rolls away.

Shaking with silent laughter, I enter the room, stalking toward her as she picks up another one. I crouch, steadying myself with one hand, the other pushing the bottom of the bottle down.

She glances at me, licking her painted red lips, then scowls. "Not sure if you're real."

"I'm real." She narrows her eyes, I hesitate, wracking my mind for a way to convince her, then shake my head, smiling. "I try too hard to make sexual references."

She nods. "True. Still, you could have said just about anything, and I would have believed you. Do you have your phone?"

"Yes."

"Great. Is there a music ability to it?"

I pull it from my pocket, unlocking it, pulling open an application. She takes the phone, taps, then the speakers crackle with heavy metal music. She shoves the speaker next to her ear as she returns to chugging the liquor.

My little star may be an alcoholic. It's well-earned at the moment, although her words percolate.

Grabbing the bottle, I remove it from her grasp as she mewls, trying to cling to it. "What did you mean, you didn't know if I was real?"

She scowls. "If I answer without sass, do I get that back?"

"This, and a follow-up."

"Oh, goody, more games. 'Cause the last one was so fun." She rolls her eyes. "I kept seeing you, but knew you weren't real."

I frown. "What did you see?"

"I saw you naked. I saw your dick. It was very scary."

I push air out my nose in an annoyed scoff. Someday she's going to know my cock is straight. "I assumed 'bent dick' was in reference to Tony."

She points at the bottle. "I'm not intoxicated enough to answer that."

I give her the bottle back. She upends it, her throat bobbing as she drains the liquor into her stomach. Others are trickling back into the room, lingering at a safe distance. I glance at them, then turn to her as she chucks the empty bottle to the side. It clatters then rolls away.

She stands up, swaying from side-to-side. "I saw Tony, Sasha, my father, you, a lot of pretty smoke, and some snake thing with too many heads that bit me, and after biting me, the snake think kept turning to ash and regrowing."

"Shadow serpent," I say, standing.

She glances around, and asks, "What's going on?"

I laugh. "Little Star, you smited that shadow serpent to the bitter afters twelve circles down. We all ran for our lives."

"Oh." She nods, eyes glazed over. "Good."

I rub my mouth. "I was under the impression that smiting wasn't an option." I grin. "Can you do it for me again?"

"Right now?" She shakes her head. "Ever? I don't know. I didn't know what I was doing I just..."

Tucking loose hair behind her ear, I ask, "Are you okay?"

Her silver eyes find mine, then her face screws up with malice. "You're fucking joking, right?"

The King's voice rings out, "Callahan."

I curl my lip at her, then turn with a blank expression. "Yes?"

"Well done."

Disgust stirs in my gut. Natalia had done it, not me. She survived. She smited. I sat there and watched. I may see her as an equal, but a proper contract means I get all the credit. It's never irked me before.

I internalize my ire and incline my head at the King, not saying anything.

"Strike Callahan's loss. Give him a win." He smiles, then turns away. "Someone cleanup this mess."

My attention returns to my little star. I extend my hand. She lifts hers, laying it in my open palm. She tilts her head at our hands, then scowls, like she didn't mean to do it. It's a reflex I've been trying to ingrain in her, and it appears to be working.

Pulling her in close, I swing her into my arms, giving my Dark leeway. It screeches as it spills out of me, reaching for her, but it's howl of agony changes to a purr in my mind, a queasy pleasure sliding through me as the black tendrils wrap around her.

I start across the room. She sighs, curling into me, face in my chest. Inhaling deep, she goes limp. "I can walk."

"I'm not sure how you made it to the alcohol."

She snorts through her nose. "Alcohol was a necessity."

"I don't know if you'd have that kind of determination to make it to the room."

I scan faces as I cut through the crowd. They all keep their distance, moving out of my way, watching, but smart enough to back off. I search for Massimo. I doubt he was eviscerated by the smite. He had been the first to realize what was coming and ran.

I crane to check our contract is still present, relaxing at the lines across the back of my hand. Massimo will find his own way. I have Natalia to worry about, and she's already unconscious.

CHAPTER 37

CALLAHAN

G<small>ETTING HER BACK TO OUR SUITE,</small> I <small>NUDGE HER AWAKE WITH MY</small> shoulder. She groans and moans then picks her head up. "What the fuck do you want? I smited. Me, Lightning Bug. Bzzt, flash. Let me sleep."

I smile, setting her on her feet. "You need to change, and I need to know you're not dying."

She is unsteady, reaching out, putting a hand in the middle of my chest. "A, I'm not even going to be able to get out of this dress. B, I'm most certainly dying, just at a much slower pace." Her eyes lift to me as she drops her shoes. "Get me out of this thing."

I intake my breath sharply at the idea of peeling her out of the gown. It's what my cock has been begging for the last few days. "Talia."

She turns around and points at the zipper. "Just pull."

With thick, shaking fingers, I grip the small tongue of the zipper, drawing it down. It releases a soft whiz through the air as it slides along her back to the top of her butt, the two sides peeling away to expose her skin.

I slip hands under them, pushing them over her shoulders to

guide the dress down her torso, my hands grazing her skin down to where the fabric gets tight around her hips. As the urge to latch on and yank her against me rises, she steps out of my grasp.

Grabbing the fabric, she shimmies it down, wiggling her perky butt. I damn near lose control as her gown pools on the floor around her feet, moving my eyes to follow the markings along her spine to the little dimples in her lower back. I ache, my cock throbbing as I stare at the round curve of her ass.

Gritting my teeth, I turn to the wall. This is a torturous try of my considerable strength of will, and my Dark rolls ideas of what to do with her lithe body and perky tits through my mind with quick efficiency. I crack my jaw open, breathing through my open mouth.

Natalia limps and stumbles to the bed where she crawls to the pillow. I track her, searching for signs of wounds. Blood is smeared and dried, staining her skin pink in places, splotches of heavier, darker pools of primal fluid gathered in other places.

Staring at her ass covered in black lace as she lays face down tempts me beyond reason. I squeeze my hands into fists and take a deep breath, trying to clear the haze of desire in my mind.

I snap at my Dark, demanding restraint and compliance, and remind it our little star went through misery and the last thing she needs is for us to dissolve into being another monster.

It quiets, vibrating with indignation that I would suggest we would take advantage of her vulnerable state. *"We want her. We are horny. We want to play. I wouldn't desecrate."*

Finding a resolve in the notion of taking care of her, I concentrate on the fact she is covered in blood. I walk to the bed and slide my arms under her, rolling her back into my arms and against my chest.

She groans as I cradle her, carrying her to the bathroom. "You need a shower, Little Star."

"I'm sleeping."

"I know, but you're covered in blood. Just a quick rinse, then you can sleep." I set her on the sink top, leaving her there to turn the shower on and pre-warm the water, before turning back. I frown at her, slumped over with her chin to her chest. With regret, I shake her. "Little Star, wake up. Rinse off the blood."

She moans, slipping off the counter and crumpling into a mess on the floor. A noise wafts out of her, a sob, that I feel in my chest.

I crouch next to her, as she shoves up, blinking at me and whining. "I can't do this. I'm too tired."

I grit my teeth. Respect is getting hard, my cock harder in response to her breasts on display. I pull her to her feet and point to the shower. "Clothes off, scrub, rinse, dry. That's it. Five fractions, then I'll take care of you from there."

She blinks barely opened eyes, her body drooping like a flower wilting without sunlight and water. I'm not sure if she's conscious, but she nods, so I leave the room.

Checking my watch, I count the fractions of the rune. At four, there's a thud and I give up, moving back into the room. I glance at the black lace on the floor, then at the shower. Natalia is a heap on the floor, water raining down on her, steam fogging the glass walls.

Trying very hard to figure out how to not look at her, I open the door, and shut the water off. "Talia?"

She groans.

I sigh, grabbing a towel to cover her, then wrap her up and pull her off the floor. Setting her on the floor, I collect a few extra towels and move back into the bedroom. Pulling the bed's duvet cover back, I spread the extra towels on the sheets, returning to gather her up and deposit her on the bed.

Throwing the cover over her, I leave her to sleep. I change, then pour three fingers of bourbon that I down in a single gulp. Massimo enters my room as I'm refilling the tumbler.

He leans against the doorframe, jerking his chin at Natalia. "How's our little lightning bug?"

"Our?"

Massimo cocks a brow. "The?"

"Mine." I turn away, pouring another drink for Massimo. "She's alive, that's about all I can say. She chugged two bottles of alcohol, gave me sass, and passed out in the shower."

"She's in bed?"

"I'm an asshole, not a fucking sick prick."

"Wasn't suggesting you were." Massimo takes a drink. "She smites."

I shake my head. "I'm done being polite. If Marius isn't dead, he will be in the next round, along with anyone else I get my hands on."

Smiling, Massimo looks to the ceiling. "I think everyone is going to be avoiding Natalia. Smites hurt."

I empty my glass into my mouth. "Leopold Baron, his son is Lazarus Baron. I should have picked up on the lineage name. I want you to find out what you can."

"Will do," Massimo nods. "Anything else you need from me right now?"

"No, just do your job. I need a heads up, like Natalia's dinner."

"Ah, that," he closes his eyes, tipping his head back to face the ceiling. "That was a fucking shit show."

"I'm pissed. I'm fucking pissed about that, about watching Marius touch what belongs to me–his fucking magic–the King double-dosing her to feed her to a fucking shadow serpent–all of it. They've all been set on killing the Light, but she's my fucking contracted."

"Mm," Mass hums, facing me with desolate eyes. "You should have foreseen that."

"I presumed my clout and worth would override a lot."

"Idiot."

"I'm aware. Say something useful."

"She smites and called firelight?" He lifts his eyebrows and chuckles.

"Smiting is good," I grumble, covering my mouth with a hand and rubbing. "But *firelight*?"

We stare at each other.

Massimo takes a deep breath, his broad chest swelling. "It's interesting."

"No, that's fucking terrifying. What the fuck is she? Not Magia, that's for damn sure, but..." I crane over my shoulder to stare at her in my bed.

"What are the odds that the Magia managed to get ahold of a Seraphinus child?"

"And we didn't hear about it? Light or not, that would reach our ears." I scowl at her, the Light over her skin dimmer than ever before. "Regardless of anything else she is, she's half fucking dead right now."

"Not full dead, though."

"I'm tempted to fucking kill her for taking the hit when she should have let me take it for her."

Massimo spins the glass in his hand, a trace of a smile to his lips and words. "You knew she wasn't going to take the easy way out."

I sneer. "In the future, she's going to. I'll deal with that. You deal with giving me a heads-up when I'm walking into a fucking mess."

"It's Gathering Shadows, you're walking into a mess, heads-up given." Massimo finishes off his drink and sets the empty glass on the small table. "I'll see you in the morning. There's only five days to go. Keep your head on." He nods, leaving to shut the door behind him.

I tug my shirt over my head before sliding into bed. I'll show enough respect to keep my joggers on, but I hate sleeping in clothes. Settling in, I lay on my side, facing Natalia, staring at her in the soft glint of her Light crawling across her skin.

No matter the yearning to pull her close, to hold her and feel her against me, I won't cross that line without her being aware. Closing my eyes, her Light illuminates through my eyelids. For the first time in my life the Light calms me. If she is shining, she's fine.

CHAPTER 38
NATALIA

WAKING UP SETS ME ON HIGH ALERT. THE WEB OF LIGHT OVER ME goes from a dim shimmer to bright illumination. I jerk upright, frowning.

I'm in our in room. Cal is next to me in bed. He stirs, sitting up to rest a hand on my shoulder. I grab the sheet to my chest as he grunts.

His eyes are squinted, face weighed down with sleep. "Talia," he mumbles.

The cool of his Dark magic twists over me, dimming the Light. I turn to him. "I know where I am, I think, but how?"

He shifts closer, moving his hand to the space where my neck and shoulder meet, massaging sore muscles. "What's the last thing you remember?"

I scowl at my bent-up knees then shake my head. "Dinner. Well, you ate. Then, the King," I say before taking a deep breath. "Marius."

"Lay down."

I do, shifting my butt down and laying on my back. Cal nudges me, so I roll over, damp, terrycloth beneath me. I shove the towels off the bed in search of smooth, soft sheets. The silky bedding slides against my skin as I get half over on my front, my back to him.

He digs his thumb through aching muscles. "Marius," he says.

I shudder, my whisper soft. "I know I shouldn't have fought back."

"No," he says, his voice hard as he shifts closer. The heat from his body is palpable, but he doesn't press against me, just props up on his side, his hand running down my back. "If anyone ever touches you, if you ever feel like you're threatened, violated, if you aren't comfortable with it, you have free rein to do whatever you want to them. You never have to accept someone violating your body."

I nod, breathing out slow as he continues the massage. "Okay."

"What else?"

I blow out hard. "The King sinking his claws in me, and then... things getting hazy. I know pieces, Tony, Sasha, saying things."

He massages the side of my neck. "What things? You said it was me too. What did I say?"

I groan, shifting an arm beneath me. "Doesn't matter." The contracts stings in my forearm. "Damnit, that's not fair."

"You have to answer to me. What did I say?"

I sigh, opening my eyes. "I remember Tony and my sister mostly, just a bunch of stuff about Sasha being better, how that's why he couldn't ever love me like her, that I was shitty seconds in comparison."

His thumb keeps working down my back, dragging along my spine. "What did I say?"

"Something about wanting to use me but I'm too weak." I frown, trying to remember, "You said I wasn't able to handle myself."

He exhales, "So I don't scare you?"

Snorting through my nose, I smile. "No."

"And it wasn't my dick?"

Laughing, I crane to see him over my shoulder. "No?"

He applies pressure on me to encourage me to lay flat again.

I go, happy to let him continue the massage. "I hurt like fuck."

"Fucking isn't supposed to hurt. I'm concerned that you think otherwise with that statement."

"Eh, according to Ness I have terrible luck with men. That's why she keeps telling me to sit on faces. In no way, shape, or form have I ever had that pleasure, so she's encouraging me to."

His hand stills. "Excuse me? Are you telling me a man has never…"

"Oral sex? Yeah, no."

"I'm really disappointed with your life choices right now."

I wince. "Pretty much what I remember being the point of everything you, Tony, and Sasha were telling me. Oh, my father too, I remember that now. He said the wrong children died. I think that's the point I realized I was hallucinating, because as much as he thinks that he won't even talk to me, and then it–like the whole world went pretty smoke and stars and there was this snake thing biting me, you all telling me how fucking worthless I am…I lost it not being real somehow."

His hand slides up my back to wrap around my throat. He doesn't hurt me, just gives a squeeze. "Little Star, you are far from worthless. You are strong, a fighter. You fucking called firelight and smited that shadow serpent. I can think of a thousand ways I can use you and will."

My voice is squeaky in shock. "I smited?"

Chuckling, he draws his hand over my shoulder and kisses the side of my neck. "Yes. Your Light went out. You weren't moving. We all thought you were dead, but then you lit up and firelight started to cover you. Massimo's the one who realized what was coming next, taking off before anyone else. It took me a few fractions to get my head around it."

"You thought I was dead?"

He presses his lips against the ball of my shoulder. "Yes. Marius had infected you with nightmare already, and the King infected you a second time. You started talking to thin air, so I knew it was working. To be fair to your Magia skills, it doesn't try to kill you, and you got double dosed."

"What did they put in me?"

"Nightmare," he says. "There are different races of Seraphinus with different abilities. Nightmares have a toxin they can infect others with. It's referred to as nightmare."

"Original."

"Mm, it twists reality and forces the infected to suffer hallucinations of their worst fears."

I lay there, woozy and aching. His large, warm hand caressing my bruised body. "I feel like I survived my worst nightmares."

"If you ever have the option to let me take a hit or take it yourself, you are going to let me take it."

I bury my face in the pillow, groaning. "He was punishing me for Marius. That wasn't your fault. Besides, my contract says I'm supposed to protect you. I thought shoving something like that your way would have breached it."

He grumbles from his chest, his nose in my hair. "I'll kill Marius if you didn't."

I shrug. "I wasn't trying to kill him. I wanted to hurt him."

"If he's not dead, the next time I see him in a game, he will be. Fuck the objective." Cal's hand rests on my hip. "You're supposed to protect me when necessary. That wasn't necessary and I'm amending the contract, so you have no choice. The next time you have the option you're going to defer any lash back to me. Do I make myself clear?"

I can't breathe, my chest restricted. "I can handle–"

He straight growls like a wolf, rumbling from the back of his throat. "I don't fucking care what you can handle. This isn't about how strong or capable you are. This is, I thought you were dead, and I couldn't handle that." His fingers curl around the front of my hip bone, digging in with a brutal force that throbs. "Do you have any idea how close I was to losing my mind?"

"No. Apparently, I was dying."

He presses his face into the side of my neck and hair, his voice a ravaged whisper. "Little Star, don't fucking tease me right now."

I giggle, stretch out, and sigh, relaxing into the mattress on my stomach. "I really set myself on fire?"

He kisses along the top of my shoulder before pulling back, starting to massage his way from my hip up. "Your Light went out. I was trying not to lose control of my magic when you covered yourself in firelight. It's an effective skill. It spreads quickly if it touches you, so don't ever do that too close to me."

I scoff. "I didn't really do it. I was done. It all went black. I was so close to letting go, then 'Combat' popped in my head, that it was all just in my head, what I was afraid of. Then that line, 'set myself on fire to keep the demons at bay', played in my head, and I just...I got pissed at Tony just telling me how much better Sasha was, then I..." I frown, "I don't know from there."

"You yelled something about Ness being right, you're ten thousand times better than her—I assume 'her' is Sasha—that she couldn't do what you could, and that's when you started calling a smite so I ran."

I giggle. "Mother, I'm so sorry I missed that."

He presses his smile to my shoulder, working on my lower back. "It was chaos. Every single person in that room was terrified of you, while only fractions before we all thought you were dead."

"Serves you fucks right."

He snickers, trailing his fingertips up my spine. "The King gave me a win, and I got you out of there, carried you back here. You told me you could walk, then passed out on the way. When I got you here, you asked me to get you out of your dress."

"Explains why I'm naked."

He chuckles. "I forced you to rinse all the blood off, and you passed out in the shower. I did my best to be polite."

My face burns, but I smile. "Thanks, but I don't remember it anyway."

He lays down, his hand resting on my lower back. "I need to sleep. You're okay, right? I've been stuck somewhere between sleep and naught, worrying if you needed something."

"I'm okay. Thanks for taking care of me."

"It's the contract."

I blanch but do my best not to react. Here I am in dreamland fantasizing about the massage and kisses when it's just the contract. "Yeah."

He rolls against me, half lying on top of my torso. His skin melds against mine, hard lean muscles pressing against me. As much as I want to enjoy it, my hope is sniffling and pouting. Even my Light flickers and dims.

He nuzzles his nose into my hair. "It's what I told you I would do, what I agreed to, and you don't have to thank me." He curls his arm around me, pulling me to my side for him to wrap his body around mine. Spooning me, his lips curve against my neck. "The only fucking reason I even have to is because I'm using you, so I don't want you to thank me for that."

I shift, snuggling in closer, his hand pressing against my stomach. "I can–"

"I," he says, cutting off my words. "I am your alpha. I take care of what's mine. That's you. My woman. My star."

I'm not sure if I'm dreaming. Maybe I died and this is a beautiful, lovely afters crafted for me by the Mother. "Cal." I wiggle further into him.

He bites my shoulder, causing tension to pull a string from my breasts to between my legs. My nipples harden into tight peaks as arousal pools in my lower abdomen, an ache demanding to be filled.

"Don't do that again."

I hold my breath. "Oh."

His dick starts twitching and throbbing against my butt.

"Damnit, Little Star," he grumbles, reaching between us to adjust himself. "I need sleep."

"Mhm." I nod, closing my eyes.

He doesn't move away, even dropping his arm over my waist. I fight a grin, as his breathing evens out. He'll stay.

CHAPTER 39

CALLAHAN

4TH EVERGREEN'S DAY, HEATWAVE, 4049 6TH MILLENNIUM

I WAKE UP WITH MY STIFF ERECTION PRESSED INTO THE SOFT CURVE of Natalia's ass and tighten my arm around her. My Dark unfurls from me, spilling out to lash around her and pulling her torso back against me, I rock my hips forward. She makes a soft noise but doesn't fight or seem to wake up.

My Dark purrs, soaking in her Light. *"She's so soft."*

I bury my face in her hair and breathe deep. She is okay. She'd woken up sometime in the night. I'd been waiting for it, glad of it. It meant my little star was recovered from the nightmare and all the power it took to ignite the firelight and the smite she called.

She wriggles against me, grinding her ass against my hard cock. "Mmm."

"Little Star." I groan. My Dark begs to play.

"Hm?" She does it again.

I grin. "I'm trying to be respectful, but you're making it hard."

"Not the only thing," she whispers, wiggling that perfect, perky ass.

I nip her neck, and she moans. Damn her. She is supposed to stop me. I grab one of her breasts, thrust my hips forward.

"Best you got?"

I'm going to lose it. My mind. My self-control. Respect. "One more fucking sass," I manage through my clenched jaw, my cock pulsing.

Her cute giggle fills the air. "You'll put me in my place?"

I'm going to put her somewhere, a few places in fact. On my face, then on my cock.

I shove my hand lower, reaching between her legs. My fingers find her clit. It's already slick. I pinch it hard, pulling on it, my grip slipping over the pulsing end.

Gasping, she arches against me, which only succeeds in shoving that perfect ass into my erection harder. She lets out a soft warbled, "Oh."

I force my thigh between hers, pressing it up between her legs to put pressure on her, opening my mouth against her neck. Breathing out, I draw a circle with my tongue, sliding my hand up her torso, my fingers circling a hard nipple.

"Cal."

My name on her lips clouds my mind with desirous need. I press my leg harder into her throbbing clit and nip her earlobe. "When you come I want to hear you say my name." She whimpers as I roll to my back. "Get on my face."

She shoves herself up and turns wide eyes to me. "Um?"

"Now," I say. "It's an order." I might be crossing the line, abusing that clause in her contract. I don't care. This is happening.

As she gets to her knees, I trail my eyes lower down her perky breasts and toned stomach to between her legs, my Dark twisting around her. It's a breathtaking sight, her naked and glowing wrapped up in my Dark. Natalia's next to me, lifting a leg to straddle me while I lick my lips, having played this fantasy in my head so many times before.

There's a knock on the door. She freezes. I glare at the door, shouting, "The fuck do you want?"

Massimo's voice carries a laugh as he answers. "You're late."

I snatch my watch from the bedside stand and grimace. "Fuck."

I toss it back to the wood surface then sit up. I grab her face, crushing my mouth to hers, my tongue invading her mouth. Breathing hard I pull back, "Later, Little Star."

She gapes at me, letting out a small yelp of shock as I roll to my knees, grabbing the back of her thighs and lifting her against me. Her long, lean legs wrap around my hips, my Dark coiling around her to bind her to us. I almost decide it's worth the punishment to skip out on the games this morning.

"Death," my Dark reminds me. *"The punishment is death, and we won't ever get to fuck our little star a second time."*

I walk on us to the edge of the bed on my knees, then get my feet under me, carrying her into the bathroom before I put her down. We brush our teeth, then I turn the shower on.

She gets in before me, and I join her. Neither of us says a word as we rush through getting clean and ready for breakfast.

I shut the water off, snagging towels to throw one at her. Leaving the bathroom to give her space, I dry and dress. She exits the bathroom as I'm tucking in my shirt. She's wrapped in a towel, hair and makeup done.

The towel drops from around her and I turn my back while threading my belt on. I'm already going to have blue balls.

I can't help but sneaking a glance, though. She shimmies her butt to get black fabric over it, causing my cock to twitch. Today is going to be a long day of trying to concentrate rather than staring at her ass. I'm in no state to be fighting for my life. I might die staring and fantasizing. It would be better than a lot of ways to be sent to the afters.

The dress is short, a loose skirt obscuring her ass. It would be easy to bend her over and push it out of the way. Ignoring that idea from my Dark, I brush her hands out of the way to zip her into the fabric instead.

"Thanks." She turns around, eyes low.

I take her face in my hands again. Her lips separate in a small

301

gasp, eyelids fluttering half-closed. Tipping her head back, I want to taste her again, but meet her gaze. "Are you okay?"

"Sure."

I smile. "Take it easy today. Don't push yourself. I'll take care of you."

Her eyebrow lifts. "You know I don't know how to do things the easy way."

"Today, you're going to learn." I release her face, turning to retrieve a pair of heels. I hand them to her, helping to steady her as she puts them on, then lift my hand. "Right now, everyone is going to fear you. Let that ride. I don't want you pushing yourself. I'll take care of everything."

She takes my hand and I pull her with me out of the bedroom. Massimo is gone, probably already at breakfast. I hurry, stopping to scoop her in my arms so she doesn't struggle to keep up in the heels. She huffs and mutters, but I ignore her, carrying her to the threshold of the great hall.

I pull the chair out next to Massimo for her, then sit on her other side, so she's tucked safely between us.

The table has a couple dozen scattered empty chairs left vacant, the previous occupants having lost their lives in games. I scan for Leopold Baron's son, trying to recall his face as I eat the eggs. Massimo trades his un-touched plate with Natalia's empty one, ensuring sure she'll get enough food. My little star burns through fuel at an incredible rate.

Massimo is going hungry, but I'm not going to worry about that. He can get food at any point during free time.

Natalia eats in a hurry, inhaling food so quick I doubt she tastes anything. I set my hand on her thigh, and she glances over. I wink, slipping my hand under her skirt. She rolls her eyes, returning to scarfing her meal. Shaking with a contained laugh, I focus on my own plate.

The far end of the room illuminates in brilliance. I turn with every other head to the source of it. I am confused. My little star is next to me, safe and sound. There shouldn't be another Light source in this city.

Squinting into the glow, I make out three Light Seraphinus walking through the hall, escorted by Dark warriors in royal garb.

One man leads the Light, tall, with long, blond hair pulled back in a bun. The Light winds around him in thick strings of gold over his pale skin as he walks with his head held high, at ease despite being flanked by enemies. I know his face. It's one I long to break, and it torments me every time I'm dosed on nightmare.

I clench my jaw, rage seething from me in tendrils of black at the square face and regal features. My magic lashes several tendrils around Natalia, wanting to protect her as apprehension gnaws at me. There aren't many Light Seraphinus who would dare to come this far into Ilbuio, but Pierre Bordeaux is one of them.

My appetite is gone, replaced with vehement hatred as the Light fuck walks past me on the other side of the table. I follow him with my eyes, every muscle in my body tensed from acting on impulse to kill him.

He killed my father.

Pierre doesn't so much as spare a glance at the table, striding toward my King. His heritage is second only to the Light Queen's, their structuring based upon heritage and age rather than merit. As much as I loathe the monster, I know he's capable and powerful.

Pierre stops to stand before the Dark King. The Dark warriors fan out in aggressive stances, ready to defend the King, but the two men with Pierre standing at attention a pace behind Pierre at either shoulder, arms limp at their sides.

The King makes no sign of acknowledging them, continuing to eat his breakfast.

Lifting his chin and voice, Pierre says, "It has come to our attention you have something that does not belong to you."

The King points his fork at Pierre, not bothering to look. "The

303

only thing that does not belong to the Dark here is you. Begone with you and yours."

Pierre smiles. "I will take what is mine and we will be on our way." Without any sign of respect he turns, coming back up the table to stop opposite of me.

I glare at him, lifting my chin because of his height. His prominent brow furrows, his straight nose flaring as he squares his broad shoulders. With a polite smile, he focuses on Natalia with his blank, white eyes. "You belong in Izul."

Natalia blinks, looks over at Massimo, turns her head over her shoulder, then to me before twisting to glance behind us. She feigns surprise and lifts her hand to the base of her throat. "Me?"

Pierre's eyes flicker, then narrow. "A Dark contract taints your flesh? That is blasphemy."

She lifts her hand away from her chest to glance at my contract on her forearm. "What's wrong with my contract?"

"Who here would dare to force you into servitude?" Pierre shifts his gaze between Massimo and me.

I squeeze her thigh. "The contract belongs to me, as does she."

"You will release her, or I will kill you to release her. That is the right of Light."

Natalia laughs. "No, I'm fine where I am."

Pierre leans back, frowning. "Your magic holds no danger for me. Light does not burn out its own kind."

I could argue that is what started our involvement, but the Light is staunch. They have rules against killing their own kind, and regardless of what my little star claims to be, she is the Light. She will be forced to answer to the laws of Light.

Natalia turns to me. I lift an eyebrow back at her. She puts her hand up, and I press my palm to hers. My magic sighs, the Dark twists around her fingers and wrist as it slides from my core. As much as it takes from her, it seems happy enough to play fair and let her take from it.

I frown as her eyes filter to black. The skin around her eyes darkens with them, like deep bruises. It's eerie to see her so Dark.

She drops her hand and stands up, "I'm going to tell you the same thing I told Cal. I'm not the Light. I took this contract for my own reasons, not because I had to, and I don't fucking need you."

"You are covered in the Light," he sneers. "How can you deny what you are?"

"I'm not denying anything. I'm telling you. I'm not the fucking Light. I'm not the Dark, either. I'm Magia."

"Magia," he repeats, then takes a half-step away with a look of horror.

I've never loved the sight of fear more in my life. Natalia might be the best decision I have ever made. Sitting back, I grin at Pierre in a gloat. "She belongs to me, and there's nothing you can do about it."

Scowling, Pierre meets my eyes. If he recognizes me, there's no sign, although his sight lingers on me before he turns to his men. "We are leaving."

"Sir?" One steps forward, frowning and looking to Natalia. "The Queen of Light was clear. Are we to leave our own?"

"For now." He glances back at Natalia, his voice low and thin. "I have something I need to do."

I smirk. "Forever. Don't come back."

With lips pressed tight, Pierre stares at Natalia. His head shies to the side, then he turns to the one who spoke. "Now," he snarls, low and harsh, fury evident.

The three walk out the way they came in.

Natalia sits down. She slips her hand to the back of my neck. Dark entwines my throat then seeps below the surface of my skin, my magic rejoining.

She blinks, her eyes returned to silver. "Neat. I've never tried to give it back like that before."

I lace fingers in hers and twist our wrists to kiss the back of her hand. "I told you to rest."

"No, you told me not to push myself." She shrugs. "I didn't, or the contract would be pissy."

Sighing, I drop our hands against my leg, prevented from retorting as my King calls out, "Who dared?"

I glance around at lax faces. This inquisition excludes me. Not one eye falls upon me as everyone searches the table, waiting for the one who betrayed the Dark to confess.

A woman stands at the far end of the table, a few seats down from the King. "I did. I did it. She almost killed us all. She's a danger to the Dark and she belongs in the burning afters or Izul."

A Dark warrior slips from the side of the King as he lifts a hand, pacing toward the woman. The royal guard grabs hold of her. Although she struggles, the warrior drags a dagger across her throat with little resistance.

It drops her body, sheaths its weapon, then picks up the corpse, taking it away.

The King lifts his chalice toward me then returns to eating his breakfast.

CHAPTER 40

CALLAHAN

NATALIA SHAKES HER HEAD. "GUESS THAT WAS A BIG NO-NO."

Massimo leans forward, meeting my gaze. His is full of question and concern. I shake my head, and he settles.

I push my half-empty plate toward her. She'll eat it. "It goes against our honor code and tenets. She betrayed the Dark to the Light, which is inexcusable."

Natalia rolls a pancake up, dipping it in syrup before she takes a bite. "Who was that?" She jerks her chin. "The Lighter? Do you know?"

I take a deep breath. "Pierre Bordeaux," I say, then try to rid the taste of his name from my mouth. "He's a high ranking Light. Almost two centuries ago he wiped out an entire Dark contender list, including my father."

She curls her lip. "I should have taken a shot."

I chuckle, shaking my head. "No, he's mine."

"Your father was a contender?"

Sitting back, I drop my gaze to her hand in mine. Here I sit, holding the hand of a Light, willing to protect her life with mine, going crazy in lust, and yet, I condemned my father for the same

actions. "Yes. Most expected him to be the next Dark King, but..."
My throat constricts around the truth.

She nods, giving me a tight pulse of my hand. "Pierre killed
him."

There's so much more to the story, however, I won't discuss
this with other present. Not even Massimo knows the truth.
There are too many secrets I have kept about those events. "Yes,
so when the time comes that I have a shot to take, I will."

"Still should have made him take a hit." She picks up her coffee,
taking a drink before settling back, one knee bent up with her
foot on the edge of her seat. She taps her thumb against the
handle of the mug, scanning the table. Her features twitch.
"Marius."

I follow her line of sight to Marius striding across the hall.
Between watching him violate my little star and seeing Pierre,
I'm ready to sling blood with my claws. "He's a dead man
walking."

She shakes her head. Marius must feel our eyes, turning to us.
He smirks as he sits at his father's left hand.

Natalia sighs. "I need vodka."

Massimo chokes on a chortle. "You drink almost as much as
you eat."

She shrugs. "When life hands me lemons I like to cut them up
then squirt the juice into my vodka. It gives it a kick."

The King raps the table with his cane, and the room falls silent.
He gestures Eloise forward. She starts on the opposite side of the
table, going around the room, offering a deck of cards to each
player.

Every player draws one, and I slide the top card off the stack
when it's my turn. Flicking it over between my forefinger and
middle, I see the number one in silver on a black background. I
toss it face down on the table between me and Natalia.

When Eloise makes her way back to the King, she still holds
cards in her hand. It's usually a sign of a weighted deck, indicating

an uneven division. She stands at his elbow to set the deck down before him.

He draws one and hands it to Eloise. Taking it, she inspects the face then nods. "Ones, stand."

I let go of Natalia's hand to stand. A few others stand, including Marius. When we make eye contact, my magic hisses, coming alive and coiling around me. It's hungry to repay him for touching what belongs to us.

Eloise motions to the empty side of the room. "Collect your partner. Stand facing each other."

I look down at Natalia while a smile. "Breathe, Little Star. We're going to be fine. I'm pissed, and I'm done pulling my punches."

She stands, smoothing her skirt. "Lovely. I'm both excited and terrified by that statement."

We move to where we were instructed. I pivot, standing in front of her. Her hair hangs in loose in waves of white-blonde. The strands closest to her face are pinned back, which will help when fighting.

Meeting her gaze, I stare into her silver eyes. She claims not to be the Light, yet, like Pierre, her hair and eyes lack color, her skin without a trace of melanin. There's no distinction skin color plays in magic types, yet the similarity to Pierre is a rude reminder that I'm attracted to the Light.

Not just attracted to it. I'm half in love with her cute sass and power. My magic squirms like eels, slithering with pleasure in my chest. That's the sickest part of my infatuation. My Dark desires the Light as much as I desire Natalia.

Someone steps next to my little star, and she cuts her eyes to them before twitching. My gaze shifts to Marius at her side. I could threaten the man, but that would be stupid. Marius is a coward. He'll hide.

His lips twist to a coy smile, his voice low. "No hard feelings, Light Bug."

"Keep your disgusting magic and hands to yourself."

Marius's partner stands at my side. Jacques grins wide at me. "I hate bloody team games." He rolls his shoulders, using a hand to stretch his head toward his shoulder. "Guess I'd rather fight with your Light bug than against her after that smite, though. That was a smite, right? Thought it was going to bring this place down. Never been near one that strong before."

I clamp my jaw. As excited I am that my star can smite, I'm burning alive from the inside out over the abuse inflected on her.

Hiro steps to the other side of Marius, almost a foot shorter. "Cal." He inclines his head, blinking his deep set, hooded eyes at me. "Glad I'm with you instead of against you."

Thames takes his place next to Jacques. He's wiry and tall with fair hair and paler skin than even Natalia. "Damn right, baby."

Eloise calls out, "Twos stand."

The rest of players rise from the table, including Telra, and I clench my jaw. Eloise moves past them further up the table to gesture. "Bring your partners and collect here."

The table is borderline empty, all players moving away with their partners. The various vassals present, yet uninvolved in the games like Massimo, remain behind. The twos line up, despite lacking instruction to do so.

I count. It takes a while. Sixty-four players stand in a row, mirrored by another sixty-four. There are only twenty ones. There are one-hundred-and-twenty-eight twos.

Natalia glances behind her at the twos, wincing. "Fuck."

Acker snickers on her other side. "We have you and Cal, Marius and Jacques, and Hiro and Thames. We'll be fine."

Checking my team again, I search the opposite collection. Sterling is grinning over his shoulder, his dazzling white smile widening as we connect eyes. I'd feel better if he were on this team. We could have fun if he were.

Eloise says, "One partners, hold hands. Left-to-left."

I reach my left hand for Natalia's. Eloise moves from one pair to the next, binding hands in metal cuffs attached by four links. I smile at Natalia, watching her frown. I almost laugh. My little star is tethered to me, safe and secure within reach.

Eloise moves back up the line, shoving headbands on the people standing in line across from me. A pair of rabbit ears gets slipped onto Natalia. She widens her eyes at me, absolutely adorable. I lose my composure at Marius with a set of antlers on his head.

"Shut up." Marius glares at me. "Everyone looks stupid in these."

"This will be a hunt," Eloise says. "Ones are prey, marked by animal features and cuffed together. Twos are hunters. Hunters, kill that which wears the mark of an animal. The trophy you take is to be stained with the blood of your kill. Leave the other alive."

Natalia's eyes roll up like she's trying to see the rabbit ears on her head. As cute as she is wearing them, I'll take those when this game begins and my Dark vibrates with an agreement.

"Prey, good luck surviving until Dawn rune to earn your point. One point will be awarded per individual that survives. Anywhere in this palace is fair game for you to hide."

I check my watch. Eight runes to stay alive and hunt down Marius. My sight settles back on Natalia, watching her face shifting in little flinches at each new rule.

"Consider the guard to be poachers. If any guard finds two preys without one wearing the mark of the animal, both parties will forfeit their lives. Prey found out of bounds will forfeit their life. Prey found untethered or without their animal marker will forfeit their life. Prey are not excluded from killing other prey to win additional points. Hunters will not be tethered and are allowed to steal the trophy of another hunter. Hunters do not have markers, and therefore killing hunters awards no additional points."

Jacques curses under his breath, dragging it out. "Fuck me."

I agree with the sentiment. This is a free for all, and I have a target on my back in the shape of rabbit ears. Natalia's gone a bit paler in a spectacular feat of nerves.

She reaches a hand up to scratch at her head next to the head band, adjusts the ears.

"Prey are granted ten fractions to run as hunters select their weapons. I remind you all, there is no shifting outside of the arena. Let the hunt begin."

A horn sounds off.

I grimace. Weapons are going to make this harder, another unfair advantage to the hunters. "Lose your shoes."

The other teams shuffle around, figuring out the metal cuffs.

Marius throws the antlers at Jacques. "You're fucked."

He slips them on with a laugh. "Always."

They take off.

Leaning forward, Natalia slips one heeled shoe off. I slip the ears from her as she gets the second off. I shove the headband on, and she stands, looking at me with a frown. "Those were mine."

"We're going to run now, Little Star," I say with a smile, grabbing her hand tight. I turn, realizing why they had us linked by the same side. It's not conducive to moving. We laugh, spending precious time figuring out how to twist together so we face the same direction, then we run.

CHAPTER 41

NATALIA

Cal runs. I do my best to keep up, bare feet slapping against the cold stone. We reach a flight of stairs, and Cal opts to go down. I don't offer to help. I don't know the palace.

"How big is this place?" I pant, following him down the steps.

He stops, stepping in front of me a step lower. "Get on."

Half-leaping, I throw my arm over his shoulder and wrap my legs around his hips. He grabs my left wrist with his left hand to accommodate the cuffs, pulling it over his shoulder, then starts jogging down the steps.

"Not big enough. Technically it ends at any of the bridges that connect to other buildings that lead out of the palace, so we can't cross any of them into the additions made from the original cathedral."

"Cathedral?"

"It was the original heart of the Dark, which made the palace. It doesn't matter." He hits the next level, then walks up a corridor in long, quick strides. I rest my chin on his shoulder, and he squeezes my wrist, his thumb rubbing the back of my hand. "You're going to be okay."

I turn my nose into his neck. "These games suck."

He chuckles. "Sometimes. I like this one." He stops, checking the other halls of the intersection, then makes a left.

"You seem to have an idea of where you want to go."

"Marius has a hiding spot he favors, and I'm going to kill that prick."

The blare of a horn echoes in the distance, causing my heart rate to pick up. "Shit."

"This is just another game, and you've been shining in them."

My lips twitch. "Did you just make a pun?"

"Maybe, but don't panic on me," he says with a grin. "Can you do that for me?"

"Yes." I nab the ears and shove them on my head.

He jerks to a halt. "Little Star," he says with worn patience. "No."

"I can heal myself a lot easier than I can heal you."

"Whoever wears those is the target. I'm not letting you wear it. I'm asking you, put them back or I will order you which will give you no choice."

"They look better on me," I say, settling down against him, chin on his shoulder.

Behind us there are screams and whoops of excitement. Cal tenses, spinning to face a group of four approaching us. They slow, grinning and brandishing weapons.

Mattingly nocks an arrow in his bow. "We're just here for the bunny."

Cal reaches up and rips the ears from my head, forcing the band over his. "Come get me."

Another one wiggles his eyebrows. "I think the ears were on the Light."

"That's what I saw," another answers.

The man out front grins with wicked joy. "You know, I think you're right." He draws back. "One little hole in her head, you hand over the ears, and you'll get to live, Cal. Fight back and who is to say it wasn't a poacher that killed you after we killed the rabbit?"

Cal turns his head, voice low. "I'm going to put you down."

I slide down his back, my bare feet meeting the cold stone. My arm jerks on his, and he grunts, swinging me around to stand in front of him.

Mattingly looses the arrow. I throw a shield, the arrow contacting it and glancing off to the side. He pulls another one, while the others start to encroach. "Looks like we're going to have a fight."

Cal shifts me against him as the three other men chuckle and laugh. Our linked hands cross over my stomach, Dark crawling over me, fine tendrils snaking and crisscrossing. The Dark races out of him, expanding and those approaching hesitate.

Mattingly glares, standing at the back, aiming his projectile. "There's only two of them. What the fuck are you waiting for?"

One snaps back, "It's Cal."

"I'm so sick of everyone here being so fucking scared of him. He's not that tough. That lightning bug he contracted seems tougher, and I'm going to put an arrow between its eyes."

Cal rumbles with a laugh, low, under his breath. "I guess maybe I've been lazy this year."

Dark magic streaks from every Darkling surrounding me. I blast at the tendrils with Ki, preventing any from reaching us. Every one of our attackers is wound up in Cal's magic, which slam them into the walls.

Mattingly lets several arrows sail through the air, which I deflect.

Cal's hand leaves my stomach, black racing from his palm. It streaks into one, then bursts with orange flames. The man roars and crumples.

I grunt, shielding from Dark. "What the fuck was that?"

"Fight now, ask later."

I blast another one with Ki who is getting too close with, Light flashing. Cold that burns slithers around my ankle, yanking my leg from beneath me. I fall, rushing feet forward. Cal follows, the cuff snapping my wrist, the metal biting into my skin.

Cal grunts, and flexes. We jerk to a stop as an arrow embeds in my stomach. A shrill squeal of quick pain makes it past my lips before I can stop it.

His arm slips beneath my shoulder, and I'm yanked backward into Cal, squeaking again.

Mattingly laughs, nocking another arrow. In the glow of the Light, I can see the shadows leaking from him. The others are getting up. "Nowhere to run, nowhere to hide, time to go out, Light." He aims.

Cal grabs the arrow in my gut, black threading together around us, encasing us. He snarls in my ear, his breath warm against my skin. "Through or back out?"

"Out," I say, the Dark bubbling and warping around us.

"One, two," he wrenches it free. I groan. He tosses the arrow to the side, and he holds me tight. "Let me know when you're ready."

The shield trembles and sucks in. He's breathing hard, heart hammering against my back.

I ask, "Are you all right?"

"Heal."

I lean my head back and find my Ki, forcing it to heal the puncture. It burns worse than the wound, followed by the telltale easy flow of healed flesh. I nod. "Healed."

"Now glow."

"What?"

"Glow, burn bright, and whatever happens don't let go of me." He laces his fingers in mine.

I enjoy the feel of his hand holding mine. He'll stay.

Warmth spreads beneath my skin, his Dark answering with cool bliss on top. It starts to sting, the Dark digging in like honed blades. I scream and Cal's hand tightens, the world exploding around us in inky midnight blues and glimmering orange flames.

I blink, hollow and battered. Cal drags me to my feet, his arm a steel bar pinning me to him. The hunters are sprawled on the floor, motionless. "Cal," I manage, doubling over his arm.

The world sways, everything whirling around me. Woozy, my knees buckle, and the world begins to tunnel before me.

He flexes his arm against my torso, then cradles me. "Breathe, Little Star."

I shudder, the empty space in my chest icy cold and throbbing like a deep, inflamed wound. My voice is a harsh rasp. "What was that?"

Cal turns away, carrying me up the hall. "Your use."

He slips into a room and kneels, setting me on a couch. His fingers press against my abdomen, his sight on the hole in my dress. "Are you all right?"

I wince. "I mean, that hole is gone, but overall? Not so much. What the burning afters did you do to me?"

He drops his hand to my thigh and lifts his eyes to mine. "My lineage eats Light. Those different kinds I mentioned? I'm a Mandolux—a Light eater. I've been feeding off you since you signed my contract, absorbing your magic."

I shake my head. "We can talk about that later, but if you have been, it wasn't that." I point my free hand over his shoulder. "What was *that*?"

"I'm not like you. I can't take a hit then send it back. I have to touch you to take it."

"*Mhm*," I bob my head, eyes wide with serious intent. "You took my magic?"

He gives me that adorable, feigned innocent half-cocked grin. "Yes."

"This is what you wanted me for." I lift my hands, staring at the Light. My fingers shake, the hole ripped through my core shrinking. "The Light, because you can use it, but you need me to generate it."

"Yes. I was hoping I could wait longer before doing that, but

317

I'm fighting with one hand tied behind my back while trying not to die." He lifts our cuffed wrists.

I nod, dropping back to slump into the couch. Last night and this morning, I was in a fantasyland. I'm just a weapon and a food source, an expendable tool.

"Your Light is alive, the same as my Dark. I'm sure it's angry right now, but it will heal."

Sitting up, I study his flawless, ruggedly handsome face, then reach for the rabbit ears.

His hand snatches mine and he scowls. "No."

"That's the trophy. It's what they're coming after, and I can heal."

"Don't make me use the contract," he says, giving me a weak half-sided smile.

I roll my eyes. "I'll be the target they come after. I'm your tool, so use me. I'll heal myself easier than if you take a hit, leaving you free to fight."

"No." His grin turns up a notch, giving me those dimples. "I'm keeping the ears, even though you probably look better in them than I do." He shifts around, his left hand pulling mine cuffed to it over his shoulder. "Come on. We need to move."

I get on his back again. He stands, his left hand wrapped around my wrist, the other cupped on the back of my thigh, his hand warm against my bare skin under the short hem of my dress.

His hand leaves, opening the door before returning. He sticks his head out to peer up and down the hall, then slips out, moving us along. Dark circles my waist and hips, tying me to his back as his thumb caressing my skin as he carries me through empty, dimly lit corridors.

The sweet, soft touches and the desire in his eyes are a ploy. I wrap my heart up, building thicker stone walls around it. I don't need to fall for a man who only wants to use me. I could go back to Tony if I wanted that misery.

Callahan starts checking rooms, then reaches a dead end. He

stops, staring at the wall, tipping his head back to sigh before turning back. "Fucker isn't here."

"Marius?"

"Yes." He stops at a cross-section. "For now, we move."

I hum. "Wouldn't it be smarter to find somewhere to hide?"

He shakes his head. "That's a good way to get pinned down or backed into a corner. Like behind us, I don't want to get stuck without an escape route. It's a good way to end up dead."

I drop my head on his shoulder, relaxing against him. "Okay, then we move."

CHAPTER 42
CALLAHAN

Two runes crawl by. We have worked our way through every level of the palace, up and down stairwells. Fatigue is settling in, tension winding tighter and tighter in my Dark at being hunted.

Natalia stirs behind me. "Um, Cal? I have to pee."

I sigh, having been trying to ignore that fact present in myself as well. "Yeah."

"Are there breaks to this? Like, at any point is there a bathroom break? Dinner?"

I stop, craning my head to see her. "You heard the rules. Survive until Dawn's rune. I'll find a bathroom. You just need to accept you'll have zero privacy," I say. "I need to put you down for a fraction anyway."

"Fucking Mother." She sits straighter before arching into me. "I'm so hungry."

"The best I can do is get you food as soon as this game is over." I start checking rooms, moving down the hall. I approach the end of the corridor where it splits into a horizontal section.

A check of the hall reveals occupants. I tense. Hiro and Thames see me and freeze. Hiro, wearing an identical set of rabbit ears on his head, lifts his chin.

Thames grins. "Hi, Cal."

I lift an eyebrow. "Thames, Hiro."

Hiro lifts an eyebrow. "Are we ignoring each other then?"

"Depends," I say. "Do you want to die?"

"No." He laughs. "Don't want to waste energy either."

I nod. "Then we ignore each other."

Hiro points at me. "Buddy, I hope I don't look as fucking stupid as you do, wearing these things." His index finger redirects at his rabbit ears.

Natalia giggles. "I keep telling him I look better in them, but he won't let me wear them."

Thames rubs the back of his neck. "Same, baby. He's set on being the mark."

Hiro shoves him and they stumble a few steps to the side in unison, linked together by cuffs. "You're not getting your neck wrung for me, Sugar Bear."

Thames's face flushes pink. He shakes his head, turning back to me. "Have you had a run-in with any hunters yet?"

"Just at the beginning." I lift my chin. "You?"

"Telra," Hiro says. "Woman is fucking crazy. I don't know how you ever dated her. She's still alive. We managed to run, in case you were thinking about trying to work things out."

Natalia tenses a bit on my back. I grin, shaking my head. "I'm not. I've tried to make my point with her, even threw a melrag at her recently, but she's still calling. It's a bit more crazy than I can handle."

That's the truth, albeit abbreviated. I'll skip over the gritty details, the way I've had to shield myself, dismiss vassals even to protect myself from her.

Thames laughs, and Hiro points at the ears on his head with his free hand. "We should go. Two prey sitting still?"

I nod. "Don't die."

"You too," Hiro says, dragging Thames away. Thames gives a salute as Hiro laces his fingers into Thames's of their connected hands.

I watch them disappear around a corner, counting to ten before I turn my back. Hiro is a good guy, and the rules of engagement state if we agree not to fight, then we don't. If he takes a shot now, he breaks those rules, but I don't trust anyone in a game.

"They're cute," Natalia says. "Make an adorable couple."

"Hiro's mother is oblivious. She doesn't know, thinks it's like any other contract."

"What about his father?"

"Dead."

"I'm seeing a theme here."

"The contractor is in charge of their lineage. Even in union contracts one of the pair is contracted to the other, so they don't face each other in the games. His mother transferred the lineage to Hiro after his father died to save her life. It's a stain on him and his lineage, an act of cowardice."

"Your father was a contractor, and when he died you got it all?"

I nod my head, chest aching. There's so much I want to say to my father, to ask him. "Yes."

"And your mother?"

"Died of the sickness." I bite down on nothing.

"What was your father like?"

There's no way I can discuss my father without doing something stupid, like telling her the truth. The games build trust between the partners, everyone knows that, but this attachment weaving in me to my star is deeper, more profound than anything I've ever felt.

"Okay, you just got really tense."

"Yes." Pressure is building between my ears.

"Dude, you aren't contracted, well, sort of, but you don't have to answer."

I clear my throat, making a turn and checking behind doors. "I will. I'll tell you, just not right now. Not during a game. Just know, every single player here is a powerhouse. They're strong enough to be both high born and contractors. In the Dark, you're either a player or you are contracted to a player. If you're under contract, you're ineligible for the games due to conflict of interest."

"Why?"

Moving away from the topic of my father, I start to lose my tension. I check a room, find a bed and two more doors. I slip inside. "There were too many under contract throwing games, misconduct, skewing the results, helping or hindering players, so those under contract are excused. You're either player or contracted."

I open the first interior door to find a closet. Checking the second one, I discover a bathroom. I bend my knees, and Natalia slides to the floor.

She steps to the toilet, and I move with her. She stares at it, then scowls at me. "There are like, thirty-seven steps in a relationship before you're allowed to pee in front of each other, and we aren't even dating."

I grin. "Welcome to the games, Little Star. I warned you that you'd have no privacy. Massimo and I are very well acquainted."

She snorts through her nose. "You've seen his dick."

"Dick, balls, ass, the insides of his guts." I shrug, going limp to let her pull on me and move how she needs, then it's my turn.

Having made our way through the awkwardness of the whole situation, we exit the bathroom. I nudge her to the bed, sinking into the mattress to bend my knees and take a moment to relax.

Natalia sits next to me, face turned away. She's been quiet since I used her and confessed to eating her Light. I check my watch, running a hand down my face. "Roughly six runes to go, a little more than half left."

She lays back. "We should move."

I smile down at her. She's a fast learner. "You're doing great."

Propping up on her elbows, she curls her lip. She glares at nothing before her, then gets up, holding her hand to me. I meet her eyes and smile, taking it. Throwing her weight back with a half-step, she hauls me to my feet. "Come on, Master-Owner."

Dropping my chin to my chest, I lift my eyebrows. "What's wrong, Little Star?"

The cuff burns and we hiss in unison. Smoke wafts from the metal, spelling out words: "Prey is limited to floors two through seven."

I sigh. "We just lost four floors."

"Oh, good, they're closing the net. I was afraid this would be easy." Natalia rolls her eyes while she rubs her wrist.

My little star could probably make a joke in the worst moment. It's a good sign. Annoyed and throwing sass is fine. She's not breaking yet.

"Come on. There's a secret stairwell we can use to avoid the obvious ways to get to the right floors."

CHAPTER 43

Natalia

I PUSH THE PANEL OUT INTO A CORRIDOR, FINDING TWO DARKLINGS waiting. They fixate on me with grins, and I hesitate, a twelve-foot painting trying to swing shut and crush me. "Uh, not so secret."

Callahan shoulders past me as the hunters adjust their grips on swords. "Balter."

One rolls his head on his shoulders. "Cal. I've been looking forward to a chance to pay you back for that last game."

I take a deep breath, centering, and pulling myself into alignment to draw Ki. "Any chance that payback is in the form of a witty insult?"

The men attack, ignoring my reasonable inquiry. I kick the blade from one as he gets close. He gapes at me, which leaves him open for a solid kick to his jaw.

Callahan blocks Balter, his sword breaking against Cal's shield. I step to slam an open palm against the man approaching me once more, square in his chest.

He grabs my wrist, twisting it, barring his teeth. I release a wave of Ki. Light flashes and his grip releases. There's a sickening crunching of bone as I blink, eyes focusing. My attacker is crumpled at the base of the wall opposite.

Callahan punches Balter. Dazed, he stumbles back, but Callahan grabs him by the throat, pulling the hunter in closer. He flips his grip, twists Balter around. They scrap, but Callahan drops to a knee and gets Balter backward over his leg, bending the man in half. Bone crunching ripples through the air, and Balter goes limp.

Shoving the body away, Callahan stands, glancing at me. "You okay?"

"Great."

He pulls me close. "Then let's move."

"I'm having so much fun." I laugh, but it rings hollow.

Spinning me under his arm, he nuzzles my ear. "I'm happy to hear that."

I snort. "Ever heard of sarcasm?"

"I have. I'm choosing to ignore it."

We walk for a bit, then round a corner, colliding with another pair. One stops short, the other panic swinging.

Callahan dodges out of the way with a glare.

The one who pulled back hisses, grabbing at the attacker to drag him further from Callahan and his reach. "Oh, shit, it's Cal, run!"

I laugh as the two stumble a few paces away. The one who swung looks at Callahan with a scared gape. "I did not mean to... sir."

Callahan rubs his face. "Turn around and go. Massimo is looking into you for a contract."

"Yes, sir," he hangs his head, then they both scurry away.

I stare after them with an open mouth. "What the fuck?"

Callahan gives me a smile. "What?"

"That was the most pathetic, saddest exchange of this whole game. I'm calling it now."

"I hope he's as smart as he claims, because I can't use him to fight." He snickers, shoulders shaking. "That was the worst punch I've ever seen."

I giggle. "It was so bad, and the other guy was ready to run from you on sight."

He glances over his shoulder. "I almost cracked up at that."

We keep walking, me a pace behind, shuffling at an angle. The cuffs clink in the silence as we move, and I inspect the paintings and artwork along the corridors and dozens of doors, sneaking glances at his butt on occasion. Damn my weak self-control.

Callahan stops. "Get on." I hop on his back, and he grips my wrist linked to his again. "I just saw Marius. We're going to find him."

Jogging, he heads up the hall, and makes a turn, his head shifting back-and-forth in quick succession like he's searching. He slows, returning to a walk.

Coming to another cross-section, he stops, breathing out hard. "Fucker."

Tension eases between my shoulder blades and I relax into him. "It's okay."

"It's not!" The abrupt rage in his words carries a harsh growl. "He touched you, let his magic run all over you. You don't even realize—," he stops. "You're mine, and you weren't okay with it. I'm going to fucking rip his head off when I get ahold of him. He knows it, too. He's running from me."

"That's sweet. Every woman wants a man who will murder someone for her."

His head twists to the side. "Would a woman think it's romantic when I rip his spine out through his mouth?"

"Maybe. You'd have to clean it up, then put a bow on it before you give it to her."

Chuckling, he makes a left turn. "I can do that. I could carve some poetry in the bone with my claws to make it really romantic."

Smiling, I rest my chin on his shoulder. "Perfect Lover's Day gift right there."

The glow over my skin picks up, and his Dark coils in a long strand off his shoulder, wrapping around my forearm. The tip caresses my skin over the contract in gentle strokes.

CHAPTER 44
CALLAHAN

MARIUS SAW ME. I KNOW MARIUS SAW ME, AND HE TOOK OFF. THE fucker is annoying, slippery even, but he's not stupid. We both know what he did, and we both know I'm out for blood for it.

I keep walking through the halls, moving down to the next floor. We encounter a few hunters, nothing difficult to handle.

I wind through the halls with Natalia on my back. I dodge a few traps laid by hunters, weaving without a destination in mine. Time ticks by, fraction after fraction.

I adjust Natalia higher in my grip. "You okay, Little Star?"

She yawns. "What time is it?"

"About halfway through Night's rune, so we have a little less than four runes to go."

"Mother." She drops her head against my neck. "I've done nothing all day and I'm tired. How are you still carrying me?"

I hoist her higher as I shrug. "You weigh nothing. I took a break."

"Hm," she hums, yawning again. She hisses, accompanying the cuff searing around my wrist again, setting off a plume of smoke.

"Prey is limited to floors three through six."

She groans, forehead dropping to my shoulder. "Think the hunters are getting notifications too?"

"I don't know. They aren't cuffed, so if they are, I don't know how. I should have asked the kid before I sent him off." I stop and glance around. "We're on the fourth floor. Stay or go?"

"What's your objective here?"

I smirk. "First and foremost, the goal is not death. Second, kill Marius."

She laughs. "You're really out to kill him."

I tighten my hand on her wrist, turning my head to flash teeth at her. "You're mine, Little Star. Watching him touch you? The way his magic—" I bite off my words, clenching my jaw.

Magic is finicky. It is its own entity, but the host links to it. The two meld as one, surviving together. It's natural that magic joins in, playing and enjoying physical encounters of all sorts. I grind my teeth. He might not have taken part in a sexual act, however, his magic did. Everyone watching knows it, the only one who doesn't is her.

"You mean how it went everywhere and *under* my clothes?"

Maybe she knows. I unhinge my jaw. "He's dead."

"Lovely."

"I will say it again for your thick skull. If anyone violates you, if you aren't comfortable, if they touch you, you have every right to do whatever you want in response."

"Great, but I shouldn't need your permission for that."

"You don't, but you also don't listen, so again, Talia, if—"

"Got it, thanks. Moving on, we're on the fourth floor? We have three to six now? Go down, start on three, and work up." She sits up a bit higher as the headband leaves my head again. "But I'm taking these."

"Little Star, no. I don't want you anywhere near those ears. Now put them–"

"I'm not fighting with you on this anymore. I can heal myself.

You worry about protecting me. I'll worry about staying alive. Deal? Deal. Good, glad we have that cleared up, 'cause I make a cute bunny."

I chuckle. "You are cute."

"Great, thanks," she drawls, disgust heavy in the words.

I cock a brow. "I'm not sure where I went wrong with that comment."

She hums. "Maybe I can keep them when this is over."

"For what?"

"I don't know, a costume party for Magic Night?"

"Magic Night?"

She giggles. "We celebrate the night that the Mother set loose her magic in the world, bringing alive all the clay dolls of the Ancients. In the old days, everyone would wear a costume during the celebration to disguise themselves from her magic on the same night every year to keep from being turned back into mud."

"That's fucking stupid."

"That's the Mother religion." She sighs. "I could go as a bunny this year, give myself a cottontail, paint on some whiskers."

Natalia in black, lace lingerie with bunny ears and cottontail materializes in my mind. "We'll keep the ears."

I start down a narrow, spiraling staircase carved from stone. Steps echo up at me, so I stop, and wait. I want to have a clear exit. I'd prefer room to move if we have to fight.

Telra appears around the bend, lingering a few steps below me. Her features pinch, like she knows I was daydreaming about fucking my little star.

Yasmin waits at Telra's back, smiling wide as she purrs, "Hello, Cal."

Telra brushes her long dark hair away from her neck, leaning against the wall to toy with a dagger. The blade twists, three edges that are honed sharp. It's the worst–and best–possible weapon choice, depending on which end one is on.

Voices behind me bounce off the stone, getting closer. "–taking too long. Just lock everyone in the arena. Fuck this shit."

Telra's eyes dance, crinkled at the corners with restrained humor. "Have you thought any more about my proposal?"

I tighten my grip on Natalia as the steps behind us stop, the voice laughing. "Well, well, looks like a little bunny's trapped."

Natalia taps me on the shoulder, and I let her go. Her body slides down mine. Under normal circumstances I'd enjoy it. Right now, it stirs turmoil in my stomach. I'd prefer to keep her where I know she's safe, wrapped in my Dark and pinned to me.

Her back presses against mine, our arms stuck between us. The cuffs proving yet again to be an inconvenience. "I'm cute, right?"

Telra asks, lifting an eyebrow and batting her eyelashes. "Well?"

Natalia shifts against me, and I wiggle my fingers into hers. I lift my chin at Telra. "I have someone else in mind."

Her eyes flash, her lips pressing together. A different voice, male–judging by the baritone decibel–speaks at my back. "What are we waiting for? Wait long enough and the lightning bug will call another smite."

"Her?" Telra asks, pointing the dagger at the center of my chest. "You're already fucking her, aren't you? I mean, it's brilliant. Play with her, pretend to care, capture her heart, and she'll be loyal to a fault. I bet she'll let you do just about anything you want to use her."

My fingers tighten in Natalia's. "That might work," I say. "I get the same from a contract, which is a lot less messy."

Natalia's free arm shoulder twists from my back. My torso jerks and I sway as a combat starts behind me. I grit my teeth, my left arm yanked at an odd angle setting my shoulder alight with pain.

I focus on Telra, certain if I turn to help Natalia, she'll stab me in the back. Losing my balance, rocked by Natalia slamming into me, I fumble a step closer to Telra.

"Ow, you fuck!" Natalia yells. "Stabbing hurts."

My heart skips, a tinge of pain echoing in the next beat. She's panting, then there's the sound of flesh and bone cracking against the stone.

Telra curves her lips with malice and glee. It's an expression she's mastered beautifully. "Aren't you going to help your poor little bunny?"

"Natalia can handle herself."

Tipping her head back, Telra laughs. "Her head just bounced off the wall. I think Mars and Luis are going to earn that trophy."

"You think?"

There's a blast of magic, and I squint against the Light Natalia unleashed. Telra and Yasmine shy away with narrowed eyes. The brilliance dims, and I rock as Natalia resumes fighting. There are physical blows echoing around the stairwell, then a loud whimper from my little star. The tang of blood fills my mouth.

I'm tense enough to shake. "If I turn my back to help my partner, are you going to stick that in me?"

The corners of Telra's painted black lips curl up. "That depends, darling. My proposal? We were good together."

The sex was good, although things went stale in that department after half-a-decade. Besides, the woman is sadistic. She likes to torment, draw blood, play mind games. It was fun for a while, but I grew tired of it and her tastes.

There's a deep groan belonging to a man behind me mingled with a heavy thump.

Turning my head, I call over my shoulder while keeping eyes on Telra. "You okay?"

"Fucking Mother," she curses, her tone miffed. Light flashes in a few quick pulses, then she says, "I'm fine, just a few extra holes. The fuckers had swords."

"We're going up now."

"My proposal, darling? I can let you go so you can sign a contract of union, or I can take those ears." She smiles with closed lips, lifting a hand to pretend to hide her mirth. "The choice is yours."

"Bring it," Natalia calls out. "I'm not that easy to kill."

I flash my teeth at Telra. My little star is a badass, a cute one too. "I'm going to have to pass, baby."

Telra pouts. "I really liked you."

"Yeah, sure, he's got a great dick. What's not to like? Can we move this along?"

I struggle to not laugh, since Natalia is enflaming Telra enough. "Up, Talia."

She takes a step. I follow, but so does Telra. The cuffs pull as Natalia takes another step and I don't, wanting to avoid running into other hunters. Telra is dangerous enough on her own, and I just pissed her off.

Sneering, Telra's features turn cold. "You're really going to choose that over me?"

"Yes," I think in unison with my Dark, but I stay quiet, eyeing the blade in her hand. I'm not going to ask to get stabbed.

I know what she's capable of, and I know it's not enough on a level field. The blade she wields, though, is enough in anyone's hands. The three edges inflict damage that can causes its victim to bleed out in fractions.

She lifts the dagger, purring at me. "Accept my proposal. It could save your Light's life, and I'd let you continue to use her, it would help us after all." She tosses her hair, flipping it over her shoulder. "After I broke her in, of course. I do detest how she looks at you."

Natalia's hand grips tighter as I chuckle. "I'm not making a union proposal under threat of a fight during a hunting game in a stairwell."

"She's glowing. Blood is in the air. Some women might consider it romantic."

Natalia laughs. "I'm afraid of the kind of woman who thinks this is romantic."

Telra's expression turns nasty. "You should be afraid, Light whore. Make your choice, darling."

Laughing, Natalia says, "You're trying too hard. If you have to beg a man this hard to marry you, he's not interested."

"I'm not begging," Telra snaps. "Last chance, Cal."

"Pretty sure his answer was no, twice already, maybe three times? I don't know, I got stabbed. I was distracted."

I'm grinning, shaking with the laughter that I'm swallowing. When Telra is irritated, she's vindictive at best. "I'll take my chances," I tell her. I give Natalia's hand a couple of pulses. "Remember earlier?"

Telra scowls. "Earlier when?"

Natalia's Light gets brighter behind me while Telra's face twists with fury. She lunges at me, and I swing my fist in response. Her head slams against the wall, where she crumples.

I inhale and wince, my muscles clenching, trying to pull me over. Pain and warmth are drenching my abdomen, every breath flaring with muscles and nerves screaming in protest.

I grunt, glaring at Telra as Yasmin helps her up. Blood is trickling from her temple beneath her glossy black hair, but her eyes lower and she exposes her teeth. Her voice is airy, despite the putrid rage. "You really should have accepted my proposal."

I lower my eyes to the dagger off to the side of my navel, fatigue claiming me. "No means no, baby," I pant, woozy, yet still managing a chuckle. She never did understand that sentiment.

Blood is soaking my shirt, the fabric heavy and sticking to me. Yasmin is no longer at Telra's back, the hair at the nape of my neck tingling.

Natalia lets out a shrill scream, although it's muted, like it's caught in the back of her throat. I'm thrown off balance, falling forward.

Telra flattens against the wall, ripping the blade from my side as I topple. The metal bites and tears with blazing agony, then Natalia and I roll and collide, slamming into the sharp stone edges of the steps and bouncing off the walls as we fall, spiraling downward.

I hit level flooring, groaning as the world spins, bright spots floating in the air, mixing with the scent of blood and sweat.

Natalia rolls down the last step, whimpering as she stills. She's half on top of me, pushing up while hissing and cursing. Her glow is brilliant, stinging my eyes, the ears on her head casting long shadows.

I try to sit and clench my teeth at the screaming pulse in my side, the blood-soaked shirt peeling and pulling my ripped torso. The wound screams to remind me of its presence.

Telra and Yasmin stand on the steps above us, Telra covering her mouth as she giggles. "I can't wait to cut the ears off this little rabbit."

I get to my knees then collapse against the wall, faint and breathless. "Don't...fucking," I pant between words, lethargic. "...touch...her."

Yasmin laughs, her shrill humor echoing off the walls. "You're really in no position for demands, or to be trying to protect your little bunny."

Telra purrs, "Can you feel my venom? I laced the blade with it for this little game. You remember how it feels?"

She's dosed me probably a thousand times, and I've never developed a tolerance. That's the trick of a Venominx. They're smaller than every other Dark Seraphinus, but they're nimble, agile, and have a venom that's potent.

The paralytic toxin in my blood is shutting down my system, my mind muddling, my energy depleting.

Natalia gets up, her hand linked to mine closes around the

links and pulls, fingers crawling along the chain. I try to get my arm to lift, wanting to take her hand. My arm twitches, useless at my side.

She lifts her chin. "I don't know what toxic shit you carry or what you've done to Cal, although knowing your personality, I'm assuming it's seriously caustic but I'm fucking adorable with these ears, and I plan on keeping them."

Telra steps down toward us. Natalia gets her hand on mine. My fingers wiggle, my mind and magic screaming at the digits to move. Dark streaks at Natalia, and she lifts her untethered hand to shield.

I let my magic loose, the tendrils crawling along the stone of the walls and steps. I'm dying, but I'm not dead yet. Telra's venom is slowing me, but I'll be damned if I don't help my little star.

Yasmin shrieks, recoiling. Natalia breathes hard. Telra stops a pace away, saying "Oh dear little bunny, looks like you've no place left to hide."

Natalia flips her off, and Telra strikes. Light glimmers, throwing Telra back up the stairs. Metal clinks as something small rolls across stone. The dagger.

Telra lunges for it like a furious cat, and I command my Dark to intercept. It streaks out, latching onto her, tangling with her limbs to delay her.

"Glow," I manage to say over Telra's shrieks as she tries to break free. My magic is stronger than her, though. It winds tight, binding her against the wall.

"Don't move," Natalia answers. Her hand tightens on mine.

Yasmin picks up the dagger as Natalia's Light intensifies. I begin to draw on it, but it rushes into me, coursing like a riptide, faster than I can control. It burns, suffocating the Dark in me, pulsating faster than I can absorb. This isn't my doing or magic, it's hers. She isn't letting me use her or take from her. She's forcing her Light into me. It's too fast, too much.

The pain lessens under the flow of her magic. I can breathe

easier, her Light giving me strength back. Yasmin slices and cleaves at tendrils of my magic. It screams in my mind at the assault, and I growl, the rumble stuck in the back of my throat.

I draw my Dark in, protecting it. I can't afford it wounded too much in my current, limited capacity. Telra and Yasmin advance. Natalia sends a burst through me, and I lose control.

A roar rips from my chest as the burning Light overwhelms me. My Dark bursts, unable to absorb the Light, expelling it as quick as it comes, like her magic is rippling through mine as if it were a filter.

Her Light and my Dark explode, flinging all of the women away from me. My arm wrenches out of its socket, threatening to rip clean off as Natalia hits the end of our tether. It pulls on my arm, stretching out my shoulder and torso, the wound in my side sending a searing reminder it's there. Natalia screams with me.

I keel over, my arm useless, but weight pulls on torn muscles because I am still connected to Natalia. My shoulder throbs, pain coursing through me with every cursed beat of my heart. I watch Telra as she gets up, doubling over with an arm to her stomach. "That hurt, darling."

"Good." Panting, I make a pathetic attempt to stand, my knees giving out. My left arm hangs useless at my side in an awkward angle. Natalia's is bent wrong.

My Dark snarls and begins pooling on the ground, preparing to defend us.

Telra kicks at Yasmin who doesn't move. "Useless. Oh well." She pulls another dagger from a sheath on her leg, shaking her head. She's bleeding, looking about as good as I feel, but limping forward. "I can still cut those ears off."

I get to my knees, at least upright, but Natalia is barely stirring. I set my magic loose at Telra which she blocks and diverts. It pulls back on the defense as Yasmin gets to her feet.

Tsking, Telra shakes her head. "Don't make me kill you. I still think we could work this out."

I laugh, my side twinging. "You're fucking sadistic."

She grins, stepping closer. "Why thank you." She bats her lashes as Natalia gets to her knees.

She groans. "What the fuck?"

Telra flicks her wrist, the blade flying loose. Too late, I form a shield. Natalia falls back, choking as deep red fluid bubbling between her lips.

"Talia," I yell, grabbing for her.

Tendrils wrap around my arm, preventing me from reaching her, the shadows plunging me into a blistering cold that freezes my skin. More Dark slams into me, and I snarl as my dislocated shoulder rips further out of place while Natalia and I are flung across the floor.

I push up with my good arm, disoriented. Telra crouches over Natalia, pulling the ears from her. My ex rips the blade out of out my star's chest, cleaning it off with one of the ears.

"You should hide for the rest of the game, darling. Wait it out, survive. I don't want you dead. Maybe I'll make you my queen if you ask nice." She blows a kiss at me, turning away, taking the ears with her. Yasmin grins at her as they start to jog up the steps, leaving me broken and bleeding.

I crawl to Natalia, staring down at her. The Light is dim, the tendrils disappearing like smoke, receding in towards the wound in her chest.

Pulling her against me, I drag us to the wall to lean against the cool, rough stone. Bending my knees, I get her between them, her back to my torso, although I'm moving sluggish under the effects of Telra's venom. "Come on, Little Star, heal," I manage, the words sticking in the back of my throat. "Heal for me."

The Light over her skin goes out, leaving me in darkness.

"Fuck," I yell, voice cracking. The sting of my loss breaks my mind free of the drug, and I make a fist with my free hand the floor, slamming it next to me on the floor, stone cracking like the splintering cold shredding through my chest.

I cuddle her, pressing my nose against her hair, my lips finding her temple to press a kiss. "You said you'd heal," I whisper, my throat thick with a lump stuck in the middle. "Fuck, you promised me you'd survive." Closing my eyes against the burn in them, I try to stop the wail of agony from my Dark from spilling out of my eyes.

"You promised me," I manage, coming apart at the seams. Wounds inflicted over centuries pull at the stitches.

All my years rush over me in an instant. I've broken bones, split skin, and shed blood aplenty, always fighting, always afraid. I have endured pain, but nothing like this. I thought Natalia was my salvation.

Taking a deep breath, I blink my eyes open again and swallow the misery. I can't stay here no matter how I long to shield myself with my Dark and quit playing the game. All I want to do is keep her close.

I kiss the side of Natalia's head, and then move her to the floor with care. It's not impossible to survive games alone. Others have done it. Sterling has several times over.

I wait, debating if I need to sever our bond. The thought sends bile up the back of my throat. I need to get up. I need to move, keep going, but her Light had gone out once before.

Maybe she's not...

A deep red glow in the center of her chest sparks to life, growing and expanding into a vibrant orange. Brilliant silver Light shines out of the wound in her chest. I stare, not breathing, too afraid if I move her Light will go out.

The air zaps, glinting with electric blue *zzts*. My Dark coils around my body, the tendrils quivering in fear.

"Don't you dare fucking smite me, Little Star."

The Light shining out of the wound ceases as the Light races and swirls out across her skin in delicate silver, the orange racing away through the rest of her body before fading out until all that's left is the lace pattern.

"Talia?"

She stirs, then sits, rubbing her chest with her free hand. "Ow." Turning to me, she makes a fist, smacking at me with cute little strikes, her face scrunched up. She screams, punctuating every word with a whack. "I. So. Regret. That. I. Saved. Your. Life."

I drop my back against the wall while a laugh shatters my chest in exhaustion and relief. "You're hard to kill, Little Star."

CHAPTER 45
NATALIA

"I did tell you that." I wrinkle my nose at him. "You look like death."

He nods. "Thought you were gone again."

I shake my head, eyeing his loose and broken arm. "You have no faith in me." I grab his arm, lifting it. He bites back a groan. "Yeah, shut up, your girlfriend stabbed me. I hope it hurts."

"Not my girlfriend." He chuckles.

I hold his arm out straight, pressing a hand against his shoulder and close my eyes. Centering, I find the dwindling Ki flickering within me.

Feeding it into him, I pull on his arm and sinew snaps, his socket popping into place. He makes a noise of pain, and I push more into him, trying to make sure the wound in his side is healed.

"That," he whispers.

My eyebrows pull together as I frown. "Shut up. Don't move. Don't talk. Don't do anything."

He falls quiet as the Ki pulses through him. When it flows smooth and even, I let go, slumping forward into him. He catches me, grabbing the back of my neck and kissing the top of my head.

"What did you just do?"

"I channeled Ki, used it to heal you."

"Did you do that when I told you to glow?"

I hum, not wanting move or even speak, but the contract demands I answer him. "Yes. You were bleeding out."

He kisses my head again, squeezing me. "You and I are going to need to work on that. You overwhelmed me to the point I lost control. My Dark couldn't handle that much at once."

I sigh, shifting in closer to him, cuddling against him in a ball between his legs. "I was glowing for you to take the Light. The Ki I was feeding into you to heal you."

He wraps his free arm around me as we catch our breath. "It was like pure, raw power."

"I guess. Ki is the energy of the spirit, so, sure."

Callahan holds me, his heart slowing, and I sink into his solid warmth. Fatigue pulls me down, threatening to overcome me, so with effort I sit up, putting a hand on his chest.

As his eyes find mine, I flip him off. "Stop making me regret saving your life."

He tries to smile, more like the idea crosses his features before they fall into place. "I'd say I'll try, but that would be a lie, and you know the Dark doesn't lie to you." He yanks me into him again.

"Well, fuck you then," I mutter to the solid muscles of his chest.

He laughs, but it's weak. "Little Star."

"What?" He doesn't answer. "Little Star what?" I repeat louder. "What? Behave? Be a good little vassal? Sit, stay, *bzzt*, *bzzt*, flash, smite, and let you *eat me* without saying a word? You should've taken her deal and let her break me if you expect that."

He makes a strange noise, like a sobbing moan. His hand yanks on mine as he grabs my head, prying my face from his chest. With sudden, crushing force, he rams his mouth against mine.

I melt. Damnit.

His tongue glides against mine, then he pulls back. "I'd rather

343

stick myself with a thousand hot irons than mate Telra, and I only expect you to behave for me when I say."

"Even that's a stretch of my abilities." I sigh, trying to get up while he keeps me pressed against him.

"Yes, I know, but I need you to behave for me. Behaving has to be better for you than breaking your mind."

"Fine, I am. I'm trying anyway. Where are we?"

He glances around. "Out of bounds." He scrubs a hand down his face. "We also lost your ears. If the guards get ahold of us, we're dead."

I nod. "Great. We need to move. How much time did we burn?"

He checks his watch. "Little more than a full rune's worth since I last checked."

"We've had two fights, time to heal, and it was only a rune? Sure, that's fucking great." I throw my free hand up. "Fuck these games, dude. Couldn't we just play beer ball or some shit? Like, oh, hand-eye coordination, sure that guy can hold his alcohol and see straight, he'd make a good king. Isn't that enough?"

He chuckles, tucking hair behind my ear. "Is there ever a point I should be aware of that you aren't sassy, like if you're sick?"

"No. If I'm out of sass my ass is dead."

"Noted. Come on." He takes my hand.

We start up the steps, moving slow. On the third floor we work our way through the halls, walking hand-in-hand, each facing a direction. Every so often we switch which one walks forward leaving the other to shuffle backward. Cal tenses at my back with an intake of air.

A female yells, "Show your mark."

Cal whips me in front of him and over his shoulder in one move, then takes off running. I can't help but giggle, watching the guards pursue.

"If they catch us, they kill us."

"Yeah," I manage, still chortling. "But the way you just manhandled me and took off was pretty impressive."

He scoffs, breathing hard as he sidesteps, shouldering into a wall and stepping into a small alcove. The wall swings shut with a soft thump. The heavy boots of the guards stomp past as we hold our breath, the sound of them running receding up the hall.

I let out a whoosh of air and glance around. "Where are we?"

"Hidden room," he says. "There are dozens in the palace. This one I found when Sterling blasted me into it maybe a decade ago? We can't stay here long, though. He knows about it. Telra, too."

"You fucked her in here, didn't you?"

He rolls me off his shoulder. "Want to try it? We need to waste some time."

"Gross," I say, faking a laugh.

Wrapping an arm around my waist, he pulls my back against him. "Because of Telra?"

Wrinkling my nose, I say, "I mean, she's gorgeous, but not my type."

"You told her I have a great dick." His lips whisper against my ear before dropping to open against my neck. "Do you want a chance to find out?"

I about damn whimper, my abdomen clenching with an ache that needs to be filled. "Are you hoping you get to close your eyes and pretend I'm her?"

He bites the shell of my ear hard enough it stings, his voice terse. "No." He steps away with a sigh. "Let's move."

He gets me on his back and takes off. We end up moving through several floors, ending on the sixth floor.

The cuff sears. "Prey is limited to floor four to five."

"Fuck," I groan, dropping my head onto his shoulder. "This is feeling a lot less like a hunt and more and more like we're supposed to die."

Cal slips into a room to put me down. "We need to move, but I

345

need a fraction." He checks his watch. "Two runes, Little Star. Think you can hold on for me?"

I glare at him. "I so regret all of this. Tony and being a baby-maker is sounding better by the rune, and I'm considering burning out your contract."

Cal tenses, shoulders lifting as his eyes darken. He moves faster than my exhausted and addled brain follows, pulling me against him then walking me against the wall before I even open my mouth to protest. I'm pinned against him, his hand linked to mine grabbing my hip, the other wrapping around my throat.

Dark coils around me, hissing in a soft warning as it constricts and pulls Cal in closer until I can't distinguish where his skin ends and mine begins. His mouth finds my ear. "Don't ever threaten my contract again, Little Star, or I'll put you somewhere only I will ever see your Light again."

His teeth sink in my earlobe hard enough to hurt as his hand tightens to jerk my hips toward him.

I release a breathless whimper. "Shit."

He goes on in that deep, rumbling growl. "You're mine, and I'm never going to hear about that disgusting pig or the thought of him touching you ever again."

His mouth moves to my neck, opening against it. My body shivers, tension coiling in my lower stomach. I grab a fistful of his blood-stained shirt as he forces his leg between mine then presses up, lifting me onto tiptoes. As I fall into him his mouth brushes against mine.

"Um," I breathe, staring at his mouth. "Pretty sure your girl-friend isn't going to like this."

He scoffs. "She's not my girlfriend, Little Star. I ended that years ago."

My heart is in my throat, my stomach in my knees as I throb against his leg. "Not so sure she knows that."

His free hand cups my jaw, his eyes intense. "I don't care what she thinks." His thumb runs across my lower lip. "We had a relationship. I ended it because she's a sadistic bitch, and I'm not interested in that. I'm looking for something else."

"Yeah?" I swallow, trying to steady myself. I'm not going to let him know he's getting under my skin. "What's that? Maybe you want to swing the other way. Masochist saint? Oh, or maybe you just want to swing the other way? Is Marius more what you want?"

His eyes flare wider, and his hand tightens, forcing my jaw to lift. "I'm hoping for a sassy star."

In my chest, my heart does a little flip of joy. Maybe I'm crazy, or maybe he wants me too. I smile, "That's a terrible idea."

"You're funny. I like that."

I tilt my head. "Not particularly."

"You're beautiful."

"So's your girlfriend," I say managing to hold back my laugh. His face flares with a sparked rage. "How'd that work out for you?"

"Don't tease me."

"I thought you were the one who liked the anticipation?"

"I thought we agreed we liked the act itself more."

"I mean, I remember I said I liked the satisfaction of the act itself. You gave up, 'cause you can't handle this."

He chuckles. "Even one-handed I seem to handling it." He rocks my hips forward against his leg. My eyes cross in response to the jolt of pleasure.

"Mother," I whisper, panting with desire.

He grins against my lips, tilting his head, "Still like things the hard way?"

My skin ripples, the muscles in my stomach and legs clamping down. All I can think about is him, hard and going hard. "Um."

"Who can't handle what, Little Star?"

I swallow, fingers curling into his shirt, "Shouldn't we be moving?"

He laughs, dropping his leg and letting me fall on trembling

347

weak ones. He pulls me from the wall, cracking the door open to check outside. He pulls back, twisting his arm behind him, pulling my arm up and over his shoulder.

"Come on, we need to hurry before guards find us."

I jump on his back, giggling. "Not quite the ride I had in mind."

He chokes on a laugh as he carries me out the door.

We manage with a little bit of luck to get on an acceptable floor, although hunters and guards are everywhere. Cal breaks out a few tricks to keep us out of sight of the guards, hiding out in hidden alcoves and rooms. We survive another few skirmishes with hunters, leaving them unconscious.

He swivels a painting and slips inside, leaning against a wall to catch his breath until I'm yawning and relaxing.

"You okay?" He shrugs his shoulder a few times to rouse me.

"Tired. I've about wiped out my Ki."

"What happens if–" the cuff burns, hissing, then dropping from around our wrists "–you run out?"

Smoke wafts up, twisting out to spell out more words. "Prey is limited to the great hall".

I yawn again. "Fuck that, and not much. When I'm out, I'm out, no healing, no channeling it. I'm just out of magic to burn. If I try to draw more than I have, I draw my life force, soul, spirit, whatever. The Assembly always warned me it kills you."

He slips me off his back and checks his watch. "It's Hope's rune. Just give me one more rune."

"Until the next game." I roll my eyes. "It's not like I really have a choice anyway. I'm your vassal. You say do it, and I have to."

He gives me that charming grin. "But we're having such a great time."

"Are we though?"

"I'm with you, so yes." There's a weight to his words, no teasing to be found.

I'm in more danger from my Darkling than these stupid games.

I can't help the smile twisting my lips. "Babe, you might be, but I'm not sadistic like your girlfriend, and I'm no masochist either, so I think these games suck."

CHAPTER 46

CALLAHAN

S<small>HE CALLS ME BABE AND</small> I <small>GRIN, PUSHING THE SECRET DOOR OPEN</small> to step into the corridor. "Great hall, *babe*," I say, holding my hand out. "And no more fighting with one hand behind our back."

She steps out with me, lifting her arms and rolling her head on her shoulders. I drop my hands to my hips, letting her stretch.

"Mother, feels good to move."

She drops low, one leg bent the other out straight to her side, then switches between legs. Next, she stands, arches back, her arms over her head, then goes through a backflip.

I extend my hand again. "Come on, there's nowhere left for Marius to hide."

"Or us." She grimaces taking my hand. "I need my ears back. I make a shit bunny without them."

"I'll figure something out."

She puts her hand behind her head, two fingers up, giving herself rabbit ears. "Think they'd notice?"

"Yes," I chuckle.

We head down a flight of steps, weaving through the corridors to work our way to the grand hall while avoiding the guards sweeping the area, closing the net.

It's easier separated, without a chain rattling to draw attention, but she shines in the shadows like a beacon. She is lithe on her feet, though, moving without sound, and my Dark is content to cloak her as much as possible.

Reaching the hall that leads into the room, I pull her next to me against the wall, leaning to check around the corner, surveying the room while staying out of sight. There are a couple groups of hunters milling about.

I scan the faces, noting some dangerous players waiting. By the look of things, the hunters were somehow getting the same messages as us prey. Telra is holding the headband she took from Natalia. She spins it on her finger, laughing with Yasmine.

Turning back to Natalia I grimace. "There's no way to hide anymore, and guards are closing in. We're going to have to fight."

She sighs, shoulders slumping. "Your girlfriend in there?"

"Telra," I stress, "is, and I'm going to ask you quit calling her that."

"Sure." Natalia kicks away from the wall. "Excuse me, while I go kill your girlfriend."

I grab her by the hips before she can walk into the room, pulling her back to my chest. "Stop, think." I press the side of my face against hers, my chin hanging over her shoulder. "We need a plan."

"I have one. I'm going to punch her in the face and see what happens."

I laugh, knowing it's only going to encourage her. My little star might be as crazy as Telra. I have a type, apparently.

"I was thinking something a little different..." I trail off as footsteps slap against the stone, coming closer.

Thames is running in a full sprint, carrying a limp Hiro. As he gets to us, his legs give, and he stumbles. Hiro spills out of his arms and tumbling across the floor as Thames catches himself to keep himself from face planting.

"Guards," he pants. "Poachers, whatever, right behind...out of bounds." He waves a hand behind him.

I scan for the guards.

Thames gasps for air, collecting Hiro in his arms. "Oh, gods. Are you still breathing?"

Natalia pulls away and kneels next to him. "Is he alive?"

Thames sobs, bobbing his head. "Not for long. That bastard Chlem got him good and took the ears." He draws a rattling breath in. "Then the guards came for us. We fought, but he went down. I just grabbed him and ran."

I eye the hunters approaching us, no doubt drawn to the commotion.

"He's not going to make it to the end. He's going to bleed out before Eloise can get to him."

Hunters stalk forward with wicked glee, lifting weapons.

I roll my shoulders back. Hiro's a loss, but I'm not joining him in the afters. "Get up and fight or we all die."

Natalia says, "Go. Cal's right. The only way we get through this is if we fight. I'll take care of Hiro."

"Talia," I warn. "You're fighting too."

She doesn't answer. I glance over, seeing her eyebrows pushed together, her glow feeding through her hand in a soft pulse.

An arrow sails through the air, past Natalia, wide. I reach out, forming a barrier around us with my Dark.

Hiro stirs with a groan.

I frown. "What are you doing, Little Star?"

"Healing."

Thames gasps, "Can she do that?"

I tense and scowl, ignoring him. "You said you were out."

She opens her eyes, glaring at me. "I have enough for this."

I grip my fists knowing she'll push her limits. "You need it to fight. Save your magic." I grunt, my head jerking to the side, a reflexive flinch to my magic taking a hit. It stings, leaving my temple throbbing. "We need to fight now," I say, my magic

352

recoiling and hissing in my mind. "I can't hold this many for long."

Hiro blinks, searching his blood-stained chest. He frowns, sitting and glancing around. "Yeah, makes sense I'd die, and my worst afters is the games."

Thames laughs, pulling his lover to his feet and into an embrace. His eyes are on Natalia with shining adoration. "I don't know how you did that but thank you."

Natalia shrugs and stretches. "I'm going to get my ears back."

I shake my head. "No. Telra's sadistic and crazier than you. Just stay alive, don't worry about the ears. I don't care about points. I'm dropping the shield now, get ready." I nod at Hiro while I reach a hand toward her. "Get ready."

He grimaces, tucking Thames in close.

When Natalia takes my hand, I pull her close, whispering in her ear, "Glow, without feeding me this time."

She nods her forehead against my shoulder. "All right, but fuck, it hurts when you do this." The Light over her skin blends and merges together, a soft orange spreading through her beneath the glimmer of her skin. It burns my eyes, yet I don't want to look away from her radiant beauty.

My father fell in love with a Light Seraphinus, even mated her. It irked me, leaving a bitter taste between us. I regret that. There's so much I regret between my father and I, as I share his adoration of the Light now. My little star is brightening something I didn't realize existed within me.

Telra was convenience and fun. This is something else.

My magic screams in sweet agony, the Light searing my Dark as it slithers over her skin, hungry with desire, sucking the Light in with delight.

Thames gawks. "Holy shit."

Hiro scoffs. "He's a Light eater. It's what he does."

"You shut up, baby. It's not like we've ever seen it before, and you so you do not get to take that sour tone with me. You almost left me, and I was going to have to follow you to the afters to find you."

I collect my magic, dropping the shield drops. Hunters press forward, I grin. I set my magic loose. It explodes in midnight blue and dusk shades of turquoise intermixing with orange flames. The shock wave flings the bodies into the great hall. Only half are stirring and starting to rise.

Natalia steps away, cringing and doubling over. She bares her teeth at me. "I hate when you do that." She flips me off and takes an uneasy step into the room. Her head shifts, inspecting the damage, and she whistles low. Her eyes narrow, and I follow her line of sight to Telra.

"Talia," I say with warning, reaching for her, but she ducks my attempt to grab her and rushes into the room. I hurry after her, several hunters closing in. I narrow my eyes, setting my jaw and loosing magic.

Natalia runs straight for Telra, yelling, "Give me back my ears, you sadistic bitch."

Telra gives her a bewildered look, others parting away from her in humor, and Natalia punches her in the face.

Telra lurches from the impact, then turns back, while her eyes start to glow green. "How the fuck are you alive?" Telra screeches. She swings back at Natalia. "I killed you, you Light whore."

I turn from them, catching a hunter and hurling it into the wall, trying to get closer to my little star. Someone hurls magic at Natalia. She recoils, sending it right back. "Stay out of this. It's personal, okay?" She kicks Telra in the face, backflipping away from her retaliation.

Telra launches at Natalia screaming and they go down, sprawling. Chaos ignites around me, and I can't watch anymore. There are too many bodies between Natalia and me.

I come to blows, fending off swords and daggers with my magic, my Dark acting on instinct to take a blow or pry weapons away from my attackers. I swing my fists. A hunter blocks, and I move in, getting in a few hits.

I get knocked from the side. Thames helps me up, rolling to press his back to mine. "Your Light is crazier than Telra. She just took down Sterling then went back to kicking her ass."

I grunt, slamming my elbow in the side of someone's jaw, hurling magic into them. The poor bastard drops to his knees, my magic oozing from his eyes. "Natalia's fucking nuts, but she can handle herself." I wait for the hunter to go limp before pulling back, turning to dive, roll, then form a shield to protect Hiro and myself with from a bolt of purple erupting from Chlem.

"Thames!" Hiro roars, throwing black haze toward his lover that engulfs him as he gets attacked from several sides.

There are others joining us, fending off hunters, but one is missing. Marius is absent in the fray. He should be helping. I use my Dark to force hunters away, Acker kicking someone down next to me as I scan the room.

I spot him, lurking in the shadows against the far wall with a grin on his face. I take a blast in the back, pain rippling through me, skin splitting with a violent sting. I roll, an inky bolt flying over me as I reclaim my feet.

A woman's scream rips through the air, followed by Telra's laugh. My chest constricts. I turn, grab Hiro, and throw him at Thames. I cross my arms, wrists together to take the next hit of purple from Chelm square with a block. I force it back with my Dark, sending tendrils of fire at Chlem that sends him sailing through the air.

Elsewhere, Light glows brighter and a feminine scream pierces the din. I try to see, but the Light hurts my eyes and there are too many advancing on me.

I back into someone, glancing at Thames and Hiro behind me. I throw a forearm to block, and hit back, growling in the back of my throat as I erupt with flames. My Dark laden with Natalia's Light, spreads out into a smoldering ruin around me.

Those attacking retreat, those not fast enough caught in tendrils of Dark begin to burn with flames. With a moment of freedom, I hurl fire at Marius. He ducks and laughs, but I've given away his position, and with Jacques still wearing his antlers, some of the eager hunters still hoping for extra points turn on him and Jacques.

Fatigue burns through me. My Dark detonates, booming as it explodes in a ring around Hiro, Thames, and me.

The fire dies away in shimmering tendrils, and I breathe hard, cursing at the hunters advancing in on us again despite several lying prone and unmoving.

Thames laughs at my back as the ring of hunters closes back in. "Any last words, love?"

Hiro answers in a snarl. "I'm glad you're dying with me."

I snap at them. "Fuck both of you. We're not dying."

My eyes search for Natalia. She and Telra are exchanging hits and blocks, but Natalia forces her hand out and Light flashes. I have no more time to watch, forced to fend off a hunter, a faceless no one right now. I put them down and get punched from the side.

The world spins. I latch onto whoever and throw them, getting up and boxing someone else, throwing a burst of Dark at them. They howl and recoil, my magic setting them on fire.

Thames's voice is thin as he pants between smacks and thuds of flesh meeting flesh. "This...would be...so...much...easier–ow– If I...could...just fucking...shift."

I force my magic to twist into another translucent shield, but Chlem's blast of purple shatters it and hits me in the shoulder. Growling at the infliction, I send tendrils out that pierce into him, forcing every bit of my temper through to ignite them with heat, and he crumples, screaming in agony and writhing.

A horn trumpet blares through the room, and I stop, pulling my magic in.

Chlem pants and gasps, clawing his way to his feet to grin at me. "Few more fractions, and you might have had me."

I scoff. "You're not that easy to get rid of."

CHAPTER 47
CALLAHAN

My eyes scan for Natalia, seeing her on top of Telra, her chest glowing orange with firelight flickering. She holds that three-edged blade at Telra's throat, stopped by the horn. Her lips move, although her voice doesn't carry.

The din and confusion have ceased in an instant. Eloise hurries into the room to tend to the fallen who need her assistance. I grit my teeth, needing to be healed, but I'll wait for Natalia.

My shoulders sag, my back on fire. I step toward Natalia, desperate to be in her Light and hold her hand. She rolls off Telra, dropping the blade as she stands, the sunny glow dissipating from her chest as she plucks up the rabbit ears nearby.

She turns back as she puts them on. "You're lucky time ran out or you'd be dead, bitch."

She spins, head bobbing and twisting. When she meets my gaze, she grins ear -to-ear, pointing at the rabbit ears on top of her head. Pride swells in me, as I chuckle.

My little star starts gimping toward me, beginning to wilt.

Telra pushes up, grabbing the three-edged blade from the ground.

I move quicker toward Natalia, my Dark and me anxious to have her safe, but Telra is there first. She grabs Natalia's shoulder from behind, sneering at me.

Natalia shrieks, toppling forward.

"No," I roar, running.

Others lurch forward, shouting about cheating, about breaking the rules of engagement, about dishonor. Sterling drags Telra away, flinging her to the floor and leaning over to bellow at her.

None of it matters. What's done is done.

Telra shoves to her feet, screaming with laughter. "Whose dead now, Glow Whore?"

I slide into Natalia on my knees, lifting her torso as she chokes and spits blood. My hand searches her back, finding the dagger embedded to the hilt, off to the left-side.

Her heart.

Mine twists and rips, stringy black veins stretching to a breaking point, threatening to snap. My magic twists around her, echoing the shattering agony in my chest.

"Move," Eloise commands, shoving me away. Natalia hits the floor, face down as Eloise takes my place. "Let me see."

She rips the blade out of my little star, and I clamp my jaw at the scream it elicits from Natalia.

Eloise rests a hand on Natalia's back over the wound gushing blood.

She's shuddering and wheezing, each breath gurgling, as she spits out more blood.

Eloise's mouth pulls tight. "The heart was pierced. There's nothing to be done. It is already dying, and she's infected by minx toxin. Telra's venom is potent. I cannot heal this."

Natalia flails at Eloise. "Way," she manages. "Get...away." She coughs and splutters, shaking violently. She glows bright orange, the air charging around us. "Go." The word is a snarl in a voice I've never heard, harsh and full of electricity.

I take a few hesitant steps away. Staring down at her in wonder, I watch the Light suck inward to the middle of her torso. If I hadn't seen it before, I'd think her dead. Now I know it's the Light is collecting, protecting itself first, then its host.

Electricity zaps like little pulses in the air while everyone is shuffling away. My little star is too stubborn to die. She may someday, just not today. When she dies, she'll flip both middle fingers in the air then walk backward into the afters on her terms, and no one else's.

Telra's scream is full of fury. "I stabbed her in her fucking heart!"

I turn to her, the little hairs on my body standing up in the charged air. It thickens and hums as I take one step toward her, but Eloise smacks a hand to my chest, staying me. "She broke the rules. She'll answer to our King. Do not break the rules as well, Cal." She turns away, rushing for others that need healing.

My hands clench to fists, every muscle in my body tenses. The zaps in the air are increasing in volume, crackling quicker. I collect my Dark in preparation of a smite, unsure of what is coming.

Natalia screams, the marks down her back turning to lines of pure silver Light, illuminated beneath the back of her dress in beautiful geometry. Everything goes white, her entire body pure Light, as the air rushes past me in toward Natalia.

I blink to refocus my sight, and see Natalia is upright on her knees, swaying. She collapses over, and I'm ripped forward, before I realize it, my Dark racing for her. I get her over on her back, my arms beneath her as I lift, cradling her against my chest and in my Dark. "Talia?"

She groans and flips me off. "Fuck you, your stupid girlfriend, and these games. That was awful, and I'm going to sleep now."

There are a few strangled laughs around, the loudest from Thames, who turns to Telra. "You're a dead little Venominx in the next round."

Chlem yells, "No one gets away with cheating."

Next to me, Sterling kneels on one knee, bracing himself with fingertips to the floor. He frowns at me, "Is she all right?"

I nod.

"Good." Smirking, he stands, looking to Telra. "You couldn't take her down in a fair fight, so you cheated? You deserve to be disgraced for this shit, and you're out of respect now."

Telra snaps back. "Fuck you, Sterling. I still am owed respect for doing what we all should have. I did what none of you would risk your life to do."

"You're a cheat."

"You're a pathetic rat if you side with the Light."

"I side with Cal," he shouts back. "She's his contracted."

"She's the fucking Light!"

Ignoring them, I drop my face close to Natalia's, whispering, "You said you were out. How did you heal?"

She twitches, eyes closed, voice throaty. "You know what I said I shouldn't do?"

I sigh, shifting her, standing with her in my arms. "Yes."

"Well, I did, and it hurt," she says with a pout. "Like a big, sparkly, pink dildo shoved in the ass with no lube."

"You are ridiculous."

"And sober," she whines. "I want vodka. A dozen bottles."

I turn to Telra. Her eyes are glassy, her face red with rage. She snarls at me, held between guards. "A human would be dead." She twists, trying to break free of the Dark warriors holding fast. The Dark emitting from them wraps her tighter, while she screams at me. "She's a Light Seraphinus! She must be! She should be dead! She should've been dead when I put a blade through her the first time. You lied! You're a fucking liar!"

I scowl, shrugging my shoulders, the split skin down my back twinging. "I didn't stab someone in the back when the game was over."

She sneers. "I was trying to save you from yourself. She'll turn on you. Light burns out the Dark until it doesn't exist."

Natalia sounds like she's trying to laugh while still dying. "You're a fucking moron if you think Cal needs to be protected from me."

The Dark King makes his way over, leaning on his cane and Marius helping him. I'm pleased to see him bloodied and limping even as he supports his father.

Everyone peels away to allow him to approach. He stops, stares at me, then turns to fix on Telra. "You broke our rules. You stabbed another player in the back after the game had ended."

She bares her teeth. "Guilty as charged."

The King turns back to me. "Put your Light bug down."

I set Natalia on her feet, helping to steady her. The King accepts a blade from Marius, and extends it as an offering, hilt to my little star. Her hand lifts, trembling as she accepts it. She sways, so I tighten my grip on her shoulders.

"You have the right to retribution in kind. You may stab her in the back." He snaps his fingers and the guards force Telra down on her knees.

Natalia doesn't say anything, the blade shaking in her grip. She shakes her head. Her voice wobbles and she hacks like she's trying to laugh again as she drops the blade. "I don't take cheap shots. When I kill her, I'm going to do it fairly."

Natalia crumples, and I catch her against me, following her down to get my arm under her knees before lifting her in my arms to stand once more.

"Callahan?" The King turns a questioning eye upon me.

I nod at the King, Natalia limp as a rag doll. "The Dark shows respect and courage. We do not break the rules of combat or cheat for unfair advantage. Me and mine follow the honor code, and Talia has every right to refuse stabbing a player in the back when they cannot fight back outside of a sanctioned fight."

The King lifts his eyebrow, his lips twisting to a smile. "Grant

Callahan an extra point for this game. If your Light bug stands as the Dark and is willing to face a contender on even ground, you deserve it."

I intake sharply. Contenders aren't marked or revealed. It makes us a target, like the Light ruining a good shirt, cappuccino, and my morning. That instance may not be the best example, given it led to Natalia's contract, and my own personal star.

The word wasn't a slip of the tongue either. As a contender, I'm already in possession of knowing who my fellow compatriots are.

Sterling smirks at me, arms crossed over his chest. He nods his approval. I tip my head to him.

The King grins at me before turning to the room. "The rest of you check in, see Eloise if you need, trade in your trophies or marks for your winnings, and clean yourselves up. Breakfast is in three runes."

CHAPTER 48
NATALIA

CAL HAS ELOISE HEAL HIM, THEN TRADED IN MY RABBIT EARS MUCH to my disappointment. Afterward, he carried me back to our suite, and shouldered us inside. Massimo lurches up from the couch, stepping to us. He throws his arms around us.

"You two give me anxiety," he says low, stepping back and frowning at me. "How'd the hunt go? Our little lightning bug looks half-dead."

"Bloody shit," Cal responds. "The Baron boy took a swing at me when I walked into him."

"Lazarus, goes by Laz. From what I can tell, everyone says he's brilliant, he's just weak. He has a few contracts, mostly those who served his father that remain loyal to him, plus a friend." Mass smiles. "It sounds like you and me."

Cal grunts and shifts me. "I'm not doing the walk down memory lane shit with you. Smart I can use though. Couldn't find Marius, but I'll get my hands on him sooner or later. Walked into Telra. She propositioned me for a union contract again." He sighs. "She laced her blade with her venom."

Massimo laughs. "Typical hunt."

"Except this time, Telra took a cheap shot after the game ended which almost killed Talia."

I tip my head into his shoulder. "That hurt so bad."

Cal says, "You should have taken the shot."

"There was no way. I could barely hold that dagger. Besides, now your girlfriend gets to live knowing I spared her life, that's going to eat at her."

Massimo chuckles. "Girlfriend? Have things changed again? Or did you accept the union contract?"

"No," Cal says with a worn voice. "And fuck no. I'm not signing a union contract with her ever. I'll send myself to the afters before I do that. Talia thinks she's being cute."

I pick my head up, managing to lift my hand enough to give myself rabbit ears. "I had bunny ears. I was cute."

Massimo smiles at me, his arms crossed over his bulky chest, biceps bulging against his short sleeved, black shirt. "I'm sure you looked better than I ever did in them."

My jaw drops and I try to glare up at Cal. "You let him wear them?"

He ignores my question, saying, "Breakfast is less than three runes. We need to clean up, change, maybe get a couple runes to sleep." He pushes past Massimo into our bedroom, kicking the door shut, and moving into the bathroom.

He sets me on the counter, cocking his jaw. "Are you healed?"

I sag against the wall. Giving in to fatigue, I let my eyes close. "Think so, but don't tell me to heal again. I'm out, completely drained, and I don't know if I'll survive trying to heal again right now."

Taking my face between his hands, he kisses my forehead. "Stubborn woman." He lets go, moving away and I slump, eyes falling shut.

The shower starts. The water sprays in a heavy rain, echoing around the room and warm steam fills the air with humidity.

Cal's large, warm hands run up my thighs. "Talia."

I groan. "What?"

"Up."

"Isn't that the man's job?" The words are a soft mumble from my lips. I'm stuck somewhere between sleep and conscious thought, burrowed deep inside myself, cut off from the outside world.

His hand slides along my jaw, his lips brushing against mine. "Little Star, chose your next words carefully. If you sass me…"

I snort, groaning to show my displeasure as he forces me up straight. "Let me guess, you'll put me in my place?"

"Oh, I'm going to put you somewhere," he says with a smile in his voice. "I'm going to put you on my cock."

Wide awake and on high alert I open my eyes, a throb pulsing between my legs. My skin tingles.

I must have been having weird, lucid dreaming moment, so shake myself awake. He's watching me with desire, leaving me to shiver, nipples hardening. "What? I think I dozed off for a fraction."

His eyes drop to my mouth. "What do you think I said?"

I arch my back, stretching my eyes wide, and yawn. Holding a hand to my mouth, I shudder, saying, "Something sexual."

He stares back at me, his black eyes drinking me in. "It was, now get up."

I slide off the counter and realize he has lost his clothes. I drink in his reddish, tawny skin across his broad shoulders and toned abdomen. He could be carved from marble, muscles sculpted. "Um."

"No sassy comment?" He slips an arm around me to pull the zipper of my dress down.

"I could go with the cliché insult to the size of your penis, but I'm so tired I haven't even managed to take a look yet."

He smirks, pushing my dress off my shoulders. "It's straight."

I crack up. "So, it's average?"

Putting his hands on either side of me, he leans forward,

blocking me in against the counter. His eyes are on my mouth as he says, "You'll like it."

"You think," I respond, but my voice shakes. Given the way it felt pressed against me half hard, I'm betting he's right.

"Yes."

"Your girlfriend must really like it given how crazy she is about you."

His eyes narrow, one of his hands clasping the back of my neck, his mouth comes down on mine. My mouth opens, his tongue snaking inside.

A breathless whimper trickles up my throat into his mouth. He steps forward, pinning me against the counter with his body, his hands wrapping tight around my waist.

I tilt my head, reaching out to press hands against his hard chest. The muscles jump and twitch, then he's pressing his legs between mine, lifting me onto the counter. The steam is wafting around us, kissing my skin with humid heat as his Dark slithers across me in cool caresses.

It's everywhere. My thighs. My stomach. My shoulders, neck, even my breasts. I shiver, desire clenching in my lower stomach. Unlike Marius's magic, I revel in Cal's.

His fingers dig under the waistband of my underwear, peel them down, then throw them to the side. His mouth leaves mine and I gape, shocked as he drops to his knees.

"Oh!" My head tips back as I gasp in a breath as his tongue flicks my clit, then I breath out, "Fuck."

He chuckles, the vibrations stimulating my sensitive flesh. Turning his head, he kisses my inner thigh, which leaves me wanting more and a throb between my legs. I hook one leg over his shoulder, trying to press him back to where I'm craving with my heel.

Snickering, he turns to kiss higher on my other thigh. I grind my teeth. "Anticipation fucking sucks, asshole."

"Not always."

"Fine, but I've already waited thirty years."

He laughs, licking my clit again. I lean back, fingers wrapping over the edge of the counter and moan to let him know he hit the button I wanted. His tongue is like wet, smooth velvet.

My eyes cross as he circles my pulsing clit and gives it a sharp flick at the end. "Oh," I whisper. Ness told me it was incredible, but this is better than that, better than a vibrator and my fingers combined. It's never felt so good, and I know all the right things to do to that I like.

I grip the marble harder as tension coils, muscles tightening and quivering. "Oh, Mother," I whimper, hips jerking as everything explodes in exquisite pleasure under his tongue. "Cal."

It doesn't stop. My eyes cross, and my hips buck, but his hands keep my legs open, his magic holding me in place. I'm on edge, my body demanding to feel that again. It's overwhelming, and as long as I've wanted this, I'm begging him to stop.

He doesn't, and the world explodes from the inside out. His name rips from my throat in a hoarse cry, and then he pulls back. I groan, wobbly muscles as useful as rubber chickens trying to hold me up.

His hands slip around my hips, one running up my back to force my torso upright. My eyes flicker open. "What the fuck did you just do to me?"

He chuckles, his hands wrapping tighter around my hips to pull me to the edge of the counter, his hard dick pressing against my thigh.

He kisses my neck, while his hands slide along my ribs to unhook my bra and remove it. His head drops, his mouth covering one nipple. I arch into his touch, another moan escaping.

I reach between us, my fingers wrapping around the thick shaft of his hard dick, causing him to exhale hard. Pulling my hand away and moving it to his shoulder, he clutches his dick. The head presses against my clit then slides in.

I hiss at him as he stretches me, tipping my head back with

eyes closed to enjoy the sensation. Both of his hands grab my hips and pull as he thrusts himself deeper.

"Fucking Mother." I wrap my legs around him.

His palms skim up my legs to grab my ass, squeezing. "Hard enough for you, Little star?"

"Not yet," I manage, half laughing. He yanks me forward and I gasp at the rest of his length sinking in. "Fucking straight? You went with straight instead of massive? No wonder your girlfriend is crazy about you."

He closes his hand on the underside of my jaw, fingers gripping my cheeks. "Stop talking," he grinds out, pulling back and thrusting with his full body.

"Mhm." I nod, clutching his shoulders as he lifts me off the counter. He spins us and slams me against the wall, one hand clutching the back of my thigh, the other closing around my throat, and he pulls back, ramming in hard.

I'm helpless to do anything, dissolving to a quivering, twitching mess under his assault. I come at least once, or maybe it's all one long incredible orgasm, or maybe it all just feels as good as any orgasm I've ever had. He's a machine, and I'm just trying to hold on and remember how to breathe.

"Cal."

His hand tightens down on my throat, cutting off my air supply. I mewl as he speeds up, his thrusts shallower, jerkier. I slip down a bit, which results in him dragging in and out against my clit. I whimper. My fingers dig into his shoulders, my body pulsing with pleasure.

He growls, slamming all the way into me as he reaches his own release. His hand drops to grab my ass as he stops. Breathing hard, he presses his forehead against mine.

My heart races, my body throbbing as I droop against him. "I don't know what you just did to me, but I think I liked it. I'm not entirely sure, though. Maybe. I need to experience it again before I make a final decision."

He's fighting a grin, shaking like he might want to laugh. "What the fuck does it take to turn off your sass?"

I smile. "Maybe like, six more of that?"

He stands up, pulling me away from the wall. "We don't have time for that."

"Depressing," I say. "Although I'm not sure how you even managed that after carrying me around for runes and kicking ass. I certainly couldn't have."

He opens the shower door, stepping inside. Pulling out, he sets me on my feet. My legs give out.

On the floor in a heap, my forearm in his grip, I laugh. "I think you broke something."

CHAPTER 49

CALLAHAN

4TH THISTLE'S DAY, HEATWAVE, 4049 6TH MILLENNIUM

SITTING AT BREAKFAST, MY MIND IS A FLOATING HAZE, STILL IN THE shower, warm water sluicing over me, Natalia naked, soapy, giggling at her own jokes.

I'm riding high on endorphins, blitzed out from fatigue, crashing from the adrenaline of yesterday and the fighting a couple of runes ago. The hall is silverware clinking, soft knocks and scrapes of shuffled movements, the players coasting and going through the motions. The hunt was a rough marathon and today is going to be tough to get through. Come what may, I'll keep Natalia by my side, although having tasted her, it's going to be even harder to focus on the games instead of deciding what I'm going to do to her later.

She's glimmering, the silver threads lacing over her skin shinier than ever before. I sit back and watch her, my eyes half-mast as my brain steeps in organic chemicals. My little star still seems oblivious of how tight I'm winding her in threads of Dark.

She should have stopped me, said no, not mewled and begged for more. She didn't. She belongs to me in every possible way now. My talons are sunk so deep I'm never going to be able to pry them loose to let go if I tried.

Not that I think I'll ever want to. I want a mate.

She stares at me, frowning. Her eyebrow lifts, although she keeps her mouth shut. I should have punished her for flipping me off, clamped down on the cute sass, but she was on death's door, and between coming back from a blade laced with Telra's poison embedded in her heart and the previous smiting, I doubt anyone is going to push me.

No one can fault me for giving her a bit of reins to run. She'd stood against Pierre, declaring she's not coerced, that she didn't need me, but kneels subservient to my will, and has more than enough ability to hold her own.

Hiro and Thames sit in open seats across the way. Thames sips on a flute of bubbling, clear liquid and Hiro crosses his arms, leaning on the table toward me. "We need to catch up, have a drink after the festivities. Come to my home."

I incline my head. Thames is a lot like Natalia will be, tied to his lover in service freely, yet capable on his own. They make for a deadly, charming team. Somehow Hiro has evaded both death and the contenders list, which is impressive and satisfying. I don't want to have to kill him.

"Your place it is," I say with a smile. "Let me know when is convenient for you."

"At your leisure. Thames keeps his home impeccable."

Thames nods at Natalia. "I owe you. For Hiro."

She cocks her head like she's confused. So has so much to learn.

I rest my hand on her thigh and squeeze. "I'll take that debt." She cuts her eyes to me, and they narrow. I grin, brushing my fingers against her bare shoulder. "You belong to me, so any debts or favors are forfeited to me."

"Sure." Thames laughs. "But I'll pay her one too. You saved him. I couldn't ever replace him or thank you enough."

Natalia smiles. "Let him have it. I don't need anything from anyone. It was a selfish act anyway. One more able fighter to stay alive."

Hiro chuckles. "You took down others, including Sterling, and still kicked Telra down. I don't think you needed me."

"Eh, I was dwindling out of—"

"Stop," I snap, preventing her from continuing that statement. I'm aware of how her magic works, but I don't want others to know. They'll take advantage of the knowledge.

Hiro waves a hand. "I'm swearing in, here and now, to be clear."

"I'll consider you and yours," I drawl. I never commit to anything as fast as I did Natalia, but there's not a high chance of me turning away Hiro, especially with Thames figured in.

Thames shrugs. "You can have me, baby. I'm not leaving him," he says, jerking his head sideways to Hiro. "Everyone knows it by now except his mother. Useless witch, either stupid or delusional, not sure which."

Hiro turns to him with a smile. "She's stupid."

"Yeah, calls me your best little vassal." Thames rolls his eyes.

Reaching out, Hiro takes his hand. "Sugar Bear, I really don't know what else to do to try to make her understand. I signed you for life, and I mated you. Does it really matter?"

Thames downs his drink and Natalia turns her face away from me. Her head tips back, her eyes to the ceiling, the same expression on her face as when the seowolf pup was being served up to her. I'm not sure why.

I was sure she would have come up with some witty quip, instead her lips are pressed together as she scans above us.

Hiro nudges Thames. "I'll find you in the afters."

Beaming, Thames glances around then kisses Hiro's cheek before ducking his head and turning away.

Natalia's still staring at the ceiling.

Hiro fights a grin. "Don't do that again. I don't want to put you down for stepping out of line publicly." He clears his throat. "You hear the rumors?"

I meet his gaze and narrow my eyes. "The Ancient, yes. Any idea what games are set for today?"

Hiro nods, then sighs. "No. Hope it's easy. I'm exhausted from the hunt."

Natalia gives a half-scoff. "Easy? That's a joke, right?"

No one answers as we descend back into the quiet stirrings of others finishing their breakfast. The tensions of bitter storms on the horizon have been swirling around for a few years now. Rumor is, there is an Ancient up and walking this world.

Seven millennia ago, the Light and Dark banded together to eradicate the Ancients. Death certificates were tracked with care to ensure complete annihilation. Unlike the Magia, who were never considered a threat, the Seraphinus feared the Ancients.

The records have a few dozen inconsistencies. There were Ancients never accounted for without being proven dead, although they disappeared. Until now. It could be fear, there may not be an Ancient walking among us. Nonetheless, I'm not going to be so arrogant as to ignore the potential threat.

A war beyond the Dark Throne is coming. That I believe. It's blowing in with the tide of the looming death of the Dark King. His death is going to change everything, I can sense that in my Dark.

I finish my cappuccino. My little star is going to have to withstand the games before we face anything else though, and she's already tried to die three times. Things are grim from where I sit. I have no choice except to continue to push her to see if my little star can withstand it, or if she'll burn out.

CHAPTER 50
NATALIA

THE DARK KING CALLS THE ROOM TO ATTENTION. "I'M SURE MOST of you are tired from the little game yesterday, but I find myself lacking empathy for your affliction."

I sigh, sinking lower in my chair. I'm not in the mood for another fight. I'm not sure I could manage a proper swing, kick, backflip, or even have Ki left to channel. I'm not the only one slumping and scowling either.

Thames looks on the verge of tears as he stares back at me.

"However, I'm reminded tired players equates to boring displays, so instead you'll entertain me in any way you chose."

I perk up a bit, turning to Cal, not sure if this is a trick. He smiles.

Thames shudders and leans his head against Hiro's shoulder, sobbing. "Please, baby, no. I'd rather fight."

"Telra!" The King snaps his fingers and points. "Cheaters don't get time to prepare. Entertain us."

I grin wider at Cal. Had I stabbed Telra in the back it would have been an eye-for-an-eye, and no one would have looked back. Instead, she was let off with a finger shaken at her for breaking the rules. There doesn't seem to be anyone, including the King, satisfied with it.

Winking at Cal, I mouth 'girlfriend'.

His eyes narrow, his jaw clamping tight. The muscles jump at the corners before he leans in close, turning his head toward me to breathe in my ear. "Do it again, Little Star, and when it's our turn, I'll fuck you for everyone to watch as their entertainment."

I sit straight and swallow, widening my eyes and pulling my ears back. I'll be a proper vassal to avoid that act. I'm not denying I'd enjoy it, but that would be awkward. Exhibitionism is not a kink of mine.

Cal and I had sex. I'm not sure what this is between us, if what happened was proximity and convenience. It wouldn't be the first time I pounced on a man in an adrenaline fueled rush to be alive, but it feels like more.

Telra walks into the open area of the hall beyond the table. She stops, turns back, and bows to the King. "May I have music to perform for you?"

He chuckles. "You're welcome to provide it as well."

Telra nods, a bit grim. "Yes, sir. Yasmin, fetch my tambourine."

I tilt my head to the side. "Is this a game? If you fail to entertain, you get your head chopped off?"

Cal shrugs. "Yes."

"Lovely, can't wait. This is a bloody nightmare like all the rest."

He nudges his knee against mine. "You can sing. I'll send Massimo for your guitar."

"I got you, Little Light," Massimo says, as he pushes his chair back with a scrape.

I glance back at him and realize he isn't the only one sneaking away. There are plenty of others leaving with heads down. I sigh, "Shouldn't you be the one performing?"

Cal gives me a grin, more chagrin than honest. "Why would I flounder through something when I can have you do it?"

376

"*Mhm.* What do you normally do?" I eye Telra stretching. "Or is this not normal?"

Hiro laughs. "Normal, but he's shite. Bloody wanker just conjures fire then walks away after a few fractions. It's downright pathetic. Cal is great at a lot of things, but performing is not one of them."

I grin and shake my head. "Singing it is."

Yasmin comes sprinting over to Telra, tossing the tambourine to her, and panting a bit. She tries to turn away. Telra grabs her arm, leaning in to say something. She shoves Yasmine back and then turns to face the table.

She starts swaying, tapping the instrument against her hip. Her body twists and her hips roll. Telra crosses her legs, spinning as green smog rolls away from her across the floor.

Swaying and twisting, Telra glides across the floor, weaving in and out of the fog while keeping tempo with the tambourine to her sultry moves.

Telra moves with grace and ease through her dance. Her beauty and movements are alluring, sexy, almost hypnotizing. I want to melt into my seat and disappear from this city.

She finishes, the smoke dissipating away. She bows low to the King, who chuckles. "It is always a pleasure to watch you, Telra."

"Thank you, sir." She straightens, turning her head to wink at Cal.

I fight the urge to slip under the table and hide. I can flip and stretch my body, yet I'll never be able to move like that. What Cal sees in Telra is a lot clearer.

Tilting my head, I scowl at him. "Just know, if I ever have to dance like that to save your life, you're going to end up dead."

He chuckles. "I don't think that's ever going to be an issue."

The Dark King's voice calls out again. "Chlem."

He walks to where Telra danced to tell a story, creating little smoke puppets to enact out the tale. Then Marius plays the violin. I curse that he performs so well since I'd prefer to see him fail.

Glass is turned molten, little figurines fighting to the death.

Massimo slips back delivering my guitar. I hold it close, dragging my fingers over the strings, up and down the neck, feeling every inch of the instrument in search of comfort.

There's a lot of instruments played, and a few more dances performed.

Hiro drags Thames to the floor, and they square up, laughing at each other as they stumble through a couple of steps. I smile, and start to strum, playing a song for them as they waltz.

They make an adorable couple. Cal and I make a mess.

A few more are called up, then the King scowls. "Callahan, you're next, and if memory serves correct, I told you to do something different this year, or you'd forfeit the game and I'd have your head."

I struggle not to laugh, standing up with my guitar.

Cal snags my wrist as I start to walk away. "Stay."

I lift an eyebrow. "What?"

"The song," he says. "Stay. Your favorite."

I frown, disgusted with Ness for sharing that song with him, and shake my head as Hiro and Thames give intrigued glances. "No."

Cal nods. "Yes, I want you to play 'Stay.'"

"It's 'I'll Stay' and no," I say, tugging free.

"Talia."

I shake my head. "I hate that song."

Stepping around the table, I'm aware of everyone watching me. My heart beats in hard, heavy even strokes that feel like hammer strikes in my chest.

I sit on the floor, and cross my legs, situating the guitar before finding the rets, and start to strum. I clear my throat, close my eyes.

Telra calls out with snark. "Any time now!"

I sigh, shoulders slumping. The light pools in my fingers as I hold tight to the melody and the words of the song I intend to perform. Focusing, two balls of light form in front of me, melding into human form.

They come alive, seeing each other for the first time, and reach out for each other as I play the opening notes.

"I felt your wreckage
Like a tidal wave
You were so infectious
Like a disease, slowly killing me
Left me in the dark so breathless
I laughed at the demons, when they tortured me
Holding your hand was so reckless..."

The figures are dancing, coming together then moving apart, a thin thread of Light connecting them.

"Hanging by a thread
Standing on that ledge
It was almost love...

"But we never hit the ground
It left me so confound
Because it was almost love, almost love..."

The Light figures come back together, returning to their playful dance.

"Hanging by the noose
One last time, dance with me
Three feet off the ground
I never heard such a sound
You never wanted this curse
It would only make things worse
And still you dragged me down

Calling to me like gravity
We were always meant to be a travesty

"Teetering on the edge
Standing on that ledge
It was almost love...

"But we never hit the ground
Instead I fell in deep an' drowned
Because it was almost love, almost love...

"So say goodbye, and when I die
On my last breath, it's you I'll see
Dancing with me, we were never meant to be
But we came so close
It was almost love
Yeah, almost love...

"Hanging by a thread
Standing on that ledge
It was almost love...

"Teetering on the edge
Standing on that ledge
It was almost love...

"But we never hit the ground
It left me so confound
Because it was almost love
Yeah, almost love...
It was almost, almost love..."

The two figures pull apart, leaving each other as I pluck the last notes. When I stop, they dissolve. I clear my throat, starting to stand.

"Stop," the King says.

I plop back down into place.

"Did your contractor specify what song to perform?"

I curl my lip. "He made a request."

"Did you comply?"

"No. It wasn't an order."

"Play the requested song, or it's an immediate forfeit for disobedience."

I grip the neck of the guitar, clenching my jaw. "Is that death?"

"Yes."

"Fine," I snap, lifting my voice and rolling my eyes at the ceiling. "I'll fucking stay."

Sneering at my guitar, I take a deep breath and hold it, counting to ten. My eyes close, my fingers find the right chords in muscle memory.

I strum, hatred boiling through my veins. I can't refuse. However, I'm going to play the song the way Dark Marrow wrote it, not the version I created that Cal heard me sing.

"I'm so tired and cold
So alone
So old

"My heart's in pieces
My body, it aches
I feel like I'm shattered
Broken, and battered
Still searching, for home

"Lover, I know
You're scared I'll leave you alone
But I'll fight when I feel like dying
Just trust in me

I won't let go
Just hold onto me
Hold onto me
And I'll stay

"There's a light on at home
But you're not here to hold
This is getting so old
This fight is dragging on
And I can't breathe
when you're gone

"I'm so scared, I'm all alone
All I want is to find my home
But I won't give in
I won't let go
Darling you know
I'll fight when I feel like dying
Just trust in me
I won't let go
Just hold onto me
Hold onto me
And I'll stay

"Just hold onto me
Hold onto me
And I'll stay

"All I've wanted
was a home
All I've needed
was a home

"You were my fucking home

"But you didn't take my hand, you let go
And Lover, I know
Now I'm all alone
I'm fighting but I feel like dying
I would have took on everything
If only you trusted in me
But you're not home
You left me all alone
I try to let go
But it holds onto me
Holds onto me
And I can't stay

"Darling, you know
I would have been the star that guides you home
I would have fought when I felt like dying
Lover, I know
You're no longer scared to be alone
And I can't keep you close
I tried not to let go
But you're not home
so I'll go..."

Without waiting, I get up, stalking back to sit between Callahan and Massimo. I flop into the chair and flick the back of the guitar in my lap, a hollow *thunk* accompanying the strike. My eyes focus on the air between Thames and Hiro, who both frown at me.

Callahan's voice is low. "You changed it."

"I didn't, actually." I answer like a good vassal that answers to her contractor.

"The end was different."

"That's the song." I laugh with a nasty twist. "The real song. I rewrote it one night messing around. Ness tends to forget that the real version is a shitty song."

He stares at me. I can make that out from my peripheral as I keep my face forward. The weight of his gaze is frigid and heavy.

I'm not sure why I'm trying to punish him. I hum with anger as Telra's dance repeats in my mind. I can't compete with that. All I do is sing other people's songs while I hope to stay on key.

I'm a vassal, Callahan's servant. He is using me, which I forgot for a moment. It's hitting home, settling in my chest to percolate through me as fragile hope breaking apart.

Another is called forward, the King adding, "Something a bit more cheerful, too. I think the lightning bug has depressed us enough for the morning."

I don't pay attention to his snide remark or the following acts. I agree with Thames, I would have preferred to fight.

Callahan's hand slips to the back of my neck behind my hair as he leans in close. "Why didn't you play it the other way?"

"You asked for the song. The King demanded it. I gave you all the fucking song," I retort between clenched teeth.

He sighs, pulling away to sit back in his chair. He asks. I answer. Then he's done with me. That's the way it works.

CHAPTER 51

CALLAHAN

4TH MOON'S DAY, HEATWAVE, 4049 6TH MILLENNIUM

NATALIA HAS BEEN FULL OF SASS AND SARCASM FOR THE LAST FEW days, in responses three words or less every time. I've kept my distance, when possible, not sure where the change from cute to frosty came from.

The upside is she isn't pulling punches. The downside is, I may have created a monster. She's been wicked in the games. She'd put Sterling down, even kicked down Hiro and damn near killed Thames without remorse. I caught attitude from Hiro for it at dinner tonight. Natalia didn't say a word.

We arrive back at our rooms to settle in for the evening, and Natalia heads straight into the bedroom. The door snaps shut. I scowl at it, narrowing my eyes.

Massimo sighs. "That blew up a lot quicker than I thought."

"What?"

"You fucked her."

I cock my jaw, hands on my hips. "Yes." Massimo gives me a long, hard look. I glare back. "What? I know she's the Light. You don't approve. I don't fucking care."

Rubbing a hand over his mouth, he tries to hide his wide grin. "Ah," he clears his throat. "That wasn't my point."

Glaring, I square up to him. "I'm too fucking annoyed to play guessing games."

"I don't care that she has the Light. She's proven herself enough, watched your back, and kept her promise." He shrugs. "The Light might be within her, but our little Light bug isn't exactly Light in any way that we hate."

Crossing my arms, I ask, "Then what?"

"Mixing business with pleasure always burns you."

"I plan to make her my queen."

Massimo features go lax. "That's—" He stops and drags a hand down his face. "That's not what I expected."

I lift my chin, staring him down. "Deal with it."

Chuckling, my friend shakes his head. "You misunderstand. I'm in favor of it, if you can wrangle her. But she's been rather—" he stops, peering with narrowed eyes, "cold?"

"That's one way to put it. Telra looks kind right now." I shake my head, turning my gaze to the door. "Reasons I hate women."

"She might be struggling with the contract."

"Everyone gets a contract." I gesture at Massimo. "That's how it works. Even you have a contract."

Smiling and rubbing his hand over the script, he says. "Things weren't always as smooth as they are now. You screwed her. Maybe she wasn't sure she could say no."

"I told her she had every right to say no, and she has three rules, answer me, let me use her, and don't talk to Tony, and only two are even relevant."

"Don't talk to Tony?" Massimo asks, eyebrows lifting.

"He annoys me."

"Jealousy is a rare color for you."

I snap my jaws at him, the skin of my nose crinkling with a snarl. "I'm not jealous. There's nothing to envy about the clay pot. I'm a hundred times better in every way and I have Natalia. She's mine."

Massimo fights a grin. "She signed a contract, and you fucked her, but she was going to union with him. That monkey got further than you have."

"She was only doing it because she felt like she had to."

"Yes, and a contract doesn't make her feel obligated in the least."

My fingers curl, as I press my lips. "My little star is *mine*."

"Tomorrow is the end," Massimo says. "You're going to need her."

Nodding, I rub the side of my jaw. "The maze."

"It's going to take two. We've been through it enough times to know. Now is not the time for you two to be fighting. It'll kill you."

We aren't fighting, although something is off. She took a major hit from Sterling for me earlier in a game despite everything, so I'm not concerned about her performance tomorrow, but the maze is deadly. We need to be at least on speaking terms to make it through alive.

Natalia is fond of reminding me she took the contract of her own volition. The smoragon was something she could have handled, at least survived without assistance, and she's repeatedly informed me she was using me for my contract. "I'm going to get answers."

"Should I be concerned?"

I smirk, dropping my arms. "With Natalia? Always. We don't know what she is capable of, and she makes me act crazy." I throw out a hand in exasperation. "As evident in the fact that I both contracted the Light and fucked it."

Massimo lifts his eyebrows, mirth evident in his face and tone. "Is that all it is?"

No, and we both know it.

"Shut up," I snap, heading into the bedroom, shutting the door behind me. She's in the bathroom, the door closed and the shower running. I leave her alone, changing into sweatpants, forgoing a shirt and laying down.

Closing my eyes, I wait, spreading out to take up the whole bed so she can't ignore me when she comes out. I'm half-asleep when she does, her Light glowing behind my eyes. She moves and shifts in the room. I'd wager she's getting dressed, then she tries to get in bed, ignoring me.

She's small enough she manages to get on her side of the bed, curled up with her head on the pillows. It's clever, cute, and maddening.

I roll over, moving higher to lay next to her. "Talia."

"Yes, Master-Owner."

"Talk to me."

"Topic?"

"What is going on with you?"

"Nothing."

Laying on my side, I prop my head on one arm. The other I snake over her waist, hauling her against me. "You suddenly started giving me attitude and I'm supposed to believe nothing's going on with you?" I brush hair back from her face, kissing the corner of her jaw. "Talk to me, Little Star."

"You don't have to do that," she says, shifting away to put space between us.

I tense, staring down at her. "What?"

"I'm doing what you want. You get to use me. That's not necessary."

"Oh, fuck no," I grind out, yanking her back into me with a growl. "I have two-hundred-and-eighty-eight contracts and every single one of them answers to me and obeys me. Unlike them, and you, I don't do a fucking thing I don't want to."

She doesn't answer. She's tense, her Light flickering, dimming then coming back up. It's like a weird heartbeat. The Light is talking. I just don't know what it means. I still don't understand the Light.

Easing my grip around her, I scowl. "Little Star, what the fuck is going on?"

"Nothing."

Stubborn, she is beyond the word. Then again, she's been used and beat down her whole life. She's developed that articulate muscle more than any other I've ever encountered in this world. Something is amiss with her, even if she isn't forthcoming.

This adjustment came after the song I requested. I cuddle her in tight and get comfortable. "Why did you play the song differently?"

"I played the exact same chords."

"Why did you change the lyrics," I try again.

"I didn't. Those were the right ones."

I sigh. "You know damn good and well what I'm asking. You can give me sass, but you must answer me."

"I don't know what you mean."

"The end was different than before. Why did you go with that version?"

Her Light stops flickering, settling on the dim setting. "Fuck off."

"No."

"I'm just your stupid vassal. Why does it matter?" Her words end with a slight uptick of breath, evidence the contract is warning her of contempt.

I nuzzle her. "Of my nearly three hundred contracts, I wear precisely three. You aren't just a contract, you aren't stupid, and if any other vassal dared to talk to me like this, I would set them on fire. You're trying my patience, so for the last time, why did you switch the ending?"

"I'm curious. Are you going to set me on fire before or after you push me out of bed?" She tenses, her arm wearing the contract twitching as the black words swell, edged in red, though she makes no attempt to respond further.

I breathe out slow. Natalia needs to be put in her place. The question remaining is how I do it. This mess is my own fault. I allowed her to fester with the idea that she is willingly abiding, not that I have her bent to my will.

I had this same fight with Massimo. He was my first contract, and the discord with Massimo came because I didn't know what I was doing. This time I should have known better.

I could alter the contract, except she might end up putting herself so far in contempt she dies. I can't lose her, not after everything I've seen she's capable of in the games. While there are various options for physical punishments, the idea of hurting her is like barbs embedding in my lungs, and she'd heal in fractions from anything less than permanent damage.

She whispers, "It fucking hurts."

"Answer me. You have to answer, then it will stop."

"I hate that song. I hate that song because it's true. I hate my version for the beautiful lie it sells, and I hate the real version for the truth it tells. I just really fucking hate that song."

I shift, pushing up on an arm to gaze down at her, a tad stunned she'd decided to cooperate. The Light is weak, the illumination over her skin all but gone, her voice laden in breathless pain.

"Vanessa said it was your favorite."

She snorts, tilting her head to my chest, "It is. It's a gorgeous song."

"You make no sense. That's contradictory."

Natalia sighs. "I'm not like some people. I don't just hear a song and think, oh, that's a good song, then move on. I lose myself in music. I connect to it. It gives me goosebumps and chills. It can change my mood on a dime."

"Yes, I noticed," I say. "For about the last two days in fact."

"That song has a hundred meanings to me, and I didn't want to play that song for about half of them."

"So, this is a tantrum?"

"What? No. You asked me why I played it the right way. I'm telling you because this contract hurts."

"And the attitude the last few days?" I brush her hair back, running my fingers through it and kiss the ball of her shoulder. The Light sparkles where my lips touch, then then dims again. "Hm?"

"Oh, I'm sorry, did I do something wrong? We won our games. Pretty sure I saved your life earlier, which hurt too, by the way. I'm fine, though, thanks for asking."

I open my mouth against her neck, a chuckle lodging in my throat as I press my teeth to her thin skin. "I'm not liking this attitude."

"Is acting how you want me to part of the contract?"

"Something is making you pissy. I want to know what, and I want it to stop."

Natalia snickers. "I've kept my end of the contract, my mouth shut, did what you told me to, so …" She tenses, pushing her shoulders together to breathe out in a hiss. "Damn you. That hurts! You know what, fine, just—Ow!"

I wrap my hand around her forearm, sending my magic to snake around it in tendrils to ease the burn. She's fighting the contract. The more she fights the more volatile it will become, and her continual rejections to answer only cause each next contempt to hurt her more.

"Answer me," I whisper against her ear. "Get the words out and it stops."

"Asshole," she mutters, squirming.

"Tell me." I tighten my grip around the contract, my body bending around hers. I could change the contract, stop this, but she's out of control. I need her to accept this, accept me.

She accepted Tony. It's time she accepts me.

The contract is growing, inky Dark crawling up her arm. Its tendrils break free of her skin, then pierce back through like dozens of thin needles. Where it covers, her Light goes out, receding from the Dark, not fighting it.

I frown, not sure why her magic is giving in. "Talia."

391

"I hate you," she grinds out, her jaw clamped shut, panting through her nose. "I hate you like I hate that song."

I slide my other arm beneath her, wrapping it around her neck as she whimpers. She's sweating and breathing hard, arching into me. The contract threads in and out of her shoulder, dragging a half-scream from her.

I tighten around her, cuddling her in close like I can protect her from this. "Damnit, answer me. Make this stop."

"Fuck–you. I'm not–I can't." She sobs.

The contract is writhing, furious Dark that pulls back and stabs into her shoulder, then begins stretching across her chest.

My lips find her ear. "Tell me. Just answer me, and it ends."

She grabs my arm, her nails biting into my flesh. I press my face into the hair against her neck. Depressing little sobs wrack her as she starts shaking.

I growl. "Just fucking tell me!"

"I don't know."

"The contract wouldn't hurt you for something you don't know."

She groans, twitching with soft whimpering. There are two options. I stop this and let her win, or I hold my ground, and let her suffer, maybe to death. If she lives, she needs to answer to me. Letting this go is a slippery slope. If she can win now, she would fight when it came to harder choices.

The contract is threading through the skin of her chest while she's making pitiful noises. I need to end this. The song is the answer, so maybe I can get enough information to solve the riddle.

"Why give me that version of the song when I didn't know it existed?"

"'Cause it's true." Her voice is thin.

The contract stops its progression as she answers me. It lashes and shifts, waiting, ready to cut into her heart. It's now or never. One more breach of contract and my magic is going to kill her.

I hold my breath. "What is true?"

She grits her teeth, not answering, so one thin tendril pulls back then stabs back in. The resulting scream sticks in the back of her throat as her body jerks.

"Fuck," I yell, and for one horrible heartbeat, I think that was the end. Then her breath rattles as she sobs. I breathe out in relief. My voice is lower, laced with fury. "Just fucking answer me. Why is this so hard?"

She breathes raggedly. She must be in agony, but she is still fighting. As annoying as it is, it's also impressive. "You can use me. Own me. You can make me do what you want, fight, kill, glow." She stops to work air in and out. "This? This is me, my heart, a part of me, and I'm keeping it safe."

I laugh, grinning while I nuzzle her ear. "Little Star, there's no part of you that I'm not claiming. There's no part of you that you get to keep, and not keep *from me*. You're mine, all of you."

"No." She whimpers.

"Yes," I kiss her temple, "All of you is all mine. I want you, every last part, and I'm going to take it. Why is it true?"

She sobs as she draws in air. "You're never going to be my home."

I drop, tension evaporating from my muscles with relief. I accept the answer. The contract beginning to pull back, sliding beneath her skin. I follow it as much as possible with little kisses in its wake.

She relaxes, and I twist her tighter against me, pressing my lips to her clammy skin as the Light twists over her, glimmering bright silver again. Her magic had pulled back, hidden itself away. It demanded she speak as much as my contract had, leaving her to suffer. It's a curious mystery.

Her breathing evens. She twitches when I stroke hair from her face, smiling at her as she's fading out of consciousness, limp against me. "You're wrong, Little Star. I am your home. I'm the only home you'll ever have."

CHAPTER 52
NATALIA
5TH STAR'S DAY, HEATWAVE, 4049 6TH MILLENNIUM

I HATE MYSELF FOR GIVING IN. THE CONTRACT WAS PISSED AS I HELD out for as long as I could withstand, furiously stabbing and weaving through my skin, spreading out with ice and fire alike. It had been too much to endure, so I caved, weak and pathetic as usual.

I'd confessed, suspended on the doorstep of the afters. Not even Ki had been able to protect me or lessen the misery, leaving me exposed to Cal's contract's torture. I spilled my guts, and the affliction vanished in an instant, abandoning me to unconsciousness.

I detangle from Callahan. He reaches for me, muttering to go back to sleep as he rolls to his stomach, an arm over the empty space I occupied. Not wanting to face him or deal with the fallout, I slip into the front room, closing the door behind me with a soft click.

Too many mixed emotions swarm inside me. My gorgeous Darkling is wicked. He could have stopped the pain anytime. He didn't.

He's not mine. He holds my contract. He owns me with the

intentions of using me. I forget that when he holds my hand or kisses me, but he made his position clear last night.

I want to sit on his face, both for my pleasure and to smother him to death. It's a complicated feeling.

Flipping off the door alleviates some of my weird rage, then I collect my guitar from the corner of the room to settle on the couch. I curl with my back to the armrest, trying to prepare myself for whatever fresh misery is waiting for me today.

I hum and strum a few times, then give up. My mind isn't recalling notes or lyrics, it's flashing between the memories of the hot sex pinned to the bathroom wall and the agonizing misery last night was. It's a dizzying teeter-totter.

Taking the contract, I thought things would be different for me. I had hoped that I'd be more than a tool. For a moment, Callahan let me believe it, but it was fallacy.

I lift my forearm, eyeing the contract. At least it looks normal. There's no evidence of the pain it caused as it rests in its usual state, no scars left behind from carving through my skin.

I narrow my eyes, menacing it. "Someday, I'm going to burn you out of me. Maybe I'll run away. I can leave the Light, the Dark, and the Magia to kill each other and find somewhere by a beach to live."

There is no answer from it, the magic not twisting alive to inflict pain for the threat. I drop my arm on the guitar and glare at it.

There's a chuckle. I glance over my shoulder at Massimo approaching me, dressed for the day with hands in his front pockets. "That is ill-advised at best." He sits on the couch across the low table. "I tried once, to get rid of mine." He holds up his hand.

I splutter. "Seriously?"

Rubbing the back of his neck, he grins. "Yes, I hated being contracted even though I did it voluntarily. I could have tried standing on my own, being a contractor when my father died."

"Why didn't you?"

Shrugging, he shakes his head. "Cal had been a friend before my father's death and when he asked...We were young, Cal's father had just died a couple of years before, we came to terms, and I signed up for life. No big deal. I knew what I was getting, but..." He drops both his gaze and hand with a heavy sigh, leaning over to rest elbows on his knees.

Massimo is cool, rich skin that's a shade above black wrapped around a stocky build, and the scar on the side of his face is imposing. Even when his face is at rest, he still seems to be glowering. A shroud of brute strength adorns him, and by no stretch of the imagination could be considered a small man, but the way he's folded over on himself, exhaustion plaguing his voice, he seems to shrink.

Shaking his head, then lifting his face, he meets my gaze. "I thought I signed up freely. It was a good contract, and I'd thought I would be free enough in the position I was to hold in his life, that I was serving of my own accord, but having to answer to the contract?" He trails off with a chuckle.

"Is annoying and frustrating and makes you feel like this thing to be used rather than a person?" I offer, rolling my head and eyes alike with disdain.

"I was putting my life in his hands. Our first Gathering Shadows together we almost died in the games. Cal managed to finish it half-dead, and Eloise got to me in time." Shaking his head, he exhales, chest deflating. "I was done answering, or wanted to be, so I tried to tear it out." He shows me the back of his hand again. There's glossy white scarring under the black lettering I've never noticed before.

"Clearly, it didn't work."

"Worse than it didn't work, it turned on me. Cal's magic is some of the strongest out there. I came to blows with Cal, I was given three options, which I'll skip over, but I accepted my contract, again, and I was bitter for a while," He rubs his forehead, studying the table. "But then we got better at the games, we both grew up, got stronger, figured it out, and now it's a distant memory."

I shake my head, turning to my instrument. "How distant?"

"Just under two hundred years."

"Yeah, I'm not going to live that long." I run a hand down and up the neck, settle on a chord, and strum. I'm not going to give up on the idea of freedom.

"Can I give you some advice?"

I wrinkle my nose at him. "It's not like I'm a captive audience or anything."

"Accept the contract. Cal is one of the better ones to sign up with, and he turns away as many as he accepts because he considers carefully, although he went searching for a reason to sign Vanessa for your benefit. He wants to take care of you."

I scoff, plucking at the strings. "No, he wants to use me. Ness got a contract not for my benefit, but because it's leverage against me." I lift my gaze to Massimo as he flinches. "I'm not stupid or ignorant. People have been trying to use me my whole life."

"You wanted her to have a contract."

I stretch my head to the side, flicking my gaze away from him. "That is true." Looking to him again, I say, "But you two are idiots if you think I didn't realize why he wanted her to have a contract." He opens his mouth to respond, and I press on in a hurry. "It's fine, whatever. I'm glad she got the deal because otherwise she'd probably be dead."

The door to the bedroom I share with Cal is wrenched open. He stands in the doorway, glaring. Black pants are slung low on his narrow hips, his carved abdominal muscles highlighted under my silver glow.

His chest swells as his black eyes settle on me, narrow. He fixates on me, his black hair a mess. Rage burns in his face as he closes the door again.

"I'm guessing you didn't mention you were leaving the room?" Massimo asks with a smile.

"He was asleep." I shrug.

"Whatever has been going on the last couple of days needs to stop, Lightning Bug." He settles into a slump against the back of the couch. "It's bothering him and what's coming today is going to require you to work together."

"Well, he should have put something in the contract against me bothering him," I retort, while plucking at the strings. "And I'm well aware how bothered he was given the contract damn near killed me last night."

He winces. "I was worried what he was going to do."

"Make me answer to him, if you really want to know, which I eventually did like a fucking pathetic princess." I roll my eyes and find a new chord to play.

Massimo watches with hesitant distrust. "Little Light Bug, if that contract wanted you to do something I am well aware of how much pain that is, and there's nothing pathetic about it."

"Sure." I strum and hum a few notes.

"There is something wrong in your brain."

"Probably."

Leaning forward, he tilts his head as he frowns. "I'm serious. If you expected yourself to be able to withstand that…" He drags a hand down his face and stares at me. "The Magia must have really made you fight to earn anything."

I laugh. "I know they made things harder for me because they didn't want me earning Pinnacle. According to Tony, the deck was stacked against me for the last seven acts."

"According to Tony?"

"Yeah, we talked about reaching Pinnacle. What the Assembly members made him do and what I had to do were two different things entirely." I play a B-sharp. "And that doesn't include the fighting I had to do to prove my right to earn the chance to try for Pinnacle."

"Lower your standards," he snickers. "You can't win against the contract. You'll either cave or it'll kill you."

I shift, bracing my arm on the top of the guitar to point at him. "Yeah, but I couldn't even hold out long enough for it to kill me. That's the sad part."

He tips his head back and laughs. "Probably for the best. I wouldn't want to be anywhere near Cal if you died."

"I'm sure he'd be pissed. He said it would be hard for him to find another Light source to use."

"It would have nothing to do with you being a Light source."

Callahan opens the bedroom door, scowling, and checking his watch. "What are you talking about?"

"The weather," I say, focusing on the guitar, playing a few notes to 'Taste of Sugar'. Callahan tastes like sugar laced with cyanide. "I was worried it might be sunny because I don't have any sunglasses."

Massimo grins ear to ear, shaking his head. "You two are going to kill each other."

"Talia."

"Yes, Owner-Master."

"Get dressed."

He withdraws into the room, leaving the door open. I set the guitar on the table, and head for a shower, then to shimmy into a dress.

Callahan is sitting on the edge of the bed, bent over with his elbows on his thighs, hanging his head. I stand in front of him, arms crossed. "I'm dressed, Master-Boss."

He sighs, lifting his eyes to stare at me with a desolate expression, then he yanks me into his lap.

"Dude," I sigh, straddling his hips in my short dress.

His hand wraps around the base of my jaw, forcing me to meet his gaze. The brush of his lips against mine is quick, then they move to my ear. "When I fall asleep with you, I expect to wake up with you."

"Noted."

"It makes me cranky when I don't."

"Doubly noted?" I lean away from him as much as possible. His eyes drop to my lips coated in red lipstick.

He sighs, hand trailing down my throat and wrapping around to the back. "Little Star, don't do that again. Answer me." He pulls my face down to kiss my forehead, then checks his watch. "We're leaving now."

CHAPTER 53
NATALIA

CALLAHAN HOLDS MY HAND THE WHOLE WAY TO BREAKFAST, HIS fingers between mine. It's nice, like I have a boyfriend, while also annoying, like we're shackled together again. It's that weird feeling returning, like I want to hold his hand, except maybe only to break every bone in it. It's a quandary I have no response to at the moment.

We make it through the meal, then Eloise comes around with a deck of cards again. Callahan draws the top card, and she moves on. He checks it, frowning as he slides it face-down on the table. He turns to me, "Last game, Little Star. Get through this and we're done."

I nod. All I have to do is survive this day, then we leave. I'll get breathing room while Callahan will have other things to do. We'll stop sharing a room, a closet, a shower, and a bed. I can stop fantasizing with my head in the clouds that this is something other than what it is.

Things between us won't be so confusing. He tortured me last night with his contract. I don't need to be daydreaming about the incredible sex or the way he holds my hand.

The Dark King stands. "Good morning. You all have your

starting points now," he indicates Eloise. "You'll enter the maze at Bloom's Rune. A failure to appear will have you hunted and killed."

I lift an eyebrow, turning to Callahan. "That's a new threat. Have people tried to avoid this one before?"

He grimaces. "It's the maze. It's the closest I've come to death, twice. It scares everyone, including me."

"Well," I blow out hard. "Fuck."

Telra drops in the chair across the way and her lips spread and curl at the ends with an air of malice in the way she bares her teeth. "Parlay?"

I curl my lip at her but turn away. As a good, little vassal I keep my mouth closed. That's all I am to Callahan. Massimo locks his gaze on mine with soft eyes and a questioning eyebrow aloft, so I face forward, trying to ignore the world around me.

Callahan's voice is drizzled with humor. "That depends. What do you want, baby?"

"Her."

"No." It's a quick, harsh response, all trace of mirth vacated from his tone.

"The maze." She purrs. "It can be difficult. Don't make me track you down to kill her. I may have to leave you for dead."

"If I we're you, I would be concerned with figuring out how to survive the maze. Leave Natalia alone. You've tried twice now, give up."

"In the vein of honesty, it's three." Telra laughs, a sweet, airy sound. "Darling, you're breaking my heart. If I take her now, it'll hurt less, and we can move on to working things out."

I give up on behaving, I meet Telra's black gaze. Leaning back in my chair, I cross my arms. "I have zero impact on whatever is going on between you two."

Blinking slow, Telra's gaze hardens and her eyes flash luminescent green. Her beautiful features move in slow motion into humor as she moves her eyes back to Callahan. "Darling! Your toy is too innocent."

He smirks. "She's usually pretty smart, but she does seem to be slow on figuring this one out."

I scoff.

"Then you aren't fucking her?" Telra puts a hand to her chest. "Do you miss me?"

Callahan's smile widens. "Fuck no."

"To which question?"

He remains quiet, grinning. I roll my eyes to the ceiling, not touching this one with a twelve-foot pole in protective equipment. I'm not about to confess to the sex with Telra's face burning with rage. Plus, it's embarrassing the way I've been walking around in delusion.

"Fine," Telra snaps, shoving away and standing up. "So be it. We'll do this the hard way. Mark my words, though. You and me, darling, we aren't done."

"I think we are," he chuckles.

She gives a dazzling smile. "You'll change your mind. I'll change it for you after she's dead."

Callahan watches her go before turning to me. "She's going to hunt you."

"Golly, gee, Mr. Master, you fucking think?"

"She'll shift, hunt you like prey, and if she kills you, Venominx like to eat the heart."

"Mine's a bit sinewy and black, so it's not going to taste very good, poor thing."

He laughs. "Better that we don't let her find out." He glances at his watch. "Two runes. I have things to get done."

Massimo leans forward. "Shall I fetch Laz?"

"Yes," Cal nods. "Bring him to the room. We'll meet you there."

Massimo knocks on the table, stands, and leaves. The corner of my mouth pulls down. "Isn't that the guy who took the most pathetic swing ever?"

"Yes." He bobs his head. "I'm giving him a contract."

"Right. Collecting useful bodies."

He takes my chin in his hand, lifting it and forcing me to meet his gaze. "He won't survive the maze, so I need to get him signed before the challenge starts so he's contracted, therefore, no longer eligible. I knew his father. He helped me once, and his father sent him to me for a contract. I don't even know what to do with him, however, I owe his father."

I peer at him. "Oh."

"I'm not all asshole."

"Sure."

Callahan presses his lips to the middle of my sweating palm. "Breathe, Little Star."

I exhale through my nose. "Breathing, Master."

He twists his lips to the side and glares. "That is going to stop right now."

"You made your point."

Lifting his eyebrows, he asks, "Did I?"

"You own my ass."

Grinning, his eyes travel down my torso, then dance with hidden laughter as he meets my gaze again. "It's a great ass. I couldn't help myself."

My eyes widen with rage, mostly because I find his quip funny.

His arm rests along the back of my chair as he smiles against my ear. "You have a contract. Because of that contract, you answer to me, and yes, you belong to me, but that has nothing to do with the contract." He nips the shell of my ear.

My spine tingles. "Pretty sure it does."

"Your service, and your life due to the length of service time, are mine because of the contract. The rest? Well," he rumbles with a low laugh. "I told you I was looking for something else."

I quarter turn my head to him, eyebrows forming that ever-deepening crease between my eyebrows. "Excuse you?"

"There's usually no excuse for me. I am what I am, and you are mine, Little Star."

I open my mouth, but I have no witty response at the ready. My lips press then twist to the side.

"You're really not getting this?"

"Getting what?"

"I want you."

"For my Light, yes, I'm aware."

He snickers. "Why the fuck do you think Telra wants you dead so badly?"

"Everyone does," I say, rolling my eyes. "They think I'm the Light."

"You are the Light." He stands, offering his hand and wiggling his fingers. "Come on, Little Star, you stay at my side."

CHAPTER 54
CALLAHAN

Lazarus exits with his partner, Aelfric. I hand the contracts to Massimo, and scrub a hand down my face, looking to Natalia. She sits at my side, where she belongs, as she has for the last rune and a half of negotiations.

Lazarus asked for the contract, sought me out because he wanted it, then he still made me work. He's too clever for his own good.

In the end he signed, Aelfric too, when I was done being polite. I'd reminded him his father advised him to do this, he'd asked me for this, and if he didn't like the arrangement as it stood, he could take his chances in the maze. Aelfric had gone pale and urged him to comply.

I force my lips into a smile, not wanting to betray the anxiety compressing my chest. "We need to change, Little Star."

She frowns, then nods as she stands. Without a word, she disappears into our room. I take the opportunity to stare at her ass. It really is a great ass.

Massimo has returned from stashing the new contracts. I'll file them away with the others when we get home. He sits on the opposite couch. "Things seem better."

I rub a hand through my hair and down my neck, slouching into the couch. "Yes."

"Get your head right, or the maze will kill you."

Torn halfway to a laugh, I smile with exhaustion. "She's really not getting it."

"Getting what?"

"That I want her to be my Queen."

Natalia scowls in the doorway to our room, dressed in tight black. "You want what now?"

I get up, moving past her on my way to change, kissing her temple. "Come here," I say, pulling her back into the room with me.

She goes like a rag doll, her facial features flickering like she's trying to solve a puzzle where the pieces don't fit. "Queen?"

Brushing hair away from her face, I hold her gaze. I don't know how else to say it. "I told you, I want you."

Confusion flickers across her pretty face, but she makes no response. That's fine. I can be patient.

I unroll a leather bundle, exposing various small knives, daggers, and my sword hilt. I grab a holster, dropping to a knee in front of her. I wrap the leather around her thigh, improvising a bit to be able to snug it down, then slip a smaller dagger into it.

"Go." I stand and give her a gentle shove to the door.

Nabbing my sword hilt, I toss it aside on the bed, then pull my shirt off to change.

Natalia and Massimo are waiting for me in the front room. I grab my little star's hand, tugging her with me. We head through the corridors then out the back of the palace into the shadows of the mountains.

Miles of constructed stone sprawls, the walls rough and hewn, fifty feet high. It looms, stilling even the air around it as the silence within stretches out to dampen the world.

Two approach us, Mattingly with William a pace behind. Mattingly stands toe-to-toe with me, lifting his chin. "Cal."

I lift an eyebrow at the comical way he's trying to act tough.

"Word is you beat this in record speeds."

"Is that so?"

Mattingly glances at William with shifting eyes, and then sighs, dropping his arms. "Are there any tricks you can provide on how to get through this thing?"

"Why should I? As I recall, you don't think much of me."

His faces flickers, then he laughs. "I may have been mistaken."

"In that case, I may tell you the best advice I can offer is to survive."

I pull Natalia in front of our entrance. She drags her feet, gaping at the walls of the maze the whole way there. Stopping, I square up to her, but turn my head to stare down the path. It's bathed in shadows that swirl and whisper in faint hisses I can't understand, ominous and lush vines of ivy covering the walls.

Adrenaline slips through me, my heart palpitating with stronger, quicker beats. "Don't touch the walls. Black ivy is carnivorous. It will kill you."

"Lovely."

I grab her hips, pulling her against me. "There are traps and the other players. The maze shifts too. It's a chaos, and a free for all. Everything in there is going to do its best to kill you."

"Great." She draws out the word. "It sounds fun. I can't wait, babe."

I haven't heard that for a while, but even that's not enough to settle my nerves. "I'm going to need that sass." I rest my hand at the base of her throat, resting my fingers along her skin to feel the pulse in her neck. It thumps in a steady rhythm. "I hate being trapped."

Her eyebrows lift high. "You're claustrophobic?" She turns toward the maze. "And we're going in there?"

"Yes, so sass, jokes, make me laugh to keep my head on, whatever you've got, it's all on the table. You have free rein."

Her eyes lock on mine, and she purses her lips. "Goody."

"Everyone is going to be shifting."

She forms her lips in a small hole, letting out a soft whistle. "We're so fucked. This is going to be awesome."

I drop my face, nudging my nose against hers. "Little Star."

"Asshole."

I grin. I'm going to be fine. I have Natalia's sass and her Light. "How are you?"

"Nauseous," she says. "I might throw up on you."

I brush my hand down her neck and over her shoulder, searching for signs of scaring. "I meant from the contract. Any lasting injury?"

Her eyes blaze. "You're a fucking prick, but no."

"Next time, answer me." I cup her face, trying to block out everything but my existence. "Don't do that again. Don't make me watch you hurt yourself."

"Don't fucking push me," she says. "I'm here, I'm doing whatever, but I have boundaries."

I laugh, "You're really having a hard time grasping this. How are the Ki levels?"

She shrugs. "Normal?"

"Anything we can do to up those? The maze will push us. I don't want you running out, having to draw on your spirit."

She closes her eyes. "Ki is a natural part of the spirit. Depending on how strong the spirit, the more strength, the deeper the well. So, unless you can make me stronger mentally..."

"That's a 'no' then." I chuckle, pressing lips to her forehead.

"I could be," she mutters with a sour tone.

Grinning against her face, "No, you damn near killed yourself last night. I can only imagine how badly that stung."

The horn sounds the beginning of the game. I sigh, dropping my chin to stare her in the eye. "Ready?"

"Fuck no."

I step back from her, offering my hand. She takes it, and I curl my fingers tight around hers. "Survive, Little Star, and let me use your Light."

"We'll gloss over having to keep you from having a panic attack in close quarters, as well as stop your girlfriend from eating my heart."

"You're going to quit calling her that." I yank Natalia to me, kissing her. She leans in, a hand against my stomach, opening her mouth to me. I taste her for the first time in days and groan.

Horses gallop closer, the sound of riders approaching. Eloise rides past, yelling, not bothering to stop, "In, Cal."

I break my mouth free, my little star pressed close, small hands grabbing at me. Opening my eyes, her Light filters through my lashes to stare down at her on her tiptoes, stretching up to me.

She is absolutely, without question, mine.

"Ready, set..." I take a deep breath, turning to the maze.

"Oh, fuck it, go," Natalia says, fingers wrapping around my wrist and tugging me forward. We step into the entrance. The earth rumbles, ten tons of stone sliding shut, and the way out disappears.

CHAPTER 55
CALLAHAN

Natalia turns and laughs. "Fucking Mother."

As the walls start to close in, my magic shrinks into my core, hissing with disgust. I crouch on the balls of my feet, one hand helping to steady me with fingers on the hewn stone breath our feet.

The path is quiet, Dark swirling in living shadows, the magic embedded in the stone stretching free of its tomb. Everything else is still, the maze taunting me. The space is closing in, squeezing the air from my lungs.

Two bright hands are shoved in my face. "Up," she says, fingers wiggling. "Now. Time to move."

I try to breathe as I squeeze her fingers for reassurance. "I don't do confinement."

"I don't do spiders or creepy crawlers. Bugs in general. Play stupid games, get stupid prizes." She yanks me further into the maze.

The Dark closes in around Natalia as we walk up the path. Her Light glows, transforming her into a shinning beacon. I adjust my hand, worming my fingers through hers.

She's the star that is going to guide me home.

The silence makes my ears ring, setting me on high alert. We reach the end, which branches with options of left or right. She looks to me. "Oh, that was scary. Which way?"

I sneer at her amusement. "This maze is thousands of centuries old, built with the blood of nightmares. The King—Marius—their race. This thing is bloody, fucking alive, and it contains the same nightmare toxin they carry. It knows your fears, and it will use them to kill you, and unlike the minor dosage you got, there's so much nightmare in these walls that it's not hallucinations—your fears are going to come alive, very real, very deadly."

"So, spiders? I'm getting spiders. Fuck."

I decide to go left, and step in front of her. "I can manage spiders. What else are you afraid of?"

"Dude, I'm not telling this death trap my fears out loud."

"It knows anyways."

A pale figure steps through the wall, blocking our procession. I frown at an apparition of Tony, but it smiles at me. "Buddy, you might as well let go of her now. Telra is going to feed on her. She's not worth protecting."

"We aren't buddies."

Tony fades with a laugh as Natalia is jerked out of my grip with a shrill squeal. I round, a massive spider dragging her closer in thick webbing. She's squirming and whimpering. "Oh, Mother! Oh, fucking Mother! I hate these games. Fuck!"

I blast a burst of magic at the spider, letting it loose from me. Tendrils race along the ground, wrapping around her as more of my Dark pierces into the creature. I dig my heels in, grabbing at my Dark webbing to play tug-of-war with the spider for my little star.

Releasing tendrils from one hand, I use it to send a fireball at the arachnid. The creature dodges and hisses, scuttling backward as it spits more web at Natalia. The front legs brace, using its sextet of other legs to pull Natalia closer.

She's muttering curses in a shrill voice as it's dragging her closer, arms bound to her sides with its web silk. It begins wrapping her up, so I stop pulling on Natalia. My Dark snarls, still tangling with the spider over our star, and I grab my sword hilt, pulling it free.

My Dark races around the hilt, seeping into it, then ignites in a flaming blade.

I run and slide, cutting the web attached to Natalia, and glide under the beast, dragging the blade through the underbelly. It screams, and so does Natalia as it pounces on her, fangs biting down into its bundled prey even as guts and blood are falling out of it.

I cut the back legs and skewer it. The arachnid thrashes, releasing a shrill shriek that bounces off the stone. It crashes sideways into the wall and then rolls to its back, legs curling up and hardening in place.

My little star squirms, encased in a glistening web and cursing. Chuckling, I drag her away from the carcass before I cut her loose. She rolls over, scrambling further from the dead spider along the stone on hands and feet.

"Nope," she says. "I want the fuck out of here. I didn't sign up for this shit. Let me out of this burning afters right now. I quit!"

I laugh, retracting my Dark from the sword hilt. The flames go out, leaving the weapon bladeless before stashing the hilt in the waistband of my pants at my lower back and catch up to her.

Scooping her off the ground into my arms, I remind her, "I can handle spiders."

Natalia trembles, gripping the front of my shirt and yanking it. "I'm serious, I want out. Out of here. Out of the contract. Out."

Smiling down on her, I dip my head to nuzzle her nose. "No. You're fine, Little Star. You have my word I'll kill any spider you ever need, big or small." I widen my smile. "I'll put it in the contract."

I take a few steps, but the ghostly figure of Tony fades to existence, halting my movement. "Buddy, it deserved to live more than she does."

I scowl. "Fuck you." Walking through the phantom, I kiss the top of her head. My little star has some twisted self-worth concerns, but I'll fix them. She'll learn what she's capable of at my side.

Another image morphs before me again, halting me from proceeding. My mother stands before me, her hair loose and framing her head like a halo of black. "You protect the Light? You risk your life for it? After everything your father did?" Her wide-set eyes bore into me with betrayal. "After what you said?"

I cock my jaw. "She's my contracted. She serves. I protect."

Scoffing, my mother turns her face away. "Careful, now. Hypocrisy is not to be celebrated."

Natalia whispers, "Who is that?"

"My mother."

"Oh."

I lift my chin and shift Natalia higher in my grip, my Dark lashing around her with possessiveness. Staring at the phantom, I say, "Ignorance breeds hatred and fear. I learned my lesson, so I still say fuck you." I'm not speaking to my mother. She's dead. This is the maze digging out agonizing wounds as a plaything to be used.

Continuing through the ghost, I walk with my head held high. I disagreed with my father about his Light lover and the abuse of his union with my mother. Regrets over words I said to my father have been prominent for days, but we are not the same.

At the next cross-section, I check the options. Natalia's not shaking as bad, and she points right. "That way."

I turn the corner, stone scraping behind us as the maze shifts, closing off the opportunity to turn back or escape. "It's got something planned for us ahead," I tell her, eyeing the Dark swirling and shifting. "What else are you afraid of?"

"Dude, it's your turn for the maze to scare the piss out of you."

"So far it seems to be focusing on you."

"Your mother popped up."

I hum.

"What was that about?"

The Dark twists then chattering laughter fills the air. The little hairs on my body stand at the noise. "What was that?"

"Um," she breathes. "If I have to guess? Clowns." The creepy giggles echo off the walls once more. "Yeah, that's clowns. Fuck."

I give her a weak smile, only one side of my face cooperating. "No one likes clowns, but you're afraid of them?"

"You," she pokes me in the chest, "shut up. They freak me out."

Setting her on her feet as the chattering and giggling gets louder with the emitter closing in. I search the path. My fingertips dig under the leather wrapped around her thigh. "Don't forget about this."

She nods, leaning over to put her hands on her knees. "All right, clowns. I can handle killing clowns." She stands up right as three brightly clad balls roll forward. "Shit."

They jingle with small bells as they pop up in unison, their uniforms standard issue strips of gold and white. The material appears dirty, but glistens in her Light. Twisted little clowns with painted faces line up, bloody, grotesque grins smeared over their cheeks and mouths exposing razor sharp yellow teeth, pointed like a child drew them. Knives at the ready, they stand in front of us.

I grab my sword's hilt, spinning it in my grip. My Dark fills the metal, channeling into the blade of flames once more. The little horrors waddle closer, the grins on their faces never waiver, but more shrill laughter courses from the Dark around us.

"Okay." I bob my head to the side. "That's unnerving." I step, swinging at one. It flips backward, does another front somersault to land on the shoulders of another, then launches at me, drawing its knife back in both hands above its head.

My magic races at it, sending it sailing back through the air.

415

Tucking and rolling, it lands on its feet, racing back towards us on little bowed out legs, the other two following. My eyes cut to Natalia as we back away from the approaching threesome. This is weird and creepy, but she is displaying petrification.

I ask, "Are you panicking on me?"

"Maybe."

I need to distract her. "What's with the acrobatic, miniature, fucked-up clowns?"

"I was, like, seventeen. It was the circus. Sasha and Tony paid fifty coin to lock me in the hall of mirrors with the clowns who pretended to be psychos. They laughed weird and threatened me and chased me with knives for what felt like runes until I was let out." She steps to blast Light at one, which cartwheels out of the way.

I glance behind us. "They're forcing us to a wall. We need to get on the other side of them before they force us into the ivy."

Grimacing and fending off one of the little clown swinging at her, she says, "I might take the ivy."

The other clowns leap at me, squealing with delight. I swing, however, they're half my height, able to evade my sword strokes with ease. They're fast too, slicing me then darting away before I can land a blow, able to spin and flip as well as Natalia. Not even my magic can latch on, sending fury through us, and causing it to screech at every miss.

Natalia leaps over her clown, then blasts at the two I'm facing. Compared to her and the clowns, I'm a slow, hulking, stone giant. The four of them leap, spin, flip, and cartwheel so much and so fast that it's making me dizzy.

The warped laughter fills the air, a rubber smacking against stone sound accompanying it. Giant, red bouncy balls with a gold star come bouncing toward us out of the Dark.

I lift my voice, "What the fuck, babe?"

Knives cut and slice, the brilliant white and gold outfits glittering in Natalia's Light in rushes of assault, mixing with the errant red blurs of the balls whistling through the air. I keep trying to fend off the clowns and duck the balls, just trying to grab hold of one of our assailants.

My magic streaks out, crashing into stone and tying itself in knots in futile attempts, signaling its frustrations in cries of outrage in my mind.

Natalia's nightmare is legitimate.

A ball knocks into me, another colliding with the side of my head before they bounce off the wall, adding to the confusion.

"Balls?" Natalia laughs. "Worst fucking addition of all time."

One ball sails through the air into the clown in front of me. It squeaks, the knife clattering to the stone. I lunge, running the flaming blade through the center of it. It lets out a shrill release of air, deflating like a balloon.

Natalia backflips, foot connecting with a ball which pegs the two remaining clowns stacked on each other, the top clown tumbling to the stone. One of the balls slams against the wall then flies into me, knocking me over.

I duck another ball, sprawling flat on the ground before I have clear air to stand. A clown launches at me, weird laughter emitting from it. I manage to grab it by the throat as its blade sinks into my shoulder. I growl and throw it into the wall. The waiting tendrils of ivy latch on, stabbing into it. It deflates with that same twisted giggle mingling with the rush of deflation.

Another giggle echoes, and a ball bounces past me. I lift an eyebrow at Natalia as she slips the dagger back into the holster on her leg.

"Those weren't clowns. Those were little freaky monsters from the burning afters," I say, ripping the blade out of my shoulder.

"Less terrifying than I remember them."

417

CHAPTER 56
NATALIA

AFTER I HEAL CAL, WE HEAD FURTHER UP THE PATH, HALTING AT another intersection. I rock back on my heels. "Your turn to pick."

He takes a few steps around the corner to the right. The wall starts closing, so Cal tucks and rolls around it back to me as it slams closed. He stands, glaring at it.

He steps to continue forward, but the wall slams closed in his face.

Laughing, I say, "I guess it wanted a turn to decide."

We start to take the left, and the maze slams the last option closed. Cal punches the wall, yanking his hand back as ivy wraps around his wrist. It screams as he sets it ablaze, shaking loose the remains. "This fucking thing is closing off to keep us from getting closer to the center."

"All right, then." I shrug, turning back to come face-to-face with another vision of Tony.

He reaches out, brushing a hand over my cheek. "Someday, Nat, he's going to realize you're not so useful."

The touch is an icy kiss against my skin that leaves my flesh prickling with goosebumps.

"You'll never be his Queen. That's Telra's fate. You're not

Sasha. He'll cast you aside for her beauty and grace–" Cal grabs me by the wrist and pulls me through the apparition. Tony's voice continues to follow us "–and you'll come back to me."

"You're doing great," Cal says. "He's never going to touch you. You're never having children with him or for the Magia. Is this what you meant when you said you saw Tony?"

I nod, taking a few deep breaths. "Pretty much it."

His hand tightens on mine. "You don't have to be afraid of the Magia anymore."

A ball clogs my throat, pressure building behind my eyes, and in my nasal cavities. I press my lips, shaking my head as I decide to take a left turn. My voice is muted as I manage to say, "Shut up."

He grabs me by the shoulders, twisting me into him and tipping my head back to force me to meet his eyes. "Little Star–"

"Don't."

That cocky smirk twists the left side of his face. "You don't tell me what to do."

"Yes, I do."

"I hold the contract. I don't do a damn thing I don't want to, unlike you," he says with humor. I open my mouth to retort, but he presses his thumb over my lips. "You are going to shut up and listen for once. The Magia don't get to have you. You belong to me, and they will never be able to pry you out of my claws. Do you understand me?"

I blink at him, the seriousness of his words offset by the mirth in his expression. Giving in to that tiny glint of hope in my chest, I close my eyes, leaning my head into his hand. "Yes."

"Good."

"But!"

"No buts," he chuckles, spinning me away and smacking my ass. "Except that one. Now move it. I want out of here."

We walk and walk, shadows closing in around us. My chest is tight, my Light glimmering bright enough to sting my eyes. I stop, heading for the wall to catch my breath, but Cal grabs my hand as

I reach toward solidity. The ivy rasps, rattles, and snakes against the stone walls, hissing as the vines twist away from the stone, trying to grab us.

We duck and bob the attempts with ease as he draws me to the middle of the path. "What's wrong?"

"I can't breathe."

He grunts, pulling me against him. "The Dark snuffs out the Light."

I nod against his chest. "I think it really is trying to suffocate me."

"Look at me."

I blink up at him, and he crushes his mouth to mine, his tongue licking against mine. I groan as his hands tighten on my hips. The world disappears as I steal the breath of life from his chest, losing myself in him, his Dark swaddling me.

He pulls back, pressing his forehead to mine. "I need you to relax."

Grinning wide I say, "Then get me out of here." I push away from him, heading up the path. Something clicks under my heel. I freeze, tensing. "Uh."

"I heard," Cal says in a tight voice.

"Thoughts?"

"A few. Nothing happened, so it's a spring-loaded trap. Something sharp is coming as soon as you let off."

"Okay, get away from here." I jerk my head at the other end of the path. "Whatever comes I can heal."

He stands next to me, shaking his head. "This thing was to separate us." He peers around. "Alone you'd be vulnerable."

A whisper of white smoke materializes as my father. He stands in front of me, glaring and unspeaking. I swallow, trying not to cower under his stern gaze, ripe with hatred and disgust.

Cal's hand rests on the back of my neck. "Who is that?"

"My father."

He sighs. "Your fears are a lot more interesting than Massimo's." The hall brightens, and I glance at his flaming wings spreading from his back. He slips his arms around my waist. "I'm going straight up."

I nod, quelling under my father's silent fury. Cal tightens, and jumps. Spikes shoot straight up after us, but his wings beat, holding us aloft, carrying us to a clear place before lowering to the ground. His wings disappear, and he twists his fingers into mine, leading me onward.

We hit another crossroads. I stop. "Is there a catch to this place, like always go left?"

"No."

I glance at him. "You okay?"

He rubs the back of his neck. "Fine."

I go left. "Question."

"Answer."

"If you're scared of small spaces, how does sex work?" I hold my hand balled into a fist to my eye, like I'm trying to see through an itty-bitty hole. "Cause, like, that's a small space."

Cal gives me a long look, eyebrow raised. "That's not even remotely the same."

"Clearly, you don't find me funny."

"I do." He flashes his teeth in a wide grin I'm certain is fake.

We hit another cross-section. I take a right this time. Scuttling against the stone wafts in the shadows, rapid tapping echoing as spiders come crawling up the walk and walls. I see a dozen, maybe more scurrying closer, the size of large dogs, and I swallow my scream of fear.

"Little Star," Cal grinds, grabbing at me as I turn to run.

The ground shakes, stone scraping.

"Talia!" he yells as Dark coils around me and yanks me backward.

I drag on the ground, knocked by a massive slab of stone hurrying to slam shut but yanked through the shrinking space before the wall slams into the other. My heart jackhammers against my ribs as a spider leaps off the wall and onto my stomach. It rears back and sinks fangs into my stomach.

I scream, my abdomen ignites with pain, and I flail, trying to dislodge it. Light flashes, and then Cal is kneeling next to me, pulling me close as his Dark tendrils fling spiders away.

"Glow."

The Light flickers as I grasp for it, but fear soaks me.

He growls as Dark shards stab into me. Another scream is ripped out of me as the piercing cold sinks into my core. It tears me apart, digging out a piece of me in shattering agony.

Fire erupts. My mind reels. The world is burning bright orange, heat searing my skin. It ends as it began, in an instant.

The spinning slows, and I come to curled between Cal's legs on the cold stone, clinging to him, shaking. His arms are wrapped around me in strong reassurance, and strokes my hair, lips against my head. "Breathe, Little Star."

"Cal."

"You're okay."

My fingers twist into his shirt for stable purchase, rooting myself to reality and him alike. I nod, swallowing the last dredges of fear.

He sighs, standing and dragging me to my feet with him. "You can't run. The maze wants to separate us."

"What did you do to me?"

"If you don't glow to bring the Light to the surface, I can dig it out of you." He takes a half-step back. "It's what I do, but that's more dangerous. If I pull too much, I'll drag the whole seed of Light out of you. I will kill you."

I press my face into his chest, not sure if he moves away that I will be capable of standing on my own. "Right," I say. "My use. You need to use me."

His chest rumbles with a laugh. "I don't need to. I can hunt Light Seraphinus, drag their magic out of them, and eat it. You're easier, I can feed in smaller increments, but I get more from you

422

than hunting, and I don't have to worry about the Council coming after me." He pries my face from him. "Ready?"

I half-laugh, half-sob, an odd mix of both working out of my chest as I screw up my face. "Mother, no, and specifically, fuck no."

His thumbs run over my cheek bones. "I promise you. It's in the contract. I will take care of every spider for you, now, here in the maze, and every day after. Okay?"

"Yeah."

Taking my hand, he leads me up the path. We navigate through the carcasses of the dozens of arachnids while I try not to pay attention. I'm wobbling, aching like I was beat half-to-death. For a moment, I crouch down, sending waves of Ki through me. It helps, although it doesn't clear the hollow yawning chasm left behind from Cal ripping away part of my Light.

Clearing my throat, I stand, catching him watching me. I flip him off. "I hate being your food source."

One side of his lips curl back. "I'll eat you later to make up for it."

Puzzled, I cock my head tilts to the side, then I realize what he's offering. Stretching my eyes wide, I open my mouth, however, nothing witty comes to mind, so I close my lips and turn away, waltzing up the path. "Fine, but I want a case of vodka too."

Following, he chuckles. "Get me through this in one piece and I'll buy you a year's supply."

We stop at the edge of a murky pool of black water that stretches as far as I can make out in the shadows. Clearing my throat, I toe the edge, "Uh?"

Cal steps next to me. "Are you afraid of water?"

I shake my head. "I'm not a fan of the idea of drowning, although I wouldn't call that a fear. I'm not excited by a lot of ways to die. Is this one of yours this time? Please let this be one of your fears."

He gives me a chagrin, mock grimace. "No. This isn't one of mine."

I groan and throw my hands up. "Great, drowning potential it is." Cal pulls off his shirt, sneakers, and socks as I glare. "What are you doing?"

"Going for a swim." He sits on the edge, then slips in, treading water to stay afloat.

"You are fucking nuts."

He makes a face of disgust. "It's cold."

"No way! I expected this maze of horrors to have a hot tub. I was hoping this was the mid-way break point to soak and relax."

He chuckles, gliding on his back further from the edge. "Come on," he says, checking behind him. "You're going to have to swim."

"What exactly are your fears?" I pull my sneakers off and toss them to the side.

A wisp of greenish, white materializes as a phantom of Sasha next to me. "Do you remember that night?"

My sister is pristine, hair pinned in an intricate chignon, wearing a tailor-fit dress with high neck and short skirt. She's even in six-inch heels, looking elegant and beautiful. It hurts to see her, my chest aching with longing for her.

Cal asks, "Who is that?"

I ignore the hint of intrigue in his voice. "Yeah, she's gorgeous."

He chuckles, "So are you, Little Star. Now, answer me before the contract gets involved."

"Sasha," I whisper.

"Your sister? Did you two not get along?"

"We did, in the way sisters do." I stare at her. "She always treated me like I was a baby, like she was better than me and I needed help."

"Hm, so she was an idiot? You need to get in."

I step to the edge, the ghost of Sasha mirroring me. She says, "Baby sister, that looks miserable. Almost like that night."

I glare at her. "What night?"

"When we all went skinny dipping."

I shake my head, frowning at Cal. He's watching, eyebrows lifted in humor. His eyes aren't on my sister, though. They're on me. No one else ever looked at me when I stood next to her, but then, that thing isn't really her.

"You remember Zander saving you?"

I tense, Cal swimming back to the ledge. "What is it talking about?"

Sasha coos, "The way he looked at you."

Flipping Sasha off, I jump into the pool, freezing water rushing over me. Breaching the surface, I gulp for air, treading water as Sasha's phantom fades away even as her voice echoes around us. "I know your secret."

Cal flips to his back, kicking away further into the pool. "Move and answer me. What's it talking about?"

"Can you wait for story time until we reach the other side?"

"I've never come across water in this maze in two hundred years. What it's referring to may be what this is about."

I kick to keep above the surface as I follow him away from the ledge. "A bunch of us went skinny dipping off the coast one Heatwave. Tony, Sasha, me, Ness, a few others–I got dragged out by a current. I was about to die, then Zander saved me."

"Who is Zander?"

"A Light Seraphinus."

Disgust twists his features as I breaststroke forward to stay with him. "And," he snarls, "what's the secret?"

I roll my eyes. "He saved me. I didn't try to kill him."

"That's it?" Cal's chuckle is low. "That's not much of a secret. You've betrayed them way worse with me."

"Fine." I breathe out hard. The water is chilling me, so I work faster, hoping the other side is close. "He and I may have fucked, which may or may not be how I lost my virginity."

"Fucking a Seraphinus? Still not much of a secret." He laughs, grinning wide. "I'm not sure how that correlates to fear, other than it being a Light fuck." He wrinkles his nose. "Clearly it was disappointing."

I shoot him a glare, having zero desire to discuss this while swimming through a death trap. "It was fine."

He flashes teeth. "You know I'm better. Millions of years of the Light and Dark fighting, and now we finally know which is the best."

A breathless laugh bursts out of me, bouncing off the stones. Something slimy wraps around my ankle, snaking up my leg. "Oh, fu–"

I'm dragged beneath the surface. Icy blackness closing around me as I'm pulled downward. I claw at the nothing above me, the water leaking up my nose and filling my ears.

Forcing my eyes open, I stare upward, bubbles floating toward the surface in my dim glow. Inky black tendrils race for me from above.

Ducking my chin to my chest, still being dragged downward, I focus on the tentacle squeezing around my leg. My lungs are burning, threatening to suck in. Dark tendrils wrap around me, twining around my torso and arms.

Cal's magic. I know it by feel.

I halt in an abrupt jerk, my leg yanked, almost torn from my body. I shriek behind closed lips, jaw clenched against opening my mouth.

The tentacle wraps tighter, tugging harder. I squeeze my eyes shut, centering to send Ki through me. The world illuminates, the presence of the tentacle disappears, and I streak upward.

CHAPTER 57

CALLAHAN

I'M LAUGHING, THEN NATALIA GOES UNDER HALFWAY THROUGH A curse with a squeal. I flip over, diving deeper to chase after her, but she's going down at a high rate of speed. I set my magic loose after her, heading for the surface. I break through, shaking water from my face as I tread water, closing my eyes and reaching for Natalia through my Dark.

My heart beats hard thirty times before I can sense her on the edge of my magic, another fifteen times before my Dark latches on. It's stretched thin. She's almost too far out of reach, but I have her. I bare my teeth at the shadows around me, snarling at my magic to bring her up.

Something is fighting against us pulling her back.

"Fuck," I snarl, commanding my magic to wrap tighter, to deal with the threat. It screams as I pulse with Natalia's magic coursing through us. She must be glowing, pumping her Light into my Dark. Fear swallows me as I try to absorb her Light as quick as she's giving it, afraid if I lose control I'll explode again. I could kill her, or my Dark might lose its hold on her.

The pulse stops in an abrupt manner, my Dark sliding into me as it recoils, bringing our little star to me. When her body breaks through the surface, I grab her, flipping her onto her back.

She chokes and splutters, water bubbling from between her lips. My magic threads and slips around her, hissing in protective fury. "I've got you, Little Star."

My Dark unwinds from my center, filling the water around us to fend off whatever is in the deep while I get her in front of me. I lean her against my torso as I recline on my back, kicking for the other side. My legs burn, but I grunt, trying to go faster.

My magic is pissed, screaming at something. It stings in my right temple as it curses.

I ram into something solid, and glance over my shoulder at the ledge of the pool. I reach an arm behind me, using my elbow as a fulcrum on the stone to leverage my torso out of the water, lifting Natalia with me.

Tentacles streak from beneath the surface, thick, black muscular arms of a water dweller with vibrant, blue, concave suckers shimmering in the dim glow of Natalia's Light. Droplets spray my face and chest as they wave, something deeper howling.

My magic responds, fending them off, binding them, and attacking. Getting my ass on the ledge, I twist Natalia free of the pool, shoving her onto dry land as far from the pool as I can manage. She rolls, flopping face down, motionless and silent.

Tentacles lash around me, thick and rubbery, suction cups sealing them tight to my flesh. I grapple at the slick stone surface as I'm hauled into the water. My fingers slip along the rough surface, singing with sharp pain as my skin shreds. I dig in, clinging to the ledge, but I'm losing my grip even as I strain with my full strength.

"Fuck it," I snarl. I don't have enough purchase to avoid being dragged into the deep for long. I take a deep breath, letting go of the ledge. The freezing water rushes around me as I am submerged in wet nothingness, descending into the unknown. Water streams past me, tentacles and tendrils battling around me.

"*Go*," I tell my Dark, setting it free from its cage, allowing it to consume me.

It whoops with excitement, euphoria cascading through my mind despite the agony shattering my body.

My skin splits along my spine as my spikes burst free. My fingers elongate, bones crunching as they break and grow into long talons. Every bone in my body following suit, snapping and pulsing with pain as my limbs alter into my true form. I roar, bubbles filling the water around me to mix with my magic.

I slice at the tentacles capturing me with my claws. My Dark unleashes its pent-up rage, and the water erupts with flames, beginning to boil. The thing howls, tentacles dissolving around me.

Free, I kick feet together surging to the surface, snarling as I brace on the ledge, prying myself out of the water and onto my feet. The ledge cracks under my weight and I tip over, flopping into the pool again as I flail at the shadows in the air.

My Dark laughs at me, and I sneer in return. Getting upright, I swim to the broken edge, prying myself out face down, my torso dragging along the stone. Unlike wet, fleshy fingers, my talons grip and cut into the path, and I claw my way to solid, stable ground.

On my feet, I stomp to Natalia, crouching low to inspect her. Slipping talons under her, I flip her over. She shows no signs of consciousness. I growl, nudging her, making sure to use gentle force.

She groans.

Withdrawing, I sit on my hind legs to wait for her to rouse. In ire, I glance behind me at the pool. I've lost my father's hilt, the weapon sunk somewhere into the abyss with the remains of my tattered clothes. I can have a new one constructed, but it won't be the same.

Returning my attention to my little star, I fume. More than two hundred years I've entered this maze during every Gathering

Shadows, and I've never encountered water. The maze is pulling out all the stops for her. I don't understand it's intense focus. It could be because she's the Light, but this has the airs of a personal vendetta.

Natalia's eyes flutter open, beautiful silver like the Light that covers her. They fix upon me, then stretch in horror. She screams, twisting over and scrambling away.

I slump, inhale, then lunge on all fours, twisting my body around her to cut off the path and stop her from running. I crouch low, forelegs bent to drop into an aggressive stance and warn her from trying to escape, tail snapping behind me in annoyance.

"Talia," I say, my voice a snarl full of ash and flame.

"Cal?" She gapes.

"Yes," I say. Even trying to keep my voice soft, it's a deep snarl. I relax, sitting on my back legs, my tailing stopping at rest on the stone.

"Mother, what–oh you're–oh fuck me. What the fuck?" She leans forward, hands on her knees to pant. Upright, she winces. "This is you?"

I stare at her, then stand on my hind legs. Her eyes travel over me as she steps toward me on shaky legs. My magic coils around me, both of us quelling under her gaze. I've never felt so exposed.

For a few fractions, she cocks her head, then leans to the side. Her jaw drops, then her eyes find mine. "You have a tail."

I curl it around my feet, almost whining as I try to hide it.

She nods, her voice a breathless whisper. "Right, you're a Darkling. You shifted."

I hunker low, self-conscious under her scrutiny. "I had to. Being in human form limits my magic."

She waves a hand. "It's fine, but you're fucking terrifying, and that is not a face I ever want to sit on."

I laugh in relief, my amusement coming out as twisted barks.

"Are you planning on changing back?"

430

I shake my head. "The maze." My tail snaps against the wall as I lash out at it. "I hate the maze. It's going to get worse before we make it to the center and my clothes were destroyed when I shifted. I'm not walking around this deathtrap naked."

"What's in the center?"

"The way out."

I turn, using my tail for balance and start up the path.

A whisper of white transforms into Tony before me. "You'd never be able to take down a shifted Darkling, Nat."

I snarl, clawing at him. There's not much that can take me down when I'm shifted. My attack goes right through the ghost.

It ripples and reforms. Tony laughs. "You really think he needs you?"

I growl and rip ivy off the wall. My talons gouging into the stone, cutting through the vines. It screeches and writhes as it breaks apart, and I fling the tangled mess towards the ghost. It sails through Tony, who disappears with another taunting laugh.

Everything the maze is throwing out is geared to Natalia. It's pissing me off. The maze has never ignored me.

My tail snaps into the wall, breaking off chunks of stone. "I do," I snarl, twisting my head toward my little star. Her head is cocked, lips twisted to the side in consideration, her eyes traveling up my body. "Need you."

"Sure, babe, whatever you say."

I stomp forward.

CHAPTER 58
NATALIA

As Cal storms further up the corridor, I eye him with my head shied to the side. "Yeah, sure. Follow the giant monster. Why not?"

His back has a row of spikes between his burning wings. They're like long exposed and elongated vertebrae formed to points, bone or hard shell I can't tell. They trail down his back shrinking in size but sharpening to razor points all the way to the tip of his double-barbed tail.

He's black skin is stretched tight over bulging muscles, with exoskeleton armor, and his legs are animalistic. His feet and hands are massive, with shiny, wicked sharp black talons.

He stops, tail swinging. I dodge out of the way as it whips around. He stares at me, his eyes glowing fire, the same fire that glows from where his limbs and joints meet.

I lift an eyebrow, head tipping to the side. "Yes?"

He points a talon in front of him, unspeaking. Staying as close to the wall as I dare, I move in front of him to where he pointed. He nudges me onward with his hand, large enough to take up my whole back.

"Easy, babe. I'm pretty sure you could break me if you flicked hard enough."

His arm bends around me, braced on the ground as he crouches. Heat radiates off him, the black skin glossy like satin, and up close the hard spike jutting from the back of his elbow looks like bone with rough, pitted surface. I'm an ant next to a beast of darkness and fire.

I breathe out slow, heart racing. "Cal?"

He snarls, "I won't hurt you."

I nod. "I know." I pat his forearm, my hand not even spanning the width. "I'm going to move now, yeah?"

He growls, lifting from around me. I take a few steps forward. He follows, his steps shaking the ground. I hum, looking around, weaving along.

I hit a dead end and stop, frowning at it. Crossing my legs, I spin myself, facing Cal. "Whelp, not this way."

The stone shifts behind me, rumbling the ground and screeching as it drags. Cal leans forward and roars, tail whipping around to smack me in closer.

I hit the pavement, and something streaks over me, the air whistling. Steel bouncing against something hard rings out, and I lift my head as the blade clatters on the ground in front of me, ricocheting off Cal.

I glance over my shoulder, expecting creepy giggles and clowns. Instead, a sleek figure with lime green wings is in a low stance, hissing. I push to my feet, turning with my hands up. A second one paces toward me, standing next to the first. They're female from what I can tell, coated in black velvet with glittering green eyes. At least these are about human size, not twelve-foot-tall monsters like Cal.

"Don't." Cal crouches behind me, one fist balled, pressing into the ground to steady him.

The first shifted Darkling stands, rolling and shimmying her body with a wide grin, exposing feline-like fangs. "Where is the fun in that?"

I know that voice and narrow my eyes at her. "Telra?"

"Hello, Light whore." Cal's tail flicks at her so she leaps back. "My, my, I did forget how well you can use your body. I miss that."

I lift my chin. "I put you down once, bitch."

Telra rolls her eyes, her eyelashes fluttering as she giggles. "Not in this form."

The one next to her scoffs. "Please, let me be the one to kill this stupid glow whore."

"No," Telra snaps.

Cal growls as black tendrils wrap around me, pulling me closer. "Don't get too worked up, Yasmin. Neither of you are killing Talia."

I eye the women, like humanoid cats. Telra lifts a hand, a soft *shnick* carrying through the air as her claws expand.

The Dark pulls me against Cal's body, his heat almost too much to bear, like a hundred-degree Heatwave season suns beating down on my skin. The tendrils race over me. I don't need him to tell me to glow. I hold tight to the thought of him smiling, the Light spreading through my chest, illuminating me from the inside.

The women hiss then lunge at us. Dark blue, twinkling haze and flames explode around us. Cal leaves me, racing forward. One of the women lurches to her feet, claws coming out. She begins scratching at him, and he snarls like a rabid dog, tackling her.

The second Venominx stands, leaping through the air, dropping on me, and her claws sink into my shoulders. We go down, me on my back, the Venominx on top of me. The bitch rips her claws out, scratching at my chest and throat.

Pain streaks through me, searing in crisscrossing agony over my chest. The Light glows brighter, the wounds pulsing alerting me to the searing, torn flesh. My sight blurs with tears of pain, obstructing my vision. Blind, I throw my hand at the Venominx chest.

Nothing happens. I'm not centered to draw on my Ki.

My heart skips a beat as it continues to tear into me. The world turning to a gray haze around the edges as sticky, wet warmth covers me. The Venominx is shrieking with laughter, still tearing at my flesh.

Cal roars.

I grit my teeth, trying to center for Ki. The Venominx claws sinking into my chest, ribs cracking and I shriek even as she screams with delight. "I'm going to eat your heart!"

Warmth wraps around my arms, long tendrils crawling across my skin. I blink, watching my Light entwine the Venominx, and it brightens. Telra yowls, hesitating in her onslaught, so I try to shove her off my chest, Light erupting from my hands in beams of energy, blasting her away.

That wasn't Ki. I gape, frozen in shock and confusion, still laying there bleeding out. I didn't do that.

"Talia!" Cal's loud snarl snaps me from the trance.

Dazed, I take one shaking breath, fighting the pain, and shoving my core into alignment. Telra rounds on her feet to pounce, claws sinking into my torso again. I dig deeper, wanting fire.

Light flickers under my hands.

I'll set myself on fire to keep the demons at bay.

The Light roars to life over me in flickering shimmers of oranges and yellows. The claws retract. I shove up, drawing my spine straight, sending a wave of Ki through me. I scream at the burn, then she is on me again.

Telra shrieks, clawing at me. "You're nothing but a glowing fuck he's playing with in boredom."

I hit back. "And you're a sadistic bitch he doesn't want."

We trade a couple of blows before I dodge low, flip over, pop to my feet, and throw out a hand. Light ripples as orange through my arm and blasts Telra's chest.

She's baring her teeth, but retreating, and doubled over. She sends black tendrils streaking out toward me. Silver vines twist away from me in retaliation. Our magics tangling together in combat.

Telra darts in and I flip through the air, my legs locking around her neck. I throw her down, landing on top of her. Drawing firelight again, I begin raining punches down on any part of her head I can make contact with as she squirms.

The flames cover me, spreading to Telra. I swing and hit her over and over again, my Light tying up her Dark and winding around her, keeping her pinned as she thrashes. I get a few whacks in as my Light finishes binding her.

I slap my hand to her cheek, pressing her face to the side into the stone as I pant. "Told you I'd put you down."

"Fuck you, Glow Whore. This isn't over yet."

I draw Ki, collecting it together. "It really is, silly kitty. You're going to stay the fuck away from Cal. He's mine."

I send the Ki through my arm, Light flashing as it blasts into her. There's a deafening crack, the stone breaking beneath us as Telra goes limp.

Shoving up, I kick at Telra. She doesn't stir. Her eyes are closed. I'm not sure if I managed to kill her or not.

I take a breath, tipping my head back as I send Ki through me to heal any lingering wounds, then scan the area for Cal.

He's sitting on his back legs, his arms bracing him as he watches me several paces away. He's like an excited puppy, his doglike head canted and tail wagging back and forth behind him. I step toward him.

His fluffy, pointed, black ears lean back flat and he growls. "You're covered in firelight."

I glance at myself, still flickering and wound tight in tendrils of

436

Light that shimmer and lick like flames. Taking a breath, I focus and center, finding an inner calm.

He lowers his head, trotting forward then lifts upright on his back legs. "Are you hurt?"

I shake my head even as one of his talon scrapes at my tattered shirt. "I'm fine. I healed already."

He pulls back. "Move." He reaches a hand toward me.

"Babe," I laugh. "I could, like, grab one talon." I push his hand to the side and head up the path. Behind us, the maze closes off. I stop, glancing back with a frown. "Pretty sure this death trap forced us to them."

CHAPTER 59
NATALIA

CAL HUNKERS DOWN ON HIS HAUNCHES TO SCRATCH AT HIS NECK with a hind leg. I giggle, holding a hand to my mouth. "Really?"

He stops in a hurry, turning his face to the wall. "Shut up."

"It's cute," I shrug. "Did you kill Yasmin?"

He grins, I think, exposing wicked, long teeth. "Yes."

My flesh prickles with goosebumps, and I shiver. "Okay then, you're a little *too* happy about that."

He growls, starting forward. "Telra?"

"Not sure if I killed your girlfriend or not. You Darklings are hard to kill." I shrug, stopping at another cross-section. "You know, in case you wanted to propose marriage after we get out of here."

His talons click as he smacks my arm. It knocks me sideways, and I stumble off balance into the wall. He snarls, Dark wrapping around me, ripping me back the other way before my mind even begins processing what happened.

"What the burning afters?" I smack at him, my palm stinging.

He yelps in sharp barks. "I didn't realize it was that much force."

I shudder. "Mother, I think you could snap me in half without effort, and there wouldn't be anything I could do about it."

Cal nudges me left. "I could break you in my masked form."

I move around the corner, saying, "Just know, if we run into another like you, I'm hiding behind you."

He snorts. "There aren't any. There are only about a dozen of my race left. I'm one, and there is one other contracted to another player, not enlisted to participate. The rest aren't in society, hiding in the Avgora Mountains."

"That's a relief." I say, then ask, "Why hiding? To avoid the games?"

"To avoid society. My race—" he stops, both talking and moving. "We were persecuted and hunted."

"Why?"

"For what we are." He takes a right.

Mirrors line the path ahead of us, a phantom Sasha stands in the middle, reflected in a thousand different ways. "I know the truth."

I catch sight of my reflection next to Sasha's and clench my fists. Even though I'm not ugly, I don't compare on the same level as my sister.

The figure in the middle of the path disappears, although Sasha remains staring at us in each mirror. She laughs. "Do you even know the truth?"

Cal crouches next to me. "Mirrors?"

I cock my jaw. "Don't ask."

He chuckles. "I already did."

I start down the path. "Mirrors don't lie," I say, keeping my eyes on my feet, movement evident in my peripheral.

"Baby sister," Sasha's voice calls out, broken and soft. "He doesn't know, does he?"

Stopping, I turn to a mirror. My reflection overlays Sasha's image. Sasha lifts her hand, pressing it to the surface of the glass, her face solemn. "You miss me, don't you?"

I lift my hand, ready to press it against hers.

Cal's tail whips out, fracturing the mirror. His Dark wraps around my middle and pulls me closer to him. "Don't touch."

Sasha's delicate laugh echoes around us. "Why would you miss me? He wouldn't want you if I were there."

He shatters another mirror.

"Is it just what he thinks you can do? Does he know how much better I was? Do you think he would have picked me instead?"

With a sigh, I admit, "You would have. She was better than me."

"No." His tail whips around, cracking mirror after mirror. "You said she didn't carry the Light. That is what I need, a Light source. I don't give a fuck about your Magia Ki shit, although your ability to heal is convenient."

I tip my head back and laugh, staring up. The sky overhead is strange. I'd forgotten we aren't buried underground.

He nudges me forward. "It's the maze, Little Star. It wants to…"

I rub my face, "Scare me, right?"

"That's what the maze does."

This doesn't seem like fear. I miss Sasha, I could be terrified that if she were here that Cal would have chosen her. If she was, the point would be moot. I wouldn't have had a reason to run.

Starting to walk again, I ignore when Sasha calls out from the mirrors as I pass by, trying not to hear her taunts and jeers. At a cross-section, I stop in the middle. Every direction is lined in mirrors. There's no escape from this bitter afters in sight.

Groaning, I turn to Cal. "Which way?"

He glances around and tenses, drawing up. I frown, the mirrors having enclosed us in a circle. Cal starts shuffling to the middle, whining, and looking around.

I hold my hands up. "You're way too big to start panicking on me."

He fixates on me, settling on his haunches, "Tal—"

Thunder cracks and lightning strikes, a brilliant streak of electricity streaking to the ground. Snarling, he stands, twisting and thrashing, tail whipping, trying to break the mirrors.

I duck, but the recoil of his tail whacks me in the stomach. I slam into a mirror, the glass cracking against my back. Groaning, I fall forward, but two hands grab me around my stomach.

"Sister!" Sasha calls with joy as she pulls me back against the mirror.

Cal is in the middle of the circle, spinning and thrashing, slamming his fists into mirrors, tail whipping into others. For each he breaks, two fractured heal, reflecting the lightning strikes raining down on him that leave sparks of electricity crawling over his body.

He shrinks from them, cowering in a ball.

The arms twisting around me tighten, cutting into my skin. I wince, eyes dropping to thin veins branching from the arms around me. Vines snake around me, black leaves swelling as the thin living ropes cut into me. "Cal!"

He whips toward me, snapping his jowls as he darts forward on all fours. Lightning strikes between us, and he skitters away, slamming into a mirror, then staggers sideways.

I fumble for the blade strapped to my thigh. I manage to grip the hilt, but more chords spiral around my arm, binding it to the wall. The vines squeezes into my arm, my flesh bulging around them as dark leaves sprout like razor blades that cut into me. Blood seeps from me, rolling across the leaves, which soak in the drops.

Cal lunges at me, clawing at the wall and vines. He growls and digs his talons behind me, ripping me free. He pulls me into the middle, crouching and cradling me close. I send Ki through me, sealing severed flesh as I hide under his protection.

He flinches and snaps at the lightning strike nearby, shying away. He slides his hand around me, his talons clicking together as he trembles. Hunkering low, one arm keeping me pinned against him, he snarls and snaps his teeth at more lightning.

I press a hand to his chest, the heart within beating like hammer strikes. "Sh," I hush him. "Sh, it's okay. I'm okay now."

There's a flash and he jerks us away from it.

As he steadies us, Cal rumbles deep in his chest, keeping me against him.

"You don't like lightning."

His tail curls around us at another crack.

I giggle. "You're afraid of lightning?"

"It's too much like smiting." He flinches, trying to get lower and smaller.

He dives, rolling us out of the way of another strike. His tail lashes out at a mirror. It shatters, causing the rest to start closing in, lightning dancing around us.

Until now, there was something to kill, to fight back against. There isn't anything to defeat this time. I turn into him. "Cal?"

He makes an odd noise like a whine. "Little Star."

The mirrors are closer still, the circle presses in so there is no room to move. Sasha walks through the reflective glass, from one to the next. I watch her, frowning. "What do we do?"

He lashes out at the mirrors with his tail without answering.

Sasha laughs from a mirror, her hands to her face in mock surprise. "What do we do? Oh no! What do we do?"

I sneer. "Shut up. You're not real."

"You're a pathetic excuse for an heiress. You can't help him."

Cal roars as lightning strikes, the crash echoing and illuminating through the mirrors. The bolt crawls over him, the charged air humming and zapping. He thrashes, throwing himself against the mirrors, beginning to claw at himself with his talons, like he could scrape away the beads of electricity racing over him.

I try to dodge out of the way, but he knocks into me. The collision sends me slamming into a mirror. It crunches and fractures, the shards piercing into my body, and I slump forward as I groan, battered and broken.

Cal stumbles, lashing out again, unleashing a scream like the roar of a fire, leaving the world ringing.

Grappling with the glass, I try to yank shards free, but it my hand slips, the fragment slicing into my palm. I try again, gripping tighter, the jagged and sharp edge biting my hand as it slips along the shard, slick with blood. I clench my jaw against the pain. It budges some, but not enough to be dislodged.

Cal spins, clawing at the mirrors. I attempt to duck his tail, failing again. The whack flings me into yet another mirror. It fractures, the crackled glass raining down on me as I fall forward to the ground. I flinch and cry out as broken slivers sink into my back and shoulders.

Sobbing, I scramble, trying to move out of Cal's way, but there's no where to go. He spins. I dive, tucking and roll out of the way. Rolling against the stone shoves the shards deeper into my muscles and flesh with a fury that stings. "Cal!" I scream through tears. "Cal, stop! Babe! Please!"

My cries are covered by the booms and cracks of lightning. Another bolt makes impact with Cal, a brilliant, fizzling chain streaking across him. He thrashes, stumbling as he claws at himself.

I fumble a few paces, limping and exhausted, spurred on by adrenaline to avoid being crushed as he crashes backward. Then he's on his feet, clawing at the mirrors, tail whipping. Broken pieces of razor-sharp mirror fly through the air, some slicing into me, others tinkering to the ground.

Another bolt of lightning, and this time when Cal fumbles to the side, I can't get out of the way. He pins me to a mirror, the fragile surface fracturing and embedding in me. I sob, pushing in a futile effort to dislodge him. "Cal!"

Thin steel-like cords wrap around me. Sasha's laughing, her image broken in the broken mirror pieces around us. "Poor Little Lightning Bug. Poor Little Star. You're no Magia heiress. You're just a poor little wingless toy trapped in the Dark."

Lightning cracks with an ear-splitting cry. It hits Cal, racing over him, leaping from his body to mine. It drags like barbed wire across my skin, and we scream in unison. I pant as warm blood soaks my clothes and rolls in droplets down my body. I go limp, whimpering and twitching in pain.

"You thought he cared about you? He cares about what you can do for him, and it looks like that's not much." Sasha giggles, vanishing from sight. Her voice whispers through the air still as Cal fumbles away from me. "If you don't have a use, how long do you think he's going to keep you? He'll throw you aside, cast you out. You're the Light, and you'll be all alone, unlovable, useless with no reason to live."

Cal sways back and forth with force. Cords are cutting into me, the ivy slicing through my flesh. It wraps me tighter into the wall, the pressure forcing glass deeper into me, sending blood oozing out of me, welling up to drip and spill across my skin. I center, forcing Ki to heal what it can, unable to seal shut any wound that is forced to remain open by debris.

Cal slams into me and I scream. His magic erupts as hard shards from him in every direction, radiating out of him like black ice. Mirrors shatter, more shards stabbing into me, and several strands of his Dark run me through.

I reach out, pressing a hand into him to feed Ki into him before he can stand up or pull away. He snarls and roars as I force more, wanting to overwhelm him. The world explodes in clouds of midnight blue and orange flames. A shrill splitting of rock rips through the air, and the ground shakes.

The world goes still. My heart beats once in the quiet, then we fall.

CHAPTER 60

CALLAHAN

POWER SURGES THROUGH ME. I CAN'T CONTROL IT. MY DARK expels it in a rush, the world exploding.

I tip over backwards, plummeting. My innards clench, my guts in my toes. I claw at the air and falling rock alike, trying to get the right way up. When I spread my wings, heavy, solid objects slam into my back propelling me faster.

I brace, flexing muscles, flapping my wings to stop falling, but further below in the dim and chaos is a brilliant glow, flickering in and out of sight. "Talia," I roar, pulling my wings back and streaking toward her.

She stops abruptly with a shrill scream. I land on top of her, boulders and broken stone slabs following. My magic shields us, every stroke of rock echoing in my head like blows of a hammer against the inside of my skull. I snarl, grinding my teeth to endure until everything settles.

The pain begins to recede. The rocks still slamming down become dull thuds. I flex every muscle, demanding strength from my body, trying to lift the slabs burying us. I strain, my talons digging into the dirt beneath us, but nothing budges. My muscles burn and quiver with fatigue and I give up, barely able to hold myself off Natalia as I pant.

Her Light is flickering at me, dim. I thrash side-to-side, but there's no room. Nothing is budging.

I can't breathe. I can't move. I'm trapped.

"Cal," Natalia whimpers, "Cal, stop, please, please just stop." Her voice is thin and trembling.

Growling, I tense and quit trying to find freedom. The air is thick, palpable with fear, and it isn't all hers. I try to find my head. "Talia."

I thought I lost her. When the maze closed in, all I could see in the mirrors was my little star crying, bleeding, dying. She'd been everywhere I looked as electricity rained down on me and zapped across my skin, but every time I tried to reach her it was nothing but a mirage in the reflective glass. I couldn't find her.

"Cal."

I breathe out in relief. She is here with me. I found her. I have her close. I inhale slow, the scent of tangy blood seeps through my addled senses.

"Talia," I snarl, eyes searching her.

A breath rattles out of her. "It's okay. It's okay," she says. "I know it's a small space, but you're okay."

"No," I snap. "Blood. It reeks of blood."

She nods. "It's okay. You'll be okay." She reaches out, her hand pressing against me as she tries to smile. "You were clawing yourself."

I shake myself, assessing the damage. My spinal spikes scrape against the stone, screeching and squealing, reverberating into me in an odd tingle. There's no pain in my body. "Not me. You."

"I'm okay." She gives another smile.

I sniff. "It's a lot of blood." My pulse races.

"Mhm, but you're okay."

I try to change my position, hitting immovable forces every-where. I snarl, digging my talons into the earth beneath us.

"You're okay," she whispers. "Breathe, babe. You're okay."

"Little Star." I groan, but it comes out as a growl.

Bloodstains are coming into clear focus over her torso, heavy, sticky splotches of deep blackish-reds, glass poking out of her all over the place. The air disappears around me. The walls of this nightmarish afters are slinking closer.

"Star," I manage, throat constricting with fear.

She smiles, lips together. "You're okay."

"Heal," I snarl. "Heal right now."

She shakes her head. "I can't. I have to get the glass out before I can. There's no way to do that right now."

"Fuck," my Dark and I scream together. I slam up into the rock over and over, trying to break us free of our tomb. Pieces break loose, pebbles and stone chips mingling with dust raining over us.

Natalia chokes and coughs, ducking her head beneath me. "Cal! Stop, stop it! You're okay. You're going to be okay."

My Dark is slithering over her, searching out how many wounds she has. It's too many for us to keep track of in our muddled brain.

She gives a weak laugh. Her other hand lifts to the side of my face. I know it's there, even though I can't feel it. She wrinkles her nose, "You're fucking weird like this. You feel like bone." She blinks, wet rolling out of her eyes. "You need to get out of here. Deep breaths, stay calm, think. I know you're scared. I know you don't like this, but you need to focus now, okay?"

"You need to heal. You're bleeding too much."

"The weak point of my healing is I can't heal with something in me. It stops it, but you're okay, you just need to figure a way out of here and you'll be okay. Focus on that, please."

I try to lift, to move side-to-side, looking for a weak point. I give up, growling. "I can't. There's nowhere to go." I lose the air in my chest again, the world squeezing me tight.

She nods. "Okay, okay, that's okay," she breathes in and out. "If brute force won't work, magic might."

"No. If I blast out, the shock force might kill you."

Silence rings as time ticks by while each beat of my heart thuds in my ears. I snap my teeth together to hear something else.

"We do something, or our star goes out," I snap at my Dark. *"Do. Some. Thing."*

Quivering, it pours out of me, slipping through crevices, navigating holes. It pushes against insurmountable weight, seeking out the cracks it can slip through in search of the surface.

"Get to the top where the weight is less. Blast us free bit by bit."

"Cal," Natalia says in a weak voice.

"What?"

"I'm sorry." She shudders, mewling. "I'm so sorry I wasn't useful."

A soft growl more like a purr wrapped thick in fury slides through my chest. The maze has been trying to convince her she is useless since we stepped inside. It's tearing her apart and it's working. I don't understand it, the maze draws out fears, preys on them, this is so much worse to her than simple fear.

I hang my head closer to hers. "Little Star, you're far from useless."

She gives a wheezing chuckle. "Sure. I've got one last use, then I think I'm done. I'm losing a lot of blood here."

"No." I try to shove up, ramming into the rock. It's too soon. My Dark hasn't found the surface yet.

"Hurry."

"I am going as fast as I can, asshole. Unless you want to crawl through these tiny holes?"

"Cal, you need to focus, think of a way out. You're not dying, just stuck. You can get out of here. You can finish this maze and get out."

"If I lose you, I lose everything."

"Liar, you've been just fine without me for years. Centuries, I think."

448

I bite at the air. "I need you for what's coming. The contest for the throne. Maybe, Ancients."

She laughs, coughing and groaning. "That hurt, don't make me laugh."

"It wasn't a joke." I grunt, muscles starting to ache from holding myself off her in the confined space. "Maybe I don't *need* you, not even your Light, but I need *you*. I need—"

"I couldn't get you through this maze. I'm fucking useless."

"Tell me you're useless one more fucking time and—" I bite off the words. It's making me crazy hearing her so defeated. I've watched her take down my top competitors and other big-name players and laugh about it like she was having fun.

"And what? You're going to put me in my place? Better make it quick."

"You're not useless, and you're not dying. I've seen you survive worse in the last few days."

Natalia shifts, her voice a soft warble in the shadows of her glimmering Light and my flickering glow.

> *"My body, it aches*
> *I feel like I'm shattered*
> *Broken, and battered*
> *Still searching, for home..."*

I close my eyes, basking in her voice. I wonder if this is love. "Keep singing."

> *"I'm so scared, I'm all alone*
> *All I want is to find my home*
> *But I won't give in*
> *I won't let go*
> *Darling you know*
> *I'll fight when I feel like dying*
> *Just trust in me*

449

I won't let go
Just hold onto me
Hold onto me
And I'll stay..."

My magic is twisting and reaching, stretched thin enough I'm dizzy with its loss, like losing too much blood. It snaps at me to stay conscious, both of us knowing if I pass out it blacks out with me. "I'm holding on. I won't let go, Little Star."

My Dark tastes fresh air, letting out a shrill scream of delight. I drop my face toward her, breathing out slow, commanding my magic to unbury us.

The desire to shift back grips me. I want to hold her, to feel her against me. I push it away. Shifting back would cage my magic, and it's pushed as far as it will go even in my shifted form. It's straining and hissing as it moves the tons of stone. We both die with her if it can't get us out of here.

Natalia's voice wafts in the air. "Cal?"

"Yes."

"Thanks for saving me from Tony."

The maze has screwed her up. I laugh at her. "You're not dying."

"Sure."

I give a shove at my magic, demanding results. It lashes back like a hammer stroke to my temple. "I didn't save you from Tony. I was just an excuse you gave yourself to leave him and the Magia."

"Ha, maybe, but do me a favor? Keep Ness. I know that–I know that was–was to..." She shudders.

I shove up. The weight gives. My magic wails, releasing a blast of power. Getting my wings free, I slide my arm under her and lift. I crouch to cradle her and launch upward.

Tendrils of Dark cleave through rock, breaking it apart and pulling rubble out of the way as I fight my way to the surface. I crawl over boulders and slabs into the clear smooth path of the maze. I kneel, setting her on the ground, and pull my magic in. I need to find a way to get the glass out of her.

Instead of returning to me, my magic snarls at me, slithering to Natalia. The shadows lick over her, searching out the holes and sliding in. She twitches and curses as it digs the glass out. The shards tinkle as they fall to the stone, retracted free of her.

"Heal, Talia," I say as my magic returns to me.

Her face screws up and Light shines out of her in radiating brilliance, then fades as the wounds heal. She blinks open her eyes, staring upward. "Oh, look, we're back in the death trap."

CHAPTER 61
NATALIA

Everything glitters. I sit. The world sways. I fall on my back as clouds spin above me. "Oh, shit, head rush."

Cal leans over me, a massive, glowing, black bone monster with a doglike face. He's some weird blend of canine and human layered with bone, shadows, and fire. "What are you?" I ask.

"I'm a Mandolux. When you heal do you heal blood loss?"

"*Mhm,*" I hum, and rock my head against the cool stone beneath my skull by bobbing my chin.

I open my eyes to stare at the twinkling clouds above us. They filter down into the maze, as a glittering dust. "Pretty."

"Damnit," Cal's snarling voice curses nearby. "Little Star, what are you seeing?"

I flounder and flop to my feet, finding him with my eyes. The flames in his eyes dance and sparks fly out of them. He shifts in-and-out of focus, blurring and doubling. Rubbing my eyes, I blink at him, closing one eye to bring him into focus.

His tail whips back-and-forth behind him. "The glass was made by the maze, part of it. You're dosed again."

I snicker. "Great, this as if this wasn't awful to begin with," I fling my hand toward him. "Seriously? You have a tail? And I can't tell if you're like a skeleton or is that an extroverted skeleton. Is that bone?"

Sighing, he shakes his head. "I'm hard to kill. Turn. Walk. I'll follow and keep you alive."

I do as he says, turning and coming face-to-face with Tony. He crosses his arms and lifts his eyebrows. "I'm curious, Nat. If he's always protecting you and trying to keep you alive, what use are you to him?"

"That is an excellent question. Ask him," I say, batting him away in a puff of smoke.

"You have your uses," Cal chuckles. "Getting dosed with nightmare takes everyone down, even me."

"You've been dosed?"

"Yes, and I'm surprised you're upright."

I stumble up the path to a section with more choices than I can count. Covering my eyes, I take a breath. When I open them, the maze is a normal cross-section. With a groan I take a step to keep going straight.

Plumes of red-tinged purple clouds appear. A black snakehead strikes toward me. I yelp and lift a hand, blasting at it. My Light shines through it and it's gone.

Behind me, Cal lets out a few yelping barks of laughter. "There's nothing there, Little Star."

"Fucking Mother."

He nudges me forward at the sound of hair-raising giggles. "That was real."

We head through the intersection, stone sliding behind us. Mirrors appear, one on each side of the path, evenly spaced as far as I can see. The chattering laughter echoing in the hall, moving toward us.

Red balls bounce from one mirror to the other, each row bouncing in an opposite direction on a loop. The smack of the rubber against stone plays on repetition, intermixing with the horrifying giggles.

From the shadows come miniature clowns in red, yellow, and white uniforms. Their jester hats jingle with little bells, their faces smeared with white paint and bloody, grotesque grins. My mouth goes dry as I watch them scurrying forward, their lower bodies replaced by the body and legs of a spider.

"Uh, babe? You tell me what's real here, m'kay?"

"Mirrors, balls–I'm interested about this ball fear, like all balls?"

"I have no idea, must be subconscious." I eye the skittering clowns leaping and racing toward us. "More importantly, what about the mini spider-clowns?"

"Real. You've got some weird fears." He crouches, one arm bracing him next to me, the other wrapping around me, "Glow."

"Yeah, well, you're scared of lightning." I take a deep breath and close my eyes. "You must love thunderstorms."

"You're afraid of balls."

"Yeah, the thought of getting smacked in the face with your balls is terrifying."

Cal's voice drawls with boredom. "Any time now."

I remember the look in his eyes as he dropped to his knees. It was pure, undiluted desire. He had wanted me. No one has ever wanted *me*.

Behind my eyelids the world turns white.

Cal roars, the Light sliding through me, like strings that yank on my core. Heat erupts around us, blowing past me. It stings my face.

Cal moves. "We must be getting close."

"Why's that?" I open my eyes, woozy with a dull ache in my core. "Um?"

"Real," he says as I focus on the dragon. "They have a nest in the center. Stay here, don't move." He steps past me, and I stare at his back. The spikes curl and move, hissing at me, and striking out like snake heads.

The wall next to me moves, sliding into itself. I take a step away as two black skinned beasts focus on me from the other side. Black horns spiral from their temples, and their fingers end in curved, black talons. My mouth goes dry with fright.

One cocks its head. I lift a hand, ready to blast Light. Its eyes stretch, the second tackling it to the side, snarling. I blast a beam of Light as the two figures dive out of the way, one rolling in closer and lifting its hand. Dark races toward me, but it contacts a shield of black tendrils.

Long, black-bone fingers curl around my wrist, forcing my hand to my side. "Real, very real, and friends."

The one shoved gets up, brushing itself off. The second pops up, leaning toward Cal to raise his voice. "The fuck, Cal? Yesterday and now this?" He points at me. "I told you I was swearing in. Control your fucking Light."

I go limp, smoke forming and twinkling around us. I watch it dance, mesmerized. It closes in around me, engulfing me in the pretty smog, disembodied voices floating through it.

Cal's voice rumbles. "Talia, this is Hiro and Thames. Don't hurt them. She's dosed, the maze probably just dumped you on her to kill you."

"Run into a Nightmare?"

"No, the maze."

"How bad?"

"Like thirty pieces of debris that soaked in her a while."

Barking laughter. "How is she upright?"

Cal chuckles. "She's stubborn. Watch her. I'll deal with the smoragon. Don't let her run off, and be prepared for acrobatic clowns, spiders, or a mixture of them."

I giggle, reaching out, trying to touch the world of purple and blue starry fog baiting me into relaxation.

A hand latches onto my wrist, a deep voice chuckling and saying, "Don't touch the ivy, baby."

The smoke clears and Tony standing in front of me is revealed. "You're not an heiress. You're barely human. A disgusting mess."

As I shrink away, something solid presses against my back. I whip around, staring into the face of my father. He glares with revulsion, and I wince, hanging my head.

Two hands grab me then shake me. Pain splits my skin, and I whimper, trying to rip free of the hands. They grip harder, rattling me enough my teeth clatter.

I blink into a confused face of a blackish-blue beast, eyes full black. It sneers at me then turns its face away. "You okay, Sugar Bear?"

"Fine. She's bleeding like crazy, though. I couldn't snap her out of it."

Cal approaches, his snarl is menacing. "What happened?"

"Weird clowns. Those are a fucking bitch," the beast with its hands on my shoulders says.

The second laughs. "True, and she just stood here."

Cal growls. "She's dosed, probably hallucinating, and fucking high. Talia," his voice calls. I blink, the maze coming into focus. Cal crouches before me, the two smaller winged creatures on either side of him. "Can you hear me? You need to heal."

I nod, my body stinging with pulsing pain. "Yeah."

My father appears before me in the middle of us, fixated on me. I tremble under his scowl, and claws slash through it without effect. My father shakes his head, unaffected. "You're not my daughter. You don't deserve to be an heiress and you don't deserve the marks we gave you."

"It's the maze," Cal says. "It's not quite real, although we're all seeing it. It doesn't matter."

I draw Ki, sending it through me in pulses so the burning race of healing spreads through my limbs and torso. My legs shake and give. I fall, smacking into the stone face down. Sharp points rest against my back. I breathe out, the cold of the stone blissful.

Cal says, "I'll make you a deal. You carry her. I'll get us out."

"Sounds good to me, baby."

The other voice scoffs. "No. She's way more important than a

456

deal like that. It's leverage." There's a pause. "I want a contract for services, jointly, and I want to keep my assets."

"I'm not negotiating a contract in the maze, but I'll say this," Cal answers. "I don't need your estates, and I wouldn't dream of tearing you two apart. Pick her up, keep up, and when I tell you to, give her to me, then shield because I'm letting loose."

There's a whistle. The talons retreat from my back. Thick arms scoop me up. I'm floating through a twinkling haze. "So pretty," I whisper, reaching out toward it.

There's a deep chuckle from above. "Yeah, she's dosed real good."

CHAPTER 62

CALLAHAN

THE MORE PEOPLE TOGETHER IN THE MAZE, THE WORSE THINGS GET. We work through it, nonetheless. Natalia's useless at the moment, which is annoying. We could all use her healing abilities. I stop when we approach the center of the maze. Smoragons are flying overhead, circling, and watching.

I glance back at Thames carrying Natalia. "If it doesn't close us out again, this is it. When we get up closer, get in far enough that the maze can't close you out, give her to me, then find something to hide behind. I'll do the rest."

Hiro inclines his head. "Will do. Anything else you need from us?"

I glance at Natalia, and frown. "Yes. See if you can wake her up. I need her to glow for me."

"Why?" Hiro asks. "Can't you take it without her feeding it to you?"

I turn away, heading up the path. "I can, but it hurts her more."

Taking long strides on all fours, I keep waiting for the maze to shut walls, redirecting us in circles again, keeping us from getting out, for some reason, though, it doesn't. At the precipice of the open circular field, I linger on the edge, holding my hands out for Natalia.

Thames lays her in my grip, "I had her awake for a fraction, but it didn't last."

Natalia stirs a bit, mumbling as she's jostled from him to me.

I cradle her. "Go, shield, and when you get the chance, run for it."

They slip away, sticking to the wall, slinking into the center as I crouch, eyeing the smoragons dropping from the sky. "Little Star." I squeeze and shake her.

"Hm?" She turns half-open eyes on me. She focuses, jerks, then steadies. "Fucking Mother, you're Cal, just shifted, okay." She breathes out hard. "I'm good."

"We're here," I say, glancing at the center behind her as I set her on the ground. "Now's when I use you."

She nods, standing, but swaying. "Right, what do I...?"

"Glow." I hold my hand out. She puts hers in it. I close around it, like a giant holding onto a child.

She closes her eyes, and the glow spreads through her. I narrow my eyes against it. My magic reaches for her, twisting around her, and feeding on her Light. She glows brighter still, while I take what she offers.

My magic shimmers in deep blues, winding around Natalia, then stretches further, slithering across the ground. Some of the smoragons are watching, others landing, sniffing the air. I wait. If the beasts are going to give me time, I'll take it.

Natalia's glow turns bright white, shimming in rays of silver Light penetrating through my Dark. My magic sucks in, drawing on the Light until it's fat and swollen. It purrs at me, and I growl, wrenching away from her before taking it all.

My Dark is salivating, wanting more, but to take all the Light from her, consuming all of her magic, would leave her as an empty husk, destroying her mind.

She stumbles a step away, breaking free of my Dark. A smoragon lurches forward, and I lunge forward to meet it. I shield from its attack, setting my magic on fire.

Half the open courtyard explodes. The smoragons screech, taking flight. Hiro and Thames run for the nest in the middle, and I grab Natalia off the stone, cradling her against me.

A blast of purple fire erupts above me. I tuck and roll, popping up on my feet, and launch into the air. My wings beat twice, then I shy to the left to avoid a diving smoragon to drop through the center of the portal.

I've never had an easier time.

Darkness rushes around me. I beat my wings to slow our progression, landing on the floor with a thump. I kneel, lowering Natalia to the ground as Massimo rushes over. He throws sweats at me and drops to one knee next to Natalia.

He grimaces. "Is she dead?"

"Dosed," I say.

Massimo jerks up. "Telra?"

"Might be dead. My little star got her."

Wagging his head, chuckling, Massimo says, "I was asking if she dosed our Light bug."

"No, that would be the maze trying to kill her."

I step away, retreating a few paces as I roll my shoulders and neck, pulling my wings in. With a sigh of regret, I clench my teeth, reeling in my magic. It lashes out, not wanting to be confined. I clench my fists, demanding its obedience. My bones and sinew begin snapping and shrinking. Shifting is always easier than reverting to human form.

Shuddering, I force my jaw to the side to crack my neck, pushing flesh and muscle into proper place. I drop my hands to brace myself in a low crouch, grimacing at an ache throbbing through me, then walk naked back to Massimo and Natalia.

I snatch the sweatpants from the ground, getting one leg in, then the other. I kick the hoodie up, catching it in the air before working it over my head. I shiver, using a sleeve to wipe at the goo on my face. I need a shower.

"Is she still out?"

Massimo nods. "She's got a ton of blood on her, but I can't find any wounds, so she must be healed." As he starts to get his arms under her, I crouch on the balls of my feet to shove him away.

"I can carry my fucking woman." I get my arms under her, and roll her into me, lifting and standing.

Following me up with a grin, Massimo shakes his head. "You want the bad news, or do you want it to be a surprise?"

"I hate surprises," I say, curling a lip and heading for the door. "I need to get into the hall to check in as a survivor."

Ahead of me, Hiro and Thames have also reverted, limping through the door together. Hiro turns back and inclines his head.

I jerk my chin at him, then glance at Massimo. "What's the surprise?"

"Pierre is back."

I come to a halt, barring my teeth at the door, then continue to walk. "What does he want?"

"Natalia. I tried to argue on your behalf."

I whip around to face him. "If you gave her to him, I'm going to—"

"I didn't," Massimo snaps. "You need to get your head right. The maze has you jacked up, and Pierre is waiting with our King for when you returned."

I growl, hoisting Natalia higher in my arms. She mumbles, snuggling into me as I move through the doorway into the hall.

The glow emitting from Pierre draws my eye and I head for him. "Fuck off, Pierre."

Pierre stands from where he sat next to my King and smiles. "Hello, Callahan. I thought you appeared familiar. You do share quite the similarity to your father."

I narrow my eyes. The quip about my father is an intentional dig. He knows my face. He's seen me. I damn near ripped his head off that day centuries ago. I'm older now, stronger, and more experienced. The next time I have a chance, he won't get to walk away.

"I'll say it again. I suggest you leave before I lose my temper. I have every right by law to protect what is mine, so fuck off."

Reaching into his back pocket, Pierre pulls out parchment. He unfolds it, displaying the gold seal with three crowns and a sword. "I have an ordnance from the Council. You are to release Natalia Swan from her contract. Further, I have been awarded charge of her. She is not yours, therefore, you have no legal recourse against me for taking her."

I scoff. "The Council doesn't have that kind of power or right."

He shrugs, twisting to toss the paperwork to the table before my King. "You are summoned to the Council here and now to report for your crimes, and you are going to release Natalia from your service. These are not suggestions."

I sneer in conjunction with my Dark as we both constrict around our star. "Fuck off. Or does piss off get through to you? I know the law, and I didn't break any rule. She's Magia. Even if she wasn't, there's nothing against Light being contracted to Dark."

"For Dark to coerce Light into servitude breeches the accorded agreements between Light and Dark."

"She wasn't coerced."

"I believe the incident involved a smoragon," Pierre says, eyebrows lifting. "Nasty things."

"I didn't summon that thing."

"You took advantage of the situation."

"Natalia accepted my contract—"

"Under pain of death from a smoragon. Yes, I'm aware of what happened."

I snarl. "Natalia took a direct hit from the smoragon prior to accepting, and if you knew anything about her, you'd know she doesn't need me to deal with one. She also has already informed you that her contract was voluntary."

"That is not the story provided from witnesses."

The only ones present are either my fellow contenders, who wouldn't ever betray the Dark, Massimo, and a Magia. I grin. "Tony? Another Magia who has already attempted to interfere with the contract. Hardly a reliable source."

"You are welcome to argue your case before the Council. Until then, I will be taking Natalia. Release her from the contract."

She shifts and stirs. "Cal?"

I drop my mouth to the top of her head, pressing my lips against her hair. "You're all right."

"Put me down."

As I set her on her feet, I never break eye contract with Pierre. "My answer remains no."

Pierre has a vein throbbing in his forehead. He clenches his fists, turning to my King. "Basileus."

My King pauses on the way to a drink and looks over. "Yes?"

Gesturing at me, Pierre says, "Would you care to enforce the rules of the Council as your station mandates?"

The Dark King lifts his goblet at me. "Callahan, are these allegations true?"

I help steady Natalia in front of me as she yawns and sways. "Natalia's contract is legal."

My King shrugs. "Then report to the Council at the appointed time and argue before them, not me." His focus shifts back to Pierre. "And you piss off."

Natalia leans her back into my chest, and I wrap an arm around her shoulders. "Talia," I say low, my mouth close to her ear. "If you need me..."

She shrugs me off. "I keep hearing my name. Why do I keep hearing my name?"

I incline my head to my King. "I will report to the Council to argue my case." I smile at Pierre. "Until they rule against me, which I doubt they will, I'll be keeping Natalia with me, under contract."

Pierre takes a step forward. "The Council has given me free rein to use whatever force necessary to ensure your compliance. Release her from the contract."

The air charges, and I grit my teeth. "I will speak with the Council at the appointed time to discuss the charges."

"Release her!" Pierre's roar thunders around the room, electricity zapping. Little pulses of Light zap and flicker in the charged air as Pierre's power builds for a smite.

I brace, calling on my Dark. "No."

The crack comes first, followed by the streak of brilliance. Natalia twists, shoving me aside.

"Talia," I scream, shielding my eyes, watching the bolt of light cut through her.

Pierre yells her name, his hand lifting, but it's too late for him to recall the smite. "No!" He takes a step forward.

I lunge, reaching for her as she falls to her knees, my Dark forcing Pierre away. I grab her, pulling her into my lap, "Talia," I say, as I shake her.

She curses. The word drags from deep in her chest, drug out on a breath. "Fuck." She lifts her chin, opening her eyes to me. White glimmering Light fills them, her irises gone, and the lace over her skin is dazzlingly bright. She lifts her hands, giggling. "Damn that felt good."

I gape. "Good? A fucking smite felt good?" My type is crazy, and Natalia's worse than Telra. No wonder I prefer her.

"Yeah," she laughs. "A lot better than taking in Dark."

I stand, pulling her up with me. "Stubborn, crazy woman," I mutter. A large, pale hand lands on her shoulder. My magic reacts, pushing back Pierre.

"Callahan, let go of her. I am taking her. I have every right to her. You breached the accords of the Council. You have coerced her and hurt her enough."

"Natalia belongs to me. There's no way I'm releasing her from my contract," I laugh.

"You will–"

"Enough," Natalia snaps. She shoves me back and rounds on Pierre. "I don't know who the fuck you are, and I don't fucking care."

Pierre smooths a hand down his front. "My name is Pierre Bordeaux and I am–"

"Did I," she cuts him off, tilting her head at him, "or did I not, just say I don't care?"

Pierre frowns. "Natalia, please listen."

"No, no I'm done listening," she says.

Pierre indicates the contract. "You were illegally forced into servitude."

I step next to her and lift an eyebrow. "Allegedly."

He shakes his head, sliding his hands in his front pockets. "The Council has awarded me charge of her. Natalia is coming with me to Izul."

She tips her head back and laughs. "No, I'm not. I'm not going anywhere with you. I'm fine right where I'm at."

Pierre ignores her, speaking to me. "Release her from the contract, Callahan. Face the Council. Perhaps they may change their mind, although I suspect not. They allowed you leniency once recently, I doubt they will do so again," Pierre says with a smile.

"You must not be hearing me," Natalia says. "I'm not going to anywhere with you. I don't care where or who you are or who says what."

"You are," Pierre snaps. "You will understand soon enough, but for now you are coming with me. Callahan."

"Yes?" I play stupid.

"Release the contract."

"No. Natalia, go sit down."

Natalia takes a step away from both of us.

Pierre grabs her by the upper arm. "You are coming with me."

She rips free. "I'm not going anywhere I don't want to, or

465

doing anything I don't want to. I signed this contract because I wanted to, but you know what fucker? If you think it's illegal, then fine."

She shines, and all that Light she received from the smite races along her skin to my contract. My eyes widen, "Talia, no!"

My Dark screams, pain lancing through my temple. Our arms glow bright before my magic can retaliate. The shrill squeal as it is burned out rips through my head.

I twist sideways like a hammer bashed into the side of my head. The world goes out of focus, agony tearing through my skull, like it's splintering into shards as a piece of my magic dies. The Light shining through the sleeve of my hooded sweatshirt accompanies the searing pain as Natalia's magic burns out the contract, and I hit the ground.

CHAPTER 63

NATALIA

Panting, I lift my forearm, Cal's contract gone. "Problem solved."

The cup falls from the Dark King's grip, clanging in the still and silence. I glance around at Massimo's dropped jaw, then back at Cal. Except Cal is collapsed in a heap on the floor.

I turn to him as my heart takes off in a gallop. "Cal?"

A hand wraps around my wrist, Pierre saying, "We're leaving now."

I throw my weight back around, swinging into a hook to clock him in the face. He recoils but doesn't let go. He makes a grab for my other arm, so I pull away, twisting and kicking him in the face. This time the combination of my weight change accompanying the strike breaks his grip.

"For the last time, I'm not going anywhere. I fixed your stupid problem, so leave." I step to Cal as he is shoving up. "Cal?"

He glares at me, slapping away my hand. "You stupid, fucking stubborn woman." He twists off the ground, putting a hand to his head, leaning to the right.

Pierre steps next to me. "If you only knew how special what

you did was." He chuckles. "I can explain it. Come with me to Izul and I'll teach you how to use the Light."

I flip him off. "You're not listening, kind of like a limp dick with too much whiskey in it."

He lifts his eyebrows. "You destroyed your contract."

Crossing my arms, I jut my hip, oozing attitude, as I watch Massimo steady Cal. "Sure, because you said something stupid about it being illegal. Coerced servitude, right? Well, now it's gone, so there's nothing illegal or forced and I'm still telling you I'm not going." I try for my sweetest smile, fluttering my eyelashes at him. "Of my own free will, I'd like to say, go fuck yourself dickwad."

Pierre steps between Cal and me, cutting off my line of sight from Cal. Pierre frowns, staring down his nose at me. "What you did should have been impossible for you."

I scoff. "You gave me a supercharge."

"You have no idea how special you are."

"You can leave now."

"Natalia, come with me, please. Give me an opportunity to explain."

I lift an eyebrow, rocking back on my heels. "Why would I do that?"

He smiles with closed lips, like trying to explain fire is hot to a child. "You burned out your contract. You are free to do anything. He's Dark. It suffocates the Light, extinguishes it until there is none. He would have used you until there was nothing left of you. Now, he can no longer use you."

I laugh, borderline hysterical. "Who the fuck cares? I'm not the Light," I lean into the scream, the words bellowing from the bottom of my lungs. Upright, I take a deep breath, "Fuck off already, Mother."

Pierre frowns, leaning back on his heels. "Natalia, I am—"

"Yeah, I still don't care."

"I am—"

"Why haven't you left yet?"

He presses his hands together, studying me. With a sigh he drops them, "When you are ready–and mark my words child, you will be soon–you have an open invitation to Izul."

"Just leave."

"When you arrive, give them my name at the gate. You have a home there as is your birthright as the Light. I will teach you everything you need to know." He bows to me and turns, walking away.

I flip off his back, and face Cal. He curls his lip at me as he steps to me. I sag on myself a bit, ready to hold his hand or get picked up. This whole day has been exhausting, and I want my Darkling to wrap me in his Dark and hold tight.

Screw independence. I'm a delicate, wilting flower that wants her man.

Cal gets in close, grabbing me by the throat. My eyes open wider as he takes me down, slamming me into the stone floor. Bones crack and snap, pain radiating through me. I cough, blood flooding my lungs and throat, lingering on my tongue as I gasp for air.

His hand grips tighter, and his knee presses into my sternum, pressing into me with his full weight until my chest cracks and splinters. A whimper works its way out of me as I spit up blood.

Cal's eyes narrow, his face closer, his words low and fast. "Don't, don't fight, don't make me hurt you." He pulls back, lifting his knee and standing. "Unless you're challenging me, stay down."

I manage to center, sending Ki through my broken body. Bones mend, tissue knits, and I breathe easier, rolling to flop onto my front and shove to my feet. "Fucking asshole."

He grabs my wrist and wrenches it to the side, yanking me in closer, his hand around my throat again. "I told you to stay down."

I grit my teeth, glaring at him. "I'm not a fast learner."

The Dark King's voice rings out, "Enough."

Cal sneers before shoving me away. He buries his fists into the front pocket of his hoodie, facing the King. I roll my eyes. Massimo shakes his head at me, grimacing.

The King calls my name. "Natalia Swan." I turn, staring at the Dark King. He stares back at me with mock delight. "You are a foolish child."

"I'm pretty good at that, but why's it this time?"

"You would dare to challenge Callahan."

I scoff, rubbing my throat. "I'm not challenging him."

"You burned out your contract."

"That Light fuck thought it was illegal, so I got rid of it."

He crooks a finger at me. "Come here."

I bat my lashes. "I not one of your Darklings, so I don't answer to you."

"He's not strong enough to claim you."

Pealing into laughter, I crack up. "You're joking." I point at Cal. "He's fucking terrifying."

"You destroyed your contract, thereby refuting service."

I narrow my eyes, determination straightening my backbone. The pulse of Light within me is building, and I begin to funnel it through my fury, the air charging with a low hum. "I serve Cal."

The King scowls. "He cannot handle you."

"No one can," I say. "It's kind of a problem in my life, but try to take me away from him, and I'll smite your ass." I force the Light to bend obey, electricity zapping in the air. It thrums in my chest, a pressurized build-up.

"Careful, Lightning Bug, you've broken your contract. You're all alone, without friends."

"Pretty typical, but I make my own choices. I'm not challenging him. I'm not refuting service. In fact, I'm choosing Cal–to be contracted to him. The only reason I did anything was to get the Light fuck to go away, so back off." I lift my hand, the Light wrapping its angry electricity around it.

Dropping his hands in his lap and leaning back in his chair, the Dark King studies me. His frown deepens, turning to a scowl. The only sound in the room is the periodic *zzts* of electricity from the Light spilling out of me, throwing a tantrum at the very idea of being taken from Cal.

Frown turning to a smile, the King's eyes flicker away from me. "Callahan."

"Yes, sir?"

The Dark King inclines his head. "Get control of your lightning bug before it kills you. I will grant you leniency, for now, but if you slip again, you will be held in disgrace."

"Yes, sir." A hand runs up the back of my neck, fingers wrapping around the side. Cal's mouth whispers in my ear. "Room. Now."

We walk out of the room, with little zaps like static electricity in the air follow me. Cal follows, hand on my neck, vibrating the whole way. The Light backs down, ebbing like a withdrawing tide, a calm settling in my core.

He opens the door to our suite, directing me inside before he slams the door. His hand retracts, and I turn as he leans forward and roars at me, his features twisted with rage. "Do you have any idea what you just did?"

I cross my arms, lifting my eyebrows. "Got rid of Pierre?"

He turns his face up and away, but I catch sight of the flicker of malice in his face. "You made me look weak. You *actually* made me weaker. You killed part of my magic when you burned out that contract. Do you have any idea how badly that hurt?"

"I hope it hurt as bad as what that contract did to me last night." I throw my hands up. "I was trying to help. I didn't know it was going to hurt you."

"There's a lot you don't know. For instance, if I can't control mine, I lose everything. You could have disgraced me."

"I'm not Dark. I don't answer to your rules, which, by the way, you never tell me those rules, then get mad because I don't know what they are and break them."

His lips twist. "If you would do as you're supposed to, that wouldn't be an issue."

"I was trying to help. I was just making a point that I'm not forced into this," I look upward and mutter, "Mostly."

"You're here to make things easier for me, not harder and you made this a lot more difficult than it needed to be, so next time, don't. I don't need your help. I don't need you."

I inhale. I knew that, but it's still like getting kicked in the chest. "No, just my Light." I try not to flinch. "My mistake."

He takes a step toward me, murder glittering in his black eyes. Dark tendrils are lashing around him, twisting in thick, opaque black tendrils. "I should throw you to the wolves and let them tear you apart. You're not useful to me when you fight me, which you do, *constantly.*"

There's a crack in my chest that widens at his words, an earthquake breaking my ribs apart. "Go ahead. Throw me out. I don't need you either. I'll take Ness and go."

"Fuck, you're stubborn," he says in a snarl. "You're too stubborn for your own damn good."

"Yeah, haven't heard that one before," I manage, my eyes stinging. I head for the door to leave.

Cal grabs me by the arm. "Where are you going?"

"To find a wolf," I say. "See if it's hungry."

"Damnit, Talia. Stop. Stop fighting for once in your life." His hand tightens as he pulls me in front of him. "Just stop."

"That's not how I work." I stare at the floor, shuffling my feet. "I don't know how."

His magic leaks from his hand, snaking over my arm as Dark streaks from his chest, latching onto my torso to yank me against him. "Figure it out, Little Star," he says, voice softer. "Or we're going to kill each other."

I frown, putting a hand on his chest. "I thought you were throwing me out."

He smirks. "I really should. I can't control you. That's dangerous to me."

"If I was supposed to be controlled, I would have come with a remote."

Cupping my jaw, he stares down at me, his face softens. "Stop fighting me."

"Stop trying to control me."

He sighs, dropping his head and closing his eyes. "No." After a moment, he shakes his head, stepping to the couch and dragging me with him "Sit." He gives me a gentle shove on the shoulder to force me down onto the cushion.

He disappears into Massimo's room, returning with a piece of paper. I throw my hands in the air, "You have to be joking!"

Cal chuckles, sitting next to me. He sets the parchment on the desk, a hand flat against it to let his magic scrawl over it. He turns to me. "Sign it."

My shoulders slump. "Seriously? This again?" I shake my head. "No. I'm not–"

"Sign it, Talia," he says, as he picks up my hand to press it on the contract.

Turning to the page, I scowl at it.

He leans in closer. "You claimed you're choosing me. You said you're deciding to let me use you, so prove it. If you're staying, you need a contract. That's how it works. No contract, no claim, which makes you fair game or worse."

"Fine," I say, "but I want—"

He emits a low, wicked growl from the back of his throat. "Sign the fucking contract."

"I don't even get to negotiate?"

"No," he laughs with a hollow ring. "Fuck no. You killed part of my magic. You don't have rights to negotiate with me. Consider us even. You saved my life, now I'm letting you keep yours."

"It'll grow back."

"Sign. The. Fucking. Contract." He glares, muscles straining like taut ropes from his neck.

I sign my name, a tendril of Light scrawling out across the page at my command before pulling it back into me. It's more elegant than my previous attempt.

Cal wipes the page, the magic collecting on his hand. "Ever do this to me again, I'll have Massimo kill you." He smears it over his forearm.

I watch it bleed in under my skin, the contract twisting to life. "Have Massimo kill me?"

'Stand at my side. Watch my back and protect my blindspot. Take my hand when it is offered. Be the star that guides me. Callahan Matteo Barraco.'

I read it, surprised that it's legible as the first never was, then lift my eyes to him, frowning. "No more answering?"

He gives me a weak smile. "Don't tempt me."

My gaze drops to his arm, which he lifts for me to read. 'Stand at my side. Watch my back. Protect me always and keep me safe. Be my home. Natalia Serena Swan.'

My heart skips and my eyes burn. Be my home. He is my home.

He takes my face in his hands. "Little Star," he drops his forehead to mine. "Stop fighting. You don't have to fight anymore. You're safe."

"Pretty sure you broke me ten fractions ago."

He bares his teeth. "I told you to behave. I told you I'd have to do something I didn't want to if you didn't." He sighs, pulling me into his lap. "I figured it was enough of a display for my kind, but with how you heal, it'd be like I gave you a paper cut."

"Yeah, sure, I can heal. That makes it okay? It still fucking hurts, asshole."

"You challenged Pierre, challenged me, burned out my contract, and destroyed a piece of my magic. I can't heal that, not even you can heal it for me. It's going to take a season to regrow that piece. You broke the contract on so many levels I can't count them all. I had to do something. If I didn't–if I can't control mine, it comes back on me." His hands slide up my thighs to wrap around my hips. "Mine get taken from me. Every written contract I have will be destroyed. It'll ruin me, and I'd be without King or Council protections."

I chew on my lip. "See, things I don't know. If you tell me these things, then I'd know better."

His shoulders drop and he rests back. "If you just behave—"

"Cal," I yell. "I don't work that way."

He rubs his mouth, sighing. "You're going to be the death of me."

"Then throw me out, I'll manage. We both know I'm not useful like you'd hoped. You don't have to deal with me. I can figure it out on my own." I lift my forearm. "Take it back, I'll go."

"No."

I shift, straddling his hips and sitting back on his legs, hugging myself. "I really can take care of myself, and it'll be less of a headache for everyone, so…" I extend my arm.

"No." He wraps his hand around my arm and the contract, pulling me against him. "You're mine, whether you decide to behave or not. All it means is when you step out of line, it's more work for me."

I lift my eyebrows. "I don't need you to take care of me."

He smiles, slow and lazy. "You're really struggling with this one. Usually, you're quicker to catch on. It's almost cute, but it's getting annoying, and I'm done waiting for you to figure this out." He sits up, sliding his hands over my hips, then behind to squeeze my butt. "So, I'm going to say this one more time, Little Star. I get all of you. Not part of you, or some of you, not pieces. All. Your secrets, your Light, your body, mind, heart, everything that is you and yours, is mine. Everything you have to offer," he says, an eyebrow lifting. "And I'll push you beyond your limits to take more than what you think you offer."

I wince.

He chuckles. "I claim you and use you, which means I take care of you and protect you. In return you answer to me, obey me, and it would be fucking nice if you stop fighting me all the damn time."

I smile, pushing away. "You're usually faster to pick up things, so, one last time, I can take care of myself. I'll figure it out. I'll be okay."

He grips my waist and jerks me forward. I catch myself with hands against his chest. He knocks his nose against mine, his voice a low silky whisper. "You can, but you don't have to, anymore. I take care of you. I figure it out. I," he holds my gaze, "am your alpha. I want you to accept it."

I stare back with a steady gaze, even though my core is shaking.

He lifts an eyebrow. "Do you even understand what an 'alpha' is?"

"A dominating asshole?"

His lips twist like he's smiling while trying not to. "I need you to be honest. Leave the jokes for a fraction of a rune. Do you know what an 'alpha' is?"

Rolling my eyes for his benefit, I say, "Yes. Dominant, aggressive, keeps the pack in line, and fights for rights to be on top." His eyebrows lift as he sucks his lips between his teeth, waiting. "It's the whole, be on top, in control, fuck shit up, as well as anyone who stands in your way, taking what you want without having to apologize for it."

"Your kind tend to be rather stupid like that."

My eyes stretch wide. "Excuse me?"

Cal cups the side of my face, his thumb brushing over my cheek as he gives me a closed lip smile. "No, Little Star, that's..." He sighs, shaking his head with his eyes closed. He rumbles with a chuckle. "The Dark was created by Mallafic. Mallafic is...evil, for the simplest word, and one the Light uses, but I'll leave that lesson for another time. Mallafic fashioned us after the beasts that lived in the shadows, so we follow those rules."

"Uh...? You're not going to like, pee on me to claim me, or something else weird, right?"

He takes a deep breath, his face bulging like he's about to explode with ire. "An alpha," he says in a strained voice with the hint of humor, "can fuck shit up and won't backdown, and yes, we can be violent or assertive, but those traits come out *only if* it's necessary. Your kind tend to mistake that." He bops my nose. "We alphas have a pack, and those in the pack answer to us. In return, it's the alpha's job to protect, nourish, and provide for the pack. I lead. I decide. I do it with the best interest of all, not just one." He gives me a dirty look, "When it goes right, it's a comforting role, not a dominating asshole."

"I can—"

"I have two-hundred-and-ninety contracts. That means I own two-hundred-and-ninety souls. That's how it works. They willingly submit to me, give me their life, and their uses, but it's an exchange."

"I'm not—"

"I have high-born contracts who are not forced by law to sign contracts. They had a choice, like you, and, like you, there are consequences for them, a price to pay. They could gamble with their if they chose not to hold a contract like I do every year. They picked me to be their alpha, which makes them my responsibility, so I tend to them."

"I—"

"Although the others have done a much better job at falling in line."

Sighing, I hang my head. "I can't."

"You can. You're just fighting it." His hand grabs the back of my neck. "You're scared you're worthless, but I think you're scared worse that you're not, that you're more than you know. More than anyone has ever told you, ever let you believe. You've fought so hard, tried and failed, and gotten back up so many times, and that means something. You're scared of your Light, your power because you're terrified not being worthless would take away everything you think you are. It won't."

I wince.

"Letting me take care of you isn't going to degrade you. It isn't about you being weak, or even about submission. It's accepting me. All you have to do is take my hand when it's offered, trust me to look after you, and stand at my side."

I hold his gaze, wobbling on an edge. My fingers are clinging for purchase while he tries to drag me from behind the walls I've built. The whole weight of my life bears over me. Temptation weakens the strength of my grip, and for the briefest of fractions, I almost let go.

I've never had anyone like Cal before. I learned the hard way, the only one I can rely on is me, but now he wants me to trust he's going to be there. It would be nice to let go, to stop fighting, to be taken care of, to trust, that when I fall, he will catch me.

The door opens and the spell breaks. I clear my throat, sitting up.

Without looking away, Cal snaps and points at the door. "Out."

Massimo freezes in the doorway. I get up, my grip on sanity doubling. Repeating the same thing over and over, expecting different results, isn't just the definition of insanity, it's stupidity at its finest.

"It's fine. I'm going to go wash all the blood off me now."

Massimo steps out and closes the door, not paying me heed. Cal turns his gaze back to me, something between fury and consideration. "You were about to say something."

"Was I?" I tilt my head and lie to him and myself. "I don't think I was."

His eyes narrow, his jaw setting. I grin wide and bat my eyelashes at him before turning and slipping into our shared room.

I lean against the closed door and tip my head back, letting out a trickle of air from my lungs. Tomorrow, we go home. I can't wait to get away from him. He is dangerous, dangling forbidden fruit that looks delicious but might be poison.

'What if I trust him and he fails?'

'What if we trust and we fly?'

I'd never been so tempted to fall as I had been in his lap. His words had struck against the walls I'd built, blazing statues painted in messy words that remind me I'm the only person in this world that I could ever count on.

On the other hand, wouldn't it be a relief if I weren't the only person I relied on. It would be a comfort to know someone else was truly looking out for me.

My eyes close against tears of exhaustion and overwhelming emotions rampaging through me. It's terrifying, but I trust him. To my core, I believe Cal can handle anything I can't. That scares me.

CHAPTER 64
CALLAHAN

Natalia had been so close to giving in when Massimo opened the door. I know it. I could feel it. She would have taken that first step. With the turn of a doorknob, it went up in smoke, gone in a blink of an eye.

She steps into our room and closes the door. Silence envelopes me, and I ram my hands into the front pouch of the hoodie before I stand up. Tomorrow, we go home. I'll lose my little star. She's going to have room to run and run she will. Trust isn't her strong suit.

I've grown accustomed to her Light shining through my eyelids as I sleep. It's going to be hard to let her go. Not that I'll let her go far, or willingly. I'll fight and claw to keep her where I want her.

I step to the front door and wrench it open, shoving my hand back in the hooded sweatshirt.

Massimo is leaning against the wall, arms crossed, one leg bent up. He lifts his face from the floor, meeting my eyes. "Is she back under contract?"

"She's under contract. She's still going to fight it, but she can at least read it now so she's not fighting the contract anymore. Thanks for the heads up."

Massimo grins. "It's my job." He stretches his shoulders. "They're all going to be coming for you."

"Let them." I jerk my head back into the room, stepping aside for Massimo to move inside. I close the door behind him. "Let them think I'm weak, that she's strong, let them underestimate me and come for her. It'll be fun."

"Pierre walked away without a fight and offered her an open invitation to Izul. That's interesting."

"He's an idiot and a bastard, but there's something else there." I rub my jaw. "See if you can reach the Magia. I think it's time I had a chat with them."

"What are you thinking?"

I drop to the couch, putting a foot on the edge of the table. "It's a hunch, maybe nothing. Something the maze said."

Dropping opposite me, Massimo gives me a skeptical grin. "It spoke?"

"A lot. It has to do with Talia's fear." I turn my head toward our closed bedroom door. "Figure out who Zander is. He's a Light Seraphinus."

"Why?"

"She fucked him."

Massimo lifts his eyebrows. "Our girl keeps getting more and more interesting."

"Mine," I correct him, rubbing the side of my neck. "That's not as interesting as how the maze reacted to her. It went after her with a vengeance."

Shrugging, Massimo kicks both legs up on the table. "Not surprising. You're possessive and protective, desperate to keep her. It would know, would hit you with hurting her."

"Maybe, but it could be my hunch."

"What's she afraid of? Worse than mine?"

I smile. "Everything is worse than yours. Who's afraid of rabbits and coconuts? Mattingly wanted to know how I get through the maze so fast. I didn't have it in me to explain my previous partner's fears are ridiculous."

He chuckles, cracking his neck. "Yes, well, you're afraid of cats, not much better."

I shudder. "Don't like cats."

Massimo smirks. "Yet you dated a Venominx."

I curl my lip, ignoring the quip. "We got buried alive. I'm not sure if that was about me or her."

"You got buried?"

"And we found water too. She's afraid of drowning, or at least not great with the idea. It dug out a memory of a time she almost drowned. That Light fuck, Zander, saved her. She has a freaky clown fear, too. They're like burning afters minions–children dressed up as clowns from a horror movie. Hard as fuck to kill."

Massimo chuckles as he shakes his head.

"They showed up with red bouncy balls. I'm not sure about that one. Mirrors and spiders were frequent. The biggest one was the maze kept spitting out ghosts of Tony, her sister, and her father. They had some things to say." I shift to slump lower, frowning.

"Is this where your hunch is coming from?"

"It's helping."

"Are you going to let me in on this hunch?"

"Natalia is not Magia."

"No?" Massimo gives intrigue. "Then…" His intrigue turns to alarm, his jaw dropping open.

I snicker. "My best guess? My little star is Seraphim *and* Magia. I can't deny she has skills Seraphim don't."

"How much should we tell her?"

I glare. "Did you get too close to the maze where a stray coconut clocked you in the head this morning? Nothing. I can barely get her to obey me as is. You want me to tell her she's more powerful than me? Maybe as powerful as an Ancient?"

"If she's Seraphim, she has the Light."

"We already knew she has the Light, but she might be both, like the Ancients were–are. Ones up and walking around, gods only know why. I can't shake this feeling it's coming for blood."

Massimo nods slowly, over-and-over, eyes unfocused and upturned. "Well, given what the Seraphinus did to them..." He rubs a hand over his mouth. "Fuck." He lets out a bark of laughter without a sign of humor. "Anything else?"

"No."

"You took a lot longer this year. Dinner's in two runes."

I curl my lip. "It was harder this year, plus when we got closer to the end, we had Hiro and Thames with us."

"Too many together," Massimo says with a grimace. "Sterling made it back before you, but Chlem and Telra haven't come back."

"Talia took down Tel and I left Yas in pieces, so I don't expect them back."

"Wicked cold of you considering you used to screw both of them."

I'm tempted to roll my eyes like Natalia. My relationship with Telra frequently included Yasmin, however, I never cared for her beyond chasing pleasure in the bedroom. "Yas was always a bitch. I left Tel to Talia. I had made my choice. She knew it."

"You sure about that, *baby*?"

"Yes." Relaxing, I shrug. "Chlem will be back. He always takes forever. Poor bastard is afraid of everything."

"Including rats."

"Everything and rats. Those things can be nasty to deal with," I snicker.

"Worse or better than the clowns?"

I groan. "Better. Those freaky little things are awful."

"I expected you back sooner, almost started to think you were dead."

"It was odd. The maze fixated on her. Usually it loves me."

Massimo laughs. "Or maybe my fears are too ridiculous for it to even try to make them deadly."

"The coconuts can be a bitch to deal with." I smile, hunkering down and tipping my head back to close my eyes. "Talia got a good laugh at my fear of lightning."

"The maze hits all of us with that. It's too easy, too much like a smite, feels like it in the maze too."

"No, it doesn't. It stings, but it's not like smiting."

Massimo stands. "I'm going to go do my job. I'll make a few calls, find a contact in the Magia."

I lift my chin, but don't answer.

"How sure are you? I mean, are we really thinking she's…?"

Lifting my eyebrow, I stare down my friend. "She fucking smites, calls firelight, and she's thirty. She's stronger than I ever was in my first century. The maze said it knows her secret, made sure to terrorize her. It wanted her alone, kept trying to separate us. I know what she is. All I need is confirmation. So, go do your job, and get me confirmation, then I'll know I bit off more than I can chew."

"We already knew that. Damn lucky our King was in a good mood."

My face twitches with disgust. "She's going to cause my demise."

"I'd prefer she didn't." Massimo grins, showing me his contract. "I have a pretty sweet deal where I do what the fuck I want. It would take me centuries to get one like this from someone else, maybe more than I have left to live."

Glaring, I say, "Love you too, *baby*."

Laughing, Massimo leaves to go be useful. Staying swaddled in sweats sounds delightful, hunkered in to shut down and recoup. I don't have that luxury, though. There is one more dinner to attend.

I DOZE OFF ON THE COUCH FOR A FEW FRACTIONS IN A SEMI-LUCID state, before unfurling. Spreading my limbs, I bend and stretch. No matter how long I maintain this form, it's always stiff and weird after shedding it for any amount of time. It's more conducive for the finer things in life, like fucking, but I'm more comfortable shifted.

Checking my watch, I realize I dozed for about a rune. There's still one rune remaining until I must report for dinner.

I head into my room in search of my little star. She is flopped on the bed like she sat on the edge and fell over in exhaustion. I stare down at her, mesmerized by the Light lacing over her skin in beautiful decoration. Several tendrils of silver vines twist free of her, waving in the air toward me.

That's new and terrifying. At first, I thought her Light was barely manifesting, then I thought it was fully matured. It turns out I was wrong both times. Her Light is still growing and learning, and she's already more powerful than I ever expected.

I'm so fucked.

Dark tendrils unravel from me, reaching out to meet her Light. The Light and Dark entwine, twisting around each other.

I remind my magic that same Light killed part of it less than a rune ago. It hisses, not caring. It wants her magic, yet it's not feeding. It's embracing the Light, desiring contact in a sick fetish.

It feels the way love is described in pretty poetry.

My father had told me if I wanted a mate to wish upon the stars, of the pieces of Adontis herself, woven into her lover, Nehil, and ask for a love mirroring her own. I had wished with every tendril of my Dark crossed in hope for a perfect mate. Maybe I wished a little too hard.

"Fuck." Rubbing a hand over my mouth, I sigh as I lean over

Natalia. Her magic winds in thin threads of itself around me, pulling me in tight, so I brace my hands on either side of her head to bear some of my weight. "Little Star," I whisper.

She groans and I cover her mouth with mine. I flick my tongue against her soft lips. They part, letting me enter to taste her. Her hands slip around my neck, yanking on me.

Her Light wraps around me, searing ropes of silver slithering beneath my shirt and across my skin.

I chuckle into her mouth before pulling back. "Dinner is in a rune."

This time her groan is louder.

Sliding my hands down her sides, I stand and offer my hand. Her eyes are closed, our magic tangling together. I wiggle my fingers, and she intakes sharply, eyes popping open to glare at me.

"Really? It's been five fractions, and this stupid thing is already annoying."

"That thing is my magic and your contract, and if you ever burn it out of you again, I'll have Massimo break your neck, and we'll see if you can heal that."

Her hand slaps into mine. "Oh, we've elevated to death threats? Lovely."

I haul her to her feet, pressing her against me to tuck her head into the dip where my chest and shoulder meet. "So that's no? You can't heal that?"

"I'm not answering that just because I can."

Grinning wide, I scoop my little star into my arms.

She squeaks, clinging to my neck. Her face goes lax, her eyes wide. "All right! No, I can't heal instant death, like if I'm decapitated, or I lose consciousness, or when there's something stuck in me, like the glass, or if I'm out of Ki."

"Good to know on all counts." I knock my nose against hers with a smile. "One more dinner. No more games."

"Fine."

I carry her into the bathroom, and together we get clean.

Leaving her to finish whatever women do, I start to get dressed, pulling clothes from hangers. I scan the dresses she has, one in particular catching my eye.

It's sheer black. I've had fantasies of what it would look like, but she hasn't worn it yet. I grab the hanger and toss it onto the bed. She's going to wear it for me tonight.

As I'm buttoning my shirt, she exits the bathroom wrapped in a towel with her hair pinned up, offset at the base of her neck. I finish with the buttons, point to the dress on the bed, and then shrug into a jacket.

Her lips press, her nose wrinkling with distaste. I kiss her temple on the way out of the room, and then pour myself a drink to wait.

Sipping my drink, I check my watch, then glance at the door. "Talia."

There's no answer. I'm playing with firelight with this new contract. It was an impromptu concept. I thought she'd cooperate better, but I'd given her too much freedom. She has free rein without my explicit permission.

Rubbing a hand down my face, I dump my drink into my mouth, swallowing three fingers of bourbon in a single gulp. "Fuck," I whisper to my Dark. "I could barely control her before. What the fuck were we thinking?"

"*You*," it laughs at me. It's unbothered, satisfied with the strength and independence of her Light.

The door opens, Natalia's Light filling the room. The gown is cut low, hugging her torso and hips while opening wider around the knees. She glitters, like a thousand stars are sparkling beneath the sheer black mesh, voiding the fabric's ability to hide any of her. Every scrap of skin, every detail of her body, is on display through thin gauze.

Great. Just what my cock wants. I'm not going to be able to stop fantasizing, and I get to sit through a five-course meal while keeping my hands and magic to myself. It's going to be at least a rune. I've orchestrated to torture myself.

I hold my hand out, and she steps forward to take it. "Happy, Master-Owner-Boss?"

"Yes." I twist my fingers in hers, my magic and hers binding us together. "Ready?"

"Hold on." She pours herself a drink, filling the glass, and then pouring it down her throat. "Gross, but all right. Let's get this shit show over with."

I turn her face to mine, cupping her jaw and running my thumb under her bright red painted lower lip. "Behave. I mean it. Not one word or eye roll, and don't you dare sass me. I need you perfect after the game you played earlier."

She pinches her thumb and pointer together before drawing them over her lips and batting her eye lashes.

"I mean it, Little Star. My King was kind, but you damn near disgraced me."

Inhaling, her eyes drop. "Explain it to me."

Glancing at my watch, I decide there's a few fractions of a rune to spare. "Dark Law states only the strongest can be contractors. Dark Law allows a contracted to challenge their contractor if they feel they are stronger."

She bobs her head, her teeth sinking into her lower lip. "Merito-cratic," she sighs. "That's what you meant about me challenging you."

"Yes. If a contracted challenges their contractor, there are two outcomes legally. The challenger wins, the contractor dying in the fight, and the challenger takes everything from the contractor. Or the contractor kills their challenging contracted."

"Legally?"

I shrug. "What happens away from the Dark Court isn't the King's business, so the discretion of the contractor is at play. It's only breaking the law if someone knows it was broken."

She smirks, "Like Mass trying to rip out your contract?"

I cock my jaw, narrowing my eyes. "He told you about that?"

"Yes, while trying to get me to just accept that I'm your contracted."

I'm going to beat Massimo bloody for sharing that. No wonder she thought she could get away with burning her contract out. "He didn't challenge me, although I still could have killed him for it. Dark Law also states I'm allowed to do anything I want with or to my contracted."

"I didn't challenge you either."

"Little Star, you made me look weak in front of players, as well as my King when you destroyed your contract. That's worse than challenging me." I pull her to the door, wanting to avoid being late. "If I'm not strong enough to control my contracted then I will no longer be allowed to have contracted. If I'm weak, I'm a disgrace to the Dark and lose everything."

"Oh," she whispers, giving my hand a gentle squeeze. "I only did it to get Pierre to back off."

The name makes my blood boil. "I hate that fuck."

She giggles. "I'm sorry but taking the smite was awesome. The one I took when I saved your life was enough to get rid of a hangover, but that one from Pierre was way more intense, maybe the best rush I've ever gotten."

I cock a brow, reaching for the doorknob. "Getting smited is better than an orgasm? If that's the case, I won't bother letting you sit on my face tonight."

Her eyes sparkle, humor filling her dainty features. "No. You owe me that."

"Only if you behave for me."

Her head tips back as she laughs. "In that case, I'll be the best damn vassal you've ever had."

If she holds true to her words, I'll have to get creative to incentivize her behavior. If she'll behave for orgasms, I'd indulge in that game. Grinning, I twist the knob as something is slipped under the door.

Natalia bends over and picks up the crisp, black envelope, checking the front. "What is this?"

"Open it."

Shaking her hand free of mine, she rips the paper to slide out the card. "Chlem Delron Dellacronte. Marius Basileus Helio. Sterling James Wellsly. Mattingly Sawyer DeBernardo. Callahan Matteo Barraco."

"The contenders list," I say. "I'm baffled that after your stint in the great hall that I'd still be named in line for the throne."

"Seriously?" She gives me a face full of exaggerated, mock horror.

"Yes. I thought for sure I'd be removed. My King must be in a very forgiving mood." I frown. It doesn't make sense. She made me look weak.

She crumples it into a ball before tossing it over her shoulder. "It's a bullshit list. There's not a single woman on it."

"Jezabelle and Telra were both on the list. You killed Jeza, I suspect Telra as well. It's your fault there isn't a woman on it."

"Jezabelle?"

"She showed up at The Gardens to try to claim you. You killed her while I was busy dealing with the smoragon."

"Oops. I set women back a several millennia. That sucks."

I hum, hands slipping around her waist. I tore Yasmine in half, so I'm certain she's dead. Telra is still an unknown. Whether she survived my little star or not is inconsequential. She broke the rules this year. She disqualified herself from the list in that act. "I heard what you said to Telra."

She rolls her eyes. "Which part?"

"To stay away from me."

Her eyes open wider, and she swallows hard. A pink blush is spreading across the bridge of her nose and cheeks. "You know, if you had time to listen, you had time to help me instead."

"Why?" I wiggle my eyebrows at her. "You don't need me."

"Nope."

My grin grows. "I'm yours?"

"Shush." She leans forward, covering my mouth with her hand. Her blush darkens, staining further across her cheeks. "We're done talking about this."

I'd told her to never do that again. It should irritate me, not make me chuckle. Pulling her against me, I rip her hand away from my face to kiss her hard, pinning between me and the door until I'm aching with desire.

My palms skim over the thin layer of mesh covering her body, to take in every inch of her. It's beyond maddening, what I want on display, just out of reach.

I'm going to rip this flimsy fabric off her, then take what I want. First, I must suffer through dinner, though. Tomorrow I'll get my freedom back, and I'll be able to tear her clothes off at my convenience.

I open the door, guiding her through it.

"Behave," I warn her, taking her hand in mine as I lead her to the great hall.

Gathering Shadows is over. We survived, but there are troubles lurking on the horizon, starting with determining once and for all what my little star is, if she's Magia at all.

Pierre delivered a summons to the Council, and I must answer. I played a game to manipulate Natalia into signing a contract. I never assumed that the Council would be involved in determining the legality of what I did, and despite the fact that I believed Natalia's claims to be Magia, she holds the Light within her. She and I are both bound by the accords between Light and Dark, and I broke the law. I'll need to be cautious in my responses. I may forfeit my life if the Council rules against me.

I remain on the contender's list, but the King's health is dire. I doubt he'll live to see another set of games, and that means I will face the contest for the throne. That's an even bigger threat to my life than having to subterfuge Pierre's claims that I coerced the Light into servitude of the Dark.

Neither of those looming threats to my life scare me as much as the rumors of Ancients in the world. If there are, they will be hungry for vengeance. Their vindication will no doubt rain blood of the Light and the Dark alike across the world. Myths and whispers shouldn't scare me, but the winds are changing. Something is weaving in the webs of fates.

Those are all problems for another day, though. For now, I have a little star to wrangle into behaving.

PLEASE LEAVE A REVIEW.

Quick reminder. I am an indie author.

I rely on reviews.

Reviews help others to find a book they might enjoy.

Reviews can control the fate of this series.

Please leave a review.

Please?
My day job is killing me.

Amazon: Gathering Shadows
Goodreads: GatheringShadows

CALLAHAN AND NATALIA'S STORY CONTINUES...

Book Two of The Webs Of Fate
Dividing Illumination

INDEX

"PINNACLE"

BASE OF NECK →

LOWER BACK →

KI

AS A BLEND OF DARK &
LIGHT, THE MAGIA
POSSESS A BALANCED
SOUL AND WIELD KI.

All Magia are given the right
to train their magic and earn
the corresponding marks
used in channeling Ki. The
highest rank achievable for
standard Magia is dubbed
'Pinnacle', however Assembly
members, both City & High,
are granted additional
training - secrets of old
magic.

All together 47 marks

1-12 marks are for healing

13-25 marks are protection

25-40 are offensive skills

41-47 are "pinnacle" marks
for advanced Ki uses

All marks are ingrained with
a single needle that is
hammered into the skin.

Jade ink is used, a compound
restricted by Assembly
members for marks only.

THE DARK

The Dark King
HONORIFIC TITLE

The Dark King is a title given in honor for their god, Malaafic. It does not revert to Queen even when a female holds the throne. The first Dark King was Diona, and she established the inheritance of the crown in their traditions of the strongest survives.

Gathering Shadows is an annual set of games to determine five individuals that will face the contest when the current Dark King dies. Five individuals compete in the contest. Only one survives to take the Dark Throne and become the Dark King.

The Dark King is responsible for ruling the Dark, settling disputes within their rank and managing the society. They act as an alpha for the entire Dark.

A contractor can challenge the Dark King if they believe the Dark King has failed to uphold their duties or is not fit for duty (not the strongest). The challenge must be issued with an audience of at least three to be valid. By the tenets, a challenge issued cannot take advantage of poor health, prior injury, etc.

The Dark King still answers to the Council if they incite conflict with the Light.

The Dark Queen
HONORIFIC TITLE
The Dark Queen is the unioned partner to the Dark King.

The Dark Queen has the full responsibility and authority of the Dark King.

Adviser(s)

The Dark King selects contracted to serve as their advisers. Typically 2-3 contracted are elevated into positions that answer to the Dark King but act in the Dark King's stead with freedom to make decisions and full authority.

Contractors

Dark Seraphinus must be high born in order to hold contracts. (see Dark Contractual Law) Contractors must answer to the Dark King but do not answer to any other. The contractors live how they want and do what they want as long as the follow Dark Law.

THE DARK SOCIETY

Emulating Nehil's beasts and following Cornu's bitter beliefs, the Dark Seraphinus live by a meritocratic code. Honesty is above all else, the most important virtue. They are pack animals in nature and follow the strongest leader they can: alphas.

THE FOUR CORNER STONES

Honesty (undefiled wisdom)

Respect.

Freedom (independence)

Desire (indulgence & gratification)

THE DARK TENETS OF GOOD STANDING

To use deceit to possess achievement is to earn nothing but sand and misery.
Take what you want. If you cannot take it, you do not deserve it.
Act with integrity and dignity. To cheat or show fear is deplorable.
Honor strength and protect those without. An alpha is nothing without a pack.
Pursue your desires. To do otherwise is to destroy your heart and live falsely.
Deal with all things logically and realistically.
Power shall be held on merit.
Respect is earned.

MERITOCRATIC

Respect is earned through proof of strength. Earn respect and the individual will be respected. Every individual has the right to earn respect and respect is to be given if it is earned regardless of high born or low born status or origins.

Some contractors may be given more respect or stature over their peers but that is determined by their peers through respect earned.

EQUAL RANK

Anyone can talk to anyone.

High and low born distinctions only apply to contracts and can be changed by proof of strength from an individual.

Contractors legally stand on level ground in society and in the games.

RULED BY ALPHAS

Kill or be killed.
Eat or be eaten.

The Dark run in packs and are led by a leader/alpha. There are numerous alphas and every high born ranked Dark has the ability to establish itself as an alpha and lead their pack.

Alphas are strong and independent. They lead for the better of all, not themselves. The role of an alpha is nurturing and guiding, but can become aggressive/dominant when necessary. A good alpha knows when to be violent and will only become violent if required.

FREEDOM

ACKNOWLEDGMENTS

I have so many to thank, but I'll start with you. Thank you for taking the time to read my book. I write stories stuck in my head to quiet the voices, but it means the world to me that someone would read my story. I hope you enjoyed it!

I have to thank my husband, Eric, for indulging my fantasies and wildest ideas, listening to me for hours on end talking about these characters and places that don't exist.

To my beta readers Renee and Amanda, two beautiful women who took the time to help me make this story what it could be, I sincerely appreciate you! I cannot offer enough thanks and praise for your time and feedback.

Thank you to Cover Craft – Fantasy Covers by Julie for the gorgeous interior artwork. Julie is nothing short but amazing.

Thank you to Gina Casto – KillingItWrite, my fabulous editor. She's beyond thorough and helpful, putting up with the fact that I never know the difference between capital or capitol.

I listen to music while I write. Songs just help me grip at emotions and spurn scenes. There are so many artists I enjoy, but most of this book was written in August 2020 over the course of five days while Folklore was on repeat to the point my husband demanded I listen to something else. Thank you, Taylor Swift, for an amazing album we all so desperately needed during the pandemic, and Bad Omens for your incredible songs.

www.ingramcontent.com/pod-product-compliance
Lightning Source LLC
Chambersburg PA
CBHW030538020726
47494CB00005B/1422